Shades of Eternity ❦ Book I

INDIGO WATERS

Shades of Eternity ❧ Book I

INDIGO WATERS

❖ LISA SAMSON ❖

ZondervanPublishingHouse
Grand Rapids, Michigan 49530
http://www.zondervan.com

Indigo Waters
Copyright © 1999 by Lisa Samson

Requests for information should be addressed to:
📖 ZondervanPublishingHouse
Grand Rapids, Michigan 49530

Library of Congress Cataloging-in-Publication Data

Samson, Lisa, 1964–
    Indigo Waters / Lisa Samson.
           p.   cm. — (Shades of eternity ; bk. 1)
    ISBN: 0-310-22368-7
    I. Title.   II. Series : Samson, Lisa, 1964–   Shades of
Eternity ; bk. 1.
PS3569.A46673I54 1999
813'.54-dc21   98-54976
                                               CIP

Interior design by Melissa M. Elenbaas
Printed in the United States of America

99 00 01 02 3 04 /❖ DC/ 10 9 8 7 6 5 4 3 2 1

Dedicated to Loretta E. Bauer, my dear "Aunt Sis."
Remembering all our walks along the avenue,
our shopping days downtown, and my first and
only trip to Radio City Music Hall.
Thanks for being a great aunt.

BOOK ONE

FRANCE

CHAPTER ❖ ONE

Sylvie de Courcey thrust a narrow foot into her dusty boot, praying that her father wouldn't notice she'd failed to polish her shoes once again. Not that it would matter for long. Today was the day! She had been looking forward to this trip to Paris for months, and now the carriage was rolling into the courtyard, ready to take her away. Keeping the Countess Racine de Boyce company in her Paris mansion promised to be great fun. The families had been close for years.

"Hurry, Miss Sylvie, do hurry!" Agnes Green, her maid, cried from the corridor outside her bedchamber. "Your mother and father are waiting in the courtyard, and the carriage has been pulled around!"

"I'm coming!" Though a native of Champagne, France, the nineteen-year-old yelled in English. She and Agnes always spoke English. It was one of the reasons the Englishwoman was hired. Maid, governess, loving advocate, sometimes judge, sometimes jury—that was Agnes. Sylvie didn't remember a time when Agnes hadn't been there.

Yanking her straw bonnet over her black hair, she caught a glimpse of herself in the full-length mirror as she sped by.

Sylvie's reflection was bony and angular and would have been worse except for the extra potato Agnes would slip onto her plate when Papa wasn't looking. Like any girl on her way to Paris, Sylvie was suddenly self-conscious. All those beautiful women and handsome men sporting about, why, she'd be plainer than a mouse in her sturdy, country clothes. A tall mouse, thank goodness, but a mouse nevertheless. Perhaps her height alone would cause her to stand out a bit. *But do I really want to stand out?* she thought, biting her lip. That was clearly a thought for later. Her father would be furious if she kept him from his work any longer.

Down the great stone staircase of Chateau du Soleil, through the large medieval hall where lords and ladies had once feasted, and beneath the portal that had once received kings and queens from all over Europe, Sylvie's feet flew. The blinding spring sunlight, the clear air of Champagne, and the dew of morning hit her forcefully and she breathed in deeply. How could anything go wrong on a day like today?

"Into the carriage with you!" Agnes ordered. "Or we'll miss the train."

"Just a moment!" Sylvie focused her attention on her parents. Armand de Courcey endured his daughter's hug in his usual stiff manner, not patting her back and barely bringing his arms up to complete the embrace. He quickly pulled away and Sylvie turned to her mother, whose response was quite the opposite. Collette de Courcey was clingy and sopping wet with tears.

Several seconds later her feet had escaped the dusty courtyard and were firmly settled on the floor of the old, but well-cared-for carriage. Rupert Green, who did double duty as stable master and Agnes's cherished husband, had wisely chosen the open vehicle for Sylvie's departure. A day like this was too glorious to waste. Agnes climbed aboard, looking and moving much like a bear with a hair bun.

"Look, there's Rupert!" Sylvie cried as Agnes's husband appeared at the stable doors and waved a large hand. She waved back excitedly, then turned to her parents. She wished she could cry and make Mama feel more missed, but she couldn't. "I shall miss you, Mama! Good-bye, Father!"

Collette de Courcey, her stiff red hair blowing in the stubborn March breeze, clung to Armand's rigid arm. "Now, Sylvie," she said, forcing a bright smile to her pale lips, "do not forget your manners! I have raised you to stand your own with any of those city ladies. Always have a handkerchief with you and please, whatever you do, excuse yourself from the room if you need to use it." She choked back a sob, immediately raising her own handkerchief to her lips. "What am I going to do without you?"

"You shall do just fine," Sylvie said. "I won't shame you in front of the countess."

"Oh, Armand!" his wife sobbed.

Vineyard owner Armand de Courcey rolled his eyes as his wife now clung to him like a helpless child. His foot tapped in agitation. Thin lips were drawn inward as he ran a large, heavy hand over his bald head. "Don't make such a to-do about this. She'll only be gone for the spring. How hard can keeping an old woman company be?"

"But Father, she's not *that* old. She's Mama's friend—"

"Go on!" The wiry man barked at the driver, extricating himself from his wife's grasp without bothering to hide his distaste. "Get her out of here, Guilliaume."

Collette fished in her pocket for her rosary. "Your father is right, Sylvie. You do not want to miss the train! Give my love to my dear friend Racine. Tell her again how sorry I am I was unable to attend her daughter's wedding." Her soft voice shook. "Write often, ma cherie. Do not forget to say your prayers! Do not forget your dear mama!" A tear slipped down her cheek. More followed.

With a shake of the reins, the driver clicked his tongue and the two black horses inched forward, then picked up their pace, leaving Collette and Armand behind. As the vehicle rolled down the hill and out of sight, Sylvie turned back. Armand was already walking quickly away. Collette was waving, the rosary dangling through her fingers, the mother-of-pearl beads jumping about.

Sylvie did her best to put them out of her mind. With her father it was easy. He had never been around anyway, always working, working—building a dynasty, married to his grapes. Thoughts of her mother, however, would be harder to put off. Collette wasn't around too much either, if Sylvie was honest. She was usually on her knees in the chapel. Only when she was enveloped in some personal crisis did she seek Sylvie's advice, warmth, and support. Collette had successfully reversed the roles of mother and daughter, mistaking Sylvie's investment for her own. If Sylvie wasn't laboring in her father's fields, she was working for her mother's sanity or taking over her duties as chatelaine. Serving her parents had become her life.

Sylvie placed her hand in Agnes's. The maid grasped it warmly and patted it. Her blue eyes twinkled as she said, "As beautiful as Chateu du Soliel looks right now, I know you're glad to be getting away for a while."

"I'm ready to leave. In fact, I should have left the place years ago." Sylvie rolled her eyes.

The village now behind them, Guilliaume granted the horses a bit more liberty with several cheerful clicks. The beautiful chestnut beasts hastened to a merry trot, their harnesses jingling musically to the accompaniment of the rhythm of their dusty hooves, their coats glistening in the morning sun. They were all glad to be leaving Chateau du Soleil behind them.

"Castle of the Sun," Aggie translated. "An apt name, especially when you're . . . leaving!"

"'Armand's Obsession' would be a more fitting name," Sylvie remarked. "The old stones must have recoiled in righteous indignation the day my father and mother moved in, peasants as they were!" Sylvie loved the old place, knew each corridor's destination, had given every room a name. But without an army of servants, fine gowns, or expensive shoes, she felt as if she didn't truly belong there. Tromping down the vast corridors in her sturdy clothes and boots, she felt more like a char-girl than the owner's daughter.

The road ribboned the delightful Champagne countryside—hills hooded with grapevines, their twisted branches weighted with dew. Wheat fields lying in wait for spring planting added contrast, a smooth texture. Almost as far as Sylvie's honey-brown eyes could see, the land belonged to her father. Armand de Courcey was easily one of the richest men in France, and probably the most frugal as well, she thought.

"Won't it be wonderful to stay in a beautiful mansion with all the fine things?" Sylvie asked. "I'm sure the countess keeps her house nice and warm."

"No waking up to a stone-cold grate and frozen water in the pitcher!" Agnes chimed. "True comfort!"

"And all the splendid gowns we'll get to see!"

"There's certainly a lot to look forward to, child. For the life of me, I cannot understand why your father has always refused to buy you the finer things. He certainly could afford them," Agnes quipped. "But here I go again, saying too much about what's none of my business."

Sylvie laughed. Agnes was always making such apologies, but never mending her ways. Sylvie hoped she never would. The fact was, Agnes was exactly right about Armand de Courcey.

Beneath the fertile earth he claimed as his own, an immense labyrinth of caverns, carved out of the chalk, housed many thousands of bottles of wine waiting to become France's premium champagne. If the winemaker wasn't exactly a patient man, his wines certainly were. Armand de Courcey had inherited his father's humble vineyard at sixteen, and by his thirtieth autumn, a dynasty had been born.

The vineyard workers, browned by years in the sun, waved as Sylvie rolled by. She sighed. "Well, I certainly won't miss the afternoons in the vineyard." Armand had insisted she spend six days a week there.

"Better to labor than risk displeasing him by your presence in the library or the gardens," Agnes said. "But that is all behind you now, love, for a while at least."

"I am off to Paris!" Sylvie cried, hugging her maid.

Agnes grabbed her hand and squeezed it tightly. "And no one deserves it more than you, Miss Sylvie. As God is my witness, I thought this day would never come."

"I can hardly believe it myself, dear Aggie. But the day has come, and I welcome it with open arms!"

"Not to mention that you'll be seeing a lot more of Guy," Agnes clucked, her fondness for Sylvie's lovable older brother evident in her eyes. Guy had been calling Paris home for seven years now as the head of de Courcey Paris.

Paris. The very name conjured up jumbled images of wealth and poverty, music and misery, religion and sin. Anything could happen in Paris, a city where every woman could find a man, every man could find a mistress, every person could find a society that fit their dimensions, however peculiar. And there were peculiar people to be found on nearly every corner!

Paris was nothing like provincial Champagne. Her heart began to thud, and she felt her scalp grow hot beneath the straw hat. She fingered the fabric of her old dress, foolishly willing it to become satin.

Sylvie groped under the seat and grabbed hold of a large box, sent from Guy a week previous and deposited in the coach in secret the night before by Rupert. It was a creation from the House of Worth, Paris's most esteemed couturier. With a joyful whoop, she pulled it out, tugged open the lid, and buried her face in the fabulous silken garment.

Agnes leaned forward and batted her hands away. "I spent half an hour packing that garment last night making sure it wouldn't wrinkle, and look at what you're doing to it. The only beautiful gown you've got and it will be a rag by the time you get to the train station!"

The perfume of Paris clung to the silken garment, still cool from its cubbyhole beneath the seat. Agnes's reprimand did nothing to stifle her excitement. Sylvie breathed in deeply, ready for anything.

CHAPTER ❖ TWO

The stars winked serenely between the soft blossoms of the cherry trees. Gentle waters trickled dark and cool from the stone satyr's urn and into a carved basin. The fragile tone of a violin hovered about Countess Racine de Boyce's ears, but she failed to appreciate the song.

"When will they arrive?" she asked no one. Unfortunately, Racine had developed a very annoying habit of talking to herself. Not that the servants which ran Maison de Fleur, her Paris home, minded. It was she herself that couldn't abide the sound of her own voice. To her ear, it always sounded too high and birdlike. But then, hadn't her late husband, Count Philippe de Boyce, always called her his little wren? How she missed him still, almost ten years after his death.

Racine was fully aware the train from Champagne wasn't yet due to arrive at the depot, but she couldn't contain her excitement. She had been rambling around the house ever since her beloved daughter Cecile had been married a week before. Having the presence of dear Sylvie to ease her loneliness during Cecile's honeymoon was something she had been greatly anticipating. Sylvie had always been such a good girl. Not a great beauty, unfortunately, but looks did not necessarily impart good company. Racine knew that beauty wasn't everything. Paris was filled with beautiful women who were simply dreadful inside. She thought of a chocolate-covered apricot she had once been given. Luscious and promising on the outside, but rotten inside. To this day she distrusted such dainties, human or chocolate.

Sylvie was another matter, trustworthy all the way in. The girl would be good for her son as well. Racine smiled at the thought of her precious Rene, now the Count de Boyce since the death of his father. Rene de Boyce, at twenty-nine, was easily the most beautiful man in France, Racine thought. He was also the most lonely, she was sure.

However, he had been in America for a year now and would be coming home soon. What wonderful timing for him, if not for poor Cecile who was quite piqued by her brother's absence from her wedding. And Sylvie would be waiting.

How could he help but not plunge headlong in love with the girl, especially once Racine had labored with her a bit? First a trip to Monsieur Worth's for a stunning wardrobe. Then Racine would turn her own maid loose on that severe hairdo the child always wore. Pascale would do wonders with that long, heavy black mane. Racine could just imagine Sylvie's milky skin framed by luscious curls. And with just a light application of cosmetics, a hint of rouge, some powder, how could Rene resist?

She wouldn't give him the chance! And that was simply that. She had been planning this match in her heart for years; even he had agreed it would be good for all involved. But it would be so much better for him if he would fall in love with the girl.

From one lonely woman to another. Racine wondered if that was how Sylvie viewed her trip. Well, she would make it worth the girl's while, most certainly! Oh, the fun that was there for the taking! Sylvie de Courcey might never recover.

Racine sauntered back into the house to jot down the ideas that were quickly filling her head. She didn't want to forget even one. Racine hurried up the marble steps, onto the wide verandah, and through one of the sets of five glass-paned doors that lined the side of the house. She remembered the first time she had walked through those doors, so many years ago. Her marriage to Count Philippe had been arranged in her childhood, but she loved him the moment she saw him, standing there on the verandah, looking at the heavens through his telescope.

Maison de Fleur was grand indeed. Sumptuous parlors and sitting rooms littered the first floor, sprouting off a wide gallery that held precious paintings and family portraits. The large music room was being used even now by one of several music students she housed in the attic during their studies in Paris. Racine de Boyce was known as a true patroness of the arts, but she knew deep down her motives were purely selfish. She loved hearing music at all hours of the day.

On the way to her personal salon, she snuck a peek into the ballroom. The lavender and white room would fairly sparkle soon, when Rene came home, and the ball she had begun planning was in full force. *Oh, Rene, come home soon.* The dear boy worried her so.

She sat down at her large white desk, plucked a pen from the drawer, and dipped it into the golden inkwell. Her hand shook just a little as she began writing a list of sites for Sylvie to see. All the usual places Racine didn't even bother to write down: The Louvre, Notre Dame, the Tuilleries, Versailles. Of course they would see all of that. Shop from one end of the Champs Elysees to the other. Remember the first Napolean at the Arc de Triomphe. But Racine was pondering other activities. Luncheon at the small café near Sacre Coeur to where she had been sneaking off since her marriage to consume a pot-au-feu for which she'd lay down her life. A definite must. Then, perhaps, she would escort her down to the waterfront on the Seine where they'd watch the ships coming in and sample cheddars fresh off the boat from England. And there were so many people she wanted Sylvie to meet! The gardener at Maison de Fleur, for one, and her friends from church, of course. How she would fit it all in remained to be seen, for she also imagined cozy evenings together in her salon, chatting and working on their handcrafts, or reading. To be honest, those were the times she was looking forward to the most. Cecile was always go, go, go. Sylvie was good company, even in the silence.

"Aunt Racine?"

The countess wheeled around at the title Sylvie herself had given to her many years before. "Sylvie! My darling!" She rushed across the room, arms wide open. "You're finally here!"

They embraced. Sylvie's long arms pulled the small countess close, and Racine felt as if she was the one who was visiting. She pulled away and stroked the girl's cheek. "Let me have a look at you! Why Sylvie, you've grown even taller! So chic and elegant!"

Sylvie blushed an endearing pink. "You are as lovely as ever, Aunt Racine. Your butler was most upset when I ran right by him, but I knew you'd be back here. I couldn't wait to see you."

Racine scooped Sylvie's hand in hers and towed her to the sofa. "How long has it been, child, since I last saw you?"

"Two years."

"My, my, my. Then we have some catching up to do. Any young men in Champagne that are crying in their stew now that you are gone?" *Please, God, don't let her say yes!*

Sylvie's brown eyes danced. "There was one boy, Aunt Racine. But his kisses became too hard and after that, I refused to see him. A field hand. Other than Jacques, I can think of no one!"

"No time for romance at Chateau du Soleil, eh?"

"Not unless it brings in more francs to Father!" Sylvie joked.

Racine smiled inwardly. Armand de Courcey was more than pleased with the proposed match between Sylvie and Rene, and what financial rewards his association with the name de Boyce would bring. She was hoping, however, to ease the girl into the matter. If she would fall in love with Rene it would settle everything. And how could Sylvie *not* fall in love with the young count? *Impossible!* Racine thought, turning her full attention back to her guest.

"Are you hungry?"

"I'm always hungry!" Sylvie laughed.

Racine examined her gaunt frame and added another item to her list of things to do. *Feed this child!* Armand de Courcey's dietary requirements for his family certainly weren't hers. Pulling on the bell cord, she summoned a servant from the kitchen, calling for every luscious treat she could think of.

Later, as Sylvie consumed the final bite of a custard tart, Racine thanked God for the opportunity to have her at Maison de Fleur. Sylvie needed to be fed in more ways than one. Some love, care, and appreciation were definitely in order.

Racine's eyes scanned the room. It had been easy to convince Sylvie that coming out with her for the evening was a good idea. Thank heavens her brother Guy had provided that stunning gown. The gowns they had ordered at Worth's wouldn't be ready for several days. Still, Guy had chosen wisely. The deep gold of the gown matched Sylvie's eyes perfectly and accentuated the excited blush that rested on her cheeks and chin. It was just a small affair at the home of her friend Monsieur Riece, listening to some music, sampling the creations of his new and very expensive chef, but Sylvie seemed to be enjoying herself. And why not? This had to be the most excitement she'd had in years!

The three days Sylvie had already spent at Maison de Fleur had wrought some remarkable changes. The new, flowing hairstyle Pascale designed for her was stunning, and the light cosmetics smoothed out the angles of her face. Now the child actually looked quite fetching. She'd never be the beauty her mother once was, but there was much more to Sylvie than the eye could see. Her beauty was deep in her eyes, waiting to be unleashed. The girl had a lot of growing up to do, so naïve and countrified. But Rene would be understanding about all that, Racine was sure.

The emeralds that the countess had lent Sylvie glimmered at her ears and throat. A lovely effect. She was weaving her way toward Racine with two crystal cups of punch.

Countess Racine de Boyce pulled her immediately to her side. "I can hardly believe we are here together," she gloated, taking her punch and setting it on a small table beside her. "When I think about your mother and I, all those years ago in convent school, I'm even happier to have her daughter for a companion!"

"Your pranks are legendary!" Sylvie chuckled, taking a sip and failing to notice the drop of punch which had fallen onto her skirt. "The evening seems to be going well."

Smoothing her thick white hair with one tiny, heavily bejeweled hand, Racine plucked a lace-trimmed handkerchief out of her evening bag with the other. The square of linen fluttered saucily, serving as visual punctuation to her speech. "Oh, yes, the quartet was positively lovely. And those little pastries are delightfully sweet. I should know, I have eaten enough for the both of us! Everyone has been telling me they are looking forward to our ball next week. I have received perfectly *lovely* compliments regarding the handwriting on the invitations! You do such lovely work, my sweet, and were so good to do them the day after you arrived!" She handed Sylvie the handkerchief. "For your skirt." She pointed to the tiny spill. "You forgot your handkerchief again, I see."

Sylvie dabbed at the spot. "Thank you. Mama warned me several times about that."

Racine thought about their school years. How different they had been! "Dear, sweet Collette. She was always worried about such conventions. We had such fun, your mother and I . . . in the old days. Back when such things as youth and health and happiness were taken for granted."

Racine was a bit relieved when one of the other guests interrupted them, regretfully bidding them good night. She was ready to leave as well. Gathering her satin purse and handing Sylvie her light wrap, she ushered her charge toward the door, queuing up with the ladies and gentlemen that flowed by their host and hostess in a long train of gem-colored silks and satins. Feathers and bows, hats and cravats, shoes polished to the sheen of a still pond, all this finery was accompanied by smiles and thank-yous, fond regards, and personal sentiments.

A heavy front of clouds cartwheeled across the inky, chilly sky as the women traveled home. The lamps in the carriage shone mellow and warm. Peaceful. The air smelled like rain.

"Ahh," Racine leaned back against the cushions. "I truly am getting to be an old woman when I would much rather sit at home with my memories than be in the company of my friends."

Sylvie leaned forward and patted her knee. "It was a lovely evening and you sparkled, Aunt Racine. As usual."

Racine chuckled at the kind but misplaced words. "My days for sparkling are long over, but you, my sweet . . . you have many days ahead of you. I wonder what you are doing here with me, being so kind to an old woman."

"You're not old. Why, you're the same age as Mama."

"'Tis true. But Collette's 'sinlessness' keeps her young! Not to mention all her worries. Good for the circulation, I suppose! It's a shame we cannot all be so dedicated."

They chuckled knowingly.

"Why did you not follow in the traditions of the church as well, Aunt Racine? I know you pray, but there are no priests who come to Maison de Fleur."

"My late husband, Philippe, was a descendant of the Huguenots. And although the revolution was a terrible time for the nobility then, now that the empire is reestablished, the religious freedom continues, and we benefit. So . . . I am a Protestant now. And though no priests visit me, I do commune with my Lord often." She took Sylvie's hand between both of hers. "You may find one day, when you are older, that there is a difference between knowing God, and being religious. I can only pray your path to that discovery will not be as difficult as it was for me."

The girl fell into silence.

"The music was lovely, wasn't it, Aunt Racine?" Sylvie's voice filtered out of the darkness, several minutes later.

"Yes, darling child. Your mother would have enjoyed such a time. She never really appreciated the balls and the dances, but she loved listening to music. It wasn't a surprise when she married Armand and moved out to the country away from all the fuss of Paris. Collette was always suited to a more bucolic setting."

"She can make a church out of any room . . . or any pasture," Sylvie said with a wry mouth. "But perhaps not a ballroom."

Racine always thought Collette would have been more suited to convent life. Even now, the woman had mass said every day, and she knew for a fact that Sylvie and Guy cut their teeth while kneeling on the cold stone floor of the family chapel.

"Was she always so religious?" Sylvie asked.

"Of course. She thrived on convent life."

"But not you, Aunt Racine?"

She shook her head, feeling a deep connection with Sylvie, wondering if God was setting the child's feet on the true path to him. "I hated it. I have never been one for schedules. And when the apostle Paul says 'pray without ceasing,' I believe that precludes a schedule. Not that I cared much about prayer then, scheduled or not. No," she said, waving a graceful hand, "convent school suffocated me. I am much too much like a little bird, and I always have been, soaring with the wind on my cheeks, and the sun in my eyes. The only difference now is that I know the wind and the sun both belong to God."

"I'm not so sure about it all yet," Sylvie admitted. "Agnes speaks about God so personally, like she knows him as she would a neighbor or a friend. Mother talks about him with such dread and fear that I have to wonder who he really is. For me, it seems like he created us, and then left it at that."

Racine squeezed her hand reassuringly as the carriage rolled toward home. Sylvie's view of her heavenly Father came as no surprise, considering the behavior of her earthly one.

C H A P T E R ❖ T H R E E

His breathing was labored, thick, slow.

The need was driving him to a slow death. He knew it. Most of the time he cared. But this was not one of those times. Not now. For if he could feel more than the need, hear more than the echoing hole hissing inside of him, he wouldn't have been where he was. Blind agitation gripped him hard as he hastened on shaky legs down the grimy Paris street. The river Seine accompanied him along the way, mocking his plight with her chilly quiet.

Paris in the spring. Caught in a spell.

How could he have forgotten his bottle?

The drizzle descended on his expensive top hat like the fine tears his mother would shed if she knew where her beloved son was going. His shoulders were silver with the stuff, but onward his feet trod. He was unconcerned that the pricey leather soles of his shoes would be ruined come morning, for the need automatically ushered him to the place he found himself all too often since the accident. His compulsion overpowered the thought of future disgust. Besides, at least there was that. The disgust. The guilt. He clung to those moments as proof he wasn't completely an addict, thoroughly helpless, utterly worthless.

The door stood before him. Once a brilliant red, the paint that overlaid the paneled surface was now scraped and scarred. Desperate hands in search of an entrance to more than just the room on the other side had ruined the glossy finish years ago. And now, the name on the lease was his own.

The knock.

Three slow. Four quick.

The door opened an inch. An eye appeared, then crinkled above a rotted smile. Sweet smoke crawled out of the opening and up into his nostrils. Obviously, Camille had already arrived.

"Mmm." He inhaled deeply, eyes closed under dark visions of the very near future. Pernicious, yet somehow good . . . very, very good.

A broader smile behind the door. "Come, master." The Chinese servant invited him with a bow.

He obeyed eagerly, entering the shabby house like a child exploding with anticipation. Its tawdriness was softened by time and the smoke of the opium pipes. On a faded settee abounding with frayed pillows, he reclined next to his mistress, her expensive garments clashing with the environment, as did his own. After the wrinkled Chinese servant presented him his pipe, Count Rene de Boyce proceeded to forget just why he came at all.

He was the first to come around from the deep sleep that followed. And there she lay beside him, curled like an infant, swaddled alarmingly tight in the bedclothes. Camille. One of Paris's newest courtesans two years before, she had caught his eye, and he had snatched her right up. Camille was breathtakingly beautiful. Rene had never seen a woman like her. Blond hair, glossy and bright, grew in waves from her small, round head. Her features were even and pleasing to the eye, but it was her eyes, large and light green, that caused even the most casual passerby to steal another glance. She was small and curvy, with a body that should have been vulnerable and was. But underneath the exterior, a sadness lived, a longing that he knew he would never fulfill. And that was all right. For Rene de Boyce loved Camille only a little, if at all.

Camille had become to him the embodiment of his opium. She had been the first to show him the warmth of the drug after a hunting accident, twisting his leg, left him in lasting pain. She knew when he hurt the most, knew what to do about it, and loved him in the bargain. He wouldn't part with her anytime soon, that much was certain. Although there were times he desperately wanted to.

She stirred.

"Are you awakening?" he asked, drawing a hand down her silky back.

"Yes." She yawned. "I think so. It was good, was it not?"

He laughed. "You, or the opium?"

"Why the opium, of course. I am always good."

His heart continually broke in pity for the woman. "Yes, you are. Even in America."

"Your dear mama would have been shocked to know you took me across the pond, my count. Ah, yes, she certainly would not like it." Camille sat up and reached over him to the bed table. She grabbed her pouch of smoking supplies and began rolling them each a cigarette. "I'm glad you told her you'd be arriving in three days' time. It's been nice having you all to myself here in my little home." He had offered to put her up in something more stylish, but Camille had flatly refused. She had grown up along the waterfront.

She suddenly frowned. "Although why you had to go see your friends earlier . . . and risk being spotted." Her full lips pouted.

He took the cigarette she offered, then lit both his and hers with a deftness that told of countless smokes made active by his hand. "Camille, how could I be in Paris and not see Youngblood and the others? It's been a year and he is my closest friend. It was just a few games of cards."

"And you probably lost scads of money, didn't you?"

He didn't want to talk about that.

Camille blew out smoke, then turned to him, contrite. "I'm sorry, my dear. That was thoughtless of me."

"Do I not care for you well enough, Camille? Has money ever been a problem?"

She quickly stubbed out her smoke and threw her arms around him. "But of course not, my count. Of course you take good care of me. I don't know where I would be without you."

And she kissed him sweetly on the mouth. Yet even as she kissed him, Rene was calculating in his mind just how much money the woman had cost him over the past two years. He pulled back from her and looked into her eyes. He saw the sadness and knew he could not, would not leave her yet. How could he do that to her?

A knock sounded softly on their door and Rene bade an entry to the servant on the other side. The old Chinese woman bowed. "Your supper, sir, is ready."

The woman and her daughter wheeled in a tea cart holding two bottles of cabernet, stewed chicken, and buttered cabbage. Camille did not like the rich food of the wealthier set and Rene was just as satisfied with the peasant fare served in her home. Not that he ate much anyway. The accident had taken away his appetite, and the opium didn't help matters either. Better than the pain, though. And it was such a lovely feeling to be stolen away on wings of ease.

He slid into his pants while Camille shrugged on a velvet wrapper. The sight of her in the sapphire softness took his breath away. Three more days, and this little home would again become a stolen pleasure. His friends would never understand the slumming he was doing. But there was something inside Rene that yearned for such simplicity.

Camille was already consuming her meal while he smoked another cigarette. "So, my count, is the time coming when you must settle down?"

She always seemed to ask that question when they were having a quiet meal together, as if such domesticity was endangered. Unfortunately, this time his answer wasn't what she would want to hear. "Yes, Camille. Mother wrote to me in America. The time is upon me. I didn't want to tell you then and spoil the trip."

"Sylvie de Courcey, then? Still?"

He drew in hard on the smoke. "Yes. It has always been Sylvie. Her mother has fought it, trying to keep her in Champagne by her side, but now she has finally agreed to let her go. According to Mama, Sylvie was becoming much too closely involved with a field hand." He exhaled through his nose.

Camille laughed, but it wasn't natural. "She sounds a bit like you, romancing someone beneath you."

Rene didn't bother to contradict her. She was right after all. "In any case, the time has come. Mama has the harebrained idea that she wants Sylvie to fall in love with me of her own accord."

His mistress took a sip of wine. "A good idea. How can she help but do just that?"

Rene smiled at her remark, but he didn't really cherish the idea of having his life mapped out by his mother. Still, it was the way of things, and Sylvie had always been a sweet child, not to mention the fact that her father was as rich as Solomon. It could be worse, so why fight it?

Besides, he could use the money. He could desperately use the money.

CHAPTER ❖ FOUR

Lord David Youngblood, Viscount Blackthorne, heir to Earldom of Cannock, rapped upon the Maison de Fleur's door with the knob of his cane. The English nobleman, a man of keen eye and ear, noticed the first signs of wear on the large mansion, and he smiled, patting his own fat purse. It had been several years since his father had shown him the door, permanently, and finally he was becoming a man of means in his own right. The Count de Boyce had been responsible for most of his good fortune. The man made an utter mockery of the card table, yet persisted in coming back for more, God bless him!

He flipped his brain over to its French side and waited to be heard. Finally a footman appeared. Youngblood was ushered into the house and accompanied back to the countess's salon where he was announced by the servant. By the way her eyebrows raised in alarm, he could tell his visit was a surprise.

The woman had never liked him. And not only did he not care, it gave him cause for amusement. If she only knew her son the way he did!

He bowed over her hand. "Good afternoon, Countess."

"Goodness me, it's Viscount Blackthorne, and a day early!"

What a shrew, he thought. *What a manipulative shrew*. The look of distaste on her face when she greeted him was fleeting but easily seen as he bent to kiss her hand. She pulled it away before his lips could touch its surface. The countess rose to her feet briefly and pointed to the sofa. Her hand reached for the bell pull. "Would you like some tea?" She stared at his mouth, but, whether her gaze was purposeful or not, he refused to become self-conscious regarding his harelip. He wasn't feeling very prickly just then, and he certainly wasn't going to engage the countess in fisticuffs over her impertinence. It was taking a while, he acknowledged within, but he was finally learning to choose his battles carefully. They were so much more fun when there was more at stake.

"Tea would be lovely." Youngblood threw himself onto the couch, fashionably loose, nobly bored.

"Rene's ship should be coming in tomorrow evening. Hard to believe all the schoolboys will be back together again. Guy de Courcey should be visiting tomorrow morning as well."

"The herd will be complete then." Youngblood was glad to hear it. The three of them had all attended Oxford together, although Rene hadn't really been his close friend then. Their friendship truly began when the French count had taken the English viscount under his wing when he arrived in Paris several years earlier. Their relationship had developed from there. Youngblood made sure of it.

The countess licked her lips in obvious delight. Youngblood knew he was in for trouble. "And you'll never be able to guess who else is showing up. Another Oxford friend of Rene's. Matthew Wallace!" Her eyes were triumphant.

He suppressed a shudder. Matthew Wallace, vicar of the Church of England, general do-gooder and God's conscience for the masses. How a man could be so devoted to an ancient book that was filled with contradictions was beyond Youngblood! He had never liked the fellow. After all, he was merely the son of a woolen mill magnate. A commoner. He pasted his warmest smile on his face. "Old Matthew, eh? Fine fellow. I remember him setting

Oxford alight with his tales of fire and brimstone. Still in the service of our Lord, then, is he?" He wanted to laugh, but the countess suddenly looked so serious.

Racine nodded. "But happy to be coming to Paris on holiday, nevertheless. Loving God does not preclude having a little fun now and then."

The urge to laugh became even more strong. "I should say. And have I heard the gossip correctly, that Guy's sister Sylvie is also here at Maison de Fleur?" Of course he had heard correctly, he was with Guy only the night before—had, in fact, missed Rene by only minutes.

"Indeed. She is staying with us while Cecile is honeymooning."

Youngblood tapped his chin, fondly remembering the girl from his visits with Guy's family during university days. She was about the only bright spot in that dreadful castle in Champagne. "She was always a sweet little thing. I am surprised she is not married by now."

"Her mother has always needed her. The child has been very sheltered from society."

"Must be miserable being Armand de Courcey's daughter." He raised his brows slightly. "All that money. Wondering if a man will ever love you for yourself." Yes, she was a pretty little filly then, of course. But who knew what puberty, always a crapshoot, had done for her? "Of course, Rene should be pleased to align himself with such wealth."

Her mouth dropped open. "You know about my plans?"

He spread his arms wide. "I am his closest friend, Countess. Of course I know. I've known for years. I shall have to congratulate her."

"You'll do no such thing, for she has no knowledge of it yet. Her father has left the timing up to her mother and now the time is finally ripe. Yet, I'm hoping Rene might woo her on his own, make her think it is her idea to love him."

"Why?" Girls in England weren't given any choice, and in France it was much the same, or so he supposed. His taste didn't normally run for debutantes.

"Because she will be a better wife if she loves him."

He rested an ankle on a knee. "Ahh. Ever the thoughtful mother. It will be nice to see her. Is she in this afternoon?"

"In the music room listening to one of my students practice. Why don't you go see her?"

Anything to get out of here, he thought, *away from this baneful parent. No wonder Rene is like he is.* Nevertheless, he left with a polite good-bye and a courteous nod.

The strains of Mozart accompanied him back up toward the front of the house. It had been a good decision to visit a day early, especially with Sylvie here. He remembered the first time he had laid eyes on the child, only ten years before. Only nineteen then, he was still trying to manhandle his way in the world. Yet this child, this little Sylvie, had accepted him, and his deformity, without so much as a blink. She took him walking through the vineyards, explained to him all she knew about winemaking, which was a surprisingly great deal, and they had laughed together in the great hall of the castle, making fun of the portraits of someone else's ancestors. It was the first time he had felt comfortable talking about other people's imperfections because his own was so clearly overlooked. Yes, indeed, Sylvie had been a most delightful child.

He had visited every summer afterwards, until he had passed his examinations and Guy went back to France for good. She had written him several times, letters filled with childish anecdotes and pleasant reports of the simple life she led. And he had returned the favor with short reports of the more comedic aspects of his life, but as often happens the letters dwindled to nothing. However, he was confident the affection would still be there. How much had she changed in almost seven years?

There she sat, head back against the sofa, eyes closed. Her hair flowed dark and lustrous over one shoulder, and it seemed as if puberty had been kind. Her body was still thin, though the foot that peeped from beneath the skirts of her gown was a trifle larger than he remembered. The thought made him smile. He motioned to the student to leave.

"Sylvie?"

She opened her eyes slowly as if she had been asleep, saw who had called her name, then jumped to her feet. "Viscount Blackthorne!" She circled quickly round the couch.

"In the flesh!" He bowed smoothly, and took her hand in his, raising it to his misshapen mouth. Not only did she accept his gesture, but she put her arms about him indecorously and gave him a hug. "How long has it been since I've seen you?" she chimed, voice now mature but still unaffected.

"Too long. You have grown up, Sylvie. And into a beautiful woman, I might add."

"It took me long enough!" she joked. "And I'm hardly beautiful. Yet you always were so kind to me, Viscount, despite my youth."

"We have always had much in common, haven't we?"

"Oh yes, especially our appreciation of fine portraiture!"

So she remembers, he thought gladly.

She wound her arm through his, and he found it quite pleasant. "Come sit down with me, then. I'll ring for tea. You must be desperate for some. I remember how you brought your own with you when you visited Chateau du Soliel."

He followed her, and sat next to her, draping one long, powerful leg over the arm of the settee. "I assume you are as happy to be away from your home in Champagne as I am to be away from mine." He recalled indifferent Armand and clingy Collette, two examples of disastrous parents. Not that his own could be remotely put on a pedestal. Both he and Sylvie were literally raised by the servants. It was the greatest commonality between them.

"You assume correctly. And I assume you are still doing your best to stay clear of *your* father as well?"

"It isn't hard anymore."

She laid a tender hand on his sturdy arm. "Guy told me of your exile. I'm sorry. He didn't tell me what precluded your fall from grace."

"It was a duel," he said simply, "over my deformity."

Sylvie's eyes suddenly flared with indignation and she opened her mouth to speak, but he interrupted her. Before God, he couldn't bear to hear her pity, his admission notwithstanding. "Don't worry, dearest, that particular fellow learned his lesson." He took her hand and laughed. "So, here I am in France. England is too small, for I kept running into my father quite by accident. My parents are very social folk, you know."

"But how do you do it, Viscount? How do you subsist without your family's wherewithal?"

He tapped his temple with his forefinger. "I live on my wits, Sylvie."

"Still waiting for the old man to die, eh?" Her laughter bounced around the room.

"We survive, Sylvie, do we not?"

"As you said, we have much in common. By the way, did the man you were dueling even have a chance?" She wrinkled her nose at him, eyes dancing.

How he liked this girl! She was an even more fetching woman than she had been a child. "Not a one, Sylvie! I wouldn't have challenged him if he had!"

"Only a coward would say such things to you."

Youngblood laughed at her loyalty. "You are still the champion of the downtrodden, eh? I remember all of those wounded animals you used to nurse."

"It's my nature." She took his hand. "Do you have plans for the afternoon?"

"I was just on my way home, but I do believe I shall stay here a bit longer with you, and have that tea." Sylvie's presence was never draining or demanding. "We have a lot of catching up to do."

"It's good to have you here, Viscount. You won't be leaving any time soon, I hope."

He took her hand and patted it gently. "Not if I can help it, mademoiselle." No, he wouldn't be leaving soon. Not at all.

Half an hour later they were sitting in the garden. He was drinking a cup of tea while she embroidered violets on a linen napkin.

Sylvie picked a new color of floss out of her bag. "Perhaps you can tell me about that English vicar who is coming? The countess mentioned him briefly. He wasn't a good friend of Guy's, was he? I don't remember hearing much about him."

"No. Rene took a liking to the fellow, and their friendship was their own. It really didn't have anything to do with Guy or myself."

"His ship should be docking in several hours, and I hardly know what to expect."

Youngblood didn't see any point in lambasting the man. Wallace's foolishness would speak for itself. "I assure you, he's a perfectly affable fellow." That was true enough.

"I've never yet met a vicar, Viscount. Even the very word conjures up odious pictures of men with long flapping coats and eyebrows resembling large caterpillars."

"You've nothing to fear from Matthew, even if he can be a bit serious at times."

"That's precisely what I'm talking about. I assume he's not married?"

Youngblood's cup stopped just shy of his mouth. Here was a tasty tidbit. "Oh no! In fact, according to Rene, has so much as vowed never to do so."

Sylvie threaded the needle with black floss. "You sound as if you're speaking of a priest, not a vicar!"

"When we were in school together, Matthew was betrothed to a most engaging young woman, beautiful, well-educated, and devoted to him thoroughly. I forget the girl's name, but she was from a good family. She died a month before the wedding. I heard he never quite got over it."

"How horrible. Especially considering they loved each other so."

"Had since childhood." *Why did I get us onto this topic in the first place*, he wondered. Too much talk about a very annoying subject always set him on edge.

Sylvie's shoulders dropped. "That love should come and be so extinguished is truly a tragedy."

"And what of you, Sylvie? Have you yet fancied yourself in love with a man?"

"Me? Why no. Of course not. Mama would not have it, though most of the girls I grew up knowing have married and some are already expecting children." Her sigh spoke volumes. "I don't know when I'll ever be freed. I visualize myself as one of those spinster women, taking care of demanding parents until she's so old there's no one left to take care of her."

"You sound so resigned to the fact. Why not break free?"

Sylvie reached for his hand. "We're not all like you, Viscount."

Youngblood covered her hand with his own. "It's a very good thing you're not, Sylvie."

"Perhaps. Yet I do so love children and babies, and to have one all my own, I daresay that even the most miserable marriage would be redeemed by the arrival of a child to call my own— one to love and defend."

He could hardly imagine this rare jewel married to a weakling like Rene. True, she would not break free from her mother's clutches, but it was strength that kept her there, strength and responsibility. Not weakness. He suddenly felt ashamed of himself. If this young woman knew half of the dark deeds he had committed, deeds that would shock even his father and ruin his friendship with Rene, she wouldn't be sitting with him now.

He decided to change the topic, and they began to recount the summer evenings they had enjoyed in one another's company. Despite his exciting life of parties, gambling, and women who ignored his mouth for the sake of his money, Youngblood realized he hadn't enjoyed himself so much in years.

CHAPTER ❖ FIVE

W hen Agnes Green received an invitation to join Guy de Courcey for luncheon, she couldn't resist. Sylvie was busy helping the countess finalize their plans for the ball the following evening and told her maid to go. So Agnes met Guy at a small café along the Seine. Her former charge smiled as he took her hands in his. It had been almost a year since she had seen him, and he hadn't changed at all. Guy never changed. He looked dashing in his perfectly cut suit of clothes, his wavy, lustrous red hair still sun-soaked. The two de Courcey siblings didn't resemble each other a whit—save for the round, absorbing eyes that Collette herself possessed. Guy, shorter than Sylvie, was powerfully built around the shoulders—a bulldog of a man. Yet his nature was anything but bestial. Unable to say no to almost anybody, he disappointed most everybody. But one couldn't help but love him.

"Mrs. Green!" He addressed her formally as he always had when she was his governess. "How delightful to see you!"

"Your English is as impeccable as ever, Guy. Why, your diction is as fine as the Prince of Wales, I'd wager to say!"

He took her arm. "I had an impressive teacher."

She swatted him on the arm. "I suppose your years at Oxford had nothing to do with it?"

He winked a blue eye and ran a hand through his curly red hair. "Maybe just a little."

They placed their food order and sat down to wait at a table outside. It was always so easy to be with Guy. One never had to talk to fill in the blank spaces. And he had a lot to talk about this day.

"Mrs. Green, I'm worried. I received a letter from Mother the other day. She told me that this trip of Sylvie's to Paris has more to it than merely being a companion to the countess."

"What do you mean?"

He leaned forward. "Have you heard anything about Sylvie and the count?"

"The count? Can you be a little more clear, Master Guy? I'm not usually so dense, but you're being a bit cryptic."

He tapped his fingers on the table. "Plans are afoot for their betrothal. Rene visited me secretly the other night. We played a little whist."

Agnes's hand flew to her mouth. "You mean he's here in Paris?"

"Yes. Don't tell the countess or she'll never get over it. He says his mother wants him to court Sylvie, to woo her."

"Is he going to?"

"Yes."

"So why are you telling me about this?"

"Do you realize what this union could mean for the de Courcey family? To be aligned with nobility?"

"It's quite an honor, I'd suppose."

"Exactly. Can you imagine what the prestige alone will do for sales? You must encourage her! Rene and I have been friends for years. I realize he's not a conscientious sort of fellow, but he'd be a good match, a kind husband. And the de Boyce fortune is well-known. Sylvie wouldn't be worried he was marrying her for the money."

For some reason, Agnes didn't like the sound of this. "Why Sylvie? Why does the countess have her heart set on Sylvie when the count could have his pick of France?"

Guy stared deeply into Agnes's eyes. "Is that really a question you need to ask? All the countess wants is what is best for her son. She wants a wife that will do her utmost to make him happy. If Sylvie could serve Mama so faithfully all of these years, imagine what she would do for the man she loved? Even as a child Sylvie's nurturing qualities were evident." That he was proud of his sister was obvious.

Agnes felt her chin stiffen. "She deserves to be loved. This worries me not because I think Sylvie is incapable of loving him, but because I don't know if he would really love her in return."

Guy scratched his temple. "Aggie, answer me this. Do you think Sylvie needs to escape Chateau du Soleil?"

Agnes nodded. "I do." Armand's drinking had been increasing over the past few months as the business grew and his responsibilities became even more demanding. And he wasn't a happy drunk either! Collette was spiraling quickly downward in the wake of her husband's neglect. Sylvie needed to get away from there.

"I received a letter from Mother yesterday filled with the tragedies of her life. If he's not working, Father refuses to leave his study. With Sylvie gone, the staff has slacked off, the household isn't running as it should, which is making Father angry and more withdrawn."

"If *that's* possible," Agnes interjected.

"Precisely. Mother feels helpless, as usual, and she's begging me to talk to the countess, to convince her to send Sylvie home right away, to call off the betrothal permanently."

"Why doesn't she ask the countess herself?"

"Mama cannot handle confrontation, you know that, Aggie."

"So she's getting you to do it for her. Typical of her." Agnes sighed. "What is your father saying about all of this?"

"When she tried to talk to him about it, he slammed the door on her face and told her the wheels had been set in motion, there was no going back now."

Actually, Agnes was glad about that. It sounded as if life at Chateau du Soliel was getting darker than ever. Sylvie needed to stay away from there for a while longer, at least long enough to grow wings of her own. If she chose to minister to her mother and keep the chateau running smoothly for the rest of her life, at least the decision would come from a more objective perspective. "So will you honor your mother's request and talk to the countess?"

"Absolutely not! I doubt if she would even entertain the wish, not with Rene's welfare involved. He comes first no matter what it means to others. Help me with this, Aggie. Encourage her to love him. You know Sylvie, if she feels she is needed more at home, she'll go back willingly and without complaining."

"A more devoted daughter you'll never find."

Guy took a sip of water. "True, but I think Sylvie stays because she has known nothing else. If her heart was opened up to love, I don't think she'd be so quick to go back."

Agnes bit into a piece of bread. "I remember the hold an aunt of mine had over one of my cousins. It was pitiful. The poor girl would leave for a spell to visit us, but it wasn't long until she would receive an urgent message from her mother, and back she would go! I'd hate to think of Miss Sylvie chained to such a life."

"I'm surprised Mother hasn't written Sylvie herself."

Agnes looked down at her hands, afraid the guilt would show in her eyes. Guy could be trusted, however, to keep her secret. "She has," she whispered softly, then looked up and smiled. Reaching into her purse, she pulled out a stack of unopened envelopes.

Guy laughed, leaned over, and hugged her.

"I'll always do what's best for Sylvie, Master Guy. You know that. At the risk of my own job, her welfare will always come first."

"So you'll encourage her as far as the count is concerned?"

"I'll encourage her to follow her heart. And I'll pray for her. You'd do well to do the same, Guy."

Guy shook his head. "There's too much at stake here to leave matters completely up to the divine. My own plans should work out just fine!"

"Oh, Agnes, what a beautiful day! I don't want to rest. Let's go down to the waterfront and watch the boats come in!"

Agnes Green loved to hear Sylvie's voice contain that element of childish wonder and excitement. It didn't happen enough as far as she was concerned. What harm could it do to go watch the ships?

The countess had told Sylvie to rest for the afternoon. Rene was coming home that evening and with the ball the next day, she would need to relax. Sylvie, however, had been in no mood to relax, and Agnes was still restless from her conversation with Guy. So she complied. Actually, it might be fun. And though her role of governess wasn't as prominent as it once was, it would be a good lesson for the girl. "Let me put on my old shoes. These are much too new to wear walking." Sylvie wasn't the only one who benefited from the Parisian shops! Wouldn't Rupert be surprised to see her in such high heels?

They tied on their bonnets and by habit, Agnes grabbed a basket from her tiny bedroom, a closet really, next to Sylvie's. Who knew what kind of fruit was coming in now? Perhaps they could stop by the market and examine all the lovely food.

Out the door and up the street they hurried. Excitement spurred them on, as hand in hand, they sought the docks. Finally, within several blocks of the quay, Sylvie could hardly contain herself. The girl would jump out of her skin if Agnes didn't do something!

"You run ahead, Miss Sylvie." Agnes allowed her beloved charge some freedom, never losing sight of the bright yellow day gown from Worth's, or the jubilant hat. She pushed down the tears. This was the way it was supposed to have been for Sylvie: pretty clothes, afternoon outings. And she prayed that the sun would always shine like it was doing just now, and that true happiness would find the golden heart of Sylvie.

But Sylvie, despite her amicable nature, was proud. A self-protective fortress of her parents' design and execution had walled her in, a fortress she herself guarded. The child possessed a hidden, inner anger, an anger that rarely surfaced and that she had learned to push down into the farthest recesses of her heart. Only God could take it away, that much Agnes knew, and she had been praying for her charge for years.

"Look, Agnes!" Sylvie cried from up ahead, turning to point into the window of the bakery. "Shall we? On the way back?"

Agnes nodded and the girl continued on her way.

The closer Agnes drew to the docks, the more she was reminded of the book she was presently reading. An English novel by that fellow Dickens. There were little Olivers everywhere, "bag-o-boneses" scurrying about the run-down tenements, seemingly oblivious to the screams and curses shouted at them by ragged women with sparse hair and even sparser teeth. Smaller children squatted like mice on the stoops and watched the activity in the street.

As the poverty increased, Sylvie's speed decreased, so that Agnes found herself walking beside her once again.

"Oh, Agnes," she whispered. "This gown I'm wearing could clothe and feed one of these children for a year."

It had given her so much joy when she had pulled it out of the box the day before. Sylvie had always hated the gowns she and Agnes made of the inexpensive, yet sturdy material Armand allocated for their use. But now, Agnes knew she would have given anything to be back inside one of the coarse wool skirts and simple cotton blouses.

"Help for the poor?"

Agnes glanced down, and there to her right sat a middle-aged woman with two young children in her lap. Sylvie immediately reached into her bag and knelt down.

"Bless you," the woman began, and Agnes detected at once the spirits on her breath.

"Agnes!" Sylvie's voice was sharp, that hidden anger rising. Apparently the odor had reached her as well.

"Yes, miss?"

"Take this money and buy the children some bread and cheese. Nothing for the mother."

"Yes, miss." She had never seen Sylvie's face quite so red.

As Agnes set to do her mistress's bidding, heading toward a baker's window displaying bread bleaching in the dry afternoon sun, Sylvie ran on toward the dock where the "Lord of the Islands" was mooring even now.

Agnes let her go.

CHAPTER ❖ SIX

Ever the observer, Matthew Wallace missed nothing. He never had, and sometimes that got him into trouble. Well, *usually* it did, but he rather liked it that way. Kept life interesting.

He disembarked from the "Lord of the Islands," a magnificent, five-masted sailing vessel launched in Dundee several years earlier. A silent prayer of thanks that the channel had been calm and the Seine beautiful had already been relayed to the One who accompanied him everywhere. Now if he could only find the urchin who galloped off with his portmanteau hanging from a grubby little fist!

These Frenchmen, so leisurely and unconcerned. Life on the continent moved much too slowly for an Englishman of his ilk. He spied a group of American industrialists growing redder in the face with each second that yawned by. At least he wasn't of the most frenzied nationality aboard. He almost pitied them and thought about offering up a prayer on their behalf, then decided against it.

"Hello, again."

He turned toward the owner of a gravelly voice, the physician who had sat next to him in the smoking lounge that morning.

Matthew himself wasn't a smoker, but he found that a man with a pipe or a cigar always seemed a bit more ready to talk, and invariably they asked him what he did. He wasn't afraid to tell them, and why.

"How are you this afternoon, Mr. Mann?"

"Good. Good. Been thinkin' about what you said in there earlier. Thought I'd get out the Good Book again. Have any suggestions as to where I should start?"

"Every page is brilliant, naturally. However, one of the gospels should do for a start. Luke has always stood me in good stead."

"Good. Good. I'll do it then. Oh, look, there's my trunk coming down now. That little prayer I muttered back there must've done the trick. Good advice, that."

And off he sauntered.

Matthew smiled. Well, a seed had been planted. And though he hated the gardening he was forced to do around the vicarage with his sister Miranda now and then, he never minded sowing a spiritual seed. He wondered where the water was going to come from with that one. No matter. God would give the increase.

Always a comforting thought.

He heeded his own advice and began praying about that portmanteau, but his attention was quickly won by the sound of a woman's irate voice.

"Let him go immediately!"

Oh, she was angry all right, standing there all yellow and glowing and stomping a booted foot three times. She was livid, in fact. Her feathered hat had slid to the side, its hatpins dragging the curly coiffure along with it; dark hair waved about her face in the breeze that fluttered off the water. Extraordinary! And what was she doing here apparently by herself?

He took a step forward and summed the scene up immediately. Two young English sailors were employing their hard boots with alarming regularity upon one hoary-faced dog with three legs, numerous scars, and a chopped-off tail. Not freshly chopped, mind you, but disconcertingly absent nonetheless. He'd seen worse.

"And what have we here? A regular Joan of Arc!" The tall seaman with a good-looking face but a decidedly cruel slant to his mouth taunted.

"Leave him alone. The poor beast." Her English was almost perfect, but she was undeniably French. That creamy skin, the lithe waist, the way she could hold her head at such a haughty angle. Hardly beautiful, but enticing nonetheless.

"He likes it, don't you, Disraeli?" said the other, tall as well, but uglier than the dog, his scars, and his tail put together. Disraeli yelped in pain as the sailor booted him in the rib cage. "It'll teach the beggar not to mess under me hammock again!"

The young lady, still in her teens, Matthew guessed, threw herself down toward the dog, catching a boot in the shoulder. Not even a wince registered on her face, she was so angry. In fact, her head snapped up and her eyes blazed with hate.

"Hey, now . . . what! We got ourselves a regular heroine here, Billy," the ugly one called to the good-looking one.

"I like a brave woman meself, Ben," Billy replied.

"Shut up, you pig! Both of you!" the girl shouted.

"A fighter too, eh?" Billy raised his brows. "Hold the old dog, Ben, while I get me the young one." He darted forward and pulled Sylvie to her feet by her hair.

Matthew roared down the gangplank. He could hardly believe she didn't scream, and when her fist shot forward and made contact with her assailant's jaw, he knew the girl was really in for trouble.

The old, familiar temper surfaced like a leviathan waking from an age-long sleep. He prayed for forgiveness in advance, pushed up his sleeves, and remembered his mother's raucous laughter when he informed her he was called to the ministry.

"Take your hands off the girl now!" he yelled in his pulpit voice.

Billy, still a bit starry from her punch, pushed her into Ben. "What business is it of yours, Parson? Go along and save some souls, but leave us alone."

He fought for self-control. "Perhaps you failed to hear me. Leave the girl be. And the dog as well, for that matter."

"Look here," the man said as Sylvie kicked against him, "this ain't none of your affair. We got no quarrel with you, Vicar."

He held out his hands, palms up. "Oh, but it is my problem. To visit the widows and the fatherless in their affliction is my duty, the reason I put up with these scratchy clothes day in and day out." Best to lighten things a bit, if he could.

"Joke all ye want, but this chit ain't no orphan," Billy scoffed, stepping forward yet more.

"Perhaps not. But a dog that old most certainly is." Matthew squeezed his fists at his side, paused, breathed in deeply. "Come on lads, let us be gentlemen about this. Let them go, and a little less sin will be charged to all our accounts today. Be sporting, mates, what do you say?" He uncurled his hands again, palms facing the sun.

Ben did as he was told and released the girl. She leaned down and grabbed the dog.

Billy's booted foot made contact yet again, this time on her bottom. Face forward, she landed in the dirt. Horrified, Matthew made his move, his temper ruling the day.

Ben disappeared into the crowd as the girl scrambled to her feet with the dog. Not lingering to watch the blows Matthew was exchanging with Billy, she disappeared into the throng. Matthew hadn't been in a fight in years, and he found it was rather like riding a horse; one never forgot how to do it. Receiving a blow to his jaw, he could only pray that his bishop would not get wind of this one!

He had been shown to his room, a good-sized chamber on the third floor. A servant offered to unpack his things, but all Matthew Wallace wanted to do was lie down and press a cold towel to his blackened eye. It had been a surprising afternoon to say the least!

Matthew had been to Maison de Fleur several times before. Five years previous, before he became vicar of St. Jude's parish in Swainswick, he had spent several months with Rene and his mother. She was a lovely woman, he thought. They had had lively discussions regarding their faith, and she had done all she could to make sure his time was refreshing for him.

He rubbed his jaw. That Billy had a nasty left hook. Apparently he needed this sabbatical he was taking more than he thought! Two months away from Swainswick would do him good. The Lord knew he loved his flock, but they were considerably draining and he found his sermons were becoming lackluster, had lost their punch—even if he hadn't! His bishop suggested he get away for a little while. And so he did, leaving his sister Miranda to tend the vicarage and entertain the visiting priests who would be officiating during his absence.

He closed his eyes.

An hour later someone was shaking him awake. "Matthew? Are you all right?"

At first, he didn't recognize the red-haired man who continued speaking. "Sorry. Can I help you?" Then recognition came to light. "Guy de Courcey, is that you?"

Guy nodded as Matthew sat up. "It's been years."

"What are you doing these days? Last I heard from Rene, you were running de Courcey Paris."

"Still doing just that. It won't be long before I head back to Champagne and take over the business full force."

Matthew was delighted to hear it. Though he hadn't been close friends with Guy, their paths only crossing due to Rene, he had always liked the fellow.

"The countess wanted me to come up and make sure you were all right," Guy apologized. "Nasty bruise you've got there."

Matthew winced as he felt the tender flesh around his eye. "Rescuing a damsel in distress."

Guy laughed out loud. "Good heavens! I thought those days were over for all of us."

"It appears not." Matthew rose to his feet and poured himself a glass of water. "She was a pretty damsel, so I suppose it was worth it."

"Who was she?" Guy asked.

"I don't know, but I wish I did. I haven't seen such spirit in a woman in years! Has Rene returned yet?"

"Just a few minutes ago. A bit skinnier than I remembered, but looking fit."

Matthew was immediately concerned. His friendship with the Count de Boyce was like no other he experienced. Rene had always come to him with his problems, and yet had given back so graciously. He remembered their many evenings together at the Lamb and Crown in Oxford, sipping ale and talking about Scripture and philosophy. Matthew cared greatly for Rene, and hadn't stopped praying for his spiritual welfare all these years, even when his friend had dipped into silence and his letters had stopped.

"Would you like to go see him?" Guy asked. "He's down in the main salon."

Matthew grabbed his coat and followed Guy downstairs. Rene was tending to his mother in the garden, and when he caught sight of Matthew he was clearly delighted. "You brought Matthew here for my return?" He turned to his mother. "I can hardly believe it!" Rising to his feet he pulled the vicar into a quick embrace, kissing him on both cheeks. "How did she ever get you out of Swainswick, old man?"

Matthew returned the hug, thumping him on the back with gusto. "How could I *not* come? How are you doing, Rene? Really?" They both knew he was referring to the hunting accident that had occurred during a visit to the holdings of Matthew's father, the accident that had left Rene's leg in constant pain. Or so the countess had reported to Matthew in a letter a year or so ago.

Rene's eyes glowed. "There are good days and bad days, I suppose. It becomes a bit easier with time. How glad I am you've come, my friend. I can't believe Mama actually brought you all the way to France for my homecoming."

Matthew had been greatly looking forward to it. In truth, he had closer friends, ones with whom he had a great deal in common. But something in his soul loved Rene, as if God had given him the affection for this man who needed a true friend so desperately, a friend that would stick closer than a brother. As if God had called him to be that friend. "Actually, your mother didn't bring me at all. I accepted the invitation and decided to make an extended holiday out of the journey."

"Well, I am glad you're here."

"So am I, my friend. So am I."

The countess smiled in obvious satisfaction. "It's a good thing you came of your own accord, or I would have dragged you here kicking and screaming."

Rene shook his head in amusement and rolled himself a cigarette. "Mother's told me many times that you're the only friend I have who's good for me."

Matthew hid his embarrassment. "Well, I don't know about that, old man, but I do know that I wouldn't have missed being here at your homecoming for the world."

CHAPTER ❖ SEVEN

Agnes poured the final pitcher of water over her mistress's head. "I don't know what your father will say about such a mongrel when you bring him back to Chateau du Soleil."

"At least the countess doesn't mind my having Disraeli up here. Although I will be sad once his wounds are healed and he'll be exiled to the stables." She stood to her feet and allowed Agnes to wrap the warmed towel around her. Agnes could tell the good food they had been eating was starting to do its job and Sylvie was looking a little less bony these days. "As for my father," Sylvie continued, "he's used to my rescues even though he's incapable of understanding the motive behind such actions. As long as I keep him out of the house we should be fine."

Agnes patted the back of her mistress with the towel. "Why it had to be such an ugly mongrel . . ."

Sylvie bent down next to the sleeping pooch and scratched him affectionately between his golden ears. "Poor darling. He's sweet. And he needs me. There's something to be said for such a combination as that, eh Agnes?"

"There are lots of people that need you without having to add his sort to the lot."

"If it's Mother you are speaking of, you're exactly right."

It was good her mistress was now in Paris, Agnes thought. Away from Collette, away from the work in the vineyard.

"Well, I need you too," Agnes said warmly.

"Only because I need you." Sylvie turned away from the dog, quickly wiping away the unshed tears glistening on the surface of her eyes. Agnes saw this, and it touched her heart. "Thank you, Agnes, for being the one constant in my life."

Agnes flushed. "We've been together a long time, I'll grant you that. It's my Rupert you need to thank . . . for being so understanding about my absence!"

Sylvie, now in her dressing gown, nodded and began roughly raking the brush through her hair. "I wish you could have had children of your own, Agnes. You would have been a good mother."

"So do I, miss. But obviously there's work elsewhere for me during my time here on earth."

"I haven't always been easy to raise, have I?" Sylvie said with laughter in her voice.

Agnes crossed her arms, remembering the headstrong toddler—those were rough years. The energetic girl—always late from her forays into the woods. The responsible, introspective, compassionate teen—spending her days in the vineyard or by her mother's side. "Once you stopped getting into your mother's face powder and rouge, it was clear sailing! Hand me that brush. I'll get the tangles out before Pascale comes to do your hair."

"It may sound strange, but I miss my plain old chignon. It was so much easier without these curls flopping all over the place!"

Agnes chuckled. "I don't. You've never looked lovelier."

Sylvie began to fiddle with the comb. "Most of these Parisian women put me to shame."

Agnes disagreed. "There's something very appealing about innocence such as yours, Miss Sylvie. And all the cosmetics in the world cannot imitate that. You may not see yourself as a great beauty, but you're a lovely girl, and that's a fact."

"But these women are so sophisticated. How could I ever hope to become one of them?"

Agnes pulled the brush gently through her hair. "Do you really want to? And will you be in Paris long enough for it to matter?"

Sylvie breathed in deeply. "I was hoping so." She turned to face her maid, tears in her eyes once again. "Oh, Agnes, I don't want to go back there. I don't want to go home." Her voice was filled with anguish and her clenched hands betrayed her feelings of guilt.

"Maybe you won't have to, love," Agnes soothed. "Maybe you'll find a way to stay here." She held her for several minutes, until Sylvie pulled away and walked over to the window to gaze out into the park. Clearly the girl was ready for a change of subject.

"The count arrived when we were out," Agnes informed her as she took the freshly pressed evening gown from the dressing closet. "One of the servant girls passed on the information when she was drawing your bath."

"I'm surprised the countess hasn't called me in to meet him," Sylvie said over her shoulder.

"She hasn't seen her son for two years. I'm sure they have much to talk about. Don't you worry, miss, you'll be seeing enough of him in the future, I'll warrant. Maybe even more than you bargained for." She chuckled. "That vicar arrived as well, sporting a black eye and a swollen jaw!"

Sylvie turned to face Agnes, eyes suddenly filled with excitement. "It was he who rescued us then? Oh Agnes, I was hoping so. What were the chances of two English vicars being aboard that boat?"

"It appears he was your savior this afternoon." Agnes was actually quite pleased with the development. "It will do you some good to be around a man of the cloth in the next few days." So far the house party was made up of Guy, the count, and that Viscount Blackthorne, not exactly spiritual bastions. At least Reverend Wallace would round things out a bit.

"I've never seen a man of the cloth with a punch like his!" Sylvie chuckled. "And did you see his eyes, Agnes? Even from a distance you could see that lovely, dark blue shade. That dark, curly hair was comely as well."

Agnes shot her a look. "You seem positively intrigued with this fellow, and you haven't even met him, child!"

But Sylvie wouldn't back down. "He saved my life, Agnes. Or close to it. Of course he interests me, and I have to thank him for intervening. Besides, when was the last time you saw a priest in a fight?"

Agnes couldn't help but laugh. "You have a point there, Miss Sylvie. Truth be told, I'm looking forward to meeting him as well."

Finally, after a painful session with the hairdresser, Sylvie was ready to go down for supper. "Let me have a good look at you," Agnes ordered, scrutinizing every inch of Sylvie's new gown. It was a stunning confection of ivory silk with gold beading on the bodice. The countess demanded a formal table in the evening, and Sylvie would fit in perfectly. She straightened out a bow near the waistline. "Just right. I declare, Miss Sylvie, your parents wouldn't recognize you." And it was true. Sylvie had been transformed from a plain country mouse into a fresh, lovely young woman, pleasing to the eye in a friendly, easy way.

Sylvie looked at herself in the mirror. "I don't look so skinny anymore, thank goodness."

"Like I said, you are just right. Now go downstairs and have a good time. Guy is already waiting, I'm sure—as well as that Youngblood character."

Sylvie eyed Agnes. "You don't like him, do you?"

Agnes shook her head. "I don't know what it is about him, Sylvie. But I just don't trust the man."

Sylvie laughed and picked up the tiny nosegay of orchids Youngblood had sent up to her room earlier. "I've always found him delightful." She kissed Agnes on the cheek and hurried into the corridor.

Agnes tidied up the room, lit a lamp, and settled in for an evening's reading. But first, she kept her promise to Guy and prayed for Sylvie. And while she was at it, she prayed for her darling Rupert as well, suddenly feeling homesick for his arms.

CHAPTER ❖ EIGHT

Making sure her long, satin gloves hugged her arms without a crease, Sylvie negotiated the back stairs, then navigated the labyrinth of passages that brought her to the music room. Two of Aunt Racine's music students were playing softly in the corner while the guests milled about the room with drinks in their hands.

Sylvie suddenly became nervous, not recognizing anyone. It had been so long since she had seen Count Rene de Boyce, and yet by all accounts, the count was supposed to be a charming, polite, gracious individual. He was eighteen when she last saw him ten years ago. He'd been slightly overweight, good at conversation, and very kind to nine-year-old Sylvie. She had been crying in the garden when he found her, her heart broken at the loss of her first dog, a cocker spaniel named Beau. Collette had confined herself to the chapel earlier in the day, and Father was busy down in the cellars. Entwining her fingers amid his own, he had said, simply, "Cry, Sylvie."

No one but Agnes had given her license to do that before. And she had obeyed. But all this time later, she could remember just his voice and the feel of his hand ... so reassuring ... so gentle as the sun set and the darkness settled over the vineyard, accompanied by her soft weeping. Later, she'd found herself tucked in her bed, not realizing she had fallen asleep on his shoulder.

But she was a child then.

She had changed . . . and so, most probably, had Rene. For better or worse she couldn't say. His friendship with the vicar could mean one of two things: he either had much in common with the man, or was seeking redemption.

Matthew Wallace apparently hadn't come down yet either.

His face flamed to life in her mind. Though she had tried to play it down with Agnes, the truth was, it had been impossible to stop thinking about him. A vicar *and* a hero. A good man. A passionate man.

And those eyes! She couldn't wait to see if they were really as blue as she remembered. Was he as handsome when he was calm as he was when he was angry? Moreover, would that brave strength be as evident under normal circumstances? Her stomach quivered as she let her mind wander again in Matthew Wallace's direction and savored the already cherished memory of her rescue.

Not wishing to mingle with guests she didn't know, she sought the countess's salon to wait for several minutes.

The light from the gas lamps caught the gilded paneling, the fringe on the cushions, and the many Limoges boxes set about on antique tables in a most bewitching manner. But Sylvie failed to notice. For when all eyes turned her way as she entered the room, the setting was hardly of importance. He was there, her rescuer, and her savior. Those beautiful indigo eyes flew open wide in recognition, and he immediately stood to his feet.

"I suppose my thanks are in order." Taking note of his black eye, she held out a hand.

"Come in, my dear!" the countess chimed from her seat on the sofa. "Pray tell us, what is it you are talking about?"

Sylvie looked at Matthew Wallace. "I owe a large debt of gratitude to Reverend Wallace"—she paused for dramatic effect, looking around at each person in the room—"for saving my life!"

Working together, Sylvie and Matthew told the story nicely, though she felt as jumpy as a kitten, standing so close to him. He even smelled good, like soap, leather, and paper.

"And so by the time that Billy character went limping back to the ship," Matthew finished up, "she was gone. With the dog in tow."

The countess trilled a laugh. "How is poor Disraeli doing now?"

Sylvie sat down next to Guy, who placed a sturdy arm around her shoulders. "He's sleeping by the fire. I don't think we'll hear from the poor beast until morning."

"What poor beast?" All heads turned as the guest of honor entered the room, none other than Count Rene de Boyce himself. He leaned heavily on his knob-topped cane, but even his severe limp could not detract from his attractiveness. His well-cut suit and his traveled air proved he was a man of high taste, and though he wasn't tall or muscular, his very presence made a statement. Bright blond hair, soft and straight, shone like newly minted gold in the lamplight, and his smile overflowed into his benevolent eyes. Sylvie would have recognized him anywhere. Her eyes were pricked by tears as she flew across the room and into his arms.

It had been a wonderful week for reunions.

"And I thought you reserved such grand hugs only for me," Youngblood drawled from the corner.

Rene kissed Sylvie's cheeks and took her hands. "Why Sylvie, you're all grown up."

"She certainly is!" piped the countess. "And lovely as well."

Embarrassment swallowed Sylvie whole, and she was extremely relieved when the butler announced that dinner was served. The group chattered like a flock of jackdaws on their way to the dining room, and Sylvie found herself seated next to Rene. Youngblood was at her other side, and Guy and the vicar sat across the table. Sylvie couldn't remember having ever had such a wonderful time. The wine sparkled, the conversation flowed, and she was the center of attention. It was extraordinary, heady.

Later that night she told Agnes all about it. "I felt like a woman for the first time in my life, Agnes. All my jokes were witty, and I never once dropped anything off my fork!" She was giddy with success. Life here at Maison de Fleur was so exciting, so much fun. Hopefully, she would never have to go back to Champagne.

Sylvie spent the next morning reassuring the countess that tomorrow night's ball would play out flawlessly. Goodness, but the emperor himself, Napoleon III, was scheduled to put in an appearance. That alone would guarantee a successful evening. Would the extravagant civilization known as the Second Empire enjoy an old-fashioned ball? Sylvie suspected they would. If only because the countess herself was so well-loved and gossip was never choosy regarding its setting.

"I wonder how you managed it, Mother," Rene remarked that morning at breakfast with a wide smile in Sylvie's direction. Surely he had lost some weight in the past ten years, had broadened some at the shoulders, narrowed a bit too much at the waist. The man was positively slender, and coupled with an almost angelic face and that sunny hair, he appeared much younger than his twenty-eight years. Only the dark circles beneath his eyes betrayed his true age. "Our emperor thinks of nothing but training his military out at Chalons . . . of expanding the empire. Yet, one little slip of paper from Racine de Boyce and he comes scampering like an eager pup. Is there something you have forgotten to tell me about you and our ruler, Mother?"

The countess trilled her youthful laugh. "Would I really tell you if there was?"

"Absolutely not!"

Sylvie chuckled at their banter, and he momentarily placed a warm hand over hers, then went back to his breakfast.

Right then, Sylvie decided that she still liked this fellow well enough. His smile was natural, his laugh was easy and frequent. They had experienced such a good time the night before. After growing up around Armand and his dour ways, she could use a friend like Rene. There was something vulnerable about him which spoke to her soft heart. For one thing, there was his limp, and he seemed almost otherworldly—aware of what was going on around him, but a tad removed from it all.

Matthew Wallace, however, was an altogether different matter. Now there was a man whose feet were firmly planted on the ground.

Ten minutes later the vicar appeared. "Forgive my tardiness," he apologized, wincing as he sat down and rubbing his rib cage, "but I had a most lovely, albeit jarring, walk along the Champs Elysees. It has been too long since Paris has cast her spell over me."

He was every bit as breathtaking as he had been the evening before, Sylvie thought, unable to keep from comparing this robust man to the wispy, fair count seated next to her. Yet the affection between the two men was evident as Rene slid the chair out next to him and greeted his friend with a smile.

"Hopefully the sights took your mind off of your aches, Reverend," the countess said with a jeweled flourish of her slim hand, ringing the bell again. "Some hot food will be brought in shortly, Matthew."

"Just tea and toast, thank you, my lady," he requested, then turned to Sylvie. "You are looking well after yesterday's unexpected adventure."

"Thanks to you, Reverend."

"Please, call me Matthew. The thought of being so formal on holiday is unbearable. And after all we've been through together!"

Sylvie felt her heart tumble. "Call me Sylvie." She quickly wrinkled her nose. "My father would hate it. A very prim man. But I'm in Paris and it's spring, so I fail to see the harm in a little friendly familiarity."

Rene cleared his throat and positioned his cane to rise to his feet. "Unfortunately, the day stretches before me with much to be done. Business that cannot be detained a moment longer."

The countess's brow creased. "Already? Can you not wait until tomorrow to throw yourself back into your affairs?"

Sylvie thought he looked a little pale.

"Now Mother, someone has to keep you ensconced in this lavish lifestyle. And since the title is mine, the responsibility is mine as well." He sighed theatrically, but winked playfully as he stood to his feet, leaning heavily upon the ornately topped cane. "Wallace, would you consider entertaining Sylvie for me today? We were going to explore the Louvre."

Both Matthew and Sylvie turned to face the countess. "Yes, my darlings. Do as he asks. As Sylvie keeps telling me, everything is ready for tonight, and there's nothing left for this old woman to do but worry."

"And then only if you feel you must," Sylvie added.

"Are you certain about this, Rene?" Matthew asked. "I came to see you, to be of some assistance while you readjust."

"You would be doing me a great favor by going with Sylvie."

Sylvie raised her brows defensively as she laid aside her napkin. "Well, if you put it that way, monsieur, perhaps I should just take care of myself. It is something I am quite good at, you know, and to be an imposition on the reverend his first day in Paris—"

Matthew put a hand over hers, squeezed, then let go. "It would be a pleasure, Sylvie. In fact, nothing would please me more than to explore the Louvre with Disraeli's savior. How is the poor mutt, by the way?"

"Been sleeping in front of my hearth ever since we came back. You must visit him, for he owes you an even larger debt of gratitude than I."

Their eyes met, and Sylvie couldn't tear her gaze from his. A new experience, and certainly one of the most lovely feelings she had ever known. But she couldn't get enough of the compelling depth of his eyes, eyes that were sending a message—somehow—a message of hope. Peace thrived in those eyes.

Footsteps on the parquet flooring quickly turned all heads in the room.

"Guy!" Sylvie rose from her chair and hugged her brother. "What brings you around so early?"

"Came to visit with the wandering count again, and you, of course, dear sister." He kissed her tenderly on the cheek.

"Do sit down with us, darling!" Countess Racine called from her perch at the head of the table. "Have you breakfasted?"

"No, madame. I was getting ready to go to the offices this morning and thought I'd bring over a bottle of this." He pulled out a bottle of wine from behind his back. "It's an 1852. Our best year by far. A more proper welcome home than I gave you yesterday, Rene."

Rene took the bottle and set it on the table. "We'll toast to us all later on with France's finest champagne!"

"And will we have you with us for long, Rene? Or will you be rushing off to yet another foreign land?" Youngblood, the final friend to enter the room, asked with a smirk from the doorway.

"I do believe I've finally come home to stay."

The countess's eyes shone as she rang the bell to have more coffee delivered to the merry, ever increasing breakfasters.

Guy sat down and unfolded a napkin. "Then my second reason for visiting still stands. I wanted to warn you to behave properly with Sylvie here under your roof."

Rene laughed. "I promise you, Guy, that no ill shall befall your sister at my hand."

Sylvie offered an explanation to Matthew as Guy and Youngblood began discussing politics. "Guy's always tried to look out for me. When Papa sent him away to boarding school years ago, I felt like I had lost my guardian angel."

"My sister Miranda is a guardian angel of sorts . . . and I suppose I play that role to her."

"Every girl needs a good brother," she stated, taking Guy's hand in her own.

Guy turned his attention from Rene back to his sister. "What's that, Sylvie?"

"Nothing, Guy. Just telling Matthew here how much you mean to me." She squeezed his hand, knowing that Guy would always be there to protect her.

CHAPTER ❖ NINE

"I t began as a library," Matthew told her, "but surely you know all about the history of the Louvre."

"Actually, no." Sylvie hated to admit it. "My father doesn't see the point in overeducating women. Other than what it takes to grow grapes, I only know what Agnes taught me. And she did give me a love for books, so I suppose the whole world is before my eyes, figuratively speaking, of course."

"Well, that is more than I know about. Your English is beautiful, and you are sweet to entertain me in my native language." Indeed, he felt he was escorting an angel this morning. Sylvie, dressed in a pale, creamy yellow and toting along a parasol, had been most engaging. He loved to hear her laugh.

"Well, with you and the viscount visiting, not to mention the fact that Guy and the count were educated at Oxford, it seems to have been the language of choice the past two days! Thank goodness the countess can work her way around it as well."

A small child suddenly careened in their direction, and he quickly pulled Sylvie aside, his hand around her small waist. She was so slender, he thought, but so lovely. By instinct, he wound her arm through his, noticing how large her hands were and how that seemed to set her apart from the small, childlike women most men found so attractive. He rather liked her height, and the way they literally saw eye to eye.

"I trust our walk down the Champs Elysees wasn't as painful as it was earlier," she remarked.

"No, it wasn't. Although working our way through the sightseers by the Arc de Triomphe afforded me several elbows in the side. I felt like one of Napoleon's veterans standing there, still suffering the effects of my battle wounds!"

Now, walking through the Tuilleries, they approached the museum, and he wanted to return to the former topic, to find out all he could about this courageous, yet gentle lady. "So you have had no formal education? No convent school?"

She shook her head. "Just Agnes, who was the daughter of a teacher. She started feeding me books from the time I was four years old. Agnes has her father send us the latest volumes from England. But I do not read very fast, I am afraid."

"And who is your favorite writer?" Matthew asked, picking up his step.

"Dickens, I suppose. His characters have to live through so much. And yet some of them survive."

"But not all."

"No." She sighed. "But then … that is life. Do you like to read?"

"Oh, yes. Anything my hands find themselves holding."

Her eyes sparkled. "I thought vicars read only the Bible."

He laughed loudly, then quickly hushed his voice. "The Scriptures are my first love, yes. But so many other works show forth the creativity that God bestows upon his people. Creativity is so exciting, so astounding in all its forms—the arts, the sciences, mathematics."

"So you were educated at university with Rene, no?"

"Oxford."

She sighed. "I always wanted to go to school. Even convent school, to be honest, would have been better than nothing."

He put his other hand over the hand she had tucked firmly in his arm. "Believe me, Sylvie, most of the learning I retained took place after university—what I read and loved myself. Keep reaching forward, mademoiselle. Moreover, for what it is worth, you seem to be a woman of keen intelligence. Shows in your eyes."

Sylvie smiled more broadly than he had seen as yet, and the sight of it took his breath away. "I do believe that's the nicest thing anyone has ever said to me."

"It is true. You remind me of my older sister Miranda—always reading or puttering in the garden. You would like her. Sees God in the small things—the beautiful things."

"I suppose it's easy to recognize God in the stars, or the bud of a flower. I just have trouble reconciling *that* God with the *people* he created."

They had entered the museum and were standing in front of the Venus de Milo. In his humble opinion, Matthew thought she paled in comparison with his escort. "There's beauty in everything," he said. "Even what some think of as ugly, can be comely in the eyes of others."

"I don't think that's always true," Sylvie whispered. "But I wish with all my heart it was."

He was stupefied. Did she really see herself as unattractive? True, she had been confined to the country life, but they had mirrors there, didn't they?

Matthew caught up to her a minute later. "Did I upset you, Sylvie?" he asked candidly.

She turned to him in surprise. "No, monsieur. It wasn't you at all. In fact, I'm finding that walking along with you is a most soothing pastime. Tell me more about the museum. Have you been here often?"

"No. Just once before. I have read about it, though. François the First began the collection, with only twelve paintings from Italy. The Jaconde was one of them."

By now they were standing in front of that very painting, staring at the enigmatic smile of the homely, mannish-looking woman who had kept people guessing for centuries. The Mona Lisa. "So she's been here all this time, eh?" Sylvie smiled. "I guess you might call her the lady of the manor!"

"A woman you can actually count on!" he joked, then bit his tongue. He hadn't meant to sound so acerbic. Staying away from the fair sex for so long after the death of his Isabelle hadn't rendered him exactly sensitive, though he was trying very hard this morning to be just that. He quickly shoved thoughts of Isabelle aside.

"Disappointed with our sex, monsieur?" Sylvie countered. "At least you are not indifferent."

"Indifferent? No. That would be wonderful." He began fidgeting with his pocket watch.

She stopped and turned to face him. "The viscount spoke of your loss many years ago. I'm sorry." She laid a hand on his arm, this woman with a soft spot for dogs and, apparently, vicars. The thought made him smile, and she breathed an apparent sigh of relief.

"Isabelle died a long time ago and still I grieve. That is the way of it for me."

"And will it always be so?"

"I suppose that is up to God. But I have not yet received any word otherwise! No other woman has crossed my path willing to forsake everything for the ministry of the gospel, and, to be honest, I haven't been looking very hard."

"Can you be so resigned to your fate? What if there's only loneliness in store for you?"

"Then he will give me the grace to forbear."

"I can't accept that so easily. When I think of a life without love, and that God would actually purpose that, it doesn't exactly endear me to him."

He stopped, turned her to face him. "Are you lonely, Sylvie?"

She turned away, but he pursued her. "Tell me, Sylvie. Tell about your fears and your disappointments. Please."

"I cannot. You wouldn't understand. Nobody understands, not even Agnes, not even Guy." Her eyes held a desperation, even a fear.

"Has somebody frightened you?"

"Yes, Matthew. *You* have."

Odd. "What do you mean by that?"

She laughed, obviously trying to turn it into a joke. "I'm afraid you might try and rescue me all over again." She turned, put her arm in his, and started off toward another exhibit.

She needed rescuing all right. From what he didn't know. But he was determined to find out.

⁓

After dinner, Rene was more than happy to spill all the details he knew regarding Sylvie de Courcey. They were sitting on the verandah overlooking the garden. Matthew fiddled with the count's pack of rolling papers while his friend smoked a cigarette.

"So she feels trapped then." He ripped out a paper and folded it into a small square.

"Her parents have kept her cloistered away in Champagne. Especially her mother," Rene offered. "Now there's a woman who I can't imagine living with." He pulled in deeply on his smoke. "It's a wonder Sylvie has turned out so well."

"How is it that a girl her age isn't already married, or at least spoken for?"

"Did I say she wasn't spoken for?" Rene lifted his brows.

"Well, no. I merely assumed."

"Sylvie's quite spoken for, old man. She just doesn't know it yet."

Matthew felt his stomach sour. "Do you know who it is?"

Rene ground out his cigarette, half-smoked, beneath his heel. "You are looking at him."

Just then Youngblood and Guy appeared. "Ready to go, then?" Youngblood asked.

Rene stood to his feet. "We're all going down to the Moulin Rouge and then over to Youngblood's to play some cards. Care to join us?"

Matthew laughed and held out the rolling papers.

Rene chuckled. "I didn't think so. But it would have been ghastly of me not to have at least extended an invitation."

"Yes, absolutely ghastly," Youngblood drawled.

"Are we off, then?" Guy asked.

"Where's Sylvie?" Rene wondered.

Youngblood pulled a cigar out of his pocket. "I was just with her. She was reading in your mother's salon."

Rene turned to Matthew. "Would you mind, old man, taking care of her tonight, until she retires?"

Matthew didn't mind in the least. And as the group dispersed, he realized that despite the lack of cards and liquor, he was going to have a finer time than all of the others put together. Rene had no idea what a lucky man he was!

CHAPTER ❖ TEN

The ballroom reminded Sylvie of a girl at a springtime party. Festooned with flowers over its intricate woodwork, it was a breathtaking display of color, light, reflection, and scent. The breezy perfume of the thousands of blossoms arranged for the celebration floated around the guests as they filled the dance floor or milled about the perimeter. The subtle buzz of even subtler conversation mingled with the music of stringed instruments and pianoforte.

"The music students are finally earning their keep, Aunt Racine," Sylvie remarked to the countess.

"Isn't it wonderful?" the countess breathed, looking absolutely beautiful in a gown of orchid silk. "All our hard work hasn't been for nothing." She hugged her. "Sylvie, thank you."

"Has the count returned yet?" Sylvie asked. Rene hadn't come home the night before, according to Youngblood's report at the breakfast table. By the time Sylvie had changed into her gown for the ball, he still had not arrived.

"Not yet! But I'm sure he'll be here," the countess said with a bit too much conviction. Sylvie could only hope she was right. Guests were arriving full force now. Yet Sylvie noticed little but the man at the other end of the ballroom. Standing out among the gem-colored silks, the sparkling jewels, wearing his black clerical garb was Matthew Wallace.

Reverend Wallace.

She put a gloved hand up to her mouth and stifled a laugh, remembering the fun they'd had together the night before, making up silly card games and eating chocolates till they were almost sick. He said he hadn't laughed so much in years, and neither had she. Matthew Wallace was like a tonic for the heart. He always knew the right things to say.

His eyes still fascinated her, so straightforward and deep. And the way the man had fought down at the docks still thrilled her! Nothing whatsoever religious about fists like that! Never before had she met someone whose heart she knew so readily. She knew *him*. She wasn't sure how she felt so close to him already, but she did, and he seemed to feel the same. They had covered miles of ground in the past few days.

Standing there alone, ostracized somewhat by his clothing and therefore his calling, his gaze smoothly scanned the room in search of a place to land. Surely he was in search of a rescue!

The azure eyes locked onto Sylvie's, delight leaping onto their surfaces.

She waved and motioned him nearer.

Sylvie watched—fascinated—as he hastened toward her. Like no other man in the room, Matthew Wallace seemed to be an entity unto himself. This broad man, dressed in black, his white shirt gleaming next to his swarthy skin, his teeth bared in a wide smile, was the largest ship on this ballroom sea. So much life, so much vitality, and that temper of his! It shouldn't have thrilled her. But it did.

He bowed. "Thank you, Sylvie," he said, lifting her hand to his mouth for a polite kiss. "I was in need of a friend just then. Nobody was asking me to dance!" His eyes, with their long, dark lashes, looked into hers, sparkling and humorous. "I am in your debt."

"After what you did to those sailors, Matthew, I do believe the scales are still tipped heavily in your favor."

Oh, he was enjoyable to look at, she decided. The warm air of the rapidly filling ballroom suddenly parched her throat, and she slipped her hand in his. "Come, let us get something to ease our thirsts, and then you may fill my ear with the wonderful sound of your voice."

He led her to a chair. "My voice? I have always hated my voice."

"Really? But it's magnificent. So warm . . . and strong."

"Yes. Well, the strong part I believe. Some members of my congregation would say it is a bit *too* strong."

"And your homilies offend your flock regularly?"

He smiled. "It would not be a worthwhile Sunday if someone was not put out a bit. But most of the flock at St. Jude's are good people."

"You love them dearly. I see that in your eyes when you speak of them, if I see nothing else."

Those liquid blue eyes softened, as did his voice, down to a husky thrum which sent a delicious warmth flowing down her spine. He loved what he did and who he did it for, and it showed. His passion for his work—for the people he served—was exciting. This man was different from any gentleman she had ever met.

"—love them too much," he was saying. "That is what Miranda keeps telling me. She says God never gave her a husband because someone has to be the brains of the outfit."

Sylvie laughed. "You are the heart and she is the head?"

"No. The Lord Jesus is the head. We both have a complete understanding of where our strength lies, of who it is that has commissioned us in the first place."

Sylvie had never heard such talk. "So you do all of this because of your love for God?"

They sat down on one of the many gilded side chairs that seemed to support the mirrored wall.

"That is the only way, Sylvie. If I did it for myself I would have given up long ago."

"So it isn't easy, then?"

"It is not just preaching a sermon on Sundays. It is visiting the sick and the hurting, planning church functions, raising money, and details, details, details. I do not know what I would do without Miranda. It's horrible of me to even say, but sometimes I selfishly hope she will never find a man worthy of her."

"At least not until you find a woman worthy of you," Sylvie declared sincerely.

His brows raised. "Methinks the lady's opinion is much too lofty."

"You're wrong. You're like no man I've ever met, Matthew Wallace. Someday you'll find your arms aching for someone, and she'll be every bit as good to you, as helpful to you, as Miranda."

Matthew reached into his pocket and mopped his brow with a handkerchief. "One can only commit these things to God. It may sound as if I should be lonely, Sylvie. And I suppose I am sometimes. But 'there is a friend'—Jesus Christ—'that sticketh closer than a brother.' My relationship to my heavenly Father has truly brought me through any trial, all the pain, I have ever had to face. And I can stand before you now as one who believes and is not bitter or resentful. At least most of the time."

"You must tell me more about this love, Matthew. You must tell me more about this love you bear for God as your Father. I've never heard of such divine intimacy. Not from anyone who seems to be a member of that family, anyway."

"Sylvie, nothing would give me more pleasure than to tell you about the One who made you."

She crossed her arms, tapped her gloved fingers—then nodded twice. "I believe you, Reverend. I certainly do."

The countess strolled over. "Hello, my sweets. Still enjoying the evening?"

Matthew stood up and offered her his chair. "Delightful, Countess. As we all suspected it would be." He looked at Sylvie. "I do not know when I was last in a place filled with such beauty."

Sylvie almost choked on her punch. Was she imagining it, or was he talking about her? She quickly downed the rest of her drink.

"Has anyone seen Rene?" the countess asked, adjusting one of the many rings she wore on the outside of her gloves. "He should have been here by now. No matter yet." She turned to Matthew, stood to her feet, and took his arm. "Take me for a whirl on the dance floor, Vicar. I want to dance with you first."

"Dear Countess, feeling sorry for me?" he joked.

She laughed. "We wouldn't want you to be left holding up the wall all night!"

Matthew smiled at Sylvie, the warmth of it causing her heart to flutter, and he hastened to the dear lady's bidding.

Sylvie watched the two weave their way through the crowd and onto the dance floor. They were so opposite in appearance—and yet they both had such faith. How could they love God like they did, when the world was like it was?

She decided the answer to that question would have to wait for another night.

One thing was certain, she thought with a laugh, Matthew Wallace was obviously a better fighter than he was a dancer!

Just then, David Youngblood blew in, snatched her into his arms, and whirled her onto the dance floor.

"I don't know how to dance!" she laughed, feeling a mild alarm, but reassured by his strong arms.

"Don't worry, little Sylvie." He held her more tightly, guiding her with practiced ease. "I will not let you fall."

"Or look like a fool?"

"Well," he chuckled, letting go of her hand to caress her cheek, "I can't promise you that. But you can make sure of that yourself, by not caring what these twits think and having a good time. It's been my secret for years!"

And that is what she did, abandoning herself to the music, the swirl of the dance. The viscount was a delight. He made everything such fun. He cut a dashing figure in his dark evening clothes, his chestnut hair loose and soft, his pale grey eyes warm and interested in everything she had to say. Viscount Blackthorne made her feel important, not because of what she did, but because of who she was.

Finally, the musicians took a break, and reluctantly she allowed Youngblood to lead her off the floor. Matthew was drinking punch on the other side of the room with Guy. He raised his glass to her and shuffled his legs a bit, a comment on her dancing she was sure. She laughed.

"Having a good time, sweet Sylvie?" Youngblood asked, indicating a chair for her to sit in. "If the flush of your cheeks or the stars in your eyes are any indication, I'd say you're enjoying your first ball immensely."

"You have no idea, dear Viscount. Absolutely no idea!"

Suddenly remembering the countess's worry, she looked around. But Rene was still nowhere to be found.

CHAPTER ❖ ELEVEN

Is the countess resting now?" Matthew glanced up at Sylvie from where he sat on the hearth rug, rubbing Disraeli on his spare stomach. After an exhausting, albeit enjoyable evening, the threesome were relaxing in a small salon at the back of the house—a quiet room done in shades of yellow and green.

"Yes. The poor dear. Has Rene returned yet?"

Matthew shook his head with a sigh. "No." Rene hadn't been the most responsible of men at Oxford, but even Matthew didn't expect such rudeness, such a lack of consideration, from his friend. The honoree had failed to show up for his own homecoming celebration. And the evening degenerated from there, for the most part. The countess had done well at hiding her embarrassment and hurt, but he'd seen it, when she thought no one was looking.

Sylvie knelt down, then sat, arranging her fancy skirts around her. Every move she made fascinated Matthew. Graceful, yet so full of life.

"I do believe you have made a friend for forever." He smiled, patting and rubbing the dog as one who had grown up with canine companionship. "Old Dizzy has certainly risen in the ranks, would you not say?"

She laughed. "I do believe I like the name Dizzy better, Reverend. It suits him now that he's a 'dog of means.' Dizzy he shall be."

They lounged in quiet contentment, listening to the fire and the sounds of servants tending to the vast cleanup. Soon after, Dizzy's soft snore lent its own quiet hum to the atmosphere. It had been like that throughout their day together. Conversation and quiet. And comfort. Matthew had never felt so much at ease in a woman's presence ... well, not since Isabelle. But Isabelle had been different, a tranquil harbor into which his stormy nature could peacefully settle. It didn't matter if the clouds were roiling up a tempest or the waves of the sea heaved and tugged around them, Isabelle's soul was always gentle, calm, and loving.

Though outwardly as gentle, Sylvie was altogether different. She had a spark of life in her that Isabelle lacked, and a reckless courage in the face of adversity. Isabelle, for instance, would have never rescued Dizzy on her own, the way Sylvie had. While Isabelle had been a woman to be adored, Sylvie was one to be admired.

He felt the young woman's eyes on his face. "It was fortunate the viscount arrived to play the host," she said.

"Yes, well, you did your fair share to rescue the evening as well."

"I simply knew what was supposed to happen at every turn. The countess was on the verge of retiring to her room when the emperor and his entourage arrived. What timing. It's a good thing she didn't go up before then."

Matthew recalled watching the two old friends as they chatted together in some comfortable chairs in the corner of Racine's salon. Louis-Napoleon's presence had been just what the countess needed to cheer her. Even so, after his brief, but appreciated appearance, she quietly retired to her suite, looking a decade older than when she had descended. Her heart had to be broken. And yet she had departed gracefully, feigning a chill. Proud and dignified, she walked slowly up the stairs, nodding and smiling. Poor woman.

Matthew was relieved Rene had not yet returned. He'd given lads a good thrashing for far less in his day. He inwardly muttered a prayer for patience, but wasn't completely sure he wanted God to answer just yet.

"The countess didn't deserve such treatment," Sylvie remarked, brow drawn, face a bit flushed.

Oh dear, Matthew couldn't help but be amused. *Another cause for Sylvie to defend.* "I wonder what kept the count away?" he asked. "It was most likely a good reason."

"The bottom of the Seine is the only place he could have been that would excuse such behavior," she snapped.

Matthew supposed Rene was now one step behind in his quest for Sylvie's love.

"Perhaps we'll find out tomorrow, after Youngblood locates him," he said hopefully, worried for his friend. Rude or not, he certainly didn't wish for any ill to befall him.

"How long will you be staying?" she asked as if it were important to her. Was she as eager for his company as her eyes seemed to be saying?

"Just three more days."

"Then we'll have to make the most of them. These three legs of Dizzy's need some exercise. Would you honor us with your company, such as we are, on a stroll in the morning?"

"It would be my pleasure."

Or my pain, he thought, wondering just what God thought he was doing.

Just then, Youngblood blew in, a swirl of cape and curl. He bowed to Sylvie, eyed Matthew who stood to his feet. "No sign of him anywhere."

"Do you think he's all right?" Sylvie asked, still rubbing Dizzy's head.

Viscount Blackthorne shrugged but looked directly into Sylvie's eyes. "He was last seen at the Moulin Rouge around eleven o'clock. I would say he is probably in good hands by now."

Matthew, much to his chagrin, felt himself draw in his breath a bit too sharply. Youngblood turned on him, derision in his eyes. "Oh, stuff the priggish nonsense, Wallace. Sylvie is not some naïve filly. While I wager she hasn't experienced much of the world firsthand, she *does* know it's out there. Am I right, Sylvie?" He arose and poured himself a drink.

"I do read quite a bit," Sylvie said, her face red. Matthew could have given the proud viscount a good shaking for causing the woman such discomfort. "So, you think he's with a ... lady friend."

"He has had several, you know." Youngblood threw the scotch against the back of his throat and swallowed, eyes returning to Sylvie.

I would swear the man is vying for her approval, Matthew thought. Sylvie was worthy of any man's favor, and that the viscount had always soothed the inner wounds of his disfigurement with the affections of the fair sex was no secret.

Sylvie dropped her eyes. "Yes. I have heard. It is the way of men, I do believe."

Matthew watched as Youngblood gently knelt beside her, taking her hand. "Not forever, though, my sweet, eh? For some men, all it takes is a good woman to reform him."

Sylvie laughed, then patted his hand. "You don't fool me, Viscount! I know of your reputation. All of France is aware of your escapades!"

Matthew was growing more and more uncomfortable. Viscount Blackthorne shot him a wicked grin. "We can't all be saints like Wallace here!"

"No!" Sylvie agreed, not unkindly, but poking fun at him nonetheless. "Sainthood is only for the pure."

So that's what she thinks of me, Matthew thought later that night as he readied himself for bed. *Saint Matthew*. It was then that he realized to pursue the likes of Sylvie de Courcey would indeed be madness.

Not to mention disobedient to the One whose will he sought so desperately to perform.

⁓

What am I doing here, torturing myself like this? Matthew thought as he looked across the boat at Rene and Sylvie. The wooing had begun. And here he was, like a fool, rowing the boat down the Seine while Rene talked softly to his intended.

Blast! This was almost more than he could take.

"Matthew," Sylvie chimed, "do stop rowing and join our conversation. You're pushing so hard over there I'm thinking this little skiff must actually be a steamboat!"

"That's right, old man. Don't keep going on our account. It's a lovely day for a drift." Rene put a cigarette in his mouth and got it going. "This isn't the Cherwell, you know."

Now he tells me! Matthew laid the oars neatly on the floor of the boat. As one of the better oarsmen at Oriel College, he had helped take their team to victory three years in a row. Apparently he hadn't forgotten the art.

"I was just asking the count how you two met," Sylvie volunteered, and he had to admit he felt better knowing he had been the topic of conversation. "He told me it was during a fight!"

Matthew remembered. "Naturally."

"How else does one meet Matthew Wallace," Rene laughed.

Sylvie joined. "That's right. Care to fill me in on the details, Reverend?"

Matthew winced. "It wasn't one of my more memorable fights, to be honest. It was before my walk with the Lord became a priority. A simple pub brawl, I'm afraid. I can't even remember how it started."

"After the room was almost completely demolished and the fight had died off," Rene reported, "he went around checking the wounded, like some battlefield physician. You see this scar here?" He lifted up the blond lock that normally fell across his forehead. "A memoir of that very night!"

Sylvie touched it, sliding a gentle finger over the line. Matthew felt his heart lurch. "That's nothing," he suddenly cried. "Look at this! Happened in one of my father's mills." He pulled up a pant leg. The others gasped at the thick, ropelike scar which snaked around his calf, over his shin, and up to his knee. "Top that!"

Sylvie reached out and lightly felt the scar. Matthew quickly pulled his pant leg down, lest his face give away his feelings. This girl was casting a spell over him, most certainly, and he didn't know what to do about it.

"I know I can't top it," Rene said, lazily flicking ashes into the water. "In fact, mine looks much the same."

Matthew berated himself for being so callous, considering Rene's ever-present pain.

"Nor I," Sylvie admitted. "And I don't want to. But one time, I broke my thumb!" She held up her thumbs, the left one more crooked than its mate. "I was playing leapfrog with Guy in the courtyard and I was going much too high and too fast, and I sailed right over him. I literally landed on my thumb!" She got such a crazy, "I'm a dolt" look on her face, the two men began to chuckle, and soon, the boat was rocking beneath their heaving laughter.

"I haven't had this conversation since I was ten!" Sylvie declared.

Rene nodded. "Remember the days of comparing scars with your best friend?"

"Tommy Meadows," Matthew remembered. "My closest boyhood friend."

"Jean-Claude St. Juste," said Rene.

They looked expectantly at Sylvie.

"Well, my sweet?" Rene put his arm around her. "What about you?"

Sylvie shrugged. "Just Guy, I guess. And Agnes." Her eyes dropped. "That's it."

Matthew suddenly understood the depths of the girl's loneliness. Apparently, so did Rene, for he kissed her tenderly on the cheek. Possessively, Matthew thought, as if it was his right to comfort her so.

Unfortunately for me, Matthew thought, *it is his right. Not mine. It isn't my right to comfort her, to make her laugh, to cling to her. You must remember that, Wallace.*

But later that day, when Rene had again left for his evening entertainment and Matthew and Sylvie sat together in the green salon with Dizzy, he knew he wouldn't be able to shove aside his feelings so easily. With each word she spoke, each joke she made, each time she laughed, Sylvie de Courcey bound him ever closer to her. The truth was, he was sent to rescue her, and the storm was far from over.

⁓

"First Guy leaves for Champagne. Then you, Matthew, up and leave for Normandy. What shall I do when you're gone? Tell your friends that you're needed here."

He could hardly believe it, but there they were standing by the train that would shuttle him to Normandy, and Sylvie was misting up with tears. He wanted to stay for all the world, but knew he could not. Reaching into his pocket, he slipped out a small book. "Would you do me a favor, Sylvie?"

"Anything. You know that. Heavens! Where is my hankie?" Her eyes began to moisten.

He fished into his pocket and handed her his, along with the book. "Take this, and read it."

"A Bible?" The book sat in her hand like a stranger in a foreign land. But even strangers became friends once you got to know them. "It's so hard to understand."

"I'll be praying that you will gain much understanding as you read it." He gently took the handkerchief and dried her tears.

"And does God listen to your prayers?"

"Always, Sylvie."

The conductor gave the last call.

"Will you pray for me in another way?"

He put his foot on the bottom step and heaved the heavy portmanteau up with him. "You know I will."

As he was handing the porter his ticket she spoke. "Pray that I forget you, Matthew Wallace. Pray that my heart will not be lonesome without you."

The train began to move. He looked back at her. Had he heard correctly? "Sylvie!" he cried. But she had turned around and was already walking back toward the station, holding his handkerchief up to her cheek.

CHAPTER ❖ TWELVE

Claude Mirreault loved what he did. He loved being owed. And he was especially fond of the fact that his record for repayment was unsullied by even one borrower. Everyone paid back Claude Mirreault.

In one way or another.

"A street rat made good," he said to his assistant, Didier Vachel, who had just gone over the books for the week. "Look at these figures. It wouldn't surprise me if I was well on my way to becoming the richest man in France!" He gazed lovingly at what he called "his beauties." His study was filled with such possessions. Affectionately, he ran a hand over a Louis XIV desk that supported solid gold antique writing implements. Turkish carpets cushioned his mammoth feet shod in leather shoes so fine they would have drawn a year's wages from a simpler man. The crystal globes of the gaslights prismed the cherry-paneled walls with tiny rainbows. He relished every bit of the wealth he had obtained. Mirreault inhaled deeply. The scent of the room was delightful. Having grown up in the malodorous slums, he promised himself he would never again be subjected to such putrid conditions. Fine incense from the Orient burned on a small table that had once belonged to Peter the Great. Peter the Great! Ha, yes, pretty good for the product of a prostitute and a farm boy's first try. Truth be told, he claimed more than the furniture of some of Europe's crowned heads, and he aimed to keep it that way.

He puffed on a cigar and watched, fascinated, as a stunning woman, dark-haired and dainty, glided into the room. Her haughty chin caught a rainbow along its delicate curve. "Didier," Mirreault directed his longtime aide-de-camp of crime who always stood ready to do his master's bidding. The two had been picking the same garbage together since childhood. "I will be expecting a guest in less than an hour. Oysters served upstairs, champagne ... from the vineyards of de Courcey, of course ... and once it is delivered there are to be no disturbances." His voice purred with culture and sophistication—well-modulated, steady and calm, articulate. He had practiced many hours, spent half a fortune to gain such a voice, such a beautiful voice, harmonious with its surroundings, incongruous with its source.

"Yes, monsieur." With a tiny bow, Didier quietly closed the door behind the woman.

She smirked, and sliced Mirreault a look so filled with venomous disdain a lesser man would have flinched. Mirreault's smile stuck as he drew in on his cigar. This was amusing to say the least. "The appropriate funds are with you, my lady?"

"Well, Monsieur Mirreault, it appears Loic was unsuccessful at the tables once again. He had the money in his hand. But then, I do not expect you to believe that." The small silver purse that hung from her fragile hands was obviously empty, perilously forlorn.

He steepled his fingers. "Ah ... one too many bets. A common enough tale. Of course, I believe you. So ... you are in all wise prepared to erase the debt? A portion of it, in any case?"

"Of course!" she snapped. "I am nothing if not a woman of my word!"

"Let me see for myself that you came prepared." He leaned back in his chair and pulled in deeply on his cigar. The lady stood motionless. "Come, come," he drawled, circling his cigar impatiently, "the day of reckoning is upon you. A bit of gratitude would become you, for I do not offer this method of repayment often, but you have a certain ... grace, shall we say? And I cannot imagine several toes missing from that delicious little foot."

"I am the cousin of the emperor." Her ice-gray eyes sought to sliver him to a fraction, but he felt harder than the flawless diamond he wore in his cravat.

He rose from the desk, circled around, and grabbed her chin with his ringless fingers. "Surely you are aware it is the only reason I'm allowing this haphazard form of retribution."

She slapped his hand away. "Allowing? *Allowing?* How *dare* you! You pig! You son of a whore!"

The words bounced off him like snowflakes off frozen glass. The accusations were nothing new. But he was the winner here, and they both knew it. That alone kept him from returning the blow. He untied the neck of the floor-length cape which she pulled tightly around her small frame. "To be so defiled by the likes of such a monster. How, my dear, will you ever bear it?"

She did bear it, with tears in her eyes, the haughty look erased. He was pleased with himself. It was a good night's work. Not by any means worth the money he had lent Loic three years before, however.

But now the woman was gone. He had plans for the evening, and there was one more matter to settle before he could finally relax. Blast Didier for permitting the gentleman audience without an appointment.

Claude Mirreault trod across the entry hall of his home, a fifteenth-century chateau several miles east of Paris, north of Versailles. Didier, having waited outside the study door, lumbered behind him. "I told him you were ... ah ... busy, sir," he explained, playing nervously with his long mustache, "but he wouldn't take no for an answer."

"What of Mademoiselle de Lunay? Has she arrived?"

"Not yet."

"For once I'm thankful for her tardiness." He barged into the salon, buttoning his vest, then tying his cravat. There sat the intruder, smoking a cigarette as usual. Mirreault yanked a bottle of scotch from a table near the sofa. "Well, de Boyce, here you are again. And to what do I owe a visit from you, all the way out here, on a night such as this?"

Indeed, the Count de Boyce was covered with sudden spring rain. "I believe you know the reason."

"I see that I am thought to be clairvoyant as well as rich," Mirreault joked, jerking back his drink. "Your last loan is as yet outstanding. Any new and ingenious plans for total retribution?"

"Nothing for you to be concerned about. In several months it should all be taken care of."

"That presupposes a worry on my part, son. You are a gnat to me, de Boyce. Do not delude yourself into thinking anything else."

Rene rubbed the tops of his thighs. "But until then . . ." His hands vibrated with nervous tension. Either that, Mirreault thought, or he was late for his opium. Mirreault chuckled, poured another drink.

"Didier!"

The small man magically appeared. "Ah . . . yes, sir?"

"The bag."

Didier disappeared, and Mirreault turned back to face his worried client. "Have no fear, my lord, you shall have your money. Your record thus far has been exemplary."

"I couldn't be otherwise, Mirreault. I am a man of honor if nothing else."

Mirreault doubted that very much, but he chose not to laugh in the man's face. The nobility and their peculiar definition of the word *honor*. "Let's hope so, son. For your sake and those that you love."

The count's brows raised. "You're threatening me?"

"Does that surprise you?"

"No, actually." He sighed. "See here, Mirreault. I am about to be engaged to Armand de Courcey's daughter. Her brother,

Guy, is my good friend. Once the betrothal is official, I will ask him to loan me the money."

"And how do you know he will give it to you?"

"Guy would do anything for his sister. She's due to inherit his entire fortune should he die without an heir."

"Are you certain of this?" Mirreault asked.

"He told me himself," the count declared.

"Interesting."

Didier materialized with an old carpetbag. Mirreault reached in and drew out a sack of coin. He tossed it to Rene. "In four weeks, plus interest. Same rate."

Ahh, another rich young fool chained to his services. One of many. He would keep this liaison going for a very long time. A very long time. He, Claude Mirreault, had only just begun to grow fat on the wealth of Count Rene de Boyce.

Rene caught the money in midair.

When he was gone, Mirreault turned to Didier with a smile, feeling like a lion finished devouring his prey. "Get a message to Yves right away," he ordered. "He's got a job to do on a man named Guy de Courcey."

"Yes, sir." Didier bowed.

"And send for Youngblood. He's due his ten percent from the job we pulled on Madame Villiers."

"Why not have Youngblood kill de Courcey?"

Mirreault glared at Didier. "Guy de Courcey is the only true friend Youngblood has. There are some things even I won't ask a man to do."

CHAPTER ❖ THIRTEEN

The countess had retired early, Agnes was asleep, and Rene was out and about as usual. Sylvie had one lone music student, a violinist, all to herself. She let his soft music wash over her as she read from the Bible given to her by Matthew Wallace. The words confused her for the most part, and she wasn't quite sure why she needed to read who begat whom in the book of ... what was it ... Matthew? She smiled, remembering when she had first sat down earlier that day with the book, wondering where to start. The choice had been obvious.

And now she was in the book of John. Something about the words "and the Word was God" pulled at her. She didn't know why, but she thought them more beautiful than any poetry she had ever read. The Word was God and he became flesh and dwelt among us. Jesus Christ had always been a vague spiritual entity, but she pictured him for the first time as a man. God become man. She wanted to know more. But the evening was winding down, and she was getting sleepy.

She didn't know how long she had been napping when she realized she was no longer alone. Pushing her hand into the softness of the sofa, she sat up straight. Viscount Blackthorne was beside her, scrutinizing her, it seemed.

"Viscount! What are you doing here?" She checked the clock over the mantel. Eleven o'clock. "It's so late!"

"Not by Paris standards. I thought you might want some company."

"Of course. Have a seat." She tucked the Bible beneath her thigh.

After pouring himself a sherry, he adjusted his tailcoat and sat in his usual, casual manner. "Wallace leave today?"

She nodded.

"And Rene is out for the evening, so you are alone."

"I'm used to it." She shrugged, then noticed a ring on his finger. It was a signet ring, his family crest. "That's a lovely piece," she observed. "I've never noticed it before."

"Funny thing about this ring. I just picked it up from the jeweler's today. It's been in my family for years."

"Did you have it repaired?"

"Yes. A couple of stones were missing—the band broke years ago during a fight."

"Gracious," Sylvie remarked, "I seem to find myself with fighters these days!"

"Yes, well, you are quite the fighter yourself, so I wouldn't point any fingers. Anyway," he continued, "I received a message that it was in my best interest to come pick up the ring, or they were going to auction it to pay for their costs in repairing it and replacing the stones."

"I see you made it in time. Or did you buy it at auction?" she joked.

He laughed. "I made it in time. But I said to the jeweler, 'Hey now, what? I didn't put it in that long ago! Only several months at the most. Why the threat?' He told me I had brought the ring in a year and a half ago!"

Sylvie chuckled. "Time flies, as Agnes always says."

"I looked at him thinking, good heavens, tomorrow I shall be seventy and by next week I suppose I shall be dead!"

"Life leaves us quickly behind," she sighed. "I always thought I'd be married with at least one child to love by the time I was nineteen. Yet here I am, the world turning faster than ever and nothing really changing for Sylvie de Courcey."

Youngblood examined her thoughtfully. "You deserve more, dearest. What are you waiting for? Someone to come and sweep you off your feet?"

"I suppose that's what every girl wants."

He stood to his feet, reached down, and picked her up into his arms. "Then here I am, your very own Prince Charming!"

Sylvie laughed. Surely he wasn't serious about it. Not a worldly-wise man like the viscount. "You're just trying to make me feel better, Viscount. Now put me down."

He did. But his smile remained. The gruesome smile she had come to enjoy. "Perhaps not. Perhaps I was serious."

"Don't play games with me, Viscount Blackthorne. I'm much too green, and I don't know whether to take you seriously or not. It's not fair to do that to me."

He sat back beside her. "Then you must forgive me. I was just having a little fun."

"Well," said Sylvie wryly, "if there's one thing you know how to do, it's how to have fun. Whoever marries you will be a very busy lady. But if I recall, you told me yourself once, many years ago, that you would remain a bachelor forever."

He laughed. "That's right, to make my father miserable."

"And will you stick to your plan?"

"My father's brother Tobin would be more than happy to assume the title someday. Assuming he lives that long. Besides, it would take an incredible woman, strong, lovely, and good, to turn me into someone worthy of a lifetime of happiness."

Sylvie knew she was none of those three things. So he had been joking all along. Of course Viscount Blackthorne didn't want to court her; he was just doing what he had done for years. He was making her laugh.

So why did she feel like crying? Only Matthew Wallace really knew the answer to that. But he had left her, leaving behind only a small black book and a hollow heart.

⁓

Agnes was staring at Sylvie with blatant disapproval.

"It isn't my fault!" Sylvie said defensively. "I've done nothing to encourage the man to do something so extravagant. I know Aunt Racine is furious." All around her the smell of gardenias perfumed the air. At least ten large bouquets, the cards all inscribed with one word: *Youngblood*. "Besides, there are no protestations of love, not even a request for my company! I hardly see where there's anything to worry about."

Agnes said nothing, just crossed her arms and tapped her toe.

"Oh, Agnes, be fair. This isn't my fault."

"Ever since Matthew Wallace left a week ago, that man has been here each evening, keeping you company. Although, why all these men feel it necessary for you to be attended to at all hours of the day is beyond me. The count is by your side all day; he mysteriously disappears in the evening—"

"It's not so mysterious," Sylvie interrupted. "He's off playing cards with his friends. Doing the things that men do."

"—then Youngblood appears with a new book, some candy, or a gift, and proceeds to monopolize your time until you come to bed at the ungodly hour of one o'clock."

"Well, if Aunt Racine is so upset about it, why doesn't she do something?" Sylvie wasn't at all pleased with this conversation. She felt like a seven-year-old caught taking a premature bit of icing from her birthday cake.

"Is there anything happening between you and the viscount that I should know about?" Agnes asked crisply.

"He's behaved like a perfect gentleman. Rene has as well."

"Well, all these flowers prove the viscount has plans, Miss Sylvie. I wouldn't expect this to happen again, though."

"Why do you say that?"

"Because the countess won't let it!" Agnes was at her most ornery. After all, a relationship with the infamous Youngblood, man-about-the-town, libertine, and general outcast from *decent* society, was something Sylvie knew her maid would *never* encourage.

"What do you mean? Why does she even care?" Sylvie was getting that odd feeling in her stomach that told her something was afoot. Time to corner old Agnes. "What do you know that I don't, Agnes?"

"Do you want to be sent back to Champagne, Miss Sylvie?"

That wasn't a question she had to even consider. "Of course not."

Agnes took her hands, squeezing them urgently. "Then heed my advice. Do not encourage any suitor other than the count."

"Is the count my suitor, Agnes," she whispered. "Is that what this is all about?" Agnes wouldn't look her in the eye. It told Sylvie all she needed to know. "So that is why I have really come to Paris?"

Agnes nodded.

"How long have you known?"

"Almost since we arrived."

"My parents?"

"Have given their blessing. Years and years ago, Miss Sylvie."

Sylvie felt sick. She thought the day would never come, she feared that she would be a spinster daughter. But now, now that she knew the truth, it was so hard to stomach. Now that she had met Matthew Wallace, it was a different matter completely. Yet, she couldn't go back to Champagne. She refused to do that.

"Why weren't we betrothed sooner then?" she asked, hoping this was all just a misunderstanding on Agnes's part.

"Your mother wasn't ready to give you up, Miss Sylvie."

"Is it the only way for me to get away?" she asked.

Agnes shook her head. "I suppose that is up to you. You could always run away, though I don't think that would be a good idea."

"Where would I go if I did?" Sylvie searched her pocket and found the small square of linen that still carried Matthew's scent.

She held it to her nose and breathed deeply. "Matthew Wallace is gone, Agnes. If only he were here, he would tell me what to do. Maybe . . ." It was a foolish thought. Matthew Wallace had expressed no opinion of her whatsoever. He had been kind and gracious and loving in that godly sort of way, but he had given her no reason to believe he was giving his heart away.

"Let me ask you this. According to my father, do I really have any choice in the matter?" she asked. "Is it Rene or no one?"

Sylvie had never seen Agnes look so sad. "That about sums it up. Just a moment, love," she said, going into her room and coming back with a stack of letters. "Here, read these."

Sylvie took the pile, dread filling her heart. "From Mother? Why was I not given these before?"

"Read them, and you'll see." Agnes pursed her lips. "You'll see why I tried to hide them from you . . . until now."

For the next hour Sylvie read the frantic words of her mother. The letters were filled with anguish, the ink was blotched from her tears. As much as it saddened Sylvie to know her mother had worked herself up into such a state, it also served as a catalyst. But there were also doubts. "Would I be a horrible daughter to not go back? To leave them to their own devices?"

Agnes sat her down on the edge of the bed and put her arms around her. "It's not your job to take care of them. It's supposed to be the other way around, Sylvie."

"It sounds as if Papa's drinking is getting worse. He never had a problem before. I mean he drank, but—"

"I know, child," Agnes said. "But with the business to run, and your mother in such a state, I guess it helps to steal him away from his troubles. Not that I'm excusing it, just trying to understand."

Sylvie felt torn in half. "I know I should return, but when I think of actually going back there, Agnes, I panic. It's as if this is the only chance I'll have to escape. I feel that it's now or never!"

Agnes kept her close. "It just may be, Miss Sylvie."

"But it's Rene!" Sylvie's heart plummeted. "He's a nice man and I know he'll treat me well, but I always hoped I'd marry someone who loved me, Agnes." She didn't know what to think, really. This was all so sudden. One day she was having an enormous amount of fun, and the next, the whole world seemed to go dark. But not as dark as it would be if she returned to Chateau du Soleil.

"Most marriages of your class are arranged, Sylvie. If you open up your heart to him, you may find it easy to love him."

"It's better than going home," Sylvie admitted, feeling sick to her stomach. "No matter what I did there it wasn't good enough for either my father or my mother. No matter how hard I tried, they never really cared about me. It was only what I could get done that mattered." Tears filled her eyes. "Oh, where's my hankie!" she cried, not wanting to soil Matthew's.

Agnes held her more tightly and reached for her own handkerchief. "I'm sorry, Miss Sylvie," she said, drying her tears as they spilled over. "I'm so sorry."

Sylvie was grateful for this woman, and the love that Agnes had always given her suddenly overwhelmed her and she cried more freely. "I don't know what I would have done all these years without you, Agnes," she sobbed.

Stroking her hair, Agnes cried with her. "I love you, child."

"At least I have you at Chateau du Soleil. If I stay here, I'll be saying good-bye to you as well." Sylvie had realized long ago that Agnes and Rupert's love had made her existence bearable after Guy left. She poured out her heart through her tears as daylight waned outside. It was a cleansing time and when it was through, Sylvie knew what she had to do.

Once again, she was trapped into living in yet another loveless home. But at least she could try to make it work, make Rene love her a little, come to love him herself. *It's happened before*, she clung to the thought, *arranged marriages have given way to love many times.*

"So be it then." She sat up straight. "I will marry Rene."

She would be leaving a home where she was needed too much, to one where she wasn't needed at all. It was a sobering thought, and she knew her work was cut out for her. But then, Sylvie de Courcey had never been afraid of a little hard work.

That night as she settled into her bed, she turned up the lamp on the bedside table and took out the Bible Matthew had given her. Her heart was heavy and sore, and life had become a burden. But the little volume offered hope when she read the words in the book of Matthew telling her to come to the Lord when she was weary and burdened, telling her he would give her rest. "Take my yoke upon you, and learn of me; for I am meek and lowly in heart: and ye shall find rest unto your souls. For my yoke is easy, and my burden is light." Could it be possible to exchange the heavy burden she was bearing for a lighter, heavenly one?

CHAPTER ✦ FOURTEEN

Getting to know Count Rene de Boyce was like becoming familiar with the main character of an autobiography. He never revealed more of himself than he wished for her to see, never made a truly spontaneous remark or an impromptu gesture. Sylvie was frustrated as well as pleased with the attention Rene had been affording her of late. They had been riding, reading in the garden, painting, singing while he played at the pianoforte, and eating almost every meal together. Sylvie could only attribute Youngblood's sudden lack of interest to the change in Rene's behavior. The viscount had considerably stepped down his late evening visits, for Rene had begun to fill in the gaps.

He wasn't as exciting to be with as Youngblood, or Matthew Wallace for that matter. Yet while Rene's conversation wasn't as humorously stimulating or emotionally perceptive as the others', it was lovely to have someone to talk to, someone who would look her in the eye—deem her worthy of the trouble, someone who placed a great deal of value upon her heart's desires and regrets. He really did seem to care.

"For two weeks he's been by my side at almost every waking hour, and he still hasn't kissed me," she complained to Agnes.

"Well, miss, do you want that?" Agnes acted neither shocked nor dismayed. "Think of how that Jacques boy's advances made you feel."

"I'd like to at least know that I'm attractive to the man. Is he wooing me, Agnes, or isn't he?"

Agnes was helping her get ready for riding in the Bois. A lovely, ink blue habit cloaked her body, now filled out nicely from all the countess's good food. A top hat with a long black scarf was perched on her head.

"Seems to me your mind was preoccupied in other areas anyway," Agnes suggested as she hung up Sylvie's morning gown.

"What do you mean?"

"Oh, just referring to the man from across the channel."

"Reverend Wallace?" Sylvie could hardly believe Agnes had been so perceptive, but she fought hard now to dispel any notion her maid might have—accurate or not. Truth was, the book he had given her had done much to bind her soul to him. She was certain it wasn't his motivation for giving it to her, but nevertheless, when she held the small leather volume in her hand, she felt as if he were in the room. "Why, Agnes, you told me to forget about him. What would I want to do with that Englishman?"

She handed Sylvie her crop. "What indeed?"

The mantel clock, obviously banished from one of the family bedrooms after a mishap or two, chimed in a less-than-melodious fashion. Sylvie gasped at the sound of the wheezy thunks. "I'm late! Quick, Agnes. Let's get me downstairs and off on my ride. Rene will be waiting."

"I doubt that." Agnes shook her head.

The count wasn't known for his punctuality. Nevertheless, she made last-minute adjustments to Sylvie's ensemble and walked her to the door.

But he *was* waiting, looking refreshed and ready to escort her. The horses were brought round, and he helped her mount. "Did you sleep well last night, my dear?" he asked courteously, settling himself on his own horse.

"Oh, yes."

"And did you dream of me even a little?"

Sylvie realized that today was going to bring about some changes. He was taking things a step further. The truth was, she *had* dreamed about him, and it wasn't at all flattering. "Actually, I did."

The horses started slowly. "And will you tell me what went on in the head of Sylvie de Courcey last night?"

She batted her eyelids at him, feeling a bit flirtatious. "No woman with self-respect would tell such secrets. My dreams, monsieur, are my own."

"Hmm." He appeared delighted with her answer. "You *have* grown up, little Sylvie, haven't you?"

"Oh, yes. You have no idea how much," she said, thinking that the past month had thrust more maturity upon her than the past two years.

"You are quite a woman, Sylvie. I'm finding that being with you is a most interesting pastime." Rene lifted her hand to his lips as they inched their way through the Bois, side by side, looking very fashionable.

"It's too early in the morning for false compliments, Rene. I know you'd rather be with Youngblood and the others. Tell me more about America!"

Rene straightened his hat with one hand, happy to oblige. "I do believe it's a lot of what we had in mind when we started to abolish the monarchy so many years ago. Unfortunately, whereas the Americans sought and achieved personal liberty through personal responsibility, we just keep setting up different forms of absolute rulership. We still don't have freedom as they do. Perhaps we never will."

Sylvie sighed. Freedom. Rene could not possibly know what the lack of it really meant. "Surely one day we will grow wise."

"Perhaps, but not as long as there is an emperor."

"You do not like our Louis-Napoleon?"

"Of course I do. But if you could just experience the American legislature firsthand, as I did. I visited Congress, you know."

"And yet it is the system we have now which allows you to be among the nobility, to be so wealthy," she reminded him.

"Being noble means nothing over there," he agreed, then went on to surprise her. "And that is exactly what I like about a republic. Any man can make his way . . . or destroy it. It's up to him. Not to say the United States doesn't have its problems. There's trouble brewing in regards to states' rights, slavery, tariffs, many issues that divide the northern region from the southern."

Sylvie was thrilled he was speaking to her about such matters. He wasn't good at throwing out compliments . . . they always sounded stiff and formal, but get him talking about politics or philosophy or art, and his speech would flow eloquently about what touched him deeply. "I sometimes think that humanity is always destined not to get along. It can be region that divides them, ideology, class, even the color of their skin. It's sad we cannot live peaceably with one another," she said.

"Do you believe that is possible, Sylvie? To be at peace?"

Sylvie thought about it, feeling that life was about being a pawn. At least hers was. And there was certainly no peace in that. Yet the Bible had talked about a peace which passes all understanding. Maybe she was just trying too hard to figure it all out. "No, Rene. I guess not."

"Mother does, and Matthew Wallace says the same thing."

"How so?"

"She talks about the Scriptures and something about the kingdom of God. Wherever that is. I used to know all that doctrine and theology as a child—but through the years, it has ceased to become important to me."

"I've never really known much about God—only what Mama and the priest have explained. But she seems so caught up in it all personally, that she has no time to share it with anyone else. I've never understood her, especially after having spent her life with Armand. Although, I guess the cold chapel floor would be more appealing than his cold heart."

He squeezed her hand. "Don't talk about him. You must not judge mankind by his example."

"It's hard not to."

"I know, my Sylvie. I know."

There was something comforting in the fact that he knew about her family, how strange they were. It was a bond of sorts.

Just then a messenger from Maison de Fleur thundered up to them on horseback. "Monsieur le comte!"

"Yes, what is it?"

"You must go back. Urgent news from Chateau du Soliel."

"What is it?"

"I do not know. The countess herself wishes to break the news to Mademoiselle de Courcey!"

~

When Sylvie saw one of her traveling bags packed and waiting by the front door, she knew something was dreadfully wrong.

The countess ran across the entry hall and gathered her into her arms. "Oh, Sylvie, oh my darling, I do not know how to say this, but terrible news has come from Chateau du Soleil." Her face was wet with tears.

"What is it?" Sylvie felt as though a lead weight dropped in her stomach.

"It is your brother, child. I'm sorry. Your brother Guy is dead."

She pushed down the heaving wave of emotion which threatened to drown her. "What happened?"

"He was murdered, child, on his way home from Paris. By a highwayman. He died at home, several hours after he was found."

"Where did it happen?"

"I am not certain. The message failed to say. I am sorry, dear child."

Sylvie's knees softened and she was about to crumble to the floor. But Rene was there to catch her. He lifted her off of her feet, cradled her next to him, and sat on the bottom step of the main staircase. He was shaking, breathing in gasps. "Dear Lord," he whispered over and over again. "Oh, dear Lord."

He kissed her hair as she cried and rocked her in an agitated fashion.

Oh, Guy! Sylvie anguished. "What shall I do without him?" she cried, feeling lonelier than she had ever felt before. And what about Guy? What had he been thinking in those final moments? Was he frightened, in pain? Did he cry out for help only for none to arrive?

Rene just drew her closer, seeking comfort as well as giving it. His friend had died too, Sylvie realized when she felt the wetness of his tears splashing down onto her face to mingle with her own.

CHAPTER ❖ FIFTEEN

Sylvie stared down at the lifeless face of her brother. Her compatriot. Her best friend. The cold hands, the pale face covered with bruises and lacerations. Spring turned to winter. Death achieved too soon. No reward, merely an ending.

He had so much to look forward to, so much for which to hope. Guy had been brilliant in running de Courcey Paris, had gone to Champagne to modernize the business, increase profits. And although he hadn't been much closer to his father than Sylvie was, the two had run the business together well, and Armand had relied on his son.

Tomorrow he would be buried.

She turned, dry-eyed, toward her mother, who rushed into the room. Collette's hair sprung matted and wild, and a soup stain as well as the greasy remains of breakfast soiled the bodice of her dressing gown. The woman hadn't bothered to put on her clothes. Sylvie examined with disgust the haggard, drawn face, then inwardly remonstrated herself. It had always been easy to trivialize her mother's emotions, but this time they were truly justified. "How did it happen?" she asked.

Collette threw herself in her daughter's arms and sobbed. "You're here. You're finally here, cherie. I've needed you so *desperately*."

"What happened to him, Mama?"

Collette lifted a tearstained face to her daughter's. Sylvie felt her strength being sucked dry, but knew she'd find more somewhere. She would have to.

Her mother spoke between sobs. "They found him ... along the road near ... the gate ... beaten and ... stabbed. We don't know ... who. Or why. He died two hours after we brought him ... home."

Collette nuzzled her small face into Sylvie's neck and continued crying. Sylvie realized there would be no grief for herself right now. If ever. Would this mean she would never escape Chateau du Soleil? She scraped her mother's matted hair away from her mouth and clumsily stroked the wild red mass. Thoughts of Matthew Wallace surfaced out of nowhere. His kind eyes, his way of saying the right words at the right time. How she wished he was with her now, comforting her, whispering to her the words of hope he was so capable of offering. She wanted to scream, she felt so agitated inside, sickened by her mother, distraught by Guy's death. If she could have been spirited away to a dark room with nothing inside it but a bed, a lamp, and that little black book, she would have considered it paradise.

Rene walked up behind her, stroking her back, saying nothing while Collette grieved. He wasn't exactly Matthew, and he wasn't exactly in love with her, but he did care, and it was what she needed. It was better than nothing. It was obvious Guy's death was haunting him in a most peculiar way. She'd heard him mutter the name "Mirreault" on the train to Champagne. But when asked to clarify his mumblings, he seemed to drift off deeper into thought, shaking his head no, no.

Armand injected himself into the room, a young maid at his heels. "Take the woman upstairs," he ordered.

Sylvie stared at the man she called father, grown more gaunt since she had left. The icy eyes, held in by a bony visage, narrowed as they shook Sylvie with their gaze, then shut down. He was clearly drunk.

The maid pried her mother from her. Collette, now hysterical, emitted a gushing wail and pulled at Sylvie's hair, the lace of her sleeves, and finally her fingers. And then ... air. Nothing. Fingers reaching—contracting.

She was gone.

More laudanum from the bottle left by the doctor would take her away even further, Sylvie thought, ordering the maid to administer the drug.

She turned to face her father. Looking straight into his pitiless eyes, she lifted her pointed chin ... and stared. Turning into a human fortress, challenging, she silently dared him to storm the walls, bombard her defenses. Her eyes felt harder than granite, sharper than a rapier. She clenched her fists. And she knew, Paris had changed her for good. There was no going back.

He turned his back on her and left the room without one word regarding Guy.

She rushed up to her bedchamber, pulled out her Bible, and sat in a small chair by the window. Too distraught to read it just then, she held it to her heart, praying, knowing that God was listening to her, and that he had been for a very long time.

Racine was pulled from sleep by an obviously frightened Sylvie. Brushing the cobwebs of repose from her eyes, she sat up. "What is it, child?"

"It's Papa. He's locked himself in his study. I hear crashings and thumps, and wails of rage. He's in a red rage, Aunt Racine."

Racine threw aside the covers and jumped to her feet. "I shall get Rene."

Several minutes later, clad in their robes and slippers, the three of them ran down to the first floor. It was just as Sylvie had said. An explosive, drunken rage was ensuing. Servants skittered about like houseflies in search of a place to land. "Go to bed! All of you!" Rene ordered harshly, and they gladly obeyed.

"I will go around outside and look through the window," Rene said, "see if he is hurting himself. It may be best to let him go until he's spent."

Racine could see the wisdom in that. "All right. Do that and we shall wait here."

Rene left them, and Racine turned toward Sylvie, grabbing her hand. "I am sorry, Sylvie. I wish you didn't have to see your family come to this."

"It's only natural Guy's death brought it about."

She could feel her heart breaking for Sylvie, and Racine took her into her arms, trying desperately to be a sea of calm in a very terrible storm. Sylvie allowed herself to be comforted, but only briefly. She pulled away and looked earnestly into Racine's eyes. "What will happen now?" she whispered.

"We will take care of you always, dearest." Racine triumphed amid the adversity. Sylvie was theirs now, it was plain.

"Get out!" Armand's roar could be clearly heard. Then nothing. The din quieted abruptly, and a minute later, Rene opened the study door, calm but a bit shaken.

"He has passed out. The study is basically destroyed."

"Will he be all right?" Sylvie's voice was small. "Did he say anything?"

"He'll be fine," Rene reassured her. "He was incapable of really talking, Sylvie. After he yelled, he just muttered, 'What am I going to do? What am I going to do?'"

Sylvie's tears silvered her eyes in the dimness. "At least Guy's death means something to him, then."

Rene tenderly took her into his arms, as Racine looked on, warmth for her son enveloping her as it never had before. Perhaps he would be a good husband after all, perhaps a little of his father was tucked away somewhere inside of him. "I know what it's like to lose a father," he said softly, kissing her forehead. "I cannot imagine what it must be like to lose a son."

"I would give him comfort if he would let me," Sylvie whispered.

Racine's heart hurt for the child who would forgive her father even now, after all these years of winter.

"I know, Sylvie," Rene soothed. "I know."

Gathering her robe more closely, Racine left them together in the corridor and went in to inspect the damage of the study. Rene had been right. One of the large iron candlesticks lay on the floor, its footed metal stand across the room. The cherry desk, once a masterful piece of craftsmanship, was scarred and battered. The drapes were pulled from the rings. Anything breakable was smashed and lay in pieces on the floor. The only object to escape ruination was the crystal decanter on the mantel, only a bit of brandy pooling in its bottom.

And there lay Armand. A pile of human rubbish if there ever was one, Racine thought right then. God help the man, she sighed, for he was the only one who could make anything beautiful out of someone like Armand de Courcey. Retrieving a lap robe from beneath a chair, she threw it over him and wiped his face clean with her handkerchief. There, that was enough.

She hastened to her room, sat down at the writing table, and penned a message to Matthew Wallace, presumably still nearby in Reims. What this family needed was a proper spiritual influence, and Collette's personal priest was too preoccupied with his charge to minister to the needs of the rest of the family.

Come to the Chateau du Soleil immediately, she wrote. *Guy is dead. We need you here.*

If anyone could appease the situation, comfort Sylvie and Collette, maybe even convince Armand to curtail his drinking, it would be the English vicar. Not only that, he was a more discreet source of aid. He'd not inform all of France of the inner tragedy of the de Courceys. She prayed he would journey in all haste. Until then, there was much to accomplish.

The first rays of morning light filtered through the window. No sense in going back to bed now. She threw on her clothing with the help of her maid and bustled downstairs to post the letter and locate the housekeeper. The castle key ring bounced heavy against her thigh. Mourners would soon be arriving en masse, and there was much to do to pull this family's cart where it was supposed to go—even pathetic Armand needed her now. Her lips pursed at the thought of him. She had tried to understand him for years, but knew it was impossible. Now it was up to her to take care of his neglected family—and see to their welfare.

So much to do, she sighed.

She breathed deeply through her nose, finding peace in the midst of tragedy and assurance she was where God wanted her to be, doing just what he wanted her to do . . . and he was supplying all her needs for the job.

Rene folded Sylvie into his arms and led her into the coolness of the garden. "We'll watch the sun rise over the fields," he said, thinking how much she needed to see some sort of beauty right now.

He had to get back to Paris, though. Camille was probably chomping at the bit. Well, perhaps Youngblood was being a good sport and taking care of her. There was no way he could leave right after the funeral. Mother would be furious. Besides, he thought, looking appreciatively over the vineyard, this was his ticket to freedom, his way out with Mirreault.

Immediately, guilt overtook him. He knew his report to Mirreault regarding Guy's estates had brought about the murder. He knew the ruthless moneylender had decided to make good on his threat regarding his loved ones. It sickened him, really, that his own loose tongue was the culprit. But he wouldn't let Guy's death go to waste. He would use Sylvie's distress to bind her to him forever.

"Ma cherie," he whispered into her hair as she sobbed, "you mean the world to me." He tightened his arms about her, not about to let go until his life was once again back to the way it should be.

Sylvie looked up into his eyes, her face broken by her grief, but her eyes lovely and luminous. Certainly, marriage to her would not be a terrible thing. He held her chin tenderly, kissed the tears from her cheeks, and when a small, sad smile slid over her lips, he kissed them too.

She tucked her hand in his. "See, Rene, the fields are lightening. A new day has begun."

Ah, yes, he thought gratefully, a new day had begun.

Her tears began afresh. "I didn't want to come back here. Guy didn't want me to come back here. Isn't it strange that he was the one who brought about my return?"

Rene swallowed. *If she only knew the truth*, he thought, but quickly pushed it aside.

"I don't want to stay here." Her voice held what he considered to be justifiable panic. "Please, don't let her persuade me to stay. I don't think I'll be able to stand firm if she corners me."

He wouldn't let that happen. "Stay with me." He brushed her ear with his mouth. "Let me take care of you." *Oh, Sylvie, Sylvie, how could you possibly know just what this marriage means to me.* "Guy is gone, but I am here with you now."

"Guy has been gone for a long time, Rene. He left this place gladly."

"He did what he had to do as a son, Sylvie, you know that."

She shook her head, eyes closed, voice weary. "I don't begrudge him his actions. But it is also true that I was the only one left to care for Mama's needs, and Papa was glad to have me there if it meant he didn't have to worry about her himself. But now, with Guy gone for good, and Mama in a worse state than she has ever been . . . will my time in Paris be cut short?"

"Stay with me," he repeated. "Let me take care of you, sweet Sylvie."

Her eyes snapped open. "What are you saying, Rene?"

Might as well do it now, he thought, *the opportunity seems heaven sent.* "I am asking you to marry me, ma cherie. I am asking you to be my wife."

Even though he had been preparing himself for this moment for weeks, he felt sick inside. *I'm getting to be as accomplished a manipulator as my mother*, he thought, wondering how this would all work out in the end. If it was to benefit everybody, he would have some serious changing to do.

At first she was speechless, then frightened. He thought she wasn't going to answer him. He could see she was thinking rapidly.

"Will you help me leave on my own?" she asked, eyes darting.

"I cannot. I'm asking you to be my wife. It's been arranged for years between our parents, and now the time is right . . . for both of us."

"All right, Rene," she whispered, her voice raspy and thick. "I'll marry you. But please, let's not tell anyone yet. Not until after the funeral."

He agreed. After all, it would take a while for Guy's fortune to be transferred to his sister. Mirreault wouldn't be sending someone around anytime soon, he knew. Now that de Courcey money would be coming his way, his patience would be stretched even further.

CHAPTER ✦ SIXTEEN

It was Guy's favorite type of morning the day the fertile soil of Champagne received his body. A crisp azure sky, clouds blown into the shape of well-worn quills, a benevolent sun, and a stricken Sylvie, all looked down upon his simple wooden coffin.

"See the day, Guy?" she whispered, audible only to herself. "Remember days like these, brother? How you'd take me fishing or we'd take a picnic out into the woods and you'd read poetry to me, or tell of Oxford."

The thought that he was there, in that box, filled her with emptiness. How could he be gone, the jovial fellow who was loved by everybody? *Well, almost everybody,* she thought bitterly, for Armand was conspicuously absent, presumably still drinking in his ravaged study.

Sylvie tried to remain strong, refusing to cry. She shot a disdainful look at her mother whose eyes were screwed shut, tears escaping from their sealed corners. Aunt Racine and Rene were literally holding her up.

Oh, Guy.

Brother. Friend. Why did you leave us so soon?

The coffin slid into the tomb, wood whispering against marble. Patrician and peasant alike overran the small, village cemetery and cried, for Guy had been a likable fellow, truly caring and good to anyone he knew or loved. Sylvie's heart was sore.

The priest intoned the words of the rite of Christian burial. Rosaries were wound round hands folded in prayer. But Sylvie heard none of this. Her own mind was crowded with prayers, prayers long overdue ... not for Guy, but for those he had left behind. The tears flowed freely now, as though God himself had taken control.

Agnes offered her handkerchief. But it was unnecessary, for Sylvie had finally remembered her own.

"What will happen now?" she whispered to her maid. "What will happen to all of us?"

But even Agnes couldn't answer her question. How could she stay here? Yet how could she leave her mother so soon after Guy's death? The answer had to be Rene. But why Rene? She always pictured herself loving a strong, passionate man, a man with vigor and commitment, a man of honor and dedication.

A man like Matthew Wallace.

But even thoughts of Matthew were quickly replaced by the yawning tomb of her brother open before her eyes. *I'll never see him again*, she wept inwardly, the bitterness of such a happening a tangible taste on her tongue. Never again. It was a thought so painful, it was impossible to lay aside.

More prayers were gargled by the priest, and it seemed so meaningless all of a sudden. Why be born if only to die? Why any of this?

Incense was bobbed around the coffin in a gilded censer, holy water sprinkled over the simple pine box. Armand's frugality had prevailed even in the choice of what would hold his only son's body forever.

Sylvie was alive and she knew this, but wondered why and for what purpose. Meaningless, this life was meaningless. Finally, the priest was finished.

It was done now. The tomb was shut and sealed, and Guy would soon cease to be anything other than the small marble edifice which held him. He would be the beveled edges, the carved inscription, the tufts of grass growing around the base, the smooth, cold marble, the heat of the sun trapped in the stone, the slickness of the rain on the top, the frigid cold of winter. Guy was forever gone. The bright red hair would no longer stand on end in the soft, humid summer rain, the humorous eyes would never tear over at a clever joke, the wide mouth would never grin mischievously in her direction. They had shared so many private jokes, so many stolen moments away from their parents, laughing, raiding the kitchen, wandering the castle after dark.

It was all over now.

Life was forever changed.

And so am I, she thought, turning away from the tomb.

"What do you mean he left everything to his sister?" Armand exploded, suddenly very, very sober. The room where the family had gathered for the reading of Guy's will turned chilly. The lawyer shuffled through the dog-eared documents.

Sylvie stood to her feet. "Are you certain?"

The lawyer, an old friend of Guy's, was unruffled. He tweaked his mustache and cleared his throat. "Of course, the final figure is yet to be determined," he said.

"That ingrate!" Armand yelled, stomping toward the door of the salon. "All I did for him, and now this!" He left the room, his rantings echoing in the corridor.

No one was saddened by his sudden absence. Least of all the attorney, who was obviously doing his best not to let his personal feelings get in the way of things.

"When will the estate be settled?" Rene asked, pulling out his tobacco pouch and a packet of rolling papers.

Sylvie was more than happy to have him take charge. This was turning out to be a most uncomfortable experience, and certainly her father was making matters far worse than they need be. Still, knowing the situation of the estates, she could hardly blame him for his frustrations.

"We can't say just yet." The lawyer shrugged. "We'll do our best to expedite matters in all haste."

More questions were asked by Rene, but Sylvie didn't hear them. She just wished her brother would come home. Finally, the lawyer was gone, and the salon seemed larger than it ever had, and Rene smaller than before.

Her lungs filled quickly, and she shook her head, wiping a tear from her eye with her sleeve.

"I'm sorry, darling," Rene whispered into her ear, the smell of soap, cigarettes, and brandy hanging about him in a heavy cloud.

"So am I," she returned, pushing him gently away. She ran out of the castle, down the hill, and into the vineyard.

Agnes poured two cups of tea—strong, piping hot tea—and spooned liberal amounts of sugar into both. She handed one to Rupert with a weighty sigh.

"I just don't like it, ducks. There's something not right about Master Guy's death."

He sipped his tea with a thoughtful expression, squeaked his fingertip around the rim of his saucer, then cleared his throat. The great black brows arched above his pearly gray eyes. "There's more word goin' about the village."

Agnes sat forward.

"Aye, luv. They're sayin' the lad's purse was still with 'im when they found 'im."

Agnes gasped. "You don't think it was a highwayman? Who then?"

"There's a lot you don't know, Aggie dear, a lot that's been happening around here."

Agnes reclined back in her mum's old stuffed chair, the only piece of furniture she had brought with her from home. That chair had received bad news many times before. "Can you tell me?"

He nodded. "I know you won't go telling everybody. It's like this, de Courcey vineyards is in grave trouble. Remember the bad harvests we had several years running . . . about five years ago? Well, we started feeling the brunt of it just last year."

Agnes couldn't have heard more shocking news. "So that's why the master is suddenly agreeing to a betrothal between Miss Sylvie and the count, and that is why Guy was so insistent the match should take place."

"I couldn't say, Aggie. But it makes sense to me. Guy also told me he was about to make some investments which would help."

"And now, the master is in no shape to set things to right."

"He was set on keepin' the land intact. Master Guy was his father's last hope."

Agnes shook her head. "So the master started drinking when the tables took a turn for the worse?"

Rupert nodded.

"And it exaggerated the downward spiral," Agnes continued her speculation.

Rupert nodded again.

Suddenly everything was making sense, and Sylvie was caught in the middle of it all.

"You know, Aggie." Rupert poured himself another cup of tea. "Maybe this union with the de Boyce family is coming along at just the right time. No matter what, though, we need to be praying."

"Of course, ducks."

And they did just that, bowing right there, lifting their burdens up to the One who had promised to shoulder them. They had faith to believe that he would work everything together for good.

A presence in the bedchamber jolted Sylvie out of a tortured sleep. Confused, she sat up, her breath coming quickly. It wasn't a happy presence, she was sure of it. Her eyes began to focus, the darkness of the room only heightening the alarm that skittered beneath her scalp. Pacing before the window, he was there, a flat silhouette with large hands and cruel eyes that scraped her body and her soul—charging the room with a hideous current. Armand, holding a bottle, shaking a finger at her. "And still you are here!" he shouted, words slurring together, barely discernible. "I told that woman—that, that, countess—to take you away from here after the funeral. But your mother . . . your awful mother. She pulls you down, refuses to let you go. She refuses to let you do your duty!"

He approached the bed, his stench winning handily the race toward Sylvie. She hurled the covers aside and sprang to her feet. "You're drunk. Get out of here. We'll talk in the morning."

"No." The bottle swung from his hand, and he wiped his face with a forearm. "He was the only reason I built this place up, the only reason I worked so hard."

"You could have at least come to the funeral."

"Shut up. Don't tell me what I could have done, girl. I could have done a lot of things. I could have insisted Guy stay in Paris. I could have made sure he took a servant along with him at all times—"

"You could have treated him as a son, not a servant," she spit out. "You could have told him you loved him. You could have made him feel significant. You could have done something other than use him all his life!"

"I won't explain myself. You deserve nothing from me."

Blinded by years of neglect, she ran forward, slamming into Armand. Looking into his drunken eyes, she saw the shock register as they fell in a twisting huddle upon the carpet.

Remembering all the kisses he never gave, all the laughter she never heard, all the stories he never told, and the love he failed to show. Remembering the times he walked away, the toil he meted out, the hunger, the cold, the despair, the gross sadness. Remembering the loneliness and the inadequacy, Sylvie threw herself at him.

But Armand was stronger and prone to do more than simply defend himself. Even drunk, he could easily overpower his daughter. The bottle of brandy slammed up against the side of Sylvie's head. She rose in a frenzy of pain, grabbed a candlestick, swung her arm up—ready to make contact, feeling as if a devil was gnawing at her innards. She received a booted foot in her stomach for her troubles.

And then he was straddled on top of her, sitting on her stomach, pummeling her with his fists. Sylvie felt a fist to the side of her neck, then her ear—misplaced intentions of a madman. Finally, he achieved his aim and slammed a punch on her jaw. Sylvie cried out as Armand was hoisted violently off her by a force she could not see for the darkness and the hot agony.

He roughly landed five feet away after striking the window. And in his place, blazing eyes filled with righteous indignation and unshed tears, was Matthew Wallace.

His feet were squarely apart, and he stood sturdy and strong. "Don't kill him, Mate," he whispered to himself. "Don't kill the despicable scoundrel."

Recalling his anger down at the docks, Sylvie knew the prayer was necessary.

Racine rushed into the room and knelt beside her in a billow of skirts and perfume, even as Matthew lowered himself to his knees. He gently caressed her hair.

"Sylvie."

Reaching for her, he clutched her to his chest for several moments. "Did he hurt you?"

She could not speak, but rubbed her jaw.

"Can you get up?"

Sylvie nodded, her fingers digging into his brawny forearms as she struggled to her feet with Matthew's aid.

"Countess, take Sylvie to your room and fetch the doctor. I'll attend to matters here."

"Matthew arrived only an hour ago," the countess explained. "We heard you cry out from downstairs."

The last thing Sylvie saw as she was tenderly led from the room by the countess was Matthew pulling Armand roughly to his feet and slapping a glass full of water onto his flushed, swollen face. He was in charge now.

Racine closed the door behind them, and Sylvie, knowing matters were now in the vicar's hands, wanted only to rest.

CHAPTER ❖ SEVENTEEN

Sylvie opened her eyes, warmed by the sunlight that dispelled the gloom of the previous, horrendous night from her room. Bewildered at first by the strange surroundings, memory burned through the haze. And then, hearing the deep breaths of sleep, she turned and saw Matthew beside her, slumped in a comfortable chair.

Matthew—yes, he had come just in time like some tenacious savior who knew just where and when to be. With a thrill she remembered the anger sparking like fireworks in his blue eyes as he hoisted her father effortlessly and tossed him across the room as though he weighed no more than a child.

Just about to waken him, she pulled back her hand. The opportunity to observe him unnoticed, to take in every detail of his person, to examine each laugh line, each mole, each perfection and imperfection, was something not to be forsaken.

She had been right all along, he was a good man. It showed in the set of his bullish jaw, now slack with slumber and supporting a heavy morning overlay of dark stubble. The comparison to a faithful, yet ferocious hound was unmistakable, a powerful, wolfish hound to be sure. Those large blue eyes—now closed—

with long, curled black lashes, the heavy jaw, the barrel chest and strong arms, the muscular thighs that made taut the material of his black pants. He was ready to spring in defense of her, and his build, his features, his heart, echoed such stalwart, inner purpose. An intense man, yes, a good man. In a strange way, Sylvie felt God had made him just for her.

A presumptuous thought, no doubt. But the fact that her heart softened around this gentle, yet powerful man, proved there was more to the cord that bound them than what was visible to the naked eye. She couldn't hurl accusations at God anymore that he didn't care, that he was indifferent. For God had sent Matthew.

Unable to wait any longer, she reached out to touch his arm, in reverent thankfulness to both him and the God who had made him so well.

The indigo eyes sprang open. "Sylvie, dearest!" He took her hand. "Are you all right?"

She smiled broadly at the concern he bore her, then winced at the pain. "I was fine, until you made me grin." But she squeezed his hand. "I'll be all right. Just sore. Bruised a little."

"I'm sorry he did that to you. I'm sorry I didn't make it in time."

"But you did, Matthew. Had you not arrived, there might have been another funeral."

"Indeed. If he had landed that blow where he intended I would have been too late." He shook his head. "I don't know who to be angrier with, myself or Armand. Oh, Sylvie. Believe me, nothing like this will ever happen again. I swear it. He will never lay another finger on you."

"Words like that can't be guaranteed, Matthew, can they?"

"In this case, yes. Let us simply say that I have much to confess after last night. Mother always said I let my temper get the better of me when someone I . . . care about is being wronged."

"Yet isn't that what being a vicar is all about? Caring about souls . . . righteous anger at the devil and the evil he stirs up?"

His eyebrows raised, and he began to wring out a fresh cloth for her jaw. "I never really thought of it like that. Temperamentally speaking, I have always thought of myself as ill-suited to the task, that the Lord has much to overcome in using me as a servant. I have always spoken with my fist much sooner than I ought." Gently he positioned the rag, and she raised her hand to hold it in place.

The touch of his fingers as they brushed hers was comforting ... and exhilarating as well. The thrill of his touch. The thrill of his compassion. The amazement of his true and utter humility. "But you love just as intensely. If I had been taught to love God as you do ... had seen God's love manifested toward me as I see it manifest in you ... perhaps I would have been at peace long ago. But too much has got in the way of all that."

Matthew sat forward on his chair. "You have had a right to be angry, Sylvie. Your father's actions have been worthy of great anger. But instead of being angry *at* God, you must try being angry *with* God. He hates your father's actions as much as you do, and he feels every bit of the pain you're feeling now."

"But why didn't he make my father to be caring and loving? Goodness, Matthew, if he just would have told me he loved me, even once, I think I could bear everything else."

"I will not offer some fancy explanation that will only serve to trivialize your situation. What I do know is this, God works through people so often, Sylvie. So does Satan. And people make choices—good and bad choices—that affect the lives of their children. But the fact is, though your parents made the wrong choices, he has sustained you, divinely so, and now that you are grown, he has sent me here. He has given you me ... and I am willingly become his hands, his feet, his heart. If I could but show you one fragment of God's love, then I count my time spent with you an honor. God does love you, though that fact may bear little comfort now. In time you may even come to see that he was preparing your heart for his love and purpose, to be fruitful."

"I believe I know what you mean. I've seen it every year, out in the vineyard. It takes a vine a long time to grow to maturity, and all the pruning that must take place along the way simply enables the vine to bear more fruit." She spoke as a true vineyard hand.

A spark flared to life in his eyes. "Jesus says exactly that in the gospels. Pain brings forth growth and character in all men. And sometimes, once we let go, it brings forth faith in those whom God has chosen. God may allow pain to come into his children's lives, Sylvie. But it is never pain without a purpose or a companion. Knowing God, loving him, walking by his side helps us to make it through ... and in the end, we know we will spend eternity with him."

Sylvie could accept that. Always aware of the condition of those around her, she never expected life to be a succession of one delight after another. That would be absurd, she thought, and utterly frustrating. She remembered the children down by the wharf—neglected *and* poor. Her life must be one of a thousand blessings to their hungry eyes.

"So how do I know him as you do, Matthew?"

He inhaled deeply and closed his eyes for several seconds, then spoke. "We are all sinners, Sylvie." He began to tell her the story of God's love and God's justice. How God sent his Son to take on her sins, how Christ's death on the cross paid the price for her transgressions. She need only repent of her sins and believe on his name.

And that is exactly what Sylvie did as the Scripture she had been reading took form and became a living thing inside of her.

Kneeling painfully by the side of her bed, Sylvie poured her aching heart out at the feet of the Savior, entrusted her soul into his keeping, and gave him her body—bruised and broken—to be used in his service. She bowed her knee at his name—as all men would someday do. But she would be bent before him as her Savior and Lord, not her judge. Her sins were pardoned, paid for by the shed blood of the Shepherd who gave his life for a precious lamb named Sylvie de Courcey.

The ultimate love was hers. And no one—not detached Armand, not needy Collette—could take that away from her. No one could separate her from the vast, unchanging, radiant love of God. Her soul was on fire, warmed by divine healing for the first time. Alight with his mercy, singing with his love, healed by his care.

After she finished her prayer, Matthew, kneeling beside her, put his arm around her. "The Bible says that the angels rejoice with each soul that enters the kingdom of God."

And when Sylvie began to weep, her shoulders heaving in silent sobs of relief and happiness, Matthew held her in his arms and wept with her.

An hour later, Sylvie found Agnes and Rupert, sitting together in the tack room while he buffed the saddles. "Remember all those times you tried to get me to read your Bible?" she asked. "And I wouldn't?"

They both nodded, wide-eyed.

"I thought your God was Mama's God. I thought he demanded subservience on a cold stone floor. But now I know better. He's a lovely God, Agnes, just as you told me when I was a small child."

Agnes stood up and ran over to her. "What has happened, Miss Sylvie?"

Rupert followed, hands in his pockets, a wide smile on his homely face. "You look radiant, Miss Sylvie."

Sylvie laughed. "I *feel* radiant! Oh, Agnes, Rupert, something so wonderful has happened to me that I find it hard to even put into words."

Agnes began to cry. "Have you come to know the Savior, child?" she asked simply, putting her arms around Sylvie.

"Yes. Tonight. With Matthew Wallace."

Rupert put his large arms around them both. "Then that is why your eyes are shining like never before," he said. "Our prayers have been answered, Aggie." He kissed his wife on the top of her head, and did the same to Sylvie.

"The angels are rejoicing!" Agnes cried, letting go and clapping her hands. "And so will I!"

Angels rejoicing. If both Matthew and Agnes said it, she reasoned, it must certainly be so.

CHAPTER ❖ EIGHTEEN

Summer arrived the next day. The sun spilled over the Champagne countryside and the restive air was softly warm. The Father was good in so many ways, Matthew thought. And when Sylvie came to him, the Bible he had given her tucked in her hand, the goodness of God was personified.

Truth was, Matthew thought, looking at her as they strolled along the large creek that bordered the western edge of her father's lands, he was already in love with her when he handed her that old Bible. It was his only way of showing that love as he was leaving her behind. And God had once again given the increase. The love of the Father never ceased to astound him, even after all these years of walking with him.

The broadleaf trees were almost fully dressed in various shades of green, and the breeze that rolled over the hills had lost all sharpness. The tight angles of winter and spring had been smoothed by the warmth of a more intimate sun. A sun, Matthew felt, that shone just for Sylvie's benefit.

She took Matthew's hand as Dizzy ran on ahead, his stump of tail jerking back and forth with canine joy.

"I know why God sent you into my life . . . and I am glad."

Matthew remembered Isabelle suddenly, the way she loved so openly, so freely. No guesses, no mysteries. Isabelle never warranted questions, and apparently neither did Sylvie. "So am I."

"You must tell me about your life, Matthew. You told me you live with your sister. But what of your parents?"

"Both still living, I'm happy to report."

"You must have come from a loving home?"

He almost hated to answer, wondering if it would cause her pain. "Yes, Sylvie, I did."

Her beaming smile caused his heart to stutter. "That makes me happy, Matthew. It means you've learned—not from your parents' mistakes, but from their good example—what it takes to love. You'll have a happy home someday, with children who will love their own children as you loved them."

"It does rather work like that, doesn't it? And yet those who don't enjoy such an upbringing can, with God's help, break the pattern. I've seen it happen many times in my ministry." Maybe that would give her hope.

He helped her across some stepping-stones to a patch of thick emerald moss where they cozied in to rest their feet. Dizzy joined them, rotating several times before lying down and resting his wise old face between his paws. Sylvie laughed as she observed the mutt dig himself into complete comfort. "He's been cleaned and clipped, but for all the fuss, he still looks like a streetwise ruffian!"

"He follows you everywhere," Matthew observed, grinning.

"Dizzy has become a most faithful companion, accompanying me anywhere he can—which is almost everywhere." She scratched him between the ears. "You were telling me about your parents," she reminded Matthew, who was throwing pebbles into the water. Remembering the large house in Leeds in which he had passed a comfortable boyhood, he grew a bit homesick. The endless rooms, the army of servants, a very round mother who never withheld a hug, an honest, fair father who was quick with a dry joke. "Mum and Dad have always been great fun. It didn't matter what Miranda and I did, Mum thought it was funny. Not good for discipline, mind you, but laughter was a common occurrence in our house." He bit into his bread and flashed her a closed-lipped grin.

"You looked like a little boy just then." Sylvie leaned forward, her dark eyes shining as she scratched Dizzy's neck. Matthew felt his face redden as he watched her hands. So full of life, those hands. On the large side for a woman, their fingers, raking through the dappled fur of the dog, were hardly graceful like Isabelle's had been. But they told him of Sylvie. Toughened by life's toil, yet capable of such tenderness.

He looked up into eyes that divulged the same story.

Sweetness beneath the calluses. So different from Isabelle, sheltered Isabelle who had known little hardship, who had been adored by all who knew her. Like honey in the hollow of a roughened oak log—hidden and all the sweeter when found. That was Sylvie. So beautiful to him now.

Her voice suddenly pulled him from his delightful musings. "What does your father do?" she continued. "Did you inherit your temper from him?"

At the mention of his temper, Matthew's laugh rang against the trees. "Yes. And a little from Mum as well, I suppose. Dad owns several woolen mills, inherited them from his father a few years ago. He's been working them all his life and operating them on his own for at least ten years—after my grandfather took sick. He always thought I'd step in his shoes, but then the Lord took hold of me, and here I sit in this scratchy black suit!"

Sylvie laughed. "Was he disappointed?"

"Heavens, no! My father was the one who showed me the Savior when I was a child. I doubt if it will ever be possible, but maybe some day you will meet them yourself. Old Dora and Mervyn are quite a lovely, fussy old pair."

Matthew's tales of growing up in the bustling Wallace household continued: work at the mills, an active life within their local parish, all the fights he had started at school on behalf of Miranda.

"What made those fights so necessary?" Sylvie asked. "Was she the type that couldn't defend herself?"

At that description of his sister, Matthew's laugh rang out. "Heavens, no! Miranda's always been capable of taking care of herself. I'd *really* like you to meet her. She's truly one of the loveliest, most industrious women you'll ever get to know. Growing up wealthy and cosseted didn't spoil her. Not a bit. But, unfortunately, she was born with a rather severe birthmark. A port-wine stain. It covers half of her face and, although I'd thrash anyone else if they said this, it *is* quite grotesque, quite purple in color and somewhat raised. In addition, she has this white blond hair which only accentuates it."

"Surely someone has seen her inner beauty?"

"Oh, yes, and to be honest, if you see past the birthmark, her features are lovely. Now that she's older, two men have tried to woo her. But the damage was done years ago in school. Miranda sees herself as unworthy of a man, and sad to say, none who have showed interest were willing to go the extra mile to convince her they were sincere. She is far too difficult a fish to catch for the average angler in Swainswick."

"And she trusts God also? As you do?"

"Miranda is a shining Christian. To be honest, if she wasn't so devoted to me and the work of the ministry, I don't know how I'd be able to carry out the task our Lord has given me."

Sylvie picked at the grass. "*Our* Lord. Such wonderful words. My heart is still weak with the thought that his grace surrounds me now . . . even upholds me."

"It always has, Sylvie." *Should I take her hand*, he wondered. Decided yes. He wanted to feel her warmth. A happy warmth. Her touch welcomed his own. "God has loved you since before you were formed in your mother's womb. He created you for a very special purpose."

She placed her other hand over his. Matthew stared at the squared nails as she spoke. They weren't pretty nails. They were splitting and peeling. He loved them all the more because of it.

"Do you believe God creates people for one another? For marriage?" she suddenly asked.

He looked in her brown eyes ... wondering ... remembering, her touch beating down the portals resurrected around his heart so long ago. How could such a simple touch, a hand in his, do such damage to the battlements he had erected so painstakingly? "Yes. I believe God has the perfect mate out there for his children. My mother and father are excellent examples."

Her hand squeezed his, and she looked down at their joined hands. Her voice was soft. "Last night, I lay in bed ... thinking ... dreaming ... and I could not fall asleep for thoughts of you, Matthew. Your face haunted me all through the darkness, and I thanked God for you, and prayed right then that you were created for me."

Matthew felt as if his heart had tumbled up into his throat. Her eyes were so earnest ... so filled with a newfound innocence. And after such candor on her part, how could he be anything but honest with her? How could he do anything but echo her sentiments and admit that each breath he drew was filled with her scent, every thought was finished with her face, every word turned into an expression of the feelings he bore in his heart. Yet wasn't love about more than feelings? "You must forget about me, Sylvie. I'm no match for you." He dropped her hand, remembering what Rene had told him in Paris. Had his friend revealed his intentions yet? It didn't matter if he had. He looked down, feeling awkward. How could he betray Rene like this? "Look who we are, my darling. You are the wealthy daughter of Armand de Courcey, and I am just a simple vicar. Of a small parish at that! You know that someday you must wed an important man, perhaps even a nobleman. I have willingly forsaken all of that."

"You mean you feel nothing for me?" She knelt before him, lovelier than the day, a new creature wide-eyed with love.

How could he refuse her the truth? This woman, whom he loved so desperately, needed so desperately to know she was loved ... even if the words could only be spoken in the present tense and only today. "It is as you say, my love. Simple man that I am, and one that is not worthy to fasten your shoes . . . I love you. With all my heart." But why go on with a charade like this? "We must be realistic, however, and resigned to the fact that most probably you will marry another."

Tears filled her eyes and she did not deny his prediction. "It is as you say. I am to be married. To Rene."

He nodded, her confession making him feel ill. "I know, Sylvie. He told me himself."

She clasped her hands tightly together, the knuckles white and stretched. "How can I marry him, when I feel like I do about you? How can I marry him when he cares nothing for me?"

"That's not true!" Matthew rushed in. "He cares for you deeply."

"But not like you do," she said, her words an accusation against himself, against Rene, against anyone that had anything to do with this situation that was obviously breaking her heart.

Matthew leaned forward, held her face in both of his strong hands, and quietly, solemnly looked into her eyes. His heart was no longer his own, but neither was Sylvie's. How badly he wanted to kiss her just then, but all the groundwork that he had done in Rene's life would be for naught if he stole Sylvie away from him. No, there was much more at stake here than his own heart. He must consider Rene's soul. "You are not mine to take," he said decisively. "You never were, Sylvie."

"You don't believe that someday we will be together?"

"You are promised to another. And besides that, Sylvie, would you really leave all this?" He swept his hand across the breathtaking landscape. "For a humble vicarage in Swainswick?"

Her hesitation told him all he needed to know, and his heart broke as she smiled sadly. "You see, Sylvie, at another time, perhaps, we might have loved much differently, more freely."

"But it *is* love, nonetheless, Matthew. Isn't it?"

"Yes. It is now and always shall be so. Someday, when you are a great lady, I can only hope you will remember me fondly as your first love."

She leaned forward and kissed him softly on his mouth, causing his head to spin. "Yes, Matthew, my first love, my only love."

"You must not say that! You must do all you can to open your heart up to Rene, Sylvie. For both of our sakes." The words he spoke tasted bitter indeed.

Tears in her eyes, Sylvie turned away, awakened Dizzy, and slowly walked to the edge of the wood. Matthew strolled by her side. He wanted to cry out that their love was meant to be, but he couldn't.

And yet, she loved him. She loved *him*. That thought alone was something he could live on for the rest of his life.

CHAPTER ❖ NINETEEN

Rene lit a cigarette, sat back on the sofa, and regarded Matthew. "I'm glad you came, old man. Your presence has been good for everyone. Especially Sylvie."

"She's a special woman, Rene."

"I am a lucky man," he said, fully agreeing with his own sentiment. After all, his fortune would certainly be improving because of Sylvie de Courcey.

"You're blessed, my friend. There isn't a man alive who couldn't see the worth of a woman like her."

Rene saw through the words. "Then you've taken an interest in her yourself," he stated. "It makes perfect sense. Sylvie is a fine catch."

Matthew said nothing, just stared into the flames dancing in the fireplace to his right.

"I have to marry her, you know," Rene continued. "I have given her parents a promise. I must keep my word."

Matthew's eyes were piercing. "Yes." His lips were tight. "You must keep your word. But I'm telling you this, old friend, if I ever hear that Sylvie's life is less than pleasant, if you are neglecting her for other ..." He was fighting for the word. "... *interests*, before God, I swear you will have to answer to me."

Matthew's passionate speech didn't surprise Rene at all. "Picking up where Guy left off?"

The vicar shrugged. "Something like that."

"Let me ask you something, Matthew," he said, stubbing out his cigarette, leaning forward in earnest. He bore no grudge against Matthew and his ways. It didn't surprise him the man loved Sylvie. In fact, now that he knew, it really did seem that the two were positively made for each other. But Claude Mirreault was breathing down his neck, and only Sylvie could beat him down. "Does she love you as you do her?"

Matthew's face deepened a shade or two, and Rene knew he would hear the truth. He always heard the truth from Matthew. "Yes."

Shoving down a mild panic, Rene reached into his pocket. "How much will it take for you to leave Champagne right away?"

His friend's face deepened even more, and he instantly regretted his thoughtless action. "I'm sorry, Mate," Rene rushed in. "I didn't mean to say that. I don't know what I was thinking."

Matthew rose from his chair. "Have a carriage sent round. I'm leaving immediately." His face was stony, expressionless.

"Old man." Rene leaned on his cane and got to his feet. "See here, I am sorry. That was thoughtless of me. But I am a desperate man. I need Sylvie far more than you ever will. Believe that if you believe nothing else."

But the damage was done. Half an hour later, Matthew Wallace was gone. Rene poured himself a quick sherry, gulped it down, and sought out Armand. He had more work to do.

Armand de Courcey was out in the vineyard, inspecting the vines. He was in his right mind, cleaned up, and ready for business. Rene took heart. The last thing he wanted was for the de Courcey empire to die on the vine. He smiled at his own joke.

"Armand!"

"Monsieur le comte." Armand bowed.

"It is good to see you back out here."

Looking so much older than he had over a year ago when Rene left for America, he ran a hand over his bald head. "I must carry on."

"And the vineyard will continue too?"

Armand nodded. "Yes, of course."

"Then may I suggest we move forward on the betrothal, as quickly as possible. Do you agree it would be to the benefit of both the de Courceys and the de Boyces to solidify the union?"

"I do," he said, thrusting forward his hand.

Rene took it, shaking it gladly. "Tonight then. We will announce it tonight."

"Fine. At dinner."

And so it was agreed. Rene breathed a sigh of relief as he walked away. If Sylvie was in love with another man, he had to bind her to himself, and quickly.

"Armand!" He turned around.

"What is it, Monsieur le comte?"

"Do we agree she either marries me, or must stay on here at Chateau du Soleil forever?"

Suddenly the man looked very wary, and his eyes narrowed slightly. "Why do you ask this?"

"I take my conquests very seriously, sir. Sylvie is mine, and mine alone." There, thought Rene, that was using words that a man like Armand would understand. Hopefully it would work. The truth was, he was leaving nothing to chance with this one. He had to make sure Sylvie, and her fortune, would be his. The girl must not be given any sort of choice in the matter. Not with her love for Matthew Wallace muddying up the works.

Armand agreed. "Now, sir, I must get back to work. It is already late in the day, and we have a big evening ahead."

"Ah, yes," Rene agreed. A big evening indeed.

⌒

"So my life is all mapped out then," Sylvie remarked as Agnes shimmied her into a dark green formal gown, one of the old ones made by the two of them several years before. It was much too tight at the bosom and a bit too short, but Agnes was afraid to ask Armand for new material to make a more demure gown than those party dresses from Worth's. Somehow they seemed out of place in such a gloomy castle whose inhabitants were mourning.

"Agnes, if Matthew Wallace had offered to take me away with him, I do believe I would have gone." She had acquainted Agnes of the entire tale earlier that afternoon as they picked wildflowers for Guy's tomb.

Agnes, tight-lipped and sorrowful at the futility of it all, nodded once. The girl was obviously in love with love, and Agnes could only pray that Matthew would fade from her mistress's mind and heart when he returned to England, or she would be in for a life of misery. Either way, Matthew would never get over it. That much about the man Agnes was sure, and her heart broke for the vicar, for she knew he was a good man. And his actions earlier in the day proved he was an honorable one. "Here, lovey, sit down and let me brush your hair." Sylvie sat, and Agnes picked up an ivory brush, drawing the soft bristles through her mistress's raven hair. "How do you feel about Rene? Is he someone you could grow to love?"

Sylvie shrugged. "Not the same way as I could love Matthew, but yes, I think he's a nice enough man. Very cordial. Attentive. I could do much worse."

Agnes snorted. "I should say! You'll be a countess."

Sylvie fiddled with the simple ivory comb on her dressing table. "The truth is, Agnes, any life is better than the one I have now."

Sylvie was silent for several moments, then spoke, not catching Agnes up on her train of thought.

"Guy wouldn't begrudge me these feelings now."

"Oh no, miss. Guy loved you more than he loved anyone else. And that's a fact."

"But we buried him only two days ago. And now I have the joy of the Lord and the secret knowledge of Matthew's love. I feel almost ashamed of myself."

Agnes tucked the final wisp of hair into the bun and patted Sylvie's slender shoulders. "There you go." She turned to get the threadbare black velvet slippers from the wardrobe. "We humans are made to feel more than one emotion at a time, miss. I remember when my own father died. He wasn't always an easy man to live with, my dad, but he loved us and showed us that love regularly, and when he passed on it was a dear loss." She set the shoes in front of Sylvie's feet. "But I remember that night—he had died in the afternoon—and we were sitting around the table just looking at each other's hands. I had got the meal together, made the funeral arrangements, and we were all gathered so quiet. Well, my dear friend Evangeline came over from the next village, as soon as she heard . . . came knocking on our door with a pudding still warm from the steamer, tears in her eyes and a smile on her face. And within a half hour we were drinking good cups of strong, hot tea, eating pudding, and laughing like Christmas." She crossed her arms over her bosom and leaned back against the bedpost. "I'll never forget that time as long as I live. And you know, Evangeline will always hold a special place in my heart, because she drove away the sadness, but not the grief. And there's a big difference between the two. It's the way we are, lovey. Grief can abide hand in hand with happiness, and that's nothing to feel guilty about."

Sylvie smiled. "Well then, down I go to see my heart's true love, Agnes." She suddenly turned toward her maid. "Am I a fool?" Her expression broke Agnes's heart.

In one of their rare moments of physical affection, Agnes put her arms around her and held her closely. "No, lamb. You've felt love for the first time, you've lost your brother, you're about to become betrothed. That you're not more confused is a miracle. God must certainly be sustaining you, my dear."

Sylvie gazed at herself in the mirror. "Why can't I leave it all? Try and convince Matthew to run away with me?"

"If you had met Matthew a year ago it might have been different. Passion blooms quickly, but commitment, the true commitment born of a deep abiding love, takes time. It's time to rely on the Lord now, my love. You've given him your heart, now give him your hand. He won't lead you to destruction, he's promised that many times."

Sylvie knew something was dreadfully wrong. Matthew was gone. And there sat Rene, and Viscount Blackthorne, come from Paris to support the family, she supposed. At least there was one sympathetic face in the bunch.

Youngblood took her hand with concern. "I went up to fetch him for dinner, and he was gone. The room was empty . . . all his things gone too. He received an urgent message, one of the grooms told me."

"Nobody knows where it came from?" Unprepared for so quick a departure, Sylvie felt her heart sink. "You all must know something about this. Matthew wouldn't up and leave like this so suddenly." So certain was she of the statement, her concern at the moment was only for him.

The countess shot to her feet—the castle keys clanging against her leg in an ominous, flat cacophony. "Sylvie, he's gone. That's all I can tell you. I had a servant call him down to supper and he was gone. It is as David says, all his things—few that they were—gone as well. I'm sorry. He left no note telling us where he had gone. I assume back to his friend in Reims."

Sylvie turned to her father, relieved to see he had tucked his right mind back into his head. Armand averted his gaze and cleared his throat. "Sylvie, I have something to tell you. It's been something the countess and I have been discussing for years, and now the day has come for it to be formal and binding. We are betrothing you to Count de Boyce."

Suddenly the room began to spin, but with an iron will, Sylvie righted it—and herself. Knowing this was coming didn't make the announcement any easier. She had made the decision to accept this proposal when she walked away from Matthew, hadn't she?

But this was her life being bandied about! She steeled herself, then spoke. "Father, I would speak with you in your study."

CHAPTER ❖ TWENTY

The study was dusty with destruction. It stunk from Armand's clothing, stale and rumpled, which lay strewn across the rubble of his wrath. Sylvie swallowed to repress the revulsion that thickened like bitter glue in the back of her throat. It was strange, to see him standing there now, cleaned up and obviously irritated. How did a disciplined man like her father lose control? More to the point, why?

How could she tell him how she felt? What was she going to say? If she didn't do this now, didn't at least try to speak up for herself, to change the direction of her future for herself, she would always regret it. He might laugh in her face, but she would take her chances.

"Papa, I would speak to you concerning this marriage."

"Say it, girl. And be quick about it. Your timing is awkward to say the least."

"Well, it's not as if you prepared me for that announcement in there. I'm carted off to Paris to supposedly keep the countess company, and now I find that was just a means to an end."

"You are perceptive."

She wasn't about to tell him Agnes had let go of the information weeks ago. "I don't think this is a good idea, Papa. I'm in love with another man."

He ran a hand over his bald head. Smirked as though he already knew. "Do you think that is important? Do you think I don't know what's best for the family, what's best for you?"

Sylvie's temper caught fire. "What's *best* for me? When has that ever been a concern of yours?" She ran her fingers lightly along her bruised, purple jawline. "Please, Father, this isn't about what's best for me. It's about you. At least be honest. A commoner's daughter married to a count—it would be the final feather in your cap, would it not?"

"I won't deny it will gain me the standing my fortune has not. Who is the lucky fellow, by the way?"

She swallowed. "Matthew Wallace."

Armand began to laugh. "So you're actually in love with that vicar? I must say, Sylvie, you've surprised me with this one. In my estimation, a man who has devoted his life to a spineless God that has distanced himself from his own creation is a fool. And yet there's something strong about him, something I can see that would attract you to him." He came closer. His reddened eyes glared into Sylvie's. "You'd be miserable, Sylvie. I've always seen how you ached for a higher social standing, for the finest dresses I could have easily given you, and your behavior in Paris solidified what I thought to be so. Who do you think paid for all those dresses at Worth's? It wasn't the countess! But I had to make sure this match between you and the count was an attractive proposition to both him and his mother. The de Courcey estates will be solidified the moment you and Rene are man and wife. That is what is at stake here. Mark my words, Sylvie. Hear them well. You *will* marry the count. And you will marry him with a smile on your face."

Sylvie knew there was nothing she could do. Matthew had left with his honor intact and no intention of vying for her love. "Is there no other way?" she asked. "Please, Papa."

But he turned his back on her and spoke, his voice gruff. "As of now, de Courcey winery will go directly into your hands upon my death. But I will change the terms of the will. The moneys shall go directly to your husband. I can't have you selling everything and running off to that vicar the moment I die."

Sylvie felt kicked in the teeth. "Papa, I would never do anything like that. You know that. Haven't I always been a loyal daughter?"

He didn't move.

"Please, answer me." She had to know how he felt, and even if he thought to the contrary, it was worth the risk.

"Yes, Sylvie. You have always been a loyal daughter." He suddenly turned, and for the first time in her life, Sylvie saw fear in the eyes of her father. Crumbling onto the couch, he leaned his face into his hands and wept.

Sylvie forgave him for that moment. Just then he needed her, and it was the first time for it. She hurried across the room, put her arms around him, and cried with him, years of pain and loneliness pouring out of her soul. "Oh, Papa, Papa," she muttered, hugging him tightly, feeling his tears soak through her gown, and she realized at that moment that he was as lonely as she.

After several minutes, he straightened up, took out a handkerchief, and wiped his face. He handed it to Sylvie. "You look a fright, Daughter."

She laughed and wiped away her own tears.

"You will marry Rene, and that's final," he declared. "If you do not, you will come back here and care for your mother, and I will approve of no other marriage."

It seemed he was desperately trying to find the edge to his voice that was always there, but Sylvie heard a difference. Just a wee difference, but therein lay the hope.

"Why, Father? Why the urgency to this marriage? Please tell me. If I am to be a sacrifice, I'd like to know just who holds the knife and why."

Armand stared into the darkened fireplace, hesitating, thinking. Then, with a shake of his head, the words rushed out. "My empire is in ruins, Sylvie. The bad harvest several years ago. And some short-sighted business deals are threatening to destroy all I've worked so hard to build. I need you to bring it back for me. Guy was going to, but now he is gone. I need your help." He choked on the last sentence.

She could hardly believe the words. "Does Rene know about this?"

"Of course not!" He was his testy self again. "And far be it from you to tell him!"

Sylvie promised not to say a word. She turned to leave the room.

"Sylvie!" he called.

"Yes, sir?"

"You're a good girl, Daughter. And you always have been. You're a true de Courcey."

It was enough right then. It had to be.

"I will marry Rene," she stated, thinking of the dynasty her father had worked so hard to build. All those hours spent away from them, all the sacrifices they'd made, all the labor she had expended would have been for nothing if it crumbled around them. Sylvie de Courcey pushed out her jaw and opened the door of the study. She hadn't shirked her responsibility to her family before, and she certainly wasn't going to start now. If the continuation of the vineyard lay in her capable hands, so be it.

On her way to the sitting room, where the guests were waiting, she stopped, breathed a prayer, and was afforded a certain peace. God was calling her away from this place, yet saving it through her marriage to Rene. Hadn't Matthew told her God has a purpose for his children?

There was nothing to do now but cling to his promises and believe that he was in control.

⌒

"May I sit with you?"

Sylvie was jolted out of her thoughts by the smooth voice of Viscount Blackthorne. A face most welcome in the dreary drawing room. "Certainly."

He chose a chair near the threadbare chaise on which she was reflecting. Tomorrow they would all be leaving for Paris to prepare for the wedding. Still reeling under the swift turn life had taken, she was trying to remember all the good reasons she had to marry Rene. Armand was working. Collette, out of guilt or embarrassment—Sylvie didn't know which—was avoiding her, and the countess was busy preparing for the return journey.

A sigh escaped without warning.

"I am sorry, Sylvie," David Youngblood blurted suddenly, eyes earnest.

"Whatever for?"

"You're going from one trap into another."

Sylvie's slow nod was accompanied by a gradual gathering of tears, and when Blackthorne took her into his arms to comfort her, she made no protest. It really was true. Living without Matthew was one thing, but going to Paris for good, to be married to Rene, was another. The family welfare depended on her, and that was that.

"One of the things that scares me the most is the countess," Sylvie admitted, always feeling free to speak her mind with the viscount.

Youngblood laughed. "You feel you'll never truly be good enough for her precious, perfect son?"

"She's so . . . so . . . ." Sylvie tried to find a kind word.

"Blind?" the viscount interjected. "Oh, Sylvie, if you only knew the half of it."

"He has a woman, doesn't he?" she asked. He had to. There was no other explanations for the way he was out all night most nights.

Youngblood nodded. "Her name is Camille."

She looked down at her hands. "Does he have any intention of giving her up once we're married?"

"I think so. Rene will do the best he can, Sylvie. You must believe that."

"The rest of my life," she mused sadly. "The rest of my *life*."

Youngblood knelt before her and grabbed her hands. "He doesn't deserve you, little Sylvie! The fool has no idea the treasure he has been handed!"

His deformed face was so earnest, so sincere, it was a beautiful thing to her. She caressed his cheek, and his eyes closed. "Oh, Viscount, you've always been so kind to me. Even when my life has been less than lovely."

He touched her hand. "You make it easy to be kind, dearest, for you are so kind yourself. So, you will marry him." It wasn't a question.

"I have to. It's the way things are done, and I haven't any other recourse but to refuse and stay here at Chateau du Soleil, and that, as you know, is something I will not do. I cannot go against my father, Viscount. Not now, with Guy's death so fresh. It would be more than he could bear."

Youngblood nodded, stood up, and sat at the bottom of the chaise. "Sylvie, no matter what happens, you can rely on me. Whatever you need, I will gladly supply it."

"We've known each other a long time, haven't we, Viscount?"

"Ah, yes, little Sylvie. Consider me your friend for life."

Sylvie smiled and put her arms around him. "I knew you were that already, Viscount. So you will still come around and cheer me?"

"Always," he promised.

Regret that her love for Matthew and his love for her would never be realized settled in for a very long stay. Nevertheless she accepted the comfort her good friend offered, so lost in her grief, she hardly felt the soft caresses of his hand upon her hair.

Youngblood cornered Rene in the wee hours of the morning as the two sat drinking brandy and smoking in the overgrown garden. "I suppose this means you are giving up Camille and her den of iniquity?" he drawled. Inwardly, however, he was broken. Here sat this man before him with the prize of the world at his feet, and he failed to realize it.

Rene stared at the glowing orange tip of his cigarette. "Oh, I don't know, David. Most men of our station have their paramours, do they not?"

"So you have no intention of ending the relationship?" In a way, he hoped Rene would say no. After all, was the count worthy of loving Sylvie in total? Of course not! If he wasn't so in love with her himself, he'd storm her defenses and take her away with him. But something deep within told him that Sylvie did not love him in return, not in the same way. He wouldn't open himself up to such rejection. If Sylvie was neglected by her husband long enough, she might someday turn to him of her own volition.

"Perhaps in time I shall put Camille aside. But I do not wish to break her heart immediately. Heavens, David, I'm not down the aisle yet."

"True, true," he acknowledged, doing his best to hide his feelings from Rene. He didn't say it, but Camille's heart would not be broken by the likes of Rene. She was only using Rene, even as he was, to line her pockets with cash and her wardrobe with lovely things.

"I don't suppose you will be my attendant, will you, old man?" Rene asked in his usual casual manner.

"And miss seeing Sylvie in her bridal regalia? I wouldn't miss it for the world!"

"There's something between the two of you, isn't there?" Rene asked. "A close friendship?"

"Oh yes, Rene. A very close friendship." Not nearly close enough, though. But maybe someday he could remedy that. He'd give himself plenty of time, however, and perhaps even Rene's lack of initiative would do the job for him. Sylvie was a woman with passions just waiting to blossom. In time, with no place for them to bloom, she would welcome a more fertile garden.

In the meantime, he would do all he could to show her he cared.

Don't scare her off, he warned himself. But something took root deep within, and, recalling her face, the way she had always accepted him without a thought to his imperfections, he knew he would go to any lengths to someday claim her as his own.

But first, he had to give up Camille himself. It wouldn't be as easy for her to lose him. For Camille loved him in her own way. Hadn't he found her in a run-down brothel, dirty, underfed, and infested with head lice? Hadn't he seen the potential of her beauty and introduced her to Claude Mirreault, who elevated her to the status of a first-class courtesan? She owed him everything she had, and as loyal in her way as Sylvie was in her own, she never wanted him to forget it. Of course, Rene knew nothing about their affair. It had all been going according to plan for two years now, and they were literally soaking the young count dry.

Now, Youngblood wondered whether it was all worth it. If he was to pursue Sylvie, however slowly, he must become worthy of her love. And he promised himself there in the garden, while agreeing to be Rene's attendant, that he would do just that.

CHAPTER ❖ TWENTY-ONE

Rene reached for Sylvie's hand as the train pushed through the countryside, past farms and villages toward Paris. The countess dozed next to her soon-to-be daughter-in-law, her soft snores hardly comforting. "You really know so little about me anymore, Sylvie. I think we should get to know one another well before the wedding. Don't you?"

Sylvie wanted to pull her hand away, but knew better. She must follow the path carved out for her, must make the best of it. Actually, the path wasn't carved at all ... she was forced to blaze her own trail across untried, rocky terrain. The ruby on her finger was an absurd reminder of the passionless life she was about to lead. The cold blue depth of a sapphire, or an icy clear diamond would have been much more apropos.

She stretched her fingers and looked at her fiancé with frank expectation. "Well, then, Rene, why don't you start by telling me why you wish to settle down in marriage so suddenly?" No sense in being cryptic. If she was to maintain her sanity, she must start this relationship on the right footing—honesty and forthrightness reigning at all times. She deserved that, at the very least.

Rene took no offense. "Wallace saved my life after I was shot in that grouse hunting accident three years ago. At his father's estates." He held up his cane for emphasis, and she noticed it was shaking a little. "If he had not taken me to the house and summoned a doctor there so quickly, I would have died. My mortality has become very real to me since then, cherie. The time to settle down has come, to marry and have children of my own. Mama has had her heart set on you since the day she was told your mother had a girl! And I can think of no one better to produce an heir than you, Sylvie."

Sylvie rolled her eyes and spared him a slight smile. She had, after all, always liked this man. He had been an integral part of her early childhood. "You make it sound *so* romantic, Rene."

He laughed. "Arranged marriages are anything but romantic. Let us not subjugate ourselves to delusion. Yet, I believe we can do well together, Sylvie. You are bright, and sweet to look upon. But more than any of that . . . you are strong." He looked into her eyes . . . through her, Sylvie felt. "We're both survivors. Though born to wealth and privilege, we both know what it means to survive."

"They say the sins of the fathers are visited upon the children. How do you know I will be such a good mother? Or wife for that matter?"

"I am not God, and I cannot say for certain that you will not follow in your parents' footsteps. But with all my heart I believe you to be a gentle soul, one that will love her children more than her pride, even her very life."

Sylvie, though she didn't know how, knew that to be so. "I don't think I'll be ready for children for a while yet, Rene. In fact the marital union has me a bit frightened. We won't have to . . . right away . . . will we?"

His smile was filled with understanding, and did she detect some relief as well? "That is up to you. I am committing myself to you wholeheartedly, Sylvie. But if you wish us to have a pla-tonic relationship until you are ready for more, I leave it up to your discretion. Who knows?" He lifted her hand to his beautiful mouth. "We may even come to love each other a little. And it will make the physical union that much sweeter and so much more worth the wait."

Sylvie knew better, remembering the man who truly kept her heart. Love with Matthew would have never been merely "sweet." He would have swept her along on the raging tide of his passions, loving her with unsullied ardor, seeking only to express the intensity of a completely committed heart. *Why did you not take me away with you*, she wailed inwardly, wishing for all the world he was there to answer her, to tell her it was not too late.

"No matter what," Rene continued, "I will be taking you away from Chateau du Soleil for good."

Sylvie raised an eyebrow. "There's certainly something to be said for that."

"And who knows when your father will come after you again? If he did it once . . ."

"Besides the obvious fact that I attacked him first, I don't believe my father would hurt me again."

"Why is that?"

"He's got more important matters to consider, and other than that, well, Matthew Wallace told me so. He had a long talk with Papa the night he came to my room."

His eyes narrowed, not menacingly so, just in intense observation—examining hers as thoroughly as he could. Then he went pale. "Ahhhh. Then if Matthew said that, it is most definitely so." He pulled out a handkerchief to swab at the perspiration that had beaded on his brow. "If you will excuse me, I shall return shortly." Rene tottered to his feet, looking almost gray. He limped away from his seat, fading into the sleeping compartment of the railroad car.

Sylvie's spine tickled in alarm. Realization assaulted her. He was marrying her because he needed her strength, not because they were survivors. But why he needed her so badly was yet to be disclosed.

Would she ever be completely free?

She doubted a treasure such as freedom would ever be hers. And she remembered the days in the fields, chatting with the men and the women, inwardly complaining about the toil her father forced her to do. Oh, that such simplicity might be hers again.

But right now, this was not to be, perhaps not ever.

Paris was before her now, but this time, anticipation had turned to anxiousness, expectation to dread.

The months of June and July flew by swiftly and unfocused. Sylvie and Rene were transformed into a Paris establishment. Invitations flooded in as soon as the betrothal was announced. After all, Rene was one of the empire's favorite sons. Having been away in America for so long, his presence was coveted at all the most fashionable functions. With the countess along as chaperone, they were the center of attention, the embodiment of the old and the new come together. The son of nobility wedding the daughter of entrepreneurial genius. The picture of France itself during the second empire, or so everyone claimed. Sylvie had her doubts, however.

While powdering her nose on numerous occasions, she was given the distinct impression she was an outsider. But there was one woman, the duchess de Laurence, who reached out to her. A small woman with dark hair and fair skin, she was possessed of a quiet beauty. And that she was a cousin to the emperor propelled her even higher up the social roster. The duchess was kind and helpful and filled with disdain for many of the more vapid members of society. One evening, during intermission at the opera, the two women talked in the lavish lobby.

"You must not worry about fitting into society, cherie." Her smile was dazzling. "The more you try to fit in, the more they will disdain you. Simply be who you are, and take no small measure of comfort in the fact that you are richer, smarter, and have by far a better-looking husband!"

Sylvie laughed. "Oh, Duchess, I'm so glad you aren't like the others. Your smile actually reaches your eyes!"

"And so does yours. But mine only does so through hard lessons I've had to learn."

"I think that's true of everyone. Your presence at these functions makes it all bearable."

The noblewoman's eyes clouded. "Do not rely on me too heavily, cherie. I may be leaving the country for quite a while."

"When?"

"Soon, I believe."

"I'm sure you'll miss your son, Loic?"

The duchess nodded. "But it is time for him to become a man. I know that now. My departure will be the best thing that could happen to him."

Sylvie had no idea what the woman was really talking about; she merely patted the duchess's arm to comfort her. When Rene came to collect her to return to her seat, she was relieved.

Up the grand staircase they walked, stopped by many people for a quick word, but finally they made it into their box. Resting on her seat was a little box. Yet another gift from Rene. Inside was yet another piece of jewelry, a fantastic pin actually, a jeweled peacock.

Each day she was lavished with more gifts from her intended. Gowns, jewels, whimsical porcelain boxes from Limoges. Never had such treasures been heaped upon her and from such an eager source. Whatever his deeper motives, Rene cared about her and had for years. When she opened his gifts with such delight, his eyes would moisten and he would say, "You should have had one of those years ago, darling." After growing up without pampering, Sylvie couldn't help but be affected emotionally by the outpouring of giving. Perhaps this marriage would not be so lonely after all. Rene de Boyce was her friend above all things, and he was proving that again and again.

Yet, he still disappeared occasionally. And during these absences, Viscount Blackthorne would appear in his place to ease her loneliness. Cecile—Rene's sister—and her new husband had returned to Paris, stealing away Racine's company. So Sylvie found herself reading her Bible more and more, lingering for hours in the library, Dizzy snoozing comfortably on the floor by her feet. And yet, she relished in the quietness, deepening her faith through many long hours of prayer.

Thoughts of Matthew frequented her mind during these hours. It was still true, she loved him. But having heard nothing from him, Sylvie wondered if the charged circumstances surrounding his visit had brought about such feelings as he professed, but only temporarily.

Absolutely not. Matthew wasn't like that. She knew he had loved her. Maybe still did. After all, it had taken him years to accept Isabelle's death.

Go to England! Her heart cried out.

FIND HIM!

Sylvie raised her chin, squashing her own emotions, defying her own heart. She would marry Rene. There would be no turning around. The plans were finalized, guests from afar were already arriving, her dress was pressed and ready.

But Rene was gone again. Probably to be with that woman.

Yet knowing men's temperaments as she did, she refused to corner him with prattling questions. Besides, the last thing she wanted to do was chain him to her by jealous interrogation and prideful worry. Her heart still belonged to Matthew, and the greater the emotional distance kept between Rene and herself, the better.

At the close of July, with the wedding only five days away, Sylvie relaxed with the countess in her boudoir. Weeks before, Rene had been banished across town to his bachelor apartments, for propriety's sake, until the wedding. It was late and he had left for the evening, leaving the women to their "frivolities," as he called them. Tatting for the countess, reading for Sylvie.

"Do you look forward to your wedding?" The countess worked her fingers, spinning lace faster than a spider spinning her web. "The truth now."

Sylvie shook her head.

"Matthew Wallace?" The countess smoothly slipped in the question, not looking up.

Sylvie hid her surprise. "Yes . . . Matthew. Yes." She hadn't spoken his name aloud in weeks now.

"I know. I suspected as much. You still love him, then? It wasn't just a passing fancy?"

Sylvie nodded, laying aside her bookmark, swallowing the tears. "I seem destined to repeat my mother's miseries."

The countess set her work down in her lap. "No. You are stronger than all that. And you will not stray from your husband." The words were more of a command than a prediction, and they puzzled Sylvie.

"I know it's wrong, loving someone else," she stuttered. "That God will not bless—"

"Shh." The countess put her knobby fingers up to Sylvie's lips. "Do not put words into God's mouth. You cannot help how you love . . . that is your own heart. But how you behave is another matter. When you give the vows, then you must never stray from my son."

"I know. I won't. Matthew is all the way in England. And as much as that pains me . . . I know it makes circumstances a bit easier, considering."

"Yes, child, yes. And Rene is the finest man in all of France. He will surely make you forget Matthew Wallace."

Sylvie suddenly turned to Racine and grabbed her hand. "Why do you do this to me? Why must I marry your son when I love another? Why do you not release me? You know you can do that, don't you? You and Rene are the only ones."

Tears filled the countess's eyes. "As much as I love you, dear child, I love Rene more. He needs a woman like you. Although he has never made it plain to you—his pride forbids it—he has loved you since he held you through the night while you cried . . . so many years ago."

"He told you that?"

"No. But a mother knows these things. You know you are free to run away on your own, without our blessing, to escape all of this. And yet you stay."

"Yes." Sylvie knew it was so. With all her heart she wished to run to the docks with Dizzy and take him with her on the first boat to England. She cleared her throat and stood to her feet. Yet she couldn't. It went far deeper than Rene, and even Matthew. It was about her father, the vineyard, about duty and honor and responsibility.

"I believe I'll retire for the night," she announced, laying aside her books. "And at least I have you here, Countess."

"Yes, my dear, you have me with you always."

Not really wanting to go to bed, but seeking solace, Sylvie hurried into the drawing room, through the glass doors, and into the summer garden. The heavy smell of roses assaulted, rather than soothed, and she wondered if there was a spot on earth that would ever feel like home. She paced restlessly.

The countess's reaction was puzzling. Sylvie had expected her to be angry, but that would presuppose a certain thoughtfulness directed at Sylvie, regarding her feelings for Rene. The countess cared nothing about her feelings, Sylvie realized, just as long as she marched down that aisle and promised to love, honor, and obey.

Suddenly, remembering all the gifts, all the attention she had received from both Rene and his mother, she likened herself to a calf . . . fattened up and ready to lead to slaughter.

CHAPTER ✦ TWENTY-TWO

Ah, darling, you have returned yet again to your Camille, eh? You may be promised to a sweet virgin, but Camille is always good enough for . . . weightier matters? Do you like my new place?"

Rene looked around him at Camille's new home. "I'm glad I was finally able to convince you to move to a more fashionable district, Camille."

She wound long, thin arms around his neck, kissed him sensually. "I know it had to cost you a small fortune. And I love you for it."

He shrugged, kissed the forearm near his chin. "Guy de Courcey's personal fortune will be at my disposal in the not too distant future. But I wanted to set you up in a better place."

"You don't have to explain it to me, cherie. I just say thank you."

"What made you want to move from the waterfront, Camille, after all this time?" he asked.

That was easy enough to answer. "I don't want that wife of yours to enjoy a better life than I do." She turned away and went over to the settee. The old Chinese woman brought them their opium pipes.

"I never promised you more than this, Camille." He drew in.

And so did she, feeling the well-being, the relaxation, the slow release from reality. Ahhh.

"I have been to see Mirreault," he reported.

"Again?" Camille sat up. Of course, she had known that. She put a hand up to her mouth in delight, and leaned into him, ready to convince him that a trip to Worth's would be worthwhile. "Monsieur Mirreault was most forgiving, eh? Now we can have a grand time! How dreary life has become lately, even in this beautiful house." She kissed him again, then pulled back, thinking of a thousand ways they could spend the money. After all, that was her job. "Let's have a party! We'll let Viscount Blackthorne plan it—he's so good at these things—and I know just the dress I'm going to need. I saw it at—"

Rene's face grew red. "Quiet! Be quiet, Camille. This is the finale to all of it, don't you see? It is why you are here in this place. I'm leaving you, but I didn't want to leave you down there, by the water. I am going to pay Claude off in entirety and tell Youngblood to pay for his own fun. I will see to it that you do not go hungry."

"But Rene—"

"It is time all of this stopped." He held up his pipe. "And while I am at it, I just might give this up as well!"

Camille said nothing, reclined back into position, and smiled, feeling like a witch's cat. She knew her lover better than anybody, and she knew that a little, innocent nobody like Sylvie de Courcey would have no positive influences over the vices of Count Rene de Boyce. Well, maybe the girl wasn't exactly a *nobody*, but she wasn't a great beauty like herself, and there was much too much thought going on behind those large eyes. Yet even Camille had to admit Sylvie's eyes were quite arresting. Enough about the competition, though. There were more pressing matters at hand, she thought. If she couldn't convince the count to squander his latest stash, Claude Mirreault would be furious with her.

Outside, the stars shimmering in the night sky were barely visible through the grimy windowpane to her left. But she picked out the belt of Orion and made a wish, the eyes, the hands, the body of David Youngblood stirring in her consciousness. The viscount had always made his feelings plain; he wasn't in love with her and never would be. Yet she still desired to do only his will, and that happened to coincide with the will of Claude Mirreault. "Forgive me, cherie," she whispered, draping her leg over his. "Of course, you must do what you have to do." She kissed him on the mouth. "But I predict, that you won't be able to discard your little Camille so easily."

Rene sighed, and her soft, green eyes must have worked their magic, for he pulled her into his arms and returned her kisses. She led him to her bedchamber and quietly closed the door.

Viscount Blackthorne interrupted the hush of the garden with a cheerful, "Good evening, Sylvie." He was dressed in black evening clothes, looking his best, acting debonair, but feeling self-consciously overstuffed. "I knew you would be alone tonight."

"I won't even ask where he is," Sylvie returned.

"You deserve better, Sylvie. Here, come sit with me in the rose arbor. They are looking a little lackluster now, but it is dark enough that we will not have to see their dreary petals."

He led her to a wooden bench. She sat as he pulled out a cigar. "Do you know where he is, Viscount?" The wedding, only three days away now, weighed heavily on him. He lit the cigar, propped one foot on the stone bench, and rested his forearm across his thigh.

"Please call me David," he invited, realizing it was time to draw her in a little farther, time to lay the groundwork for the future. "And I thought you were not going to ask." He pulled in one long drag to get the stogie going completely, then examined the glowing tip, satisfied.

It was good to be with Sylvie again. He had been on a short trip to England to see his younger sister, the only relative, other than an iconoclastic uncle, who would speak to him.

"I didn't realize you'd be arriving so soon or I would have arranged transportation from the dock," she said.

Her strange eyes pierced him. Was there a woman in the world such as this? "I am a grown man, mademoiselle. You need not worry. I can take care of such things for myself. You worry too much about the welfare of others."

Sylvie dropped her gaze. "I sometimes forget how great a family you hail from."

He waved a hand, sending her subtle scent into his nostrils. "We are all from the same earth, Sylvie, are we not? We all must breathe the same air, eat food to survive."

"We all burp," she said suddenly, unable to keep a smile from her lips. Guy had always said that to her.

How he liked this woman's spontaneity. "Yes, we do. Although some of us are better at concealing the matter than others, I daresay."

"Was your journey arduous?"

He grabbed her hand, quickly but not harshly, and sat down beside her. The time to lay the cornerstone had come. "Tell me, why do you wish to marry a man who leaves you so often? If he loved you so much, why are you alone right now?"

She whisked her hand from his grasp. "Rene does not love me in that way, Viscount. We both understand that this is a marriage of convenience . . . convenient for him and my father, that is."

"But not you?"

That shrug again. "It's not for me to decide such matters, my lord."

Play it right, Youngblood, he thought. *Don't scare her away now.* He took her hand again, raised it to his misshapen lips. "If you were mine, I should be right where I am now, doing just what I am doing. And I would make sure no other man would be vying for your affections."

Sylvie looked away, squeezed his hand, then let go. "I think we should be going in."

"I think not."

"Rene will be home shortly."

"Are you positive about that?"

"Well, no, but I . . ." Her eyes were darting in panic.

Slow down, friend. This is not the way to go about it. He tried to give as reassuring a smile as he could. "Do not be frightened. I am just trying to tell you that you are not alone, darling little Sylvie."

She sighed and rewarded him with a smile that bespoke her relief. "For a moment there I thought . . . never mind, it was silly of me to presuppose."

"What do you mean?"

"I thought you were telling me you felt . . . more . . . for me."

He raised her hand, pressed it to his cheek as if it were the rarest of roses. "As I told you before, sweet miss, some women have the power to reform even the most vile of sinners."

With that, he thought it best to quit the garden. So he did. But as he walked into the house, he turned and saw Sylvie's shoulders shaking beneath the weight of her tears. The tears weren't for him, he knew. He stopped and turned back toward her.

"Who do you love, Sylvie," he asked. "For whom do you cry?"

"Matthew Wallace," she whispered.

"This is about much more than your wedding."

"Yes." She raised her face to his, stricken, tormented. *Heaven help me*, he thought. Competing with Rene was one thing, but Matthew Wallace was another matter entirely.

⌒

Youngblood paced violently in his room. He had gone too far, revealed too much, opened up his heart much too far, much too soon. "Remember your place, sir." He said the words aloud, hearing his father's voice, having heard them ever since he could remember. *Remember that you don't belong to the world of the beautiful. Remember your lips, your deformity. Remember that your advances make Sylvie de Courcey want to vomit.*

A spasm of rage gripped his throat, as he heard the mocking voice in his mind. Always in the wrong, no matter how hard he tried. Blamed for his imperfections, or worse, ignored for weeks on end. He had had loads of time to make his own way in life, gather about him the friends who would look beyond his face—as long as he was financing their vices. He was honest enough to realize this. After all he was nothing if not a man who "knew his place." Yet he knew he could be great fun, a reckless man thought of as just a little bit insane. Most of the time Youngblood thought the title wasn't justified, but there were days when he wasn't so sure.

This was one of those times. Obviously. Oh, if he could somehow change his appearance. He'd sell his soul to do it. *You certainly can't buy a better face even if it were possible,* he sneered at his reflection. His parents had cut off his allowance years before, and yet he continued to inhabit the lifestyle he was born to enjoy.

Claude Mirreault's wretched image blurred his thoughts, and he laughed. No. He certainly couldn't sell his soul for a prettier face. He had sold it years ago to the moneylender with a face almost as ugly as his own, the devil in the fortress near Versailles. Blackthorne only acquired a small percentage of the money Mirreault garnered from the men he led down the road to destruction and financial ruin. However, he had his own ways of lining his pockets. De Boyce hadn't been the first to fall prey to him, but—Youngblood remembered the haunting dark eyes of the woman he was falling crazily in love with—he just might be the last.

Now was the time to show Lord and Lady Youngblood that they were wrong about their only son. He would make them see he was worthy of a good life, with a good wife and children of his own, that a wonderful woman could love him despite his appearance. But Sylvie was the key. Moreover, if he had to destroy Rene de Boyce in the process to claim her as his own, so be it. The slight tinge of guilt that tickled at his heart would be nothing compared to the joy he would experience once Sylvie was his. He would make life good for her. Would take away all her pain and loneliness, and she would take away his.

Unfortunately, she was getting married in two days. Even he couldn't work his will in such a short space of time. After the wedding would suffice. It would have to.

The rage subsided, leaving in its wake an undeniable thirst.

He stood apart from the rest of the group, partially obscured by a holly bush. The clothes he wore, a brown tweed suit and crisp white shirt, felt foreign, as did the bowler he had pulled down low over his brow. No one would recognize him, he was sure, for certainly in his case, the clothes went a long way in making the man. How many mornings had gone by since he had last donned anything other than his vicar's garb?

Due to the recent death of Guy, the wedding of Sylvie and Rene was a modest affair by anyone's standards. Surely, Armand was pleased with the frugal, spare ceremony, in the gardens of Maison de Fleur, Matthew Wallace thought. Family, close friends, and a few servants watched solemnly as the striking couple muttered their vows. That they were a striking couple, he so fair, she so dark, plunged the dagger more deeply into his aching heart. They would make beautiful children together, was a comment he heard several ladies make on the way in.

He stood motionless, never taking his gaze from the bride who was dressed in black, still mourning her brother. She had been draped in yellow the first time he beheld her. His heart dove fast and deep within his chest, and he vowed that never again would it crawl out of the abyss.

Never again.

Later, when the bride whisked by on her way inside, he pulled his hat down tightly over his stormy blue eyes, tucked a note into her hand, and dashed toward the gate. It was time to go home, back to England, back to Miranda, back to the life he would never leave behind.

The words swayed before her eyes as her hand, supporting the folded parchment, bobbed with the rhythm of the de Boyce railroad car. The honeymoon travels had begun. Settled inside the silk-lined sleeping compartment, Sylvie scanned the note that had been secretly tucked into her hand earlier that day.

Dear Sylvie,

Unable to stay away, I had to see you married, had to shovel the final spadeful of dirt over my heart's grave. It will always belong to you. And though I risk the sin of adultery to even write the words, I must. I am only a man, always in need of the Savior's redeeming blood.

But know this, should you ever need me, I will always do what I can to help you. My door is open to you, though my heart, of necessity, be shut off from the nurturing light of your love. Yes, I know you still love me as I love you. It will always be thus, but can never be shared. Because of your now married state, you shall hear from me no more. But my prayers for you will never cease.

M.

"Tears? And on our wedding night?" Rene crossed the car in his dressing gown and took the piece of paper. He read it slowly and handed it back. "I had no idea. You love Wallace?"

Sylvie nodded as he knelt down next to her where she sat on the bed.

He reached out, cradled her face with his hand. "Why did you not tell me?"

"Would it have mattered?"

He looked briefly away. "I would like to think it would have. I would like to think I am not that desperate a man," he softly joked, and wiped away her single tear.

"My father forbade it anyway, Rene. There was nothing you could have done. We must make the best of our lot. Remember, no delusions."

Taking her hands in his slender ones, he gazed at her earnestly. "They had this planned for years, my sweet. You knew that, did you not?"

"Every girl hopes to marry for love."

"So does most every man. I thought that now the timing was right . . . for you. I am back from America, and with Guy's death . . . it was good to get you out of there."

"I know."

"But I shall never be Matthew, shall I?"

And I shall never be Camille, she thought. "Perhaps not. But I swear to you, Rene, that I will be a good wife."

"And you are a woman of your word."

"I've always tried to be."

With the help of his cane, he rose to his feet and sat beside her on the bed. "What has wrought such a change in you, Sylvie? It's not so much your actions that have been transformed, but your outlook, your eyes."

She recounted to him the events following Guy's death, fearing he would deem her a lunatic for her newfound faith. Instead, he sighed with relief. "You will give my mother great comfort."

"She prays for you constantly, you know."

"Yes. I know. Perhaps someday I will be ready to listen. But for tonight"—clearly he was changing the subject—"we have other things to do. If you are ready, we will go to bed. Unless, of course, you still wish to refrain."

Sylvie breathed in deeply. Her limbs turned to ballast and her mouth to straw. Nevertheless, she placed her hand in his and dutifully turned down the coverlet on their marriage bed.

She had made her vows. There was no reason to hold back, to deny herself the only pleasure she foresaw in her future—the delights of motherhood.

"I am ready tonight."

"Are you certain about this?"

She shook her head. "I do not wish to wait. Let us pray this night is blessed, my husband."

He turned down the lamp and took her into his arms.

Later, the rhythmic movement of the train lulled her to sleep, and Sylvie realized that Rene's arms weren't the worst place in the world to be. Perhaps they weren't the ultimate place of fulfillment and rest, but they certainly were better than nothing at all.

CHAPTER ❖ TWENTY-THREE

The only indication of Racine's impatience was the manner in which she flexed the toes on her right foot. Thank goodness they were hidden beneath the billowing folds of her traveling gown. *When would they arrive?* she wondered regarding the honeymoon couple due to return any moment now.

She was ready to be going. An urgent letter from Collette called for her assistance. Apparently, life at Chateau du Soliel was quickly crumbling. Armand had steeped himself into the business so far he never emerged, and Collette, unable to cope after Guy's death, was falling apart as well.

Finally, after she had imagined at least twenty carriages pulling up outside, the long awaited phaeton whirled around the corner and up to the front of the house. Rene was driving, exuding a well-nourished glow and looking better than he had since before his accident. Time in the sun had turned his skin a light bronze, and his hair was bleached almost white. Beside him, Sylvie was pink with health, her hair glossy and heavy beneath a pert little green traveling hat.

Racine hurried to the doorway, bag in hand, hat snug on her head. "You're finally here!" she cried, running down the steps. "How was your holiday?"

"Mama! How do you move so swiftly these days, and in such clothing!" Rene climbed down, helped his new bride to do the same, then kissed his mother.

"How does one move so slowly coming home from the station?" Racine asked.

"It was such a wonderful time for us," he replied. "I didn't want it to end."

He bestowed on her a warm, sincere hug, and Racine remembered what an affectionate lad he had once been. Those were the days! "I am glad your stay in Nice was so lovely. You are both looking better than before. And as happy as I am to see you, I am in all haste to get away. Stay right there, Herman," she called to the driver, "we are going back to the railroad station."

"You mean you're leaving?" Sylvie asked, looking so pretty as she stepped forward that Racine pulled in a quick breath. Could her grandchild already be growing within? Oh, dear God, let it be so!

"I must. Your mother calls for me."

"Father—?"

"Is working himself to death. But the household is in a state of anarchy to put it mildly. The servants have no direction, and if one meal arrives on the table each day it is nothing short of a miracle. She cannot accept Guy's death, Sylvie. She needs someone to help her now."

Another vehicle had pulled up behind the phaeton. It was loaded with luggage, boxes, souvenirs, and two very warm servants. Agnes lumbered down from the carriage, looking as if the honeymoon had indeed been no vacation for her. "Would you like me to go with her, my lady?"

"No, no, no," Racine clucked, confident she was capable of dealing with the situation, "Sylvie will need you." *If my guess is accurate, that is.*

"Yes, my lady." Agnes nodded and walked in, but she looked back at her mistress anxiously. Sylvie waved a placatory hand. "It's all right, Agnes. I'm sure Aunt Racine can take care of everything."

Rene took his mother's hand. "But do you feel up to the task at hand?"

Racine smiled and willingly told the truth. "To be quite honest, I do. I have not felt this strong in years, my darling. Cecile," she spoke of her daughter, "will do everything she can to help you assume your duties here at Maison de Fleur, Sylvie. Perhaps it is better this way, more fitting that you should begin your proper role as a countess without your predecessor hanging about inspecting your every move."

"Talk about trial by fire!" Rene pulled her into his side with a familiar arm.

Sylvie smiled, her lips trembling slightly. "I'm up to the challenge . . . I hope."

Racine patted her hand. "I know I'm leaving things in good hands. You've always been so capable, Sylvie." She kissed her new daughter-in-law, and allowed Rene to lend an elbow at the carriage steps.

As she rode away, she was pleased to see Sylvie put her arms around Rene's waist and lay her head against his chest. *Didn't I know it?* she gushed, feeling utterly responsible and infinitely pleased about the entire matter.

Horses this. Horses that.

Sylvie thought if she ever had to hear the word "horseflesh" again she would scream. For the last three months she had been sharing this home with Cecile, and for three months she'd heard about nothing but horses.

Rene's sister was an equestrian style nightmare.

Wondering why Cecile hadn't married before the age of thirty-five, the answer soon became apparent. The woman was monstrously big, with wild green eyes and a voice louder than a factory whistle. She was an untamed creature with deeply muscled legs, sturdy arms, and flaxen hair as coarse as a horse's tail. The name Helga would have suited her much better, Sylvie decided. Rene declared she was a spitting image of their father, and Sylvie could well believe it. She couldn't imagine the man who would be right for this Amazonian amazement known comically enough as Ceci. But when she met Francois, twice as large and twice as loud as his new bride, she wasn't at all surprised. They lived on Francois' manor east of Orleans, breeding and raising fine "horseflesh" and quickly earning a favorable reputation among equestrians across the land. They had agreed to stay at Maison de Fleur for a bit, to ease Sylvie through the transition.

It was a noisy transition, mind you. For not only were they both robust in their vocals, they were heavy of foot as well, thumping all over the house at once, it seemed. The music students were always playing reels, mazurkas, and tarantellas at their request.

"Sylvie!" Ceci boomed as she practically galloped in from the kitchens to where Sylvie stood arranging a massive dome of flowers in the large entry hall of the house. "What do you think?" She turned stiffly, straight legged, for her sister-in-law.

"Breeches? You're actually wearing breeches, Ceci?"

Her mouth spread wide with pride. "I am getting bolder by the year. It was a day of riding like you would not believe, sister! A picture-perfect day. How I hate sidesaddles!" Sylvie was yanked into a hug that would have left the emperor himself breathless. Ceci was a woman with a heart as big as her calves, and she had decided she loved her new sister-in-law. Ruddy Francois was equally as accepting. "I hope you did not mind seeing to the dinner preparations."

Of course Sylvie didn't. Ceci had no creativity whatsoever, or direction, when it came to planning the daily meals. The cook had been allowed to get lazy and the kitchen staff as well since the countess had left three months previous for Champagne. Sylvie, in the throes of early pregnancy, hadn't been capable of caring what the servants were doing. But now that the extreme exhaustion had left her, now that she could keep her food where it belonged, she was demanding better. She had enough of old Armand in her to expect more from her servants.

"We will be eating in an hour, Ceci. Are you expecting anyone this evening?"

Ceci placed her large hands on her narrow hips and stared with flat eyes and a crooked mouth. Then snorted a derisive laugh. She and Francois weren't exactly social butterflies. They enjoyed each other, their family, and their horses. And not necessarily in that order!

"It's just us then, I suppose," Sylvie said, placing the last orchid in the colorful arrangement, then standing back to admire her handiwork. She placed a hand on her slightly bulging belly, the outer sign of the honeymoon child growing within. She had sent word to her mother and father of the impending birth, but doubted that either of them would care all that much.

"Unless that Youngblood beast comes calling at the last minute," Ceci grimaced, "we'll have a nice quiet dinner."

Sylvie looked at her askance, doubting they could have a nice quiet anything with Ceci and Francois in attendance. "I don't know why you don't like him. And there's nothing to worry about anyway. He was called to England a month ago—some sort of family emergency, he told me—and not likely to return until next week." Sylvie made a mental note that she would have to thank him for the lovely birthday gift he had sent from London a week ago. He had written her faithfully, twice a week, since he was called back by his father to take over the duties. Reluctant to go, but still interested in his inheritance, he swore he would someday return "to keep you company when your husband mysteriously disappears." And Rene was still disappearing regularly, without explanation. But Sylvie knew where he was, and though she wasn't in love with him, it still hurt to know she wasn't enough for him. Still, he was leaving *her* alone in the bedchamber, and that certainly counted for something!

Ceci's distaste concerning Youngblood was evident. "There's something not quite right about him. Mama sees it too. He's very predatory."

"Not around me."

"He wouldn't be around *you*, Sylvie. The man is in love with you."

Sylvie laughed. "You may be somewhat right. But he really is harmless, Ceci. The viscount would never hurt me."

Ceci picked up an orchid and began to disassemble it with absentminded curiosity. "I presume Rene showed up last night?"

Sylvie shook her head with a sigh. "No, not until later this morning." They'd had this conversation many times in the past few months.

Ceci scraped off her riding hat, spiraled the trailing scarf around her arm, and frowned at the bright scene outside—a cold day, cloudless skies. "I don't know, sister. Seems to me you should allow yourself a tighter rein with my little brother."

Sylvie nodded dully, but in truth she suspected it was better not to question her husband's nocturnal habits. After all, the more he was gone, the less she was forced to play the dutiful wife. Choking back a sob, she quickly excused herself and left the room.

Moments later, in the quiet of her bedchamber, she indulged in memories of her heart's only love.

I should have followed him, she cried silently without tears. *I should have followed my heart.*

She reached beside her and picked up her Bible, feeling closer to Matthew, feeling closer to the Savior as she opened its pages and began to read about God's love for the world. She had believed on him. She would not perish. She would have everlasting life.

If only I can get through today, Lord, she prayed. *Just let me make it through today.*

⌒

Sylvie knocked on Agnes's door. She knew her maid had been missing her husband sorely as of late, and she felt guilty for not sending her back with Racine. On a fancy plate, nestled in a lace doily, sat three chocolate truffles, Agnes's favorite treat. Maybe that would cheer her up.

Agnes pulled open her door, eyes red from crying, but she immediately saw the truffles and gave Sylvie a smile. "Well, Miss Sylvie, you've discovered the secret of coping with womanhood. If you can't have your mate with you for comfort, chocolate is the next best thing! Would you like to come in for a bit?"

She handed Agnes the plate. "Yes. Do you mind if I sit here in your chair? I'm exhausted."

"You settle yourself right there, and put your feet up on the footstool," Agnes clucked. "I'll go get us a cup of tea."

But Sylvie wouldn't have it. "You'll do no such thing, Agnes Green. You'll sit there and eat those truffles and enjoy every bite."

Agnes held the plate out. "Care for one?"

"No!" Sylvie cried. "They're all yours. It's enjoyment enough to watch you eat them. Besides, I'll be gaining enough weight as it is."

Picking one up and examining it, Agnes asked, "Is one of these raspberry?"

"That one in your hand."

Agnes quickly set it aside. "I'm saving that one for last then. I'll have it tonight before bed." She picked up another one and bit down, closing her eyes in appreciation of the smooth, silky chocolate and the hazelnut filling. "This hits the spot."

"Well, I know you'd rather be back in Champagne with Rupert, so I thought I'd try and make your stay with me a little sweeter."

Agnes settled herself on the bed, leaning against the pillows and nibbling slowly at the remainder of her truffle. "Truth is, Miss Sylvie, I miss him terribly. And with Christmas right around the corner."

"I know it's asking a great deal. But would you stay with me until after the baby is born? Cecile won't be any comfort, and Rene is never here . . ."

"Are you still feeling that lonesomeness that plagued you earlier, right after you returned?"

Sylvie remembered what it was like the first month as countess at Maison de Fleur. Rene was never home, the countess was gone, and she was so ill. Not to mention the ache in her heart for Guy and Matthew. "That was the lowest time of my life, Agnes. But, that Bible of Matthew Wallace's has become more precious to me than I could have ever dreamed."

"It's *your* Bible now, Sylvie," Agnes reminded her.

Sylvie nodded. "Yes. Yes, it is. It's been a real comfort to me. The loneliness hasn't been as acute either." She looked down at her hands. "It's funny, I always thought my loneliness would be cured by a loving husband, or children of my own, but I'm finding out altogether differently, Agnes."

"There's a difference in being lonely and alone, isn't there, child?"

"Yes. The Savior is always with me now, and I'm so aware of his presence, I cannot help but feel a sense of peace, a glimmer of hope, no matter what the circumstances are around me. So, in answer to your question, no, the loneliness isn't plaguing me much at all. It's more of a nuisance now, and all I have to do is remember who walks beside me, and lift up my heart in prayer, and I immediately feel so much better."

"So you've been praying a lot then?" Agnes asked knowingly.

Sylvie laughed. "More than ever before!"

Agnes finished the final bite of her first truffle and laid the other two aside. "Have you heard about some of the silver disappearing?"

Sylvie sighed. "Yes. The count is taking care of it himself. He doesn't want to bring the investigators into the matter. He's a very private man."

"It sounds to me like it's someone who's familiar with the way things work around here. And there's been no sign of anyone forcing their way in from the outside."

It was a matter that concerned Sylvie greatly. But she knew she must leave it in the hands of her husband.

"Well," said Agnes, "it's probably better that you don't worry yourself about a sticky-fingered servant. Especially considering your delicate condition."

Sylvie patted her stomach. "To be honest, now that the nausea is over, I haven't felt this good in a long time. I feel as if I'm doing something so amazing, so miraculous, that nothing can hurt me or make me ill."

Agnes smiled a sad smile. "You are truly blessed, child."

Sylvie wished she could have taken back her statement. Poor Agnes, made to be a mother, but destined to be childless. Some things about the Almighty she would never understand. She could only trust him to know and to do what was best. "But I still need you, Agnes," she assured her. "You may not have had children of your very own, but you had Guy and me. You took care of us."

Agnes pulled a hankie out of her pocket and wiped away the tears that had quickly gathered in her eyes. "Goodness me!" she said. "It's my day for tears, Miss Sylvie!"

Sylvie arose from her chair and sat next to Agnes, putting her arms around the woman that meant more to her than anyone else in the world. And she comforted her as Agnes herself had comforted her many times.

CHAPTER ✦ TWENTY-FOUR

Racine climbed the steep, circular staircase to the top of the tallest turret at Chateau du Soleil. As she glanced out of the windows on her way up, the dormant vineyards spread before her eyes like a woolen quilt. The vines twisted brownish gray in the December twilight, beautiful even in their winter nakedness. Even Racine felt awkward and clumsy as she looked down upon their graceful lines.

She twisted the golden bracelet on her arm as she heard the scraping slippers of Collette already inside the uppermost room. A sigh stole from her lips and she opened the door, prepared to take on the duty to which her Father had called her. Being Christian could be so difficult, she thought without guilt, knowing it was true. She should be watching her grandchild grow in Sylvie's belly, but instead she was here in Champagne, making sure two grown adults survived. At least Armand was so busy she had only to look after his meals. She had never seen him so driven, and that, surely, was saying something!

"Racine? Are you there?" Collette turned from her perch by the window, looking clean and well cared for. This arrangement had been good for Sylvie's mother. She was eating well and had even gained a little weight. But her eyes still welled with tears without notice, and she spent most of her time in the chapel.

"I am here, dear friend."

Collette's brows knit. "It is so quiet here in the winter."

Saying nothing, Racine moved to join her at the window. Several minutes later, Collette turned to her and laid a hand on her arm. "I have an idea, Racine. Why don't we go to Paris? Spend Christmas with Sylvie and Rene?"

Though she couldn't be more surprised at the suggestion, Racine could think of nothing she would like better. "I would love to do just that! Are you sure?"

Collette nodded. "I need to get away from here, Racine. I'm not well inside, and though I hate to leave, a change of scenery would do me well. Armand would be relieved to get rid of me for a while, I think."

"So Armand has given you his permission, then?"

Collette's face puckered sheepishly. "I was hoping you would ask him. He will refuse to go himself, of course. But he might allow me to travel, to leave him alone to do whatever it is he does all day."

Inwardly, Racine shook her head, but bestowed upon Collette the smile that had made her famous throughout Paris. "All right, my dear. I think a change of scenery would do us both a bit of good."

"Do you think we might find a way for Rupert to drive us?" Collette asked in a rare moment of thoughtfulness. "It has been so long since he has seen his Agnes. And it would be a lovely trip, stopping along the way . . ."

Racine raised her brows. "If he can work it out in his stables, I do not see why not. It has been ages since I traveled by carriage. I shall make sure we have enough furs to keep us warm!"

Perhaps there was hope for Collette yet, she thought, watching her friend gather her skirts and start down the steps. Racine hurried behind her, ready to get packing, ready to leave this cursed place behind.

"Come right this way!" Rene showed Guy de Courcey's lawyer into his study. It had taken quite a while, but the intricacies of his estate had been worked out, and it was time to hear the final figure.

The de Boyce's personal secretary, Jean-Francois Gauttier, stood behind the desk, brows folded in worry. Rene regarded him carefully. So far the man had questioned nothing regarding the finances. Rene had made sure enough money was always available so that their expenses could be paid off. But the Mirreault money was almost gone, and he had gone to more creative means of obtaining the funds necessary to keep up their lifestyle. The last thing he wanted to do was borrow more money from such a criminal. He had already sold off all their land in Burgundy and was trying to keep all the Paris holdings intact lest Mother find out.

Today would change all this, though, he thought. Ah yes, Guy had told him four years ago of his financial condition. He had invested wisely, and though he wasn't extremely wealthy, his estate should at least go to pay off Mirreault. And Rene promised himself he wouldn't borrow money from the man again. He would give up gambling as well. *It might mean leaving Youngblood behind*, he thought, *but I've got to stop this dreadful way of living*.

Sylvie entered the room, looking as if she'd rather be anywhere else. But she sat dutifully next to him, even taking his hand.

"Shall we get started?" Guy's lawyer asked, and the men sat on leather chairs facing the desk. The advocate sat down, pulled his small spectacles from his face, and rubbed the bridge of his nose. Rene wanted to scream.

"Get on with it!" he barked, surprised at his own outburst.

The man replaced his glasses. "It doesn't look good for you, countess," he said to Sylvie. "Once we paid off his outstanding debts, I'm afraid there's very little left of your brother's estate."

Rene could hardly believe what he was hearing. "What? Are you certain about this? What about his home here in Paris? That was worth something, wasn't it?"

The man nodded. "That was what we used to pay off his debts. His accounts severely dwindled this last year. I'm not sure why."

Rene looked at his wife. She seemed neither surprised nor upset, although she was quite pale. After more details were divulged and papers were signed, he thanked both his secretary and the lawyer, and marched Sylvie from the room.

"Did you know anything about this?" he asked.

She shook her head. "Guy never confided in me about his financial affairs."

This was terrible. What was he going to do now? "Where do you think that money went?"

As pale as she had been before, Sylvie turned a more startling shade of white. Rene grew fearful. She knew something after all.

"As your husband, Sylvie, I demand you tell me all that you know."

She pushed a dark curl from her eyes. "I didn't know you cared so much about my family's wealth, Rene. What business is it of yours whether or not my brother left me anything! You have your own wealth. I didn't foresee you were the type to steal his wife's inheritance out from under her!"

Oh, he'd never seen her like this! It was actually quite exciting, and had his world not been crashing down around him, he might have taken her into his arms. But disaster was just around the corner. "Don't change the subject, Sylvie. Why did your brother's money disappear?"

"Because my father needed it, I suppose."

"What are you talking about?"

Sylvie shrugged. "De Courcey wines is in financial ruin even now, Rene. Guy had used his money to help save it. At least that's what I imagine. Father told me the night our betrothal became official that he was in trouble financially, that I had to marry you to save the family empire."

"You mean you're penniless?"

Sylvie's eyes challenged him, and he could see she was angry. "Hardly! We still have our land, might I remind you! Father is doing all he can to keep from selling it off."

"So the match between you and I was all about money . . . from your father's perspective," he mused.

Sylvie crossed her arms. "Aren't all arranged marriages?"

He had to admit it was true. And how could he be upset with the de Courceys for viewing the marriage in the exact same manner as he? Now, to repair the damages, he'd have to put in extra effort—take up where Mirreault left off.

The sinister qualities of that thought shocked him. He felt his heart race and his mouth go dry, and he realized just how desperate he had become. He would have to talk to his father-in-law. Perhaps Armand de Courcey would go to great lengths to protect his daughter. Perhaps he would pay off the outstanding debts to Mirreault. True, he would have to sell off a portion of his lands, but if he had read Armand de Courcey with any bit of accuracy, he knew the vineyard keeper's pride was worth far more than his lands.

The thought of groveling before de Courcey sickened him so thoroughly, he decided another course of action would be more agreeable. It would be a temporary fix, but he'd rather kneel before Claude Mirreault one more time than beg before Sylvie's father. Surely the ugly moneylender would be agreeable to just one more loan. Wouldn't he?

He turned away for a moment lest his wife become privy to his turmoil. She mustn't see the agitation which squeezed at his throat and shook his limbs in their sockets.

There now. There.

He knew then he would do it; he would go to Mirreault and lay out the plan. Sylvie must suspect nothing.

He turned around and took her into his arms and kissed her on top of her head. "I'm sorry, Sylvie. Forgive me," he tried to set things right, keep her from guessing the truth. "I just thought you'd be disappointed that he left you with nothing."

"Guy never told me he was doing this in the first place. That he thought of me at all is touching. It makes me miss him even more."

"I know, dearest. I know. Now get you downstairs and plan my supper. I must say, you've made even Mother look lax in the way you run things around here."

Sylvie turned to go, walked to the door, then turned back around. The look she threw him, the puzzled expression, told him she was pondering all that had taken place, and he wasn't being seen in a highly flattering light. Well, he would make it up to her tomorrow, but there was something he had to do. Sylvie would keep until then.

He called for a horse and soon was riding westward, away from Paris.

The dusk faded into the night, and in the clear sky, diamond bright pinpoints of stars hovered like a jeweled bat above him. He pulled his hat down low over his cold brow. The breeze, hardly a wind, was thin, and somehow slapped upward at his muffler. Down the road, the warm light that seeped from the castle windows should have been welcoming. Instead, it thrust an icy hand into his insides and froze his heart with fear.

The day of reckoning was upon him.

No servant met him in the courtyard as he dismounted, so he slipped the reins of his horse through the ring of the hitching post, positioned his cane, and slowly negotiated the steps. He wondered if it would be presumptuous to pray.

Didier opened the door and without expression showed him into Mirreault's warm study.

"Brandy, sir?"

"No, thank you."

Didier thoughtfully rubbed his chin. "I'd recommend it."

Rene looked into eyes that had been without conscience for quite some time, eyes that knew the procedure, eyes that had seen virtually everything. "All right."

As Rene accepted the glass a moment later, Mirreault, fancied up in evening clothes but still ugly nonetheless, entered the study. The heels of his shoes thudded softly against the parquet flooring, then were swallowed up in the thick, burgundy rug.

"Monsieur le comte."

The man's wide smile disarmed Rene. "Mirreault." He slammed back his brandy and bit his bottom lip to quell the trembling of his face. Blast it, but this was one of the few times he wished he was more like his father.

"I presume by the state of your chin that you have failed yet again to procure the needed payment."

"Yes . . . sir." *Better to be contrite than refused.*

"I thought your wedding would take care of such matters. Your wife *is* the heir now, correct?"

"Yes."

Mirreault chuckled and straightened a cuff link. "And Guy's estate wasn't all you thought it would be when you dropped that hint to me. How did you like the highwayman bit? Not very original, was it? But I do enjoy the classics!"

Rene swallowed and nodded. "I thought Guy was well-heeled."

Mirreault was obviously finding this to be hilarious. "So you've just now found out that he was as penniless as you! You should let this be a lesson to you, lad. Next time you plan on murdering someone for their money—it would be prudent to make sure they have some!"

"I didn't murder him. You did!" Rene spat out.

Mirreault chuckled. "That, my dear Count, is a matter of semantics."

Rene ignored this jab, choosing to keep to the matter at hand. "I need more time, monsieur."

Mirreault walked toward the fireplace, then stood with his back toward the blaze. Rene was reminded of a demon emerging from the fires of hell, although he didn't believe such demons were so mindful of fashion.

Mirreault sighed. "More time. Yes, you need more time. So do we all. But time has run out, monsieur le comte. Word is,

Armand is privately investigating his son's death. So the question is, has time run out for you or for Armand de Courcey?"

Rene felt his scalp prickle. "What do you mean?"

"The land in Champagne is worth several fortunes," Mirreault said, rubbing his chin. "Though Armand isn't lolling about in hard currency, he has a king's ransom beneath his feet, and the promise of more wine to be made with the land that would remain. Therefore"—Mirreault's smile was wicked—"Armand de Courcey must follow his son to the grave. And who better to arrange it than the one who will benefit?"

Rene knew the time for begging had arrived. "Please, sir." He spread out his hands. "Do not ask me to arrange the deed. I won't be able to look Sylvie in the eyes again."

The look of disgust that appeared on Mirreault's face caused Rene to step back two paces. "It will cost you either way," Mirreault whispered. "I will do as you ask."

He stepped closer, his eyes glittering. "And one more thing, Rene. See that you take good care of your bride. We would not want anything to happen to her either." He was so calm, so matter-of-fact. There was no anger. He was a man doing business.

Rene kept his tone light. "Is that a threat, sir?"

"Naturally. I employ threats as other men use pen and paper, monsieur. Nothing personal mind you, merely the nature of the business." He was as cold as the night outside.

Rene said nothing, simply reached into his pocket and pulled out a diamond brooch . . . his mother's favorite and once a possession of Marie Antionette. "Will this do for a little while?"

As Mirreault took the heavy bauble set with a large canary diamond, his eyes lit up with delight. "It must, I suppose. You brought the right object, monsieur le comte. It will do nicely as a paperweight."

"I thought you did not use paper," Rene said.

"Oh, dear boy, you would be surprised what one can do with a piece of paper."

Rene was gone again for the evening. *I'm not a bit surprised,* Youngblood thought as he was shown back to the green salon that Sylvie had taken as her own. She did all her business from there, he imagined, as he walked quietly into the room and saw a desk littered with lists and cookbooks. Tucked into a chair, her stockinged feet toward the fire, she was emitting a soft snore. Beneath the plum folds of her satin gown, her womb was beginning to swell ever so slightly. As lovely as she looked, the sight of her pregnant with another man's child was bitter to him, indeed.

He laid his top hat upon an end table and walked across the room. Tenderly, he rested his hand upon her shoulder. "Would a visitor be welcomed about now?" he said softly, not wishing to startle her.

She sat up straight, eyes wide open. "I wasn't asleep!" Then her surroundings became clear and her face took on an expression of delight. "Viscount!" She leapt to her feet and threw her arms around him.

Would Sylvie ever change? he thought, pulling her tightly to him. He hoped not. She clung to him as if she had lost any friend she had ever had.

"You *were* asleep," he joked. "In fact, your snores could be heard round the entire house!"

She laughed. "I don't snore."

"That's what they all say!"

She pulled him over to the couch. "Come sit with me and tell me about your stay in England. The old man was trying to make amends?"

He sat down next to her, pulled out papers and tobacco, and began to roll a cigarette. "He's going on extended holiday this coming summer. He doesn't trust his secretary to keep things going as they should."

"And he trusts you?" Sylvie laughed.

"Of course not. I won't be able to touch anything. He just knows that I'll be a stupendous watchdog!"

"What do you have to lose if your father's man mishandled matters anyway? Aren't you disinherited?"

"Heavens no! As the eldest and only son, I'm the heir. There's nothing that can change that. But he can refuse to see me, or to give me anything until his death. Which, as you know, he has done. Until now."

"Maybe he's softening, Viscount, and this is his way of setting things to right."

He loved her even more just then. "Sylvie, you are the eternal optimist. No . . . he hasn't offered to reinstate any sort of allowance. I'm just needed now, and that is that."

She wound an arm through his. "So. Tell me all about your trip. Did you visit family?"

"Other than my parents and an uncle, just my sister Adele. She just gave birth to her fifth child."

"So you are an uncle many times over, then."

He shrugged. "Not a very good one, I'm afraid. She's had most of them since I moved to France. Still, Adele was always great fun, and she was happy to see me."

"When do you go back?"

"After the new year, I suppose. I'm not really needed until June."

"Then why did he send for you so early?"

He waved a hand. "Oh, that's my father. He couldn't have simply sent me a letter. No, I had to come crawling to court."

"Well, you're here now. And I am glad. The evenings haven't been at all fun." She pouted. "What do you say we play a game of whist?"

Youngblood thought of all the activities he could be taking advantage of right now. Poker, cockfights, the Moulin Rouge, Camille. Well, strike Camille off the list, she was probably working. For if Rene wasn't here, he was certainly with her. Sylvie took his hand and pulled him to his feet. "Come now, Viscount. I know I'm not the most exciting person to be with. But we'll have a laugh or two."

He forgot everything else and followed her to the small square table in the corner. Sitting down as she set out the game, he lit his cigarette. "Sylvie, you've been too formal with me for too long. Stop calling me viscount. I insist you call me David."

Her smile thrilled him. "Sometimes," she chuckled, "I quite forget that I'm all grown up. All right then, David it is."

It was a small step in the right direction, he mused. But a good one.

CHAPTER ✦ TWENTY-FIVE

My mother has never looked better, Sylvie thought as she met the countess and Collette in the entry hall. Collette's eyes were a clearer, saner green than they had been in years, and her hair was pulled back neatly.

"Mama!" she cried, taking her tiny mother into her arms.

"Dearest Sylvie." Collette hugged her tight, then let go and stood back. "Ah, I can feel my first grandchild stirring below."

Sylvie almost felt embarrassed. She laughed. "Oh Mama, you're here. It's good."

"Yes, child. Very good. Racine here was delighted at our nice long drive to Paris."

Agnes, who had been standing at the foot of the stairs, leaned forward. "Did you say you drove, ma'am?"

Collette's eyes sparkled. "Yes, I did. And we were driven by a most handsome Englishman!"

"Ducks!" Agnes hollered, sliding across the shiny parquet flooring on her heels and out the door.

"That will be the last we'll see of them for a while," Racine crowed. "Pierre!" she ordered a footman, "go fetch a groom to take care of the carriage. And please, bring all of our things up to our rooms. Madame de Courcey will be in the Coral Room."

Racine turned to them, eyes shining. She bestowed a light, but sweet kiss on Sylvie's cheek. "It was a lovely drive through the countryside. Wasn't it, Collette?"

She tucked her arm through her daughter's. "Ah, yes, my friend. Sylvie, we stopped at two of the most delightful little inns I've ever stayed in. Just lovely."

Sylvie had to ask. "How's Papa?"

To her surprise, a cloud did not appear over her mother's eyes. "He's been working hard, as usual. But he sent a present for you!"

Sylvie held a hand up to her mouth. She could hardly believe it.

Racine reached into her carpetbag and pulled out a bottle of champagne and a note. More than a little intrigued, Sylvie took the gift, then tore open the envelope. A single message, *To the Jean d'Arc of de Courcey wines*, and no signature. Sylvie laughed out loud.

"What does it say?" Collette reached for the note.

"No, no, no!" Sylvie held it up out of her reach. "It's between Papa and myself." It was the first joke he had ever made to her. Sylvie hadn't felt this much hope in years. Everything would be all right, she was sure. The Christmas holidays were now well on their way. With family all around, love to be given and received, it should be a good time for everyone. It was time to move forward, to forgive and to make amends. Papa was working hard on his end, and she was fulfilling her promise in Paris, laying the groundwork for the day Armand would approach her husband for aid. And truly, God was overseeing it all. She believed that completely.

The countess sighed loudly. "Well, I am ready to relax. Off to my salon. What about you, Collette?"

"Oh, I think I'm going to the chapel for a while before dinner. I hope it hasn't lost its consecration."

Well, thought Sylvie, *I guess some things will never change.* Nevertheless, she put an arm around her mother and escorted her to the far western corner of the house where a small chapel had been built by the original owner. At the door, she laid a hand on her mother's arm.

"Mama, how are you really?"

Collette reached forward and tucked a stray tendril of hair back into Sylvie's bun. "Why, dearest, I don't always even know the answer to that question myself. Some days I'm fine, others I'm not. Racine has been a godsend. She's taken care of everything, as you had always done, daughter."

"Do you visit Guy's grave? I long to visit his grave."

Collette shook her head. "Maybe someday I will, child. But I can't yet. Maybe someday you and I will go there together."

"Yes, Mama. We will."

Sylvie's mother padded softly into the small chapel, then turned. "Now your father, he visits the grave every day."

"He does?" Sylvie felt her eyes fill with tears.

Collette nodded, knelt down beside one of four pews, and crossed herself, though no host was present up at the altar. Her back was turned, and a moment later, she was in prayer.

The next four days were filled with Christmas preparations. Decorating, planning meals, trips around town for the right goose, the right greens. It was exhausting, but delightful. Collette accompanied Sylvie everywhere, and Sylvie couldn't remember ever having such a good time with her mother. It was hard to believe the change that Guy's death was bringing about in both of her parents.

Isn't there a verse in the book of Romans which talks of all things working together for our good? she asked herself. And promised herself she would look it up. So many aspects of her life were looking better, she decided. Father and Mother were doing better. She was feeling good, nurturing a child within. Agnes and Rupert were enjoying each other. And even though Rene hadn't checked on her in at least five days, David Youngblood was always there to comfort her. Yes, life in Paris was turning out to be not so bad after all.

"Joyeux Noel!"

Sylvie was awakened by Agnes's thickly accented French. She translated immediately to English. "Merry Christmas, Agnes."

The maid leaned down to give Sylvie a small celebratory hug before helping her out of bed. "How do you feel this morning?"

"Well, thank you. But then I haven't had many problems at all in the past month. I do believe my bony body was made to cradle a babe within."

Agnes patted her shoulder as she helped Sylvie out of bed. "Not so bony anymore. Now that you've got a bit of meat on you, I'd say you're right. The others are congregating in the drawing room around the fire. They've all had their breakfast."

She rubbed the sleep from her eyes. "I didn't realize it was so late. Is my husband there as well?"

Agnes's hands busied themselves in the wardrobe. "Yes. He must have made it home sometime during the night. Looks worse for the wear, I might add. If he loses any more weight, ma'am, I swear I'll cart him off to the doctor myself!"

Sylvie smiled, pulling on her wrapper and buttoning it over her little tummy. "You'll do no such thing, Agnes."

There was a knock at the door.

"Who on earth?" Agnes wondered and opened the door after a nod from Sylvie.

Rene rushed in. "Darling! Merry Christmas!"

His smile was filled with warmth, and yes, he was looking quite thin, as Agnes said, but he seemed so happy to see her. He took her into his arms and kissed her soundly on the mouth. Agnes left the room discreetly, shutting the door behind her.

Sylvie pulled back and looked at him with some well-deserved incredulity. "Merry Christmas to you too, Rene. To what do I owe the honor of your presence?"

He winced. "I know I deserve that, but you must forgive me, darling."

"Now that the viscount is back in town, I'm wondering if I married the wrong man!"

"I deserve that too. But you see, I am so desperately trying to get my affairs in order. And you are a wonderful girl not to be hounding me with questions all of the time. But I tell you this, my dear, after the new year begins, you will be seeing far more of me! This baby of mine needs a father who will be attentive and loving, and I will not fail him. I promise you that life will be different from now on."

All said so easily. Sylvie couldn't prevent a small frown. "But Paris tempts you, Rene. She always has, and she always will." She sat down at her dressing table. "I know more about your life than you think. What makes you believe I want you around any more than you already are? For all you've seen of me, talked to me, don't you find it a presumption to think I'd be jumping joyously about the room at your unbelievable proclamation?"

Rene pulled away and walked over to the fireplace, kneeling down on his haunches and placing another log onto the blaze. "You are beholding a man with a new mission, a new purpose, and that is to make you and our child happy." He picked up her hairbrush and smoothed it through her hair.

Sylvie wasn't sure whether or not she liked this new development. When Rene was distant or gone from the house completely, there was less required of her, less to pretend about.

"Well then, I suppose there are worse things for a wife to have than an attentive husband. It certainly should be a new experience."

He leaned down and kissed her on the curve of her neck. "Attentive, yes. And much more."

Sylvie froze, looking at her own eyes in the mirror, the blond of her husband's hair mingled with the dark of hers.

This was her lot. This was utterly her lot, and she wasn't so sure if she wanted him as such a vital part of her daily life. Yet it could certainly be much worse. He wasn't a repulsive man, and if she was ever to fall in love with him, she would have to be with him on a regular basis. Still, there was always Camille, and the thought of sleeping with him again after he had been with Camille all these months, well, it made her physically sick.

Yet in her own heart, she knew she had hardly been faithful.

But someday the memory of Matthew Wallace would fade, the feel of his kisses would be forgotten, and Rene would still be here. Perhaps love would grow in a well-tended garden.

He lifted a handful of her tresses to his nose, breathing in deeply. "Mmm, you always smell so good, Sylvie."

Sylvie, still as no-nonsense as ever, turned her face toward him. "Why all of this all of a sudden? We've hardly spent any time together since the honeymoon."

Rene returned the frank gaze. "Did you ever meet my father?"

"Yes. A magnificent man to be sure. But what does he have to do with this?"

Rene nodded. "A wonderful man. A likable man, and everyone respected him, and that respect was well deserved."

"Your mother still mourns him, ten years later."

"Yes, and nobody could blame her. We all still feel the loss. But my point is this, Sylvie. If I could even claim to be the *shadow* of my father I would be satisfied. Yet, here I am married to you—a lovely woman who carries my child in her belly ... my wife—and I am not the husband I should be. It is simply time to change my ways."

"And you can do this? All of a sudden?"

Rene inhaled deeply, an almost shuddering breath. "It will be a battle."

Sylvie decided to throw a flaming dart in his direction. This marriage wouldn't begin to succeed if he continued to hide things from her. "Don't you think you might get a better start if you tell me exactly what it is you're turning away from? I'd be a fool not to realize it's more than catching up on matters left untended while you were in America. Such work is for the daylight. Tell me about Camille."

"What?" His hands found their way to her shoulders. "How did you find out?"

"Does it really matter?"

"Of course it does, the only person I can think who would—"

"No, Rene." She felt her face go wooden. "It doesn't matter. The issue here is not what anyone else has done but you. Be man enough to at least admit that."

Rene walked away from her, put yet another log on the fire, and waited. Sylvie crossed her arms. As far as she was concerned, she had all day.

"The woman means nothing to me. She will be easy enough to leave behind."

Sylvie smirked. "That's comforting."

"Oh, Sylvie. I'm trying to make amends here." He raked a hand through his hair.

She stood from the dressing table and poured herself a glass of water. This entire conversation was making her extremely thirsty. "Rene, we've known each other since I was a little girl." She took a sip. "Do you honestly think you could ignore me for the first four months of our marriage, and all it would take for me to accept you into my arms would be a declaration of intention? Do you honestly believe that after you have repeatedly committed adultery, I would fall down on my knees and thank God you had finally seen the light? You have ignored me, been utterly unfaithful.

"I'm very happy you've decided to mend your ways. It will be good for us, and it will most certainly be good for the child. But it will take time and perseverance on your part to woo me. And, believe me, you *will* have to woo me. You've wasted too much time already."

He looked at her, studying her with a wry twist to his mouth. And then he smiled. "Blast it, Sylvie, but you are more woman than a man like me can handle. But I will try. I promise you that I will try. The question is, are you willing to forgive and forget?"

"Forgiving and forgetting are two different matters. Of course, I forgive you. I am commanded to. But the only way for me to forget is through time, and it will take a *lot* of time."

He rushed across the room and took her hands in his. "Time is all I ask for, darling. Time to show you what you mean to me. Time for us to cherish each other, and join in love."

Sylvie, having grown to accept life the way it was, was very leery about this change of events. But, before God, she had made several vows to this man, and before God, she would do her best to keep them. Still, he would have to prove himself. She didn't see any harm in that.

She allowed him to kiss her tenderly and rewarded him with a smile. "Now, Count de Boyce, get you out of my room so that I might get dressed and see about having a merry Christmas. See it is snowing?" She pointed to the window, where they could see a light snow powdering the city.

"Today is a good day for Christmas, Sylvie."

Before answering, she regarded him carefully. Uttering a small, silent prayer, she touched his cheek. "Yes, Rene. It is a very good day for Christmas."

"I'll go down and make sure the servants keep a plate warm for you. Better yet, I'll bring a tray up to you myself."

"All right," Sylvie agreed. "That would be lovely."

He started toward the door. "By the way, your mother took the first train out this morning for Champagne."

This was indeed news. "Did she say why?"

"Only that no one should spend Christmas alone. I presume she was referring to your father."

Sylvie felt her eyes widen. "Was she feverish?"

He laughed. "No, darling. Perhaps your mother is like the wines that bear her name; she might be improving with age. By the way, I'm feeling a bit of headache. Have you any paregoric or laudanum?"

"Of course." Sylvie rummaged through the drawer of her nightstand for the small brown bottle and handed it to him.

David Youngblood threw down his cigar and crushed the lighted end with the heel of his boot. Sparks skidded out of the smoking cylinder, and the aroma of Cuban tobacco flew over the garden. As pleasant as the brief, solitary interlude had been, it *was* getting cold. Despite what Claude Mirreault thought regarding his sanity, Youngblood wasn't a reckless killer at all. He carefully planned each job—for he had done many. Mostly for Mirreault. Contrary to legend, he had never killed anyone over a personal matter.

Tonight, however, was different. When Mirreault approached him, he had only hesitated briefly before replying in the affirmative. Armand de Courcey would be cut off from this world. He should not be given the chance to use his daughter any longer, he should not be allowed to further break her heart. It was a deed he would do with pleasure, but he must be extra careful to keep his wits next to his skin, now that his emotions were intertwined with his duty.

Mirreault had been specific. "Make it look like suicide."

Ah, yes. Suicide. How enjoyable it would be to look into the eyes of Sylvie's father, so like his own sire, as he realized he was being murdered and all of France would believe he had done the deed himself. Then again, with the way the man had been dealing with his son's death, he might very well thank him for relieving him of the trouble.

The Chateau du Soleil was open and waiting for him. Viscount Blackthorne stole soundlessly through the massive entryway. Below stairs, the staff was celebrating in the servants' hall. Their airy laughter wafted up the curved stone steps.

He found Armand in his study, sleeping peacefully on his couch. A halfhearted attempt had been made to clean up the place, but it still looked beyond repair. Obviously the man had been too busy to see to its refurbishment.

Youngblood opened the window that led into the garden, enjoying the cold breeze that rushed inside. His smile was feral as he rummaged through the desk drawer. Ah, there it was . . . a pistol. Loaded and ready to fire.

"This is almost too easy," he laughed deeply as he carefully regarded Sylvie's father. *Would he leave a note or not? Hmm, that could pose a problem.* He crossed the room and poured himself a small glass of sherry as he considered the question. Armand de

Courcey never had much to say to anyone, especially his family. He wouldn't care if his wife and daughter were crushed at the news. Therefore, he wouldn't leave a note. No, Armand de Courcey would definitely *not* leave a note.

He threw back the sherry and stood to his feet once again, satisfied that all was as it should be. Best to get it over with. Wasn't he doing everyone a favor? Rene would see more wealth, as then, would he. Sylvie would stop striving in her heart for her father's affection. All of that pain would be behind her. *Wish someone would do the same favor for me*, he thought, regarding his old father. Yes, this was better for everyone. And it wasn't as if Armand *enjoyed* his life, for heaven's sake.

"Wake up, old boy." He spoke the words directly into the man's ear, then sealed them with a kiss. Armand's mouth, open in a soft snore, easily accepted his pistol.

"Wake up!" Youngblood hissed. Armand's eyes opened sleepily. He felt the gun, saw Youngblood. Eyes growing wide, Armand de Courcey, tried to raise himself, but Youngblood was too quick for that. "For all you've done," he whispered. "For Sylvie."

He pulled the trigger.

A quick gasp sounded from the doorway, then a small cry, as Collette ran into the room. She looked as if she was trying to scream but was too frightened.

"Ah, the lady of the house inconveniently come to his rescue." Youngblood gloated as he quickly rose, ran over to her, and slammed her to the floor in the space of two seconds. Wasn't she, after all, as guilty as her husband? Using up the children she had been designed by God to protect and nurture?

A quick blow to the head and she was unconscious. He wouldn't kill her face-to-face as he had Armand. *I'm nothing if not a gentleman*, he thought.

Shutting the study door, locking it, he placed the pistol to her temple and shot once more. Footsteps sounded in the corridor as he arranged Armand's fingers around the gun. The gunshots had been heard.

Youngblood escaped through the window, shut it gently, and ran away into the darkness. It had been so easy to pull the trigger, to end their lives. The realization horrified him. This killing had been different. It left him feeling hot and agitated as he ran through the vineyard toward the horse waiting for him by the creek. Thoughts of Sylvie, her fear, her eyes, her laugh reminded him suddenly who he had done this for. Yes, Sylvie. No longer doomed, as he still was, to seek affection and acceptance from a man who had none to give.

Perhaps I might arrive in Paris in time to give Sylvie her Christmas present, he thought, feeling a renewed sense of determination regarding his conquest. In a year she would be his wife. It was a promise he made himself then and there. Call it a New Year's resolution, but one way or the other Rene de Boyce would have to die.

The thought disturbed him deeply, but he knew there was simply no other way.

CHAPTER ❖ TWENTY-SIX

Staring out of the window at her parents' fresh graves, Sylvie wiped Rene's thin face with a cool, wet rag. Pale as death he lay, chest heaving, a clammy sweat surfacing on his ashen skin. Finally asleep, after muttering the strange words, in a frightened voice, "Sylvie, you are pale blue."

"There now," she whispered tenderly to the slumbering boy-man. Her lot in life. Mimicking Agnes who had done the same for her countless times, she kissed him on top of the head. She rose again to her feet to watch the falling snow, brow folded in worry. "There now," she whispered again, arms hugging herself tightly. Everyone was gone now. No one left but Sylvie.

Only Guy afforded her an unadulterated grief. She tried to banish her parents from her mind for now ... until the baby was born ... until the baby was a year old ... until the baby didn't need her anymore ... until ... What was the use anyway? Even though matters with her parents had been improving, well, they were gone now. It was strange to be living back at Chateau du Soliel. Under Rene's orders, Maison de Fleur had been closed up, the staff pared down to the barest minimum, and they had all been packed up and moved off to Champagne. It was mysterious, but she supposed he had meant what he said about starting over.

"Away from here, darling Sylvie," Rene had rejoiced. "I can leave it all behind. Start anew. It will make the change so much easier."

And here they were. She now owned these lands. For reasons she didn't know, Armand had never changed the will. The de Courcey vineyards were hers to do with as she wished. She could try and save everything, or just sell a large portion of the land and pay off the debts. Still, there was a lot of time before she'd have to decide. Lawyers weren't known for their speed, she thought, glad of the fact for the first time in her life.

A knock at the door whirled her away from the waning light. "Dr. Charboneaux!"

"Dearest Sylvie." The doctor blustered in on wide, steady feet. His white eyebrows, contrasted by a face so ruddy it was almost purple, relaxed in a smooth forehead. A white goatee surrounded an almost lipless mouth. He was a kind man—born to a German mother—with a no-nonsense approach to medicine, a belief in sunshine, fresh air, and the healing power of time and prayer. He was wary of medications as well. "How is the patient this morning?"

"Not much better. I don't know what's wrong with him. He should be coming around now, don't you think? Nothing's changed since yesterday." She knotted a handkerchief in her hands. "Awful pains, stomach cramps, and leg cramps."

Charboneaux stroked his goatee, thoughtfully considered the patient, then set down his bag. He placed a practiced, steady hand on Rene's brow. "This will take a while to get over, my dear. But he *will* get better. You must trust me. There's not much I can do to facilitate the matter. He must make it through on his own."

"He cries out so."

"Yes, he would. But no matter what, Sylvie, if he asks for laudanum, paregoric, or any other medicine for that matter, you must not give it to him without consulting me first. You promise me you will do this?"

Sylvie nodded. "I ran out of it several days ago. But wouldn't some more help to ease his sufferings?"

"For a while, but in the long run it will add to it. You must trust me." He pushed his spectacles up farther on the bridge of his nose.

"He thinks I'm trying to kill him at times, Doctor. And he . . . he sees things coming alive . . . like . . . like the clock, or the curtains." *Tell me something*, she pleaded inwardly, hating the way doctors were so secretive. "He thrashes about so."

"That's all normal considering the circumstances."

"What *are* the circumstances?"

"It's a disease that's quite common, little Sylvie. Do not worry yourself. He'll be good as new in about two weeks."

"Two weeks? Will you come back?"

"Of course. I'll look in on him tomorrow. He'll be defensive toward you for a while, but it will pass. In your delicate condition I'd have someone else care for him, at least until his emotions are under control. You must consider the babe."

Sylvie poured herself a glass of water. "I suppose you're right. But what if he awakens from all of this, feeling better, and I'm not there?" She took a sip.

"Oh, believe me, when he's not sleeping, he's extremely aware of his surroundings—acutely so. That which is normally pleasurable is so intense it becomes painful. That's part of the illness. Stay in the room if you must, but charge someone else with his actual care."

Perish the thought, but Rene was really all she had now. "But what if he—"

"No arguments, my dear. I know of which I speak."

Sylvie nodded solemnly. "All right, Doctor, I'll do as you ask. But I don't like it."

He placed his capable hand on her forehead and blinked with satisfaction. "You're doing well, I see. Take care not to run yourself ragged now."

With a smile, he grabbed his bag and swung out the door.

Agnes hurried down the corridor, turned a corner, and collided with the doctor.

"Aggie!"

"Dr. Charboneaux. In to see the count?"

He tipped his hat with a nod and they smiled broadly in mutual appreciation of each other's vast store of common sense. "Yes, madam."

"I fear more for Sylvie, you know."

"Yes. And I'm glad we ran into each other." He chuckled at his own joke, his voice lowering to a whisper. "Sylvie shouldn't be caring for the count like she's been doing. You must get the housekeeper to delegate some of the staff to sit at bedside and tend him. He may get quite ornery, to put it mildly, and we don't want anything to happen to the countess, especially considering her state."

"I see."

His merry face became grave in the space of a heartbeat. "Another thing, and keep this between you and me, Aggie. Secure all the laudanum, paregoric, and any other opiates under lock and key."

Agnes could hardly believe her ears. Was he saying . . . ?

"Wipe that look off your face, Aggie. I'm sure you know exactly why such precautions are necessary. Under no circumstances are the countess and the count's mother, or anybody else for that matter, to know the true nature of his illness. I don't believe either of them could cope with such news right now."

Agnes, valuing honesty above all, laid a hand on his arm. "May I tell my Rupert?"

Charboneaux grinned. "Of course, Aggie. Everyone knows that Rupert is your only confidante."

"Mum's the word with him, Doctor. He can be trusted with any word or any deed."

"Yes. 'Tis a heavy burden you've been carrying for these folks for years. I'd be a cad not to let you ease some of the burden onto your husband."

Agnes heaved a sigh. "Well, much of the burden bearing is over now that the master . . ." She could say no more.

"I know, Aggie. Madame de Courcey gone, too. Tragic."

"I hate to say it, Doctor—but she's free now."

"That she is. And it was a long time coming. Good day, Aggie." He sauntered off to be handed his coat by a waiting doorman.

Agnes reached into her pocket for a little piece of peppermint hard candy, the final remnant of her Christmas presents from Rupert. She popped it into her mouth and went to find Sylvie. Life had turned very strange and other than pray, she didn't know what to do about it.

~

Rene had never felt so good in his life. No chains. No addictions. And a beautiful young wife, swelling enticingly with his child. Opium wasn't such a good thing after all. The pain in his leg was easier to bear than the pain his heart had reeled beneath when he realized what he could potentially do to his child. As so many men who've been squandering the gifts of health and a sound mind, the impending birth had been a jolt to an otherwise paralyzed conscience.

I'm not really a bad man, he wrote in his journal, *just weak. And yet, I feel protected. I can still look my wife squarely in the eye knowing that her parents died, not from my mistakes or by my orders. Armand did the deed himself. I am certain that even Mirreault was surprised by such a turn of events.*

Yes, life would be good from now on. He would see to it. Pressing pen to paper once more, he continued recording his thoughts.

I went into this nightmare fond of the woman I married, and I've emerged with twice the fondness and double the respect. Sylvie, dear Sylvie, was there, sitting quietly in that chair, the entire time. Thank God for the woman!

And now, I want nothing more than to please her, make her realize that her marriage to me was no mistake. It would be hopeless to try to compete with the strength of mighty Wallace, and so I dare not. But I will do better than I have before this. Her child is also my child, and that will count for something, I daresay. In any case, she is my wife, not Matthew's . . . and nothing can change that fact.

I have become a committed husband. Faithful now to my vows, loyal to my responsibilities. Do I love her with the star-crashing love of which poet's speak? I love her more . . . with an earthbound love that will stand the test of time. Passions do not collide frenetically in my heart when I think of my wife. But she is ever present, a friend, a sister, a mate, and a tender lover. Sylvie is all these things to me now. I will not miss the rush of passion when I have all of this in one woman. And she will be a wonderful mother to my children, of that I have no doubts.

But what shall I do about my past? She knows nothing of my debts to Mirreault. How could I have known the estates passed directly to her and not to her husband as is common? How can I tell her, ask her for the funds? Indeed, I cannot. To do so would only afford me her scorn. And, though understandable, it is something I dare not risk. She is a strong woman who will not abide such weakness. I must find another way—before Mirreault demands more money. To chain men to him by his wicked devices—it must be wicked good fun for him. May he rot.

How could I have let him use me thus? 'Tis true, the opium took away my will for anything else but more of the stuff. And the gambling . . . well, I was never good at that, and now that I have returned to my own skin, I wonder why I persisted in trying to gain money by luck. But now I am once again looking out of my own eyes, so to speak. Where I submerged for so long is a mystery, for opium steals a man from himself, but should God be gracious, I shall never go there again. Or to the gaming tables. Unfortunately, I believe the gaming tables will be the more difficult of the two to resist for good.

Rene suddenly looked up from his writing as Sylvie entered the room, more appealing than a ripened peach. He quickly closed his diary and arose from his seat at Armand's old desk— now repaired like the rest of the room. "Darling!"

His wife grasped his outstretched hands. "Rene. Come sit down, I've a surprise for you!"

They sat on the sofa and she took his hand in hers and placed it, flattened, on her stomach. "There!" she shouted in triumph a full minute later as he felt the kick from beneath the wall of her belly. "Did you feel it?"

Rene de Boyce had never been happier. The child. His child. He folded Sylvie into his arms and kissed her. "Yes, my darling. Our child is making his presence known, and I'd say he is most welcome."

Her smile thrilled his heart. "Yes, Rene. I do believe you are right."

Yes, this was life as it should be and he would do anything—*anything*—to make sure it stayed as it was right now.

CHAPTER ❖ TWENTY-SEVEN

Viscount Blackthorne slouched in the choir benches of Westminster Abbey. It was dusk, and tomorrow the funeral for his parents would be conducted right there.

"Leave it to them to wish to be buried here," he scoffed, remembering how the earl and his wife had always lived their lives in such a grand, public manner. No wonder they had been so appalled when their deformed little son arrived on *their* earth to mock them with his imperfection, to remind them of their frailty. Without a doubt a blemish on the family, a sore on the foot of their social standing. That was little David.

But now they were dead, killed by a mad stag on a hunting run. Naturally Lord and Lady Youngblood had been "in at the kill." But *they* were the kill. What a fitting, ironical end to two cruel, silly people. As if God himself had planned their demise.

Youngblood thought their death would make him happy. But he wasn't happy.

Now they would never see Sylvie on his arm.

"Blast you both!" he grated against his teeth. Their demands he take over the estates had kept him from bringing his plans to fruition, but not any longer. As soon as the Archbishop of

Canterbury pronounced the funeral at an end, he would embark for France, and soon Sylvie would be his. For months now he had been dreaming of the day, going over each motion, planning every detail of the operation. For weeks he had ceased to feel guilty about what would happen to Rene. They had never really been friends anyway, had they? It had all been Mirreault's mirage.

What if it all goes wrong? he wondered, then leaned back with a smile, knowing full well that matters such as these always worked out in the end.

If one was careful.

~

Two months to go. And it was a chilly, throbbing March.

Sylvie rubbed a hand over her rounded stomach, massaged an aching shoulder, and wondered if there was ever a time in her life that she hadn't been pregnant. The past few months at Chateau du Soleil had been pleasant enough, since the countess had set her hand to decorating the place as a residence befitting a nobleman and his family. Lounging before the cozy fire of her salon, growing bigger, rounder, and more content, she had been nourished and cherished by her husband. He read to her, played upon the piano, and updated her on all the goings-on of Paris as he read the newspaper. And that he always looked like a Greek god while doing so was an added benefit. When he went to Paris on necessary business, he always soon returned with her favorite chocolates and a new hat. Tired of the large-waisted gowns she donned out of necessity, Sylvie had become immensely fond of hats. Rene was almost everything she could have wished for in a mate. So attentive, caring, and . . . careful.

Was she in love?

No. Not in that way, she knew decidedly. But she did love him, cared for him deeply, and would have placed herself in between him and harm's way if the situation would arise. Even his lovemaking was pleasant, and lest she feel adulterous in her mind, she pushed aside thoughts of Matthew Wallace during those times. She concentrated on the fact that one of the most handsome men in France was sharing her bed and her life. This new relationship had to be enough. For both of them.

And then there was the baby soon to come. Agnes swore it would be a girl the way Sylvie was carrying the child so low and completely out in front. The countess thought exactly the opposite. As for Sylvie—deep down in her heart, she wished for a little girl. One that would be loved without pain, or dependency—one that would redeem her own childhood.

And they would name her Eve, the name God himself had chosen so long ago when he created womankind.

She pushed aside the thoughts of Collette and Armand. Sylvie knew she should go for her daily walk, at least place some flowers on the graves, but the cozy salon, a golden room which cocooned her from the driving winds outside, was too inviting. Instead, she picked up her copy of *Pamela* and began to read away the morning hours, wondering if heroines such as these really existed. She was not at all surprised the book was written by a man.

⁓

Agnes poured Rupert a second cup of tea and sighed. She hated sighing, it was such a ridiculous activity, but some situations warranted nothing else.

"What is it, Aggie?" Rupert asked as he spooned in two heaping spoonfuls of sugar. They were having their nightly repast in the small quarters they shared over the carriage house.

Agnes picked up a piece of shortbread. "I'm just a bit worried, ducks. More items have been found missing. It was happening at Maison de Fleur and now it's happening here."

He chewed on a small mince tartlet. "Well, what servants came back with you?"

"Only the countess and her lady's maid, Pascale. The count and Miss Sylvie, and myself."

"It certainly narrows the possibilities. Unless, of course, it is a coincidence, and we have two completely different servants with sticky fingers."

Agnes didn't like it. "I don't know why I should trouble myself about it, ducks. After all, it's all de Boyce treasure that's being pilfered."

"Naturally." He took a sip of tea. "The master didn't go for all them beads and baubles."

"Or candlesticks and paintings."

"That's what's missing?"

She nodded. "The countess brought all her valuables with her. It was certainly strange the way they shut up Maison de Fleur indefinitely. Not one servant left to care for the place. Strange indeed."

"What's being done about it?"

"The count is handling it himself. Or so that's been the word downstairs. All the house help is abuzz with the news. Apparently Countess Racine is so upset about the matter that she told him if he didn't do something about it soon, she would call in the authorities herself to get an investigation under way." She tapped her chin. "I just wonder who it could be, ducks?"

"Don't you be worrying about it, Aggie dear. We aren't paid well enough to take on the troubles of the gentry."

"Yes, of course, Rupert, you're right."

But in the pit of her stomach, she didn't have a good feeling about this at all.

⁓

Several days later, Rene entered Sylvie's boudoir, concern screwing his features into a stronger expression than usual.

"What is it, Rene?" Amid the satin pillows that rendered her chaise even more luxurious, she pushed herself up on her elbows as anxiety overtook her calm.

"The missing items. They have been found. A few of them, at least."

"That is wonderful news!" Then she saw his eyes melt under a heavy burden. "Is it not?"

He perched at the end of the chaise and jerked a hand through his hair. "Unfortunately not, darling." He took her hand. "We discovered them in Agnes's and Rupert's quarters this morning after breakfast." He paused. "I am sorry."

Sylvie went cold, pressing a hand to her now ample chest. "What will happen to them?"

"It is a clear case. They have already gone. I dismissed them several hours ago."

This couldn't be happening. Not like this! "Without telling me? Have you notified the police?"

"We just started investigating ourselves. Unfortunately the items weren't hard to find."

"Agnes?" Overcome, Sylvie dropped her face into her hands, gulping in air to dry up the tears which threatened to gather. Then she looked up wildly and grabbed his hands. "We must help them!" Sylvie sprang to her feet as quickly as her condition would allow. "She raised me! Agnes raised me, Rene. I know her better than this. She never did such a thing before this, so I don't know why she would have started now. Someone planted them there!"

It had to be true. There wasn't a doubt in her mind that Agnes was not only not immoral enough, but not so stupid as to attempt such a string of thefts. There was surely another explanation.

He clasped and unclasped his hands. "Well, perhaps it was Rupert."

"Have you still not notified the authorities?"

"No. I knew that would be the last thing you would want me to do. I saw them safely to the train. I will inform the police after I am sure they have escaped to England. But certainly I shall have to inform them to receive the insurance moneys. The items were all insured."

"Of course." Her jaw was set in a firm line, but she puffed out a sigh of relief. "I'll find out the truth. She's all I've got, Rene. Besides you." An afterthought.

He pulled from her grasp, his expression suddenly sad. "All right, darling. You do that." He paused. "I have another piece of bad news as well."

"Oh, Rene, no. What else could possibly be wrong?"

"My secretary, Jean-Francois, was waylaid in Paris on his way to the bank. He was carrying a considerable sum of money. The de Courcey payroll actually."

"Is he all right?"

Rene fidgeted with the top of his cane. "Yes. He is fine. Poor fellow."

"How much was it?"

"It was the moneys set aside for next month's payroll. But darling, I do not want you to worry."

Sylvie knew that wasn't the case, but she didn't say anything. "And we can make up the difference, so that the workers will be paid?"

"I shall take care of it. With your permission of course, as the de Courcey finances are still in your hands."

Sylvie sat back, wondering if there was something she wasn't being told. "Contact the lawyers and tell them to do whatever they must to retrieve the money to pay the workers."

"I've already done that, darling. I don't wish for anything to worry you now."

Relieved that the matter was being handled, she could concentrate more fully on exonerating Agnes. And perhaps he was right. Perhaps she shouldn't be told the full extent of their troubles. As long as there was a roof over their head, shoes on their feet... "Thank you, Rene. Guy couldn't have run this enterprise any better. I promise you, when this baby is born, I'll make myself much more useful."

"It is no trouble, darling." He leaned forward and kissed her on the cheek. "And so you do not overtax your strength, I shall set some more of my own men to finding the true thief. The truth will be revealed. I'll see to it myself."

Rene pulled a chair out for his mother and seated her at the breakfast table.

"And to think it was Agnes the entire time!" Racine reached for a bun, quickly pulled off the steaming hot top, and set it on her plate. "I would never have thought her capable."

Rene wasn't interested in food just then. "I agree. But I saw the items myself. Some of them, at any rate. Who knows how much they have already sold off? Of course both she and Rupert denied having any knowledge of their presence."

"But it makes sense. Items were missing from my house as well, and she was the only common servant between the two households. Other than my dear Pascale who would never steal so much as a hairpin." She sighed with her entire body. "I hate to admit it, but it seems to be the only explanation. The woman has stolen a fortune, and yet there is nothing else in her belongings that would testify to such an exorbitant financial gain!" She bit down into the warm crusty bread. "You are a saint to have sent them away as you did."

Hiding his discomfort, Rene gazed across the hall toward the closed door of the study. No one would enter that room now, not after the slaying and suicide. "She probably sent it all to England already, Mama, or has sold it."

Racine shook her head sadly and patted his hand. "Let us forget about it all now. The mystery has been solved, and though the paintings and jewels which were sold will probably never be found, your wife is far from financial ruin."

"In any case, I took them to the train personally, and they should be safely on a boat to England by now."

"You are a good man, Rene, to be so kind to your wife. You did not give them references, though, did you?"

"Of course not, Mama." He knew better than to tell her he'd given them two months' wages.

"I should hope not."

A servant breezed in and began to clear their plates. Another poured fresh coffee into their cups, the aromatic steam rising upward.

Racine breathed in through her nose. "There is nothing like a fresh cup of coffee early in the morning. Armand could not abide the smell. Collette loved coffee." She suddenly dropped her head, pressing her napkin to her eyes.

"There is nothing you could have done, Mama. Nothing." But he had little time for compassion. He had other things on his mind. "I must be going to Paris. Just for a day or two. Take care of Sylvie for me while I am gone." He kissed her on the cheek, and she caressed his face with her jeweled hand.

"You are a good man, Rene," She said the words again, he thought, because she finally felt she could. The tears in her eyes sparkled like diamonds.

His eyes twinkled. "You are my mother, madam. I would say your opinion is hardly objective."

Poor Agnes, he thought. She had been the scapegoat, but as the only servant besides Pascale who had served in both households, he had no choice but to blame her for his crimes. There was no way he would let his mother call in an official investigation. The Paris house was by now almost emptied of its former, glorious contents. One day, he promised himself, when he was free from his debts and a man of honor like his father, he would make it up to all of them.

It was a hollow promise. And he knew it.

Claude Mirreault reared up like a great, hairless bear, reached back, and swung with full force until the back of his hand swiped cruelly along the jawline of Camille—Rene's old Camille. "Idiot woman! What good are you if you cannot accomplish the most elementary of tasks?"

She indignantly pulled the bedsheets around her and straightened her yellow hair. "But I'll find another rich man, Claude. And this time—"

"Silence. With your wiles and charms, I thought surely you were capable of indefinitely imprisoning a man in your clutches. My word, woman, he was an *opium* addict! How much less difficult could it have been to broaden the debt a little more? I might have had him in arrears for the remainder of his lifetime! And now that the de Courcey lands are well within his reach, the bondage in which we could place him is virtually limitless. Why he refuses to grab hold of that money like any other self-destructive man would do is truly a mystery. Men have been stealing their wives' inheritances for centuries! Why is he behaving so contrary to long-established precedent?"

"Oh, the count has his good points. I should know," Camille said in a saucy manner and rubbed her cheek as she arose from the bed. "He doesn't hit women, for one." Shrugging, she poured herself a prolonged glass of brandy. "It's that wife of his, Claude. She has a certain power over him. I could see it in his eyes as clearly as a winter mile, monsieur. He's besotted with her. Told me"—she deepened her voice—"'It's over Camille, I'm married now and I'll do what is right.' When she conceived his brat there was no hope for poor Camille … or you, monsieur."

He lit a cigar, slid into his dressing gown, and reclined in a well padded chair near the fire. The gold silk damask upholstery danced in the shimmering light of the blaze. "Cease this prattle about babies. You know I cannot abide even the thought of the little terrors."

"You have enough of them," she smirked.

"All over France, girl." He smiled broadly and spread his large hands, his foul mood blown over as quickly as it had rolled across the horizon. "But that is neither here nor there. Pour me a brandy as well, come sit upon my lap, and let us put our heads together. We must do away with this de Courcey woman, we must regain the moneys once and for all, and then Count Rene de Boyce will be mine to do with as I wish. Oh, the fortune he will obtain from his wife will be enough to fill the coffers of Croesus himself."

"But who should we use to carry out the task?"

He tapped his teeth. "Who is close enough to the family, but still has an appetite for mayhem?"

Camille ran a finger over his bald head in a circular pattern. "Only one man I know of is that crazy, mon chere."

He nodded and together they spoke a single word.

"Youngblood."

Surely Viscount Blackthorne would kill one more de Courcey, wouldn't he? Claude asked himself, then smiled his broadest grin. The deed was as good as done.

~

The last person Claude Mirreault wished to see that afternoon was Count de Boyce. What a weakling! What a despicable example of manhood. And yet, the tragedy the young man had placed himself in might be worth a fortune to him someday. Inconveniences were worth it if the payoff was high enough.

And there the young count sat before him, face chapped and pale from the ride in the bitter winds that buffeted the chateau. *It must be important to him*, Claude thought, *to brave such inconvenient forces and come all the way to Versailles.*

The count slid a money bag across the table. Judging by the size of it, Mirreault knew it wasn't nearly enough. "You honestly try to placate me with this?" Claude laughed harshly in the count's face.

Rene remained calm, still holding out the satchel. "It covers most of what I owe—minus interest of course."

This was rich. "Of course. Have you any idea how much interest has been accrued over the past five years? Three times more than the original debt, is that not right, Didier?" He turned to his sidekick who was looking at a large black ledger.

"Three and a half times to be exact, sir."

Rene cleared his throat. "Yes, I am fully aware, Monsieur Mirreault. If you would extend but a little more time—"

Mirreault calmly studied his fingernails. "There will be no more time. No more mercy. We have dragged this silly affair on long enough. My patience is worn through, monsieur. I will have that money. And since you are too cowardly to demand the funds of your wife, I will see that you get them myself."

He stood to his feet in alarm. "You cannot be serious!"

"Oh, I assure you, monsieur, this is no laughing matter. Your wife will be dead by morning, and your unborn child, I might add. And when the money comes to you, you will pay me . . . to the very last penny. 'Tis very simple." He reached into a desk drawer for a bottle of laudanum and pulled off the cork. Moving as he had when a young boy on the rough streets, he reached across the desk and pulled Rene into a headlock that would have been the envy of Hercules himself. Didier followed his master's lead and lent his aid. "And while we're at it"—he forced open Rene's mouth and poured the contents down his throat—"we might just as well give you a little taste of the past. Just for the fun of it."

Rene tried to spit it out, but Mirreault plugged his nose and mouth until he swallowed. He gasped for air when Mirreault let go, filling the room with angry expletives.

Claude's wicked laughter flooded his ears. "My man is already on his way. Unless, of course, you get there first, and having gotten down on your bony knees and begged your wife for the money, have the proper amount ready and waiting."

"I cannot do that!" he gasped, mortified that Sylvie would know the truth, know that he had caused the death of her brother, know that he had been lying to her since the day he came back from America.

Less than thirty seconds later, Count Rene de Boyce was out of the room and pounding his way back to Paris. They would escape. He would take his wife and child somewhere far away, where there was no murder, no pain, no opium, no debt, and certainly no Claude Mirreault.

CHAPTER ✦ TWENTY-EIGHT

Agnes and Rupert decided they'd almost rather die than be shuffled off to England without references. And innocent like they were, well, they would have none of this being spirited off in the middle of the night! Unwilling to part France shamefully disgraced in the eyes of the people they had served so long, they never set forth on the ship, choosing instead to rent a small room near the Church of the Sacred Heart. Learning of the count's arrival in Paris the day after they were to embark, they followed him out to Claude Mirreault's chateau in a rickety cab, the driver of which hadn't bothered to stay around to take them back home. It would be a long, cold walk back to the city. But neither of them cared. More than their immediate physical comfort was at stake here.

It was six o'clock.

"It has to be the count!" Agnes whispered in the shadows, drawing her black shawl tightly under her chin. "He was the only other person both at Maison de Fleur and Chateau du Soleil besides Pascale, who wouldn't do such a thing! And after what Dr. Charboneaux said ..."

Rupert drew his hat lower and peered around the corner of the building. "We've been over this, Aggie. You don't need to justify it to me. The fact is, who's going to hire us when we *do* get back to England? We have to clear our good name. God knows our cause is just."

Rupert always pronounced God "Gawd." It was a small thing that Agnes had always loved about her husband. And just then, the remembrance of just how big her Creator was and how sovereign she had always known him to be, comforted her. She could trust him now. "I know, ducks. It's just poor little Sylvie. He's been so good to her and she's seemed so much at peace lately. I don't want to be the ruination of their marriage."

"Don't worry, lovey. God's looking out for all of us. See now!" He pointed to the door. "Here comes the master! And he's running. I wonder what happened?"

As Agnes shook her head in bewilderment, he rode away.

Moments later a carriage careened into the courtyard. From its sumptuous recesses descended one of the most beautiful women Agnes had ever seen, carrying a baby. She was small and regal, with dark hair and pale skin. Sylvie had pointed her out once as one of the few noblewomen who had truly befriended her. Agnes couldn't recall her name, but she remembered she was a duchess.

A servant brought out a basket and laid it on the doorstep. The woman settled the baby inside with warm blankets, kissed its exposed forehead, and backed away. A delicate white arm reached toward the child, then was pulled back into the velvet cape.

Agnes's heart broke as she heard the fragile, thin cry of a newborn.

Rupert tugged on her arm. "Let's go, Aggie! It's a long walk back, and I want to see what his lordship is up to now. We don't have a lot of time to waste."

She hissed a whisper. "Wait! It looks as if she's abandoning that baby! There . . . see?"

Rupert's attention was immediately caught, and he leaned further around the corner as the duchess pulled on the bell and hurried back to the coach.

"Pull away now!" she ordered the driver, who tipped his hat and obeyed. Dry-eyed and beautiful, her sad, oval face appeared at the carriage window. Longing filled her gaze, which never left the little basket. Ten seconds later, the curtains snapped shut. Agnes couldn't move at first. The air grew more silent as the coach disappeared into the darkness.

But it was a cold night, a bitterly cold night, and that baby needed attention.

By the time Agnes was at the baby's side, an enormous man in a dressing gown was standing in the doorway, hands on hips. Calmly he pointed in Agnes's direction. "What are you doing?"

"Attending to this baby!" She picked up the bundle and stood to her feet. Unfortunately she couldn't see his face, but judging from his silhouette and his tone of voice, he wasn't someone she would ever want to come up against.

"Who are you?"

Rupert stepped forward boldly and laid a hand on his wife's shoulder. "Rupert and Agnes Green, sir."

"What are you doing here?"

"It's none of your business!" Agnes snapped.

"It is my land, my house, and my gun that is pointed at you from that turret there." He pointed nonchalantly at the guard. "Now I shall ask you again, and for the life of me I do not know why I am being so generous, what are you doing here?"

Agnes jutted her chin forward.

The man blew an impatient sigh from between his lips, but even in the darkness his eyes sparkled appreciatively. "You will be left unscathed if you enlighten me as to what brings you here, but realize I utter no promises."

"Who was that woman?" Rupert asked.

"And this baby?" Agnes looked down at the homely, crude little face of the soundly sleeping infant. She wasn't about to let on she knew anything, Lord help her.

"What woman?" the man inquired, his entire body leaning forward in interest.

"The mother of this baby, I presume, sir," answered Rupert.

The man huffed another sigh. "Bring the child inside for heaven's sake, madame. The night grows chilly. Didier!" he yelled, and Agnes beheld a man who seemed to materialize out of nowhere. "Show these people into my study and bring them a glass of wine or some brandy."

"Oh, no thank you, sir!" Agnes piped up. "We don't drink either. But I wouldn't turn down a nice cup of tea." She was feeling strangely confident. Hadn't they prayed all the way here? Obviously something was afoot, and only the good Lord knew what it was.

"Tea then," Mirreault ordered. "I will change clothes and be with you shortly," he said, in quite a regal manner, Agnes thought.

Walking through the chateau, Agnes was astounded. This made even Maison de Fleur seem like a paltry dwelling. The artwork alone, Grecian urns, Roman busts, Flemish masters, and a vast amount of those Italian religious paintings lined the walls. Both Agnes and Rupert gasped and pointed their way back to a large salon. Agnes thought if heaven had a sitting room, it would look just like this one.

Blue silk lined the walls, and the ceiling was painted with clouds and angels. She had never seen anything so beautiful in her life.

The baby wriggled in her arms and let out a wail. Rupert, bless him, remembered the basket. Agnes was glad to see there was an extra supply of nappies. "The dear one is wet, I believe. We'll make this baby more comfortable, and when that Didier fellow comes back I'll ask him to bring in some warm milk and a spoon."

She laid the baby on the carpet, kneeled down in front of him, and went to work. As the oldest of eight children, Agnes Green was an expert at changing a diaper. She unwound the blankets, pulled down the thick woolen overdrawers, and unpinned the soft diaper. "A boy!" she proclaimed, quickly throwing the old diaper over him. She remembered the first brother she was given, Ralphie, and all the times she had to change herself after changing him. For certain, Ralphie had taught her a lesson or two about babies! "Oh, he's a sweet thing!" She couldn't resist picking up the soft little body, and holding him against her. He smelled so wonderful as he snuggled his face into her neck, trying to suckle. "How could she have left him, ducks? How?"

Rupert sat with his hands in his pockets, tears glistening in his eyes. "I don't know, Aggie. I've never seen a more beautiful sight in my life. But you'd better get him wrapped back up, lovey, he's going to catch a chill."

"You're right! It's hard to resist not looking at him." Agnes finished the job, enjoying it immensely. To a barren woman, even changing a diaper was deemed a pleasure. "He's a big one for a newborn. But all newborns look so tiny, don't they?"

"So, Mr. and Mrs. Green!" The voice of the man boomed from the doorway, and he entered as though accompanied by a fanfare of trumpets. "I suppose now you'll answer my questions."

"Well, I have a few of my own!" Agnes quipped as she finished up.

"Some I shall most probably answer, most I likely will not. Didier!" he bellowed. "Bring me a cognac! Now." He made himself comfortable in a chair by the fire. There was something almost grotesque about the man, Agnes thought, but his power and self-assurance more than made up for his facial features. That this man was the baby boy's father was evident.

"The apple doesn't fall far from the tree!" she said, shaking her head.

"Oh, so you've concluded that he's mine?" The man didn't even bother to lean forward. So Agnes held the baby up for his inspection. He bestowed only a cursory glance on the little fellow. "There is some resemblance, I suppose."

"Babies are always a bit puffy when they're born, but it's more than that," Agnes declared. "It's around the eyes, and see how large his mouth is?"

The man laughed. "Puffy? Do you think I am puffy?" His eyes were filled with humor. For some reason, Agnes thought, he liked her.

She chuckled.

"You've got a spunky one there, Mr. Green. I envy you."

Rupert looked surprised. "Aggie? Well, she's a lamb, sir. A downright lamb."

Didier appeared with the cognac, and the man took it off the tray. "Now, let's get down to business. Did you know the woman who deposited this infant on my doorstep?"

"No, sir," Agnes said.

"Was she dark haired?"

"Yes."

"Fair-skinned?"

Agnes nodded.

"Noble, surely?"

"Yes, sir," Agnes answered again, feeling like a traitor though she knew nothing about the situation.

"Hmm." He sat back, then smiled wickedly, apparently satisfied. Agnes felt angry, but knew better than to seriously cross this man. Little jokes and quips were one thing, judging from his apparent sense of humor, but he was a man who demanded compliance.

"And what are you doing here, then? I thought maybe you had come with the baby. A servant perhaps, sent along to make sure it—"

"*He*," Agnes informed him.

"—*he* was seen safely inside. So, if you are not stealing around my grounds due to this woman and this baby, perhaps"—he tapped his chin—"it was due to my other visitor this evening."

Agnes bit her lip. And she cursed herself that she had never possessed eyes that could hide the truth.

"Aha! So I am right?" The man slapped his thigh in triumph. "And what might the Greens have to do with the de Boyces?"

"Don't tell him anything, Aggie!" Rupert hissed.

"Come, come, I have ways to find all this out anyway. When you walked upon my land you sold yourself to me, don't you know that?"

Agnes felt herself bristle. This was a dangerous man indeed. "What do *you* have to do with the count, sir?"

He grinned. "Is that the way it is to be, then? An answer for an answer?"

"Quid pro quo," Agnes nodded, spouting out one of the few Latin phrases she remembered her father using. She smiled to soften things a bit.

The man turned to Rupert. He tapped his finger to his temple. "She's a smart one, your wife. All right, then. The count is in my debt, and that's all I will say about the matter. Now, what do you have to do with him? Does he owe you money as well?"

Agnes couldn't help laughing. "That would be a sorry state indeed! No, we are servants of the de Courceys, and I suppose, now that madame and monsieur are dead, of the count."

"Did you follow him out here?"

"Yes," she said. "We were wrongfully accused of stealing precious items from his home here in Paris as well as the chateau in Champagne."

"We are innocent, sir," Rupert broke in.

Agnes watched as the man rapidly summed up the situation. "So, you believe he was the one stealing the items."

"After what you've just revealed, I'm more convinced of it than ever."

The man rubbed his chin. "Well, it puts the count in yet another unflattering light."

"And he's been so attentive to Miss Sylvie lately!" Agnes sighed. "I thought he was finally coming around. How much does he owe you?" she asked.

"That's not for you to know, but it is a sizable amount."

Agnes felt sick. The rushed wedding suddenly made sense. "So he's trying to pay you back then?"

"Trying. But not doing a very good job at it. Now, let us get to the matter at hand."

"This *is* the matter at hand!" Agnes cried.

"For you, perhaps, but not for me. I want to know what you're going to do about this baby."

"Me?" Agnes felt her mouth drop open. "What do you mean me? This is your baby."

The man shrugged. "He'll simply go back in the basket if left in my hands."

"You wouldn't!"

"Oh." His expression took on an evil bent, and Agnes recoiled inwardly, but sought to remain strong. "I would, Mrs. Green. I like you, I do. You're a feisty, good woman, and unless you crossed me severely I would do you no harm. But I'm a hard man, and when something is in my way, I cast it aside, in one way or another."

Rupert stood to his feet, eyes glaring. "You'd do away with this bairn?"

"Simply put, I do not need such a complication at this time."

Agnes stood to her feet. "We'll take the baby, then."

"I wish you would, Mrs. Green."

She could hardly believe this was happening.

"I'd like to at least give you some financial help with this. I assume you will be taking the child to England?"

Agnes became angry. How dare the man presume! "Keep your money, sir! Just keep it! We'll do fine on our own. I wouldn't take your money if it was shoved down my throat."

He grinned wickedly. "I knew you'd feel that way."

"We'll be going," Rupert declared, shaking his head. "I've lived a long time, sir, and I've never heard tell of anything like this." Agnes's heart broke for her husband, a man who had spent his life with horses, and was still in the process of losing his innocence.

The man took another sip of his cognac. "No, sir. I don't suppose you have. Didier!" he bellowed, and the man appeared. "There is a ship in Paris, the Buccaneer, you know the one."

Didier nodded.

"See that the captain transports the Greens over to England right away."

"I won't let you pay for our passage," Agnes said, sticking her chin out.

"He will charge you a nominal fee, so do not worry your conscience over the matter, good woman."

Agnes, realizing that she was embarking on more than a journey across the channel, hugged the child to her. Motherhood was upon her. And the other child she held so dear was beyond her reach now. There was nothing she could do but place her safely in the hands of God.

They were bound for Dover.

Agnes could hardly believe it. She was to raise this child, this little boy baby with no hair, blue eyes, and oversized feet and hands. He was tiny, but had greedily taken the milk Agnes offered from a spoon as the ship sailed toward home. She thought him the most beautiful sight she had ever seen in her life. And he was hers to do with as she wished—and all she wanted to do was love him. The only order his father had given her was that he never set eyes on the babe again. "Tell him he is your own," Mirreault ordered. "He need never know you are not the one who bore him, madame."

"And do you wish for reports as to his health and welfare?"

"No. Nothing of that nature. Nothing at all."

Agnes looked over at her traveling satchel, now heavy with the silver coins the count had given her, the two months' wages obviously given as a guilt offering. The babe was sleeping peacefully, rocked by Agnes's arms and the waves of the English Channel.

Agnes caressed the downy cheek of her new son. "You can raise your own horses, eh? Maybe your brother will let us stay with them until you can get started. Surely someone will be glad to invest in such an enterprise."

"I don't know, lovey. Lord Guilford once said if I needed employment, there was always a space for me at Thistlehill Hall."

Agnes thought for a moment. "I could take in cleaning at home."

"God will take care of us. "Rupert put an arm around his wife as she cradled the infant against her breast and stroked the cheek that rested against the soft brown flannel of her dress. "God works in the strangest of ways, Aggie. What some men mean for evil . . ." he quoted. "God must have important plans for the wee fellow."

"Several hours ago we were humiliated and full of despair. And now"—her eyes shone tearfully into her husband's as she kissed his hand—"and now, ducks, our family is finally complete."

It had been difficult for Agnes to observe Sylvie growing round with her pregnancy, and now a child had been given to them. A baby to call their own.

"I'm going to call him Adam. Adam Rupert Green," she declared. "I was thinking about Sylvie naming her baby Eve if it is a girl. And if God's choice is good enough for her child, it's good enough for ours!"

So . . . Adam it was. As the boat sailed across the water, prayers were already being sent heavenward on his behalf. And that legacy of faith had only just begun. There wouldn't be a more prayed-for child in all of Britain.

That night, the dark waters lapping gently at the boat, Agnes suddenly sat up straight. "Ducks!" she cried.

"What?" Rupert rubbed the sleep out of his eyes. "Are you all right?"

She was horrified at the thought that had just come into her mind. "You don't think the count was behind the deaths of Guy and the master and the madame, do you? What if it wasn't a suicide? And what about Sylvie?"

His silence wasn't comforting at all, but after a moment his voice came out of the darkness. "She's in God's hands now, Aggie. This is the course set before us. And we must follow it. We've work to do."

CHAPTER ❖ TWENTY-NINE

Viscount Blackthorne had to wonder about his employer. Claude Mirreault was a paradoxical study of humanity. A pugilist's face with a scholar's mind. A criminal mind with a nobly clothed body. A hardened body of the street with a gentleman's voice. And around and around it went. Youngblood eyed him as he talked.

Mirreault lit a cigar. "So I put her on my own yacht and instructed Didier to tell the captain to take a bit of their money. And in the end, I am paid to get rid of my own illegitimate brat!" He laughed.

"I daresay," Youngblood drawled, lighting a cigar for himself, "it was quite a coup, Mirreault. Even for you."

"Oh, yes. Now that woman, Mrs. Green, she was an interesting old girl. I like a woman with spirit."

Mirreault knew exactly what he meant. "Unfortunately, the good ones are usually taken." *Dear Sylvie*, he thought.

"Hmm. Yes. So now, I have an urgent matter at hand for you."

"If it has anything to do with the de Courceys or the de Boyces, it's going to cost you dearly, Mirreault. I'm upping the ante this time."

"I figured you would do that."

"*Especially* if it means yet more de Courcey blood on my hands." Youngblood had known it was just a matter of time before Claude would seek Sylvie's life. She held the money, after all, and whoever held the gold, as far as Claude Mirreault was concerned, was indebted to him.

"With the money that will eventually be coming my way from the de Courceys, you will literally be worth your weight in gold, Viscount."

"Tell me what I am to do," Youngblood sighed. This was all getting positively *boring*.

"I want you to journey to Champagne in all haste and kill Sylvie de Courcey."

David faked a yawn. "Why such a rush?"

"De Boyce is on his way to his wife now. They will try and escape somehow, I'm sure. He's failed to pay up yet again, and the de Courcey fortune did not pass through to him as he expected. It went straight to his wife. After the young countess is dead, Rene will hold the entire de Courcey dynasty in his hands. He can pay me off, and then some."

"So you have future plans, do you?" Youngblood raised his brows. "Rene has stopped his opium smoking and his gambling. How do you intend to keep him chained to you?"

"I have taken care of the opium problem. The gambling will be your problem. At first, after he initially pays off the debt, he will not be chained directly to me anyway. It is up to you and Camille to help him fritter away his fortune. De Boyce never refused anybody a loan. I keep seventy percent, and you pocket the rest."

"Fifty-fifty," Youngblood declared. "Or I walk out of here right now."

Mirreault's expression didn't change. "You're finding our old arrangement unsatisfactory?"

"Highly. I do all the legwork."

"But I set you on his trail in the first place."

"That might have been worth something at first. But not after all these years. Besides, I don't really need your money anymore. The desperation is gone. Fifty-fifty, Mirreault."

The man rubbed his chin, then shrugged. "As you wish. Now, the first step is to kill Sylvie de Courcey. I think they will try to escape from France. But whether they will go south to Spain or Italy, or west to England, I do not know. He has connections in both places."

"America too, for that matter," Youngblood surmised. "So he knows you're after his wife. How does he know this? That must have been quite a slip of the tongue for you, Mirreault."

"Even I am not perfect in my dealings. When I suggested he supplicate himself to his wife, he flatly refused. I thought surely he would go for the bait. But he would have none of it."

"He fancies that he loves her now," Youngblood reported. The thought of Sylvie with Rene de Boyce made him want to tear out his hair by handfuls.

"Hard to believe the man is actually acquiring some scruples." Mirreault pulled in on his cigar.

"Sylvie will do that to you," Youngblood said.

"A pretty filly?" Mirreault looked interested.

"In her way. You know how it is with some women. Some men might find her not beautiful at all, but I find more than a few redeeming qualities in the lady."

Mirreault leaned forward. "Are you the right man for the job, then?"

Youngblood laughed a great ha! "You've known me long enough, Mirreault. Do you need to ask such a thing?"

"I suppose not."

"You suppose correctly. Now, if I am to catch up with them, I shall be on my way." He stubbed his cigar into the ashtray. "His yacht is docked here in Paris. My guess is that they shall use it to escape."

"Unless they go by land," Mirreault said.

"True. Let's be safe about this. Send Didier to Champagne, and I'll stay in Paris and wait down at the docks where his yacht is moored. If they leave by train, he can follow them, and then report back to us. I'll go do the job then. My instincts tell me, however, that they will go by boat."

"Didier!" Mirreault bellowed. And the man appeared a moment later. "Go to Champagne and keep a trail on the young Countess de Boyce. Report her every move to me." He turned his attention back to Youngblood. "So, then, that is all for tonight, Viscount. You may go."

Youngblood chuckled. "One of these days, Mirreault, you'll learn not to dismiss me so easily."

But Mirreault wasn't put off in the least.

Camille tugged at her bodice, straightened herself, and tried to look as appealing as possible. Mirreault had summoned her to his home an hour earlier and explained the situation. She was to be ready to call on Rene at a moment's notice, to succor his loss, to hold his shaking hand when he told her the news of his loss, to offer him the pipe. She was well paid to do such things.

Claude Mirreault paid her for many different tasks, and though selling herself bothered her deeply at first, the finer things it brought her had become sufficient justification. If others judged her, so be it. They didn't know what it was like to go about the streets of Paris begging for honest work, only to be turned down by the mistress of the house because "you're just too pretty, cherie. We can't have a woman like you about the house tempting all the menservants, not to mention the master."

It was better this way, she supposed.

Servicing men like Claude Mirreault and the Count de Boyce wasn't so bad, really. It could have been a lot worse. And it had been, before Viscount Blackthorne had found her one night. She had never charged him for her services. And she never would. For love was something one gave away.

Youngblood's butler had shown her into the small, yet elegant house. He went to find the viscount, while Camille waited, feeling the anticipation of the moment she would see him. It was like this each time she saw him. There was something so beautiful about his eyes, as if God had made them extra lovely to make up for his deformity. Even his mouth didn't bother her. It made him who he was, toughened on the outside, but so soft on the inside. Not that he ever really opened himself up to his tender side, but she knew it was there.

"Camille!" She heard his voice come from his study. "I'm in here, darling!"

She hurried inside, wishing she could make him love her the way he loved Sylvie de Courcey. Now *that* had been a sore revelation to be sure. Of course, when Rene had let it slip that Youngblood had been showering Sylvie with flowers and attention, he didn't realize how much the information had pained her. Hoping Youngblood would deny his attachment to Sylvie, she'd asked him about it, and he'd told her the truth. He did love Sylvie. Not her. Not Camille. For he was a gentleman and she was a commoner. He wasn't able to love her the same way she loved him. His class wouldn't allow him. *Like Mother always said*, Camille thought, *oil and water don't mix, no matter how hard you shake them together.*

"What are you doing here, Camille?" he asked, not unkindly.

"I won't be here long. I had to see you before you left. You're not going to kill her, are you?" She could not believe that of him.

He cocked his eyebrows in apparent surprise. "You have known me some time now, Camille. When have I ever let love get in the way?"

Camille closed her eyes against the onslaught of pain his words brought, and yet, with Sylvie dead, it would be better for them all. She would still belong to the viscount. "I am glad." Yet her words felt hollow as they fell off her tongue. Could she believe him? Would he really do this—kill the woman he loved for money?

He handed her a brandy, then poured another one for himself.

"Will it be soon?" She took a sip as she watched him carefully, from lowered eyes.

He shrugged, his face inscrutable. "I do not know yet. Let's talk about something else. I have until morning to meet the fleeing party down at the docks, and when Rene's yacht is released from its moorings, there will be one more person on board than they had bargained for."

"And will you come back to me. Right away?"

No promises made, Youngblood reached out his hand and began unbuttoning her dress.

⁓

Racine knew Rene's footsteps. Always had. And the boots that slid then clambered into the entry hall sounded urgent, blackened by desperation, polished by panic to a high sheen.

She rose from her chair and traversed the drawing room, relieved that Sylvie was soundly asleep in her bedchamber. Only five minutes before she had checked on her herself.

Turning the corner, she cried, "Rene?"

"Mama!"

She was thrown backward by the distraught expression in his glazed eyes, the way his entire body was wired tightly with alarm.

"Mother. Pack a bag for yourself, and one for Sylvie. We must get to the yacht immediately."

"Whatever are you—"

"No time to explain now. Do as I ask. Tell no one."

"Are you coming with us?"

"Yes. I will go and awaken Sylvie myself."

He sped up the massive stairway, four steps at a time, its mammoth proportions dwarfing him to insignificance. And yet the urgency of his motions were reminiscent of the bow of a boat cutting through the high waves of a stormy sea. Racine followed in his wake like a frivolous but indispensable dinghy.

⁓

Clutching a carpetbag and an extra shawl, Sylvie was whisked down the back stairway, sandwiched between the hurrying figures of Rene and the countess. No explanation other than "your life is in danger" had been afforded her upon awakening. The expression on Rene's face told her he was speaking the truth.

And here she was, being spirited away from her own home in the middle of the night, into a drab old coach onto the service road—bound for Reims and the train, then to Paris to board his yacht, then to England—of all places.

Then where?

She didn't know.

In the coach, looking pasty and spent, Rene assured her it would all work out fine—provided they stayed one step ahead of "the man." Whoever "the man" was, she wondered, choosing not to express her fear until Rene's constitution had strengthened a bit. Besides, a little silent prayer might do them all good, she thought, looking out into the darkness.

Finally, they were seated in the de Boyce's luxurious, private railroad car. Sylvie took off her new hat, a riotous, blue feathered confection that seemed a bit loud considering the circumstances. Without a thought for its welfare, she shoved the expensive topper into her carpetbag. "I want an explanation, Rene. And I want the truth."

"My dear!" the countess exclaimed, her eyes snapping under the strain of the hour, "are you suggesting my son has anything—"

"It is all right, Mother . . . she is right. It has everything to do with me. And it is time I own up to it . . . and it is time *you* own up to the fact that I am not the man you have always wished me to be. I am not my father."

"But, Rene," began the countess.

"No, Mother. It is time you listen to me, and that you do so very, very carefully."

And so began the tale of gambling, riotous living, opium, Camille. Debt. Sylvie felt more than betrayed, and she knew he was still holding back something.

Sylvie had never seen the countess angry at Rene, but that was the countess's state just then. "After all these years of defending you, guiding you, protecting you . . . and now, I find out, Rene, that you have been deceiving me?" Her lips were shaking, and she had gone whiter than the roses embroidered on her traveling coat. "I am shocked, Rene! And . . . and penniless! And what of poor Sylvie? Pregnant with your child. Well, I don't know what to say. I feel so, so . . . *betrayed!*"

"You have been betrayed, Mother, and I am sorry to you both."

Dread fisted in Sylvie's stomach, the fright of the situation collecting in her throat, waiting to burst forth at any moment. First the death of her family, then Agnes's departure, now this. She wondered what God was doing. But this was not the hour for more than that simple, surface question. There was much more to be digested.

"Sylvie will simply pay him off," the countess burst out. "She has more than enough. I am certain this fellow is a reasonable sort."

Sylvie dropped open her mouth, hardly able to believe her ears. Did the woman never learn?

Rene stared at his mother with no small measure of incredulity. "You do not understand his 'sort' at all, Mother. No. It has gone beyond that." His eyes were beginning to go wild. Sylvie knew he needed more opium and, feeling sorry for him, knowing now was not the time for him to tackle his cravings, she reached into her bag for a bottle of paregoric.

He took several swallows, then thudded against the seat back with a sigh. "Thank you."

"There's time for you to get over this later on. In England."

The countess, hands fisted, chin set defiantly, sat forward and took Rene's hand in an iron grasp. "What do you mean it has gone beyond this?"

"It is past the point where a simple repayment will suffice. He wants to gain a vast share of the de Courcey fortune. He means to keep me in chains through my addiction, Mother. He made that much clear when he poured it down my throat. And when I am eating opium I am gambling too and borrowing money all the while. It is a vicious circle."

"But why are our lives in danger?" Racine asked, her voice uncommonly fierce.

Rene groaned. "Don't you see? He wants Sylvie out of the way so that he can gain the fortune. He's already dispatched a man for the job."

Sylvie stiffened, then bit her tongue against the hysterical accusations that were gathering in her brain. She sought a different course, a safe course. She sought to take control of the mess her husband had made.

With a gentle, kind touch, Sylvie took his other hand. But her words were far from soothing. "I don't agree with your mother. I will not simply pay off this man. He will continue to do such to others and probably far worse. No, my father didn't work so hard to build up our vineyards to have the fruit of his labors thrown into the hands of a scalawag like . . . like . . . I still don't know why you won't tell me his name, Rene."

He pulled his hand out of his mother's and rested it atop Sylvie's. "I know you, Sylvie. You will take matters into your own hands. And I cannot risk you or the baby."

"What of the authorities?"

"I have broken too many laws myself now, cherie. Stealing the silver, holding up the payroll. It is too late to call them in without confessing to what I have done."

Sylvie knew she would never let him go to prison. He was weak, and the crimes had been against only herself and his mother. If they forgave him, it was none of the government's business. Besides, their baby needed a father. She prayed while Rene and Racine buzzed in conversation around her ears. Whoever this man was, he would be sorry he ever set his sights on the de Courceys.

Reaching into her bag she pulled out a handkerchief and began wiping at the perspiration that beaded on her forehead and neck. "I will bury him, Rene. I promise you this."

The countess gasped. "How can you say such a thing, Sylvie? To kill a man—"

"I am sure Sylvie is speaking figuratively, Mama," Rene rushed to her defense.

Sylvie was getting a little bit tired of the countess at this point, but held her consternation in check. "Perhaps I am. Perhaps I am not. It is up to God to decide. All I know is, once I find out this man's name, he'll soon be out of business."

Rene squeezed her hands, looking quite a bit worse for the wear. Sylvie felt no disgust at the man before her. Only pity. All her suspicions were confirmed, and she thanked God she never fell in love with him, had never placed the love she bore as a woman into his fragile hands. It would have been too much to have dealt with. But now, friend to friend, she was ready for a clean battle, and she hoped it would be side by side, but she rather doubted he could play any significant, commanding role in the fray that might ensue.

Rene licked his lips, eyeing his wife's carpetbag. "They have instructions to kill you, Sylvie, not to negotiate. For the present, we must get to safety, and then deal with the situation on our own terms."

Sylvie could see the sense of that. And she mustn't forget she harbored a life inside her now which must be kept safe no matter what. "To England, then." She nodded firmly, gravely. Leaning back against the pillow Rene slid behind her, she began praying yet more. She was, after all, in charge now.

There was other business to tend to across the channel as well, and she couldn't wait to see the faces of Agnes and Rupert when they heard their names had been cleared. Then she remembered—she had no idea where they would have gone!

CHAPTER ❖ THIRTY

The mantel clock chimed six times. Youngblood sat up suddenly in his chair and reached for his coat.

"Blast!"

He crushed his hat down over his curly hair as he grabbed his derringer. Jamming it into his coat pocket, he slammed out of the house. A stiletto was already tied snugly to his leg, and curled in the other pocket was a full, velvet mask. When Rene was killed, Youngblood didn't want him to know that the man who had drawn the knife across his throat and thrown him into the channel was his supposed best friend. After all, it wasn't Rene's fault that Sylvie was the woman Youngblood feverishly adored.

A small bit of regret for what would soon happen crept into his consciousness, but he hoisted his lithe body onto his horse and galloped away.

Poor Camille, he thought, lied to again. But there wasn't a chance that he would kill the only object of his heart's desire. It was time now for Sylvie to be his. With Rene out of the way, there was nothing to stop him. Sylvie would certainly need a bit of comforting when her husband died. And he would be there, to take her into his arms, to kiss her hair, to love her forever. She deserved nothing less.

When he arrived at the docks, dawn streaked the sky with pale silver light, diffusing the hard line of the city skyline with its pearly clouds. The smells from the bakeries wafted about him enticingly, but he knew better than to succumb to the temptation of warming his hollow stomach with a freshly baked baguette or a choux pastry. On the other hand . . .

Better not.

The de Boyce yacht bobbed quietly in the dark waters of the Seine. Led by the figurehead of a majestically carved sea nymph, the boat was ready to set sail. He couldn't help but smile at the count's predictability. *What a nincompoop!* And yet, what other course was there for such a dolt, he wondered as he picked his fingernails with a sliver of wood he kept in his pocket for just that purpose.

Across the dock he noticed a man. One of Mirreault's men, that blond hulk of a fellow named Yves. Youngblood had never liked him. Thought he was a ladies' man. Hmm. The man's idea of courtship was a bottle of scotch whiskey and a roll in the hay. His presence assured Youngblood that Mirreault wasn't taking any chances. It figured. He saluted him from his perch on his horse.

The de Boyce carriage rolled up, and Youngblood smiled from his place of concealment near a group of shipping crates. The count had played right into his hands. A three-legged hound sprung from the vehicle, then the ladies emerged, and finally the count himself. All looked fashionably harried. And Sylvie, so round and blooming, was obviously suffering beneath the weight of her husband's weakness. He wanted to run to her, to comfort her as he had been doing since they had reacquainted themselves last spring in Paris. But he remained unseen.

They boarded the yacht in all haste, too preoccupied to notice that the winds of morning would be in their favor. Rene hurried Sylvie onto the small ship, supporting on his arm his mother, who was seemingly growing older by the minute. She was spilling something about a note to Cecile.

"I think we have escaped them," the old woman puffed, not even bothering to look behind her. "Get me downstairs, dear boy. And Sylvie, I could do with a little of that paregoric. I just want to sleep."

Sylvie gasped. "My bag! I left it in the coach!"

Youngblood pulled his coat collar up against the stiff breeze as he watched the drama play before him from his vantage point. As soon as they were below, he would board the boat and hide himself down in the hold.

"I must get it." Rene was looking greenish. The idiot was willing to risk it all for the opium. How typical.

Youngblood donned his mask.

"No, Rene! We've got to go now. Now!" Sylvie pulled his arm toward the stairs as a rider wheeled onto the dock. "That could be the man!"

Youngblood pulled his hat down further over his brow. Rene frantically rummaged in his pocket and handed her a slip of paper. "Go there ... to this address ... if I do not make it back. Youngblood will send word when it is safe to return. If you do not hear from him by autumn, send word to his estates in Cornwall or Scotland or ... or London!" And he ran down the ramp toward the coach, and that bag which held the key to his immediate sanity.

Youngblood could hardly believe his luck. The time to strike could not be better. He jumped down off his horse, licking his hidden, misshapen lips. Why wait? He could do away with Rene now and follow Sylvie to England as soon as possible. This was the moment he was waiting for. The imbecile was storming the carriage even now. Which would prevail? His love for his wife and child, or the need for more opium? It could be the only reason he would risk his wife's very life at such a moment.

Viscount Blackthorne considered the question for less than a second. This was definitely his opportunity to strike. What a fool the young Frenchman was. A true fool. Certainly he didn't deserve a woman as majestic, as adorable as Sylvie.

He ran toward the carriage just in time to witness Rene frantically grabbing hold of the bag and backing out of the carriage with a jerk. Youngblood made his move, springing with athletic ease. But the wild-eyed count, spurred on by desperation, lifted Sylvie's bag and swiftly slammed it up against the side of Youngblood's head. "No!" Rene shouted, pushing the viscount, who went sprawling.

Blast! Youngblood cursed inwardly and scrambled to his feet. He would not let that buffoon get away so easily. Surely he could outrun a man half-lame? A split-second later he was running full pace. As sure as his name was David Youngblood, he would do away with this thorn, this pathetic excuse of a man. Today Rene de Boyce would die.

Sylvie stood rooted to the deck, watching in horror as the masked man gained on Rene.

"Cast off!" Rene ordered his captain and crew with a mighty shout. "Cast off now!"

The crew obeyed, untying the craft and pushing off as they unfurled the sails. Winds filled the canvas and the river Seine grew wider and wider between the husband and wife. His mother too.

As Rene tried to leap aboard, the assailant, knife in hand, caught him about the knees and they tumbled together down onto the dusty quay.

"Not him!" a blond man nearby yelled. "Not *him!* The girl! The girl!"

The men scrambled for possession of the weapon, bruising the ground with the weight of their struggle.

"No!" Sylvie yelled to the sailors, feeling the movement of the vessel. "Do not leave him!"

The captain laid a steadying hand on her arm. "We must obey his wishes. My orders are to protect you, madame. At all costs."

Sylvie watched in horror as a knife was raised into the air. The assassin was strong and sure, and Rene struggled, but was no match. Receiving the knife in his chest, Rene's body went limp.

Sylvie leaned into the railing, feeling it bite into her abdomen. She screamed his name.

The boat continued on its indelible course.

The figure in black stood to its feet in triumph, then wordlessly rolled Rene into the water with a booted foot. He stood tall, and to her horror, blew her a kiss. There was something familiar about his movements, but she didn't know what it was exactly.

Rene sunk into the Seine as the ship left the only country Sylvie had ever known. She was safe for now. Rene, his final gesture sprung from a true heart of courage, had made certain of it.

France was behind her. Another time for weeping had truly begun. But it was not to arrive at its fullness just yet. "God help me," she whispered as her tears were sucked dry by a gust of wind. "God help us all."

The sails filled up with no room to spare, and their speed increased. She remembered the scrap of paper handed to her by her husband, thought of looking at it, but knew she should go down and tell the countess that her son was dead.

Countess Racine de Boyce lay on a bed covered with a silken spread.

"Aunt Racine?"

The old woman's eyes opened. Seeing Sylvie's expression, they became filled with alarm.

"The assassin caught up with us," Sylvie related, feeling sick, feeling as though all the wretchedness in her life was culminating in this one moment.

"Where's Rene?"

Sylvie sat down next to the countess and put her arm around the fragile shoulders. "I don't know why it happened, but the man turned on Rene."

"Oh, dear God." The countess put a hand up to her mouth, gulping back a sob. "Is he—"

"Yes," Sylvie said, proceeding to relate what had happened.

"How much more can I bear?" the old woman wailed.

Sylvie sat in helpless silence, waiting for more questions, but they did not come. Although they would very soon, she was sure.

"Leave me, child," the countess requested, turning her head away.

"If you need me, Aunt Racine, I will come immediately."

Bestowing a kiss upon the old, papery skin of her cheek, Sylvie went back up on deck. And there she remained, looking only forward, away from the winds which ushered her onward, clawed at her back. This wasn't over. It wasn't close to being settled. Someone wanted her dead, and she didn't even know who it was.

Terror overtook her and she began to gag, holding her sides and bending forward. They would follow her, wouldn't they. They would hunt her down, and someday she would stand before her enemies face-to-face. The first mate came forward and handed her a bucket none too soon. Sylvie retched, feeling not a bit better for having done so. After several spasms, she sat down on a deck chair and cried. And cried, for her mother-in-law, for herself, and for Rene. His was the most tragic story of all, she thought. Born to privilege and wealth, doomed by his own weaknesses to throw it all away, down to his very life. So much waste, so much pain, so much sacrificed to gain so little— it was a fitting epitaph for the man she had called husband. Sylvie's tears flowed freely in her desolation. Poor Rene, that his world should end thus—and that he should leave behind him such a predicament. Sylvie couldn't begin to guess where her dead husband's dark appetites would lead her in the end.

Finally, the morning clouds parted, revealing a ray of sunlight on the horizon, a finger of light pointing the way, reminding her that there was nothing she could do, but hope was not lost. God was preparing the way for her and her child. Above the clouds the sun was shining and there was a land she knew not of, one fairer than day and filled with all the promises a young woman could only dream about. *If I can only persevere until then.*

Lord David Youngblood watched until the boat was out of sight, soaring ghostly on indigo waters. Feeling an immense sense of satisfaction, he turned on his heel, yanked off the mask, and walked toward Yves, who was possessed of a giant irritation.

"You let them go! You killed the wrong person, you deformed imbecile!"

Any good feelings at his recent success snapped in two, and Youngblood reached forward, grabbing Yves by the throat. His own throat went bitter and dry. "Never, *never* say such things to me, you putrid street rat."

Unable to breathe, Yves reached behind him, a panicked expression paralyzing his face. Next thing Viscount Blackthorne knew, a knife was pressed against his neck. Youngblood laughed and twisted the implement away as Yves cried out in pain.

"Never . . ." he whispered into the man's ear, "threaten me again. More than one man has rolled in a river at my hand."

He pushed Yves into the dust and mounted his horse. He had more important matters to consider, like just where Sylvie was going and how long it would take him to find her.

Would he find her? Most certainly.

BOOK TWO

BRITAIN

CHAPTER ❖ THIRTY-ONE

The ragged, lofty cliffs of Dover towered lordly, arrogantly haphazard, as the boat crested the horizon. Perched atop the sturdy precipices, Dover Castle rested formidable, almost more imposing than the chalky cliffs themselves. Never taken by a foreign adversary. Stalwart. Proud. A visual picture of what Sylvie thought England and the English to be.

Sylvie stared down at the scrap of paper that lay in her palm. Only an address in the city of Bath. No name. No explanation. The paper had been folded and unfolded many times during the voyage. Its creases were now soft and slightly fuzzy. Two blurred lifelines. A road sign in a foreign land. How would she convince whoever resided at the place of Rene's choosing that they should take her and the countess into their home? And she just about to have a baby! Life was growing bleaker by the hour. And there was no sign or word from the countess yet.

Rene is dead, she thought, saving the tears that threatened to gather for later, tired of crying, tired of everything. They had all sensed Rene's life wasn't what it should have been, but no one had been brave enough to hold him accountable. And now, he had destroyed himself, a young man with a good future ahead of him. Surely not a glorious one, but one of comfort and love and children and suppers and music and fires burning on the hearth.

Sylvie stopped the train of thought. There were too many other matters to consider, too many unknowns to be faced and dealt with. How would she get to Bath? Well, at least she had brought plenty of money with them. Francs, of course, but she should have no trouble exchanging them, or so she hoped.

Now here they were, England before them, the sun setting over the green hills of spring, tinting the sky to warm with its raging hues of scarlet and saffron. Sylvie was numb to all but the castle—feeling an affinity with the thick ramparts, the cold stone, the iron gates.

Never again, she promised herself.

Never again would she will her life to someone else. She had always done just fine on her own, and now, having foolishly trusted in Rene, her life was disintegrating rapidly. The only reason to hold on moved restlessly inside of her as the quay grew closer and the skies began darkening to night. The cliffs loomed inviting, so easy. But a dangerous path twisted before her now, and one that demanded she play the role of protectress, of nurse, of daughter-in-law, of mother. She must become all the things woman was capable of being. Except wife. That role was behind her forever.

Just after sunset, they docked. No rest would be afforded them. "The man" would be sending someone on their trail. They had to keep moving.

Sylvie called the captain of the yacht to her. "Return to Paris at once, and inform my husband's secretary, Jean-Francois, that you have indeed returned."

"And what about you, madame? Where will you be going?"

"For your sake, it's best that you don't know," she said. "I will send word to you when I need you to return for me. It may be to Dover, it may be to someplace else."

"We will await your pleasure, madame."

So official and dependable he was. Sylvie was truly grateful to the man who had guided her to safety. She reached into her bag for a small purse and took out several gold coins. "For you,

Captain . . . with my thanks." Then she proceeded to disembark, only looking behind her to help the countess onto dry land. With just two bags between them, they walked into town and ate a bit of bread and broth at a small public house. There were no rooms available, so they slept for several hours near the fire. Early the next morning, a willing lad with a rattletrap cart and a bedraggled horse agreed to convey them halfway to Canterbury. By nightfall they had arrived at the cathedral where Thomas à Becket was murdered.

"It would probably be safest to stay here for the night, in the cathedral," Sylvie whispered, gazing in wonder about her from where she stood at the west entrance to Canterbury Cathedral. Though the soaring ceilings were veiled in darkness, the stonework around her and the windows glittering high in the walls promised a breathtaking sight come morning. A few other weary pilgrims and travelers were already resting at various points along the nave.

The countess agreed, obviously too sore of heart and head to argue about anything. "Yes, we will sleep here. Near the tomb of the Black Prince. Such an amazing fellow he was, child. He died much too young, too."

Sylvie laid a comforting arm across her mother-in-law's bony shoulders. She was more than capable of being strong, for since she had walked into the doors she had felt the power of God in a more solid fashion, as if he brought them into his house, built of stalwart stones, to show them that his strength he would always provide.

And so they did as Racine de Boyce suggested, leaning up against the Cosmati tomb of Edward, the Black Prince. Racine whispered his tale to Sylvie in the darkness, and the two women finally let relief wash over them. Surely they were safe from the night that had already descended over England, and that which was yet on its way.

"In those days, Sylvie, even the English court spoke French."

Taking some comfort from those words, both women allowed the churchly silence to enfold them. Racine softly cried herself to sleep, but Sylvie only stared across the nave, waiting . . . waiting. And watching.

CHAPTER ❖ THIRTY-TWO

Matthew Wallace wiped the grit of sleep from his tired eyes. Normally he loved composing his sermons—the time passed in prayer beforehand, the reading, the study, forming thoughts into words that would sound beautiful both to the ear and the heart.

He truly loved this part of his calling. No men informing him how to preach, no women encouraging him to eat more eggs, no children kicking him in the shins or yanking on his robe. No people at all. Lovely. Just he and God, and a message to give to those who made his work more of a chore. Yes, he did love them all. They meted out joy with their exasperating habits and ways, and most of them truly cared about him as well. Except for maybe Mrs. Horace P. Rooney. But she had been making trouble for years. The church wouldn't be the same without the gossiping, back stabbing, and griping that Mrs. Horace P. Rooney spewed from beneath the brims of her majestic feathered hats.

But this evening, with the spring rains gushing out of the heavens, well, even thoughts of the buxom matron failed to keep him awake beneath the hypnotic thrum of the downpour.

Several lamps burned brightly around him, and the chimney stack at his back radiated the warmth from the fireplace down in the kitchen. Miranda's pleasant humming spiraled up the narrow stairs as she penned her poetry while waiting for their pudding to finish steaming. God was in all wise good. Matthew was content . . . in his lonely manner. It was his lot, and he knew now that it would always be so. Never again would he open his heart. He reminded himself of that daily.

His study, tucked in the attic of the small brick manse, was in its usual state of disarray. How he found anything at all was a veritable testimony to God's grace! At least that's what Miranda said every time she threatened to straighten his mess. So far, he'd forbidden her from tidying up anything but the teacups, and then only once a week. "For goodness sake, Matthew," she'd harp every Saturday as she clattered cups and saucers together into stacks, "how can you get any work done with these empties lying about!" And she wondered why he wouldn't so much as allow her big toe over the threshold Monday through Friday. But living with Miranda had more advantages than drawbacks. The smell of her cooking to name just one. Her pudding would soon be finished, so perhaps just a few more minutes of napping was justifiable.

Matthew rested his head back down on top of his papers, finding he napped more and more since his return from France. His dreams were filled with Sylvie, and a man couldn't be held responsible for his dreams, could he? Unfortunately, he wasn't adept at fooling himself.

"Yet a little sleep, a little slumber!"

He was yanked from his repose by his Scripture-quoting sister. "A little folding of the hands," he continued upon straightening. With a quick swipe he tidied his hair. "Speaking of folding of the hands, Miranda . . ."

"Yes, the pudding is done and only awaits God's blessing before its demise."

He arose and followed her down the small staircase, his broad shoulders brushing the walls on either side of him. "Is it a tansy pudding?"

"Is it your birthday? We always kill a tansy pudding on your birthday, Mate."

"It would not be the same if we did otherwise, Mira." Matthew gazed with appreciation around the warm, tidy kitchen his sister kept, the room in which they passed the most time together. A pot of strong tea was cozied on the small oak table near the pantry; two willow plates with the appropriate cutlery gleamed spotless in the evening candlelight.

"I think this is going to be the best pudding yet," she gloated, wrinkling her nose and winking at him. She was the consummate older sister.

Resting on his chair was a simply wrapped package, bound with the same red ribbon Miranda had been using for the past five years since they'd taken this small, mission parish near the city of Bath, in the town of Swainswick. "I thought you had forgotten, Mira."

His sister smiled a crooked grin. "As usual, 'tis a meager birthday, I'll warrant, Mate, but at your age—"

"Not so fast, or you will end up incriminating yourself!" he cautioned with a knowing smirk. Miranda was six years older than he.

"Besides," Miranda rejoined cheerfully, tucking a wayward strand of gleaming blond hair back into place, "Mother and Father won't forget. They're always just a little late. It wouldn't seem like your birthday if a present was actually . . . present!"

Inside the parcel was a small volume of poetry by John Donne. The same book wrapped up every year. This year, a new poem was marked. It was her ritual. Miranda was definitely a woman of ritual.

Holy Sonnet 14
Batter my heart, three-personed God, for you
As yet but knock, breathe, shine, and seek to mend;
That I may rise, and stand, o'erthrow me, and bend
Your force to break, blow, burn, and make me new.
I, like an usurped town, to another due,
Labour to admit you, but Oh, to no end.
Reason, your viceroy in me, me should defend,
But is captived, and proves weak or untrue.

Yet dearly I love you, and would be loved fain,
But am betrothed unto your enemy:
Divorce me, untie or break that knot again,
Take me to you, imprison me, for I,
Except you enthrall me, never shall be free,
Nor ever chaste, except you ravish me.

His eyes quickly scanned the familiar sonnet, and his quick words belied the tide of emotion in his heart. "Apropos as always. But it's all easier said than done, isn't it?"

"I suppose so."

The discussion went no further. With Miranda it never needed to.

She filled their plates with the moist pudding, poured tea in his cup, added neither sugar nor milk but liberally laced her own brew with both.

Gratitude to this woman in front of him suddenly overwhelmed him. This woman had given up her life for his work and the work of the Lord and was never lonely or dissatisfied. Miranda's eyes never went liquid with impossible dreams. Miranda truly knew what it meant to be content.

Was he sinning in his heartache?

That question might never be answered, he feared.

"How is the sermon coming along?" Miranda wondered as she sipped on her tea with delight. She had loved tea since she was two years old. Matthew suspected it was the copious amounts of sugar she mixed in that kept Miranda making pot after pot, all day long.

"When I am awake it is coming along quite well. Dying to self should be such an easy concept to talk about, but it certainly makes one feel hypocritical."

Miranda bit her lip. "I don't know how the apostle Paul really thought we could actually do such a thing. Maybe it was more about trying. Too bad George isn't around to help you out. He always has such insightful things to say about almost everything."

Matthew smiled at the mention of their good friend, George MacDonald. "I wonder how the latest little MacDonald is doing?"

"Don't know, but I'm sure there's another one already on the way!" Miranda chimed. For several years she had been friends with Louisa, the wife of the famous lecturer, writer, and former pastor. It was only natural that two men who loved God as much as her brother and George did would become such good friends after meeting at a forum in London. Mostly they corresponded by post.

"I would love to see George again. Perhaps we should have him come to speak at St. Jude's, Mira."

Miranda rose from her chair. "A marvelous idea! I'll write the letter right away and post it tomorrow!"

"Sit down, my girl! Do sit down! Help me celebrate my twenty-ninth birthday. A man only turns twenty-nine once in his life, you know."

She winked at him with a wry eye. "So do women, Mate, although some may beg to differ!"

Their cheerful laughter warmed the kitchen so that the very air almost glowed yellow in the nourishing light of good companionship. Though the storm raged outside, they barely noticed. There was much to celebrate, indeed, Matthew realized. And so much for which to be thankful.

⌒

"Tell me this, Viscount. Did you for even one tiny second entertain the thought of killing Sylvie de Courcey?" Claude Mirreault tapped his pen rapidly against the blotter of his desk.

Oh, he was piqued! And Youngblood thought it was marvelous. He loved seeing the normally unflappable Mirreault as agitated as a mosquito. "No."

"I'm surprised you have the fortitude to come here. If I wasn't such an affable fellow, I'd have beheaded you on your way through the gatehouse!"

Youngblood laughed. "You're not finished with me yet, Mirreault, and you know it." He threw a heavy money bag onto the desk. "But I am most definitely finished with you."

Mirreault stuck out his chin. "How so?"

"In this bag is all the money that de Boyce owed you before his death."

"Why?"

Viscount Blackthorne scratched an eyebrow. "I am a gentleman, Mirreault. And a rich one now, at that."

Mirreault leaned forward at the mention of money. "The old man left you well-heeled, then?"

"Heels of gold, my good fellow. Heels of absolute gold."

Holding his arms wide, Mirreault accused, "So . . . you turn upon me. You do not need Claude Mirreault now that you are a man of means. What about loyalty? What about respect?"

"Oh, come now. We've both known our association would one day come to a close. Be glad I'm paying you off like I am doing. I could have just left for England. Followed Sylvie immediately."

"I'm surprised you didn't do just that. You're not above that sort of thing."

"Well, initially I was going to. But I figured I would let Didier and Yves do all the legwork for me."

"Yves will kill her when he finds her, you know."

"Yves?" Youngblood laughed. "He's not capable of killing. I'm surprised you didn't see that yourself. Neither is Didier, for that matter."

Mirreault lifted the heavy sack of coin and chuckled. "Why do you think I brought you on board? Well." He rose to his feet and extended a hand. "Good luck, then. And just for the record, Viscount. I'd step up your search for Sylvie de Boyce. Yves *will* kill her. As he did her brother."

"Guy?" Youngblood's eyebrows raised.

"Yes, Guy. Get going. I'd say they have a strong lead over you."

This was confusing. "You won't call them off now that you have the money? Now that Rene is dead?"

"I have no way to contact them, and they have strict orders to return with proof of the girl's death, or not to return at all."

"It seems to be the case, then," Youngblood said as he stood to his feet, "that I have a damsel in distress to rescue."

"It would seem so, Viscount. Off to London, then?"

He nodded, already making plans. "Off to London."

"So you love her." Mirreault's lips curled in disgust. "I figured you were above all that, Viscount."

Youngblood winked. "You said it so yourself, Mirreault. David Youngblood isn't above anything!"

CHAPTER ❖ THIRTY-THREE

While the morning light bathed Canterbury in its most faint, most silver of rays, Sylvie ushered Racine back down the nave and out into the slowly awakening town. It didn't take long to find two women willing to trade their rough wool skirts and simple blouses for the fine silks and satins the two countesses wore under their concealing cloaks.

"We'll take them gowns off yer hands, and in exchange we'll give ye a bit o' breakfast," said Barbara, the taller, heavier woman who traded clothing with Sylvie. "Could certainly use a bit o' conversation we ain't already heard nigh unto a thousand times."

"That is fine," Sylvie agreed, ushering Racine, still stricken silent with thoughts of her son, into the small dwelling above a sweets shop. And so they had their first real taste of life in England. Barbara and Jilly, half sisters who ran the shop, chattered away, asking all sorts of questions and receiving vague answers. Not that they seemed to really care. They were happy to see two new faces, or so they must have said twenty times!

Sylvie was more than a little relieved that Barbara's skirt fastened around her bulging midsection. And soon they were ushered to the table for a bite of breakfast.

Sylvie ate a bit, for the baby's sake. The countess drank only a cup of tea. They had to be off.

Standing to her feet, Sylvie smiled for the first time in two days. "Thank you, ladies, and might I ask you not to wear the gowns until several weeks from now? It's most imperative that our presence in Canterbury be kept a secret."

Jilly folded her arms. "Well, we might could do that for ye, luv. Depends."

Sylvie reached into her bag and pulled out a small purse. She dropped several coins into the woman's hand, curled the work-worn fingers round them, and pressed her own index finger to her chapped lips. The voyage had taken its toll on her skin and hair, leaving the one dry and peeling, the other matted and coarse.

They hurried out the door and into the now-thriving traffic of the street. Choosing the most anonymous means of transportation, as well as the quickest, they boarded a train—not for London as would be supposed by those who would pursue them. They chose the southern route, through Brighton, where they spent the night. The next morning they boarded once again, continuing west to Portsmouth then northwest to Southampton and up toward Bristol.

Didier Vachel had never been more piqued. Having sailed all night across the channel, he was tired and hungry. Curse that Viscount Blackthorne! *I spit upon him!* he thought as he remembered the train ride back to Paris when he realized the de Boyces had already fled. A few of the people loitering about at the rail station had been more than eager to offer up the direction in which the count had gone.

And to top it all off, Mirreault had sent that imbecile Yves along with him to England! It was not going to be a pleasure trip, this. Now they were in Canterbury, and no one was giving them any helpful information whatsoever.

"I'm hungry." Yves shoved his hands in his pocket like an expectant brat.

"And?" Didier growled.

"I want my breakfast."

"And I want you to jump in the channel and swim back to France. But it doesn't look like either of us is going to get his way right now, does it? Keep looking."

Yves cursed beneath his breath.

"At least the young countess is pretty," Didier remarked.

"If you like that type."

"What type?"

"Pregnant." Yves smiled a wide, crooked grin, and pulled his beret down low over his brow.

"You are a pig," Didier stated.

"A hungry pig."

"Yes. Well, when you're used to eating slop . . ."

Yves said nothing. And a few minutes later he took matters into his own hands, and entered a bakery. Didier figured he'd might as well follow. He was a bit hungry, and surely they needed some sustenance if they were to keep going at such a pace. Yves was right, but Didier would never admit that to him.

Two women were serving a gentleman who was apparently quite choosy about his rolls. He sniffed each one at least three times before placing it in the sack. Didier wanted to scream. Yves growled. "Does that picky man need two of you to help him?"

The short woman laughed. "No, of course not. What would be your pleasure, gentlemen?"

With a tilted head, Yves leaned against the wall. "Oh, I can think of a few things, mademoiselle."

Her eyes widened. "Oh, one o' them Frenchies, eh? I've heard about men like you."

Didier rolled his eyes. "Coffee and choux pastries, please."

She cleared her throat and gathered their order as the other woman finished up with the other customer. She was tall, and eyed Yves as boldly as he eyed her. "I'd suggest a scone. It has more . . . substance . . . to it. Don't you agree, Jilly?"

Sacre bleu! Didier fumed. "We're in a hurry."

"Oh yes, Babs," Jilly cackled, not moving a muscle in the direction of the pastries. "Scones is much better."

Yves crossed his arms over his broad chest. "Scones for me then."

"Would *somebody* just give us our food!" Didier exploded.

Babs took down a plate. "All right, all right. But we don't sell coffee here. Just tea."

"Whatever. I do not care. We've got important business to tend to."

"Oh?" Jilly put on a kettle for the tea. "And what is that."

"We're looking for someone," Yves rushed to answer. "Two women to be precise. Two French women. Did you happen to see them in town ... yesterday, perhaps? One was old and one was young and pregnant."

Barbara rocked back on her heels. "Aye, luv, we did. Didn't we, Jilly?"

"Sure and for certain, gentlemen. Even traded dresses with us. Got the silks upstairs to prove it! Fancy digs they are too!"

Didier looked over at his counterpart, thinking he might just prove to be useful after all. "Have you any knowledge of their whereabouts? It's most important we find them."

Without looking at Jilly, Barbara replied, "Most everybody comes through here is on their way up to London. Course, they might've gone south, if you know what I mean. I just can't seem to remember what direction it was they went in when they left us, eh Jilly?"

"Me either." Jilly nodded without enthusiasm. "Even though I followed them ladyship types to the station, I'm not quite rememberin' what train it was they got on."

Without expression, Didier fished into his pocket. He expected no less. He laid a golden sovereign out on the table.

"Goodness!" Barbara whispered, sucking in her breath.

Jilly snatched it up without hesitation. "Now I can't say as for certain, but London's yer best bet. They was awfully nice ladies. Shame they was so quiet and forlorn actin'."

Didier tamped his hat down tightly his head, shoved the choux pastry into his mouth, and was out the door. "Come on, Yves. Now."

Yves winked at Barbara wickedly before he finally turned around and followed his boss with more of a spring in his step than before.

"Hey Frenchies!" Jilly yelled as they opened the door. "You forgot your tea!"

But neither man answered. Didier was already running toward the depot.

"We'll be closing in on them soon," he said, feeling that first bit of excitement work its way down through his legs.

Yves gobbled down the scone in two bites. His excitement mirrored Didier's. "You know, there's nothing so good as a good chase, whether it be for pleasure or profit."

"For the first time in my life, I agree with you!"

Didier purchased two tickets to London, bought a newspaper, and sat down on a bench to wait for the train. It would depart in three hours. Yves was gone, on the prowl no doubt. But he'd be back in time. Oh, yes, he would most certainly be back in time. Or Claude Mirreault would have his head.

$\sim$

"I thought the service went well today, Mate," Miranda said as she set his plate in front of him. "It made me want to completely lose any of myself, and give my all to the Savior once again."

"Oh, Mira, you do that every day."

She smiled, sitting down opposite him. "I have to. All my best intentions upon waking fade away, and I find myself so contrary and sore by the end of the day, my only hope is to fall at the Lord's feet."

Matthew gave her a grin. "You know, Mira, sometimes I wonder if *you* should be the priest and *I* should be *you!*"

She laughed, and cut into her cold chicken. "I noticed you failed to put a title to my position. Housekeeper? Assistant? Cook? So . . . what am I, then?"

He paused, knowing he would be diving into deep waters if he didn't say the right thing. "You are my best friend."

Miranda rose from her chair, pulled him to his feet, and gave him a hug. "Good answer, brother! You're learning after all these years!"

He kissed her forehead. "Yes, well, it's hard not to be schooled in diplomacy after seven years in the ministry."

Miranda sat back down and picked up her fork, wagging it at him. "I saw you talking to Mrs. Horace P. She seemed quite animated. What was she talking about?"

"Just about her nephew. He's graduating from seminary at Cambridge this spring and is hoping for a post in our diocese."

"You don't think she's after *your* post, do you?"

He laughed. One of Mira's few negative qualities was her uncanny ability to jump to conclusions. "I wouldn't worry about that yet." He leaned forward and pushed her typical wayward lock of hair back behind her ear. "Although, I wouldn't put it past her."

"Make light of it all you want, Mate, but she's a formidable woman. I wouldn't want her as my enemy. You know she's never accepted you since you arrived."

Matthew knew that well. Mrs. Horace P. Rooney had tried to block every change he and the vestry had implemented. Fortunately, the bishop, Jonathan Wells, didn't much care for women interfering with church business and had consistently refused her audience. "Don't worry yourself over this, Mira. You know Jonathan would never relieve me of my position at St. Jude's. Only for a larger, more influential church, I'd assume."

Miranda wiped her mouth with a napkin. "I don't know, Mate. You've already turned down several opportunities that Jonathan has placed before you. He's been magnanimous toward you from the day you entered his diocese."

"Yes. Jonathan's a good man. And as long as he's the bishop, we need not fear the likes of Mrs. Horace P. Rooney."

They finished their meal in pleasant conversation regarding the parish. It had, indeed, been a wonderful service, a banner day. The hymns were played to perfection by the elderly organist, no rain to keep away the easily dissuaded, and everyone stayed awake. A minister couldn't ask for much more than that!

He stood up and bestowed a kiss on her cheek. "Well, sister, to bed with the likes of me. Would you like help in clearing the dishes?"

She shook her head. "You know Sunday is a day of rest, Mate."

"Then leave them there till the morrow."

She crossed her arms and shot him a look. "I like doing dishes. It's not work if it's enjoyable."

"Hmm. I'll have to remember that the next time I read the creation account."

She threw a towel at him and bade him good night.

He climbed the stairs to his room, each footstep getting heavier as he ascended. Sliding out of his clothes and donning a nightshirt, Matthew pulled down the blanket with a grateful sigh. "Sunday night," he whispered to himself with satisfaction. He had made it through another week. Only by God's grace, no doubt.

His bedside lamp was cheerful and bright, and he turned the flame up yet more, then climbed into bed. He grabbed the book on the table. *Phantastes*.

"Well, George," he said aloud to his good friend, though absent, and the writer of the volume in his hand. "Finally, I pick up this book."

It had been a year since George MacDonald's novel had been published, and Matthew had been giving excuse after excuse as to why he hadn't started it yet. Now, he knew that to offer up any more would render him pathetic and not a very good friend. Besides, George would be coming through in two weeks' time, and Matthew swore he would not be found wanting again. The man could only take his friend's lack of enthusiasm as insulting.

Folding his pillows in half and making a bigger stack of their softness, he leaned back and began. But only halfway through the first paragraph, the fantastic world of MacDonald's own design blurred into one of Matthew's dreams, and the weary young vicar fell fast asleep.

CHAPTER ❖ THIRTY-FOUR

It was certainly a charming little dwelling crouched there in the rapidly fading daylight. Aged brick peeked through the dark tendrils of ivy that clung to the side of the house like stubborn babies to their mamas. Window boxes, crowded with red tulips and variegated ivy, rested beneath rather large windows for the size of the cottage. The frames were painted white. Freshly done. Everything seemed crisp and cherished, as though the occupants viewed their dwelling as part of the family.

Sylvie stood on the small porch while the countess waited in the hired coach. She knew it was late, but there was no place else to go, and she didn't want to spend yet another night in an inn. If Rene gave her the address, obviously it would be all right if they showed up at such a time. She would have been here sooner had he not mistakenly written down "Bath" as the city of destination. By God's grace the cab driver knew the road was actually in the town of . . . what did he say? Sounded something like Sinsick. Apparently not all the English spoke as clearly as Aggie! So here she stood, alone on an unknown doorstep, a gleaming black door awaiting her fist. She tapped four quick raps.

No matter where this mysterious person lived, or how the town was pronounced, Rene would have never recommended someone unkind, would he? Still, she could not quell the nervous fluttering in her stomach.

As she raised her fist to knock once more, the door opened wide before she could again rap upon its shiny surface. A face, made gruesome by the candle held beneath it, appeared out of the darkness. A face bearing the raised redness of a large, consuming birthmark.

"Miranda!" Sylvie declared with surprise and relief, remembering Matthew's description of his sister. Everything would be fine now, or as close to fine as she could hope. Rene had sent her to the one man who would never hurt her, unknowingly coming to her rescue once again. In her overwhelming relief, she stepped backward, fell off the door stone with a cry, and landed in the soft dew-strewn grass.

Miranda was down by her side in an instant, bending over her. From over her shoulder, Sylvie saw him, silhouetted in the doorway. "I heard a cry," he said in a voice still filled with sleep.

"A woman," was all his sister reported, cradling Sylvie's head in her arms. "She knew my name, though I swear to you I've never seen her before."

Sylvie knew he could not yet see her face in the darkness. And, now that he was outside in the darkening twilight, she could see only his form, the familiar, athletic grace with which he moved. The curly hair was lifted slightly by the breeze. He hurried to her side, and with Miranda's help lifted her to her feet.

"She's expecting, Mate," Miranda said tenderly. "She must need our help."

Then the lamplight spilling out the doorway reached her face. And he saw her, really saw her. He could barely choke out her name. "Sylvie." He clutched her hands to his chest. "You're here, on my doorstep." His voice was filled with wonder.

"Matthew. It's you!"

"Sylvie?" Miranda asked. "This is Sylvie?"

"Yes. I can hardly believe it. Unless of course, you and I are both having the same dream, Mira."

Without even thinking about it, she threw herself into his arms. He was here, he was her refuge. Everything she could ever want.

"No indeed," Miranda said officiously, hurrying toward the door. "I assure you, Brother, this is no dream. Let's get her inside and resting. I'll put a pot of strong tea on the boil and get some warm blankets."

Matthew swept her up off her feet, following after Miranda. Sylvie was here, in his arms! She couldn't reconcile the thought.

"Matthew, I'm so glad it was you," she breathed, her breath caressing his stubble-lined jaw. And he tightened his arms as her body went yet more limp, with relief.

"What are you doing here, Sylvie? Where is Rene?"

She sighed deeply before she spoke the words, preparing herself for more questions to follow. "Rene is dead. He sent me here, me and the countess."

Matthew laid her carefully on a sofa in the drawing room. "The countess?"

"She's waiting in the carriage outside."

"I didn't notice a vehicle at the roadside."

Miranda entered the room piled with blankets. "Say no more, Mate. I'll go fetch her. The poor dear must be tired and grief stricken."

Miranda slipped out the door. Matthew laid a hand on Sylvie's cheek. After the cold nights of traveling, the warmth it provided her was like heaven itself. She was with him! *Oh, God,* she prayed, *let this not be a dream.*

"Mira knows everything," he said, "about what passed between us in France."

"Good."

"How is the countess?"

"Not well, Matthew. Not well at all."

The front door opened again as Matthew whispered. "Mira's healing touch will see you both in good stead."

"And you, Matthew? What will you do now that we have come to stay?"

At her words an expression of joy infiltrated his eyes. "I will never leave you again."

His words covered her completely, a shelter in the storm. She didn't know if they were enough, but until she learned more about what had brought them here, they would have to be. She could trust him, and she would.

Miranda led the countess into her own room. Fresh sheets adorned the small bed, and a bouquet of daffodils perfumed the dimly lit, Spartan chamber. Obviously, the old woman noticed little.

"Thank you, child," she said, patting Miranda's hand. "You are a dear girl." The words were automatic.

"You deserve a good night's rest, my lady. I'm drawing the curtains so that you will be able to sleep as long as possible in the morning."

The countess, dry-eyed but deep-eyed, turned away and sat quietly on the bed. Miranda helped the old woman out of her clothes, dropped one of her own freshly laundered nightgowns over her head, and tucked the weary body between the sheets.

She turned down the lamp on the face of grief, now in repose. *Good, then*, Miranda thought as she shut the door. And she prayed for a healing sleep for the dowager countess de Boyce. A sleep that would refresh the body, encourage the soul, and heal the heart.

She trod thoughtfully into the sitting room, wondering if she should disturb her brother and the young countess. She decided they might both need a little distraction, and she was curious about the woman who had stolen her brother's heart.

"Well, Matthew. You must properly introduce me to her ladyship."

The woman lifted a weary hand. Sylvie. Mate's Sylvie. "Please Miranda, call me Sylvie. This is hardly the time for such formalities, and I so appreciate your hospitality to the countess and myself."

"All right, then." Miranda sat on a chair opposite the settee on which the two were somewhat awkwardly perched. The initial relief upon seeing each other had obviously turned to discomfort. "I heard you say your husband was dead. What happened?"

Matthew cleared his throat. "Sylvie . . . if you do not—"

"It's all right. If you're kind enough to take us in, you should know the risks involved."

"Risks?" Brother and sister spoke the word together, and Miranda felt the gooseflesh rise on her arms and back.

Sylvie's revelation was chilling indeed. "Someone is seeking my life, and I don't even know his name."

⌒

"If only I could have given him a proper funeral," Racine whispered to the woman who cradled her hand in her own and matched her tears one for one. This angel, this woman they called Miranda.

"There now, my lady. I know. But chances are your son's body was washed out to sea. An honorable way to be buried certainly."

Racine sniffed, dabbed at her nose. "That is true."

Two weeks had passed since they had arrived at the vicarage, and this was the first time she had ventured forth from the cottage. And the woman who had pulled her from her grief-filled stupor walked beside her, tall, strong, and yet so marred by her birthmark. It hadn't taken Racine or Sylvie long to get used to it, and now they saw right through it, choosing to concentrate on the light blue eyes and the coarse, straight, glossy blond hair.

"And he wouldn't want his death to take you down to the grave, my lady. Isn't that right?"

"Oh no! Rene . . . he loved my zest for life. As did his father. It was what attracted Phillipe to me in the first place."

"So he would expect you to carry on, like you did after the death of your husband."

Racine felt her chin stiffen a bit, her heart lighten a little. The girl was right. "It would be dishonoring to his memory to do otherwise, I suppose."

"There, that's so." She tucked Racine's arm through her own, and warmly patted the fragile hand as they continued down the cow path. "And you're here now. God has brought you to Matthew and me."

Racine knew that was so. The two had done all they could to help them, to comfort them, to love them. Certainly this was a gift from God himself. "I have always liked Matthew. He was the only friend Rene ever had that was good for him. I should not have let him get so close to some of those boys, but he always seemed a lonely sort and I never was one to say no to those eyes of his. We all want our children to be accepted." The sigh she heaved was jittery and filled with regret.

"We can't see what the future will hold, my lady. If you were guilty of being too easy on your son, well, at least you loved him, and that means more than anything."

If only she knew where his soul was now. "A little discipline might have gone a long way."

"It's too late for that now, my lady. Do not grieve over what you did wrong. Just remember him in the good times. Remember how your heart was filled with the love you bore for him. It will be much easier on you in the long run, I'm sure. What's done is done."

"Yes, you're right. I know. But I still cannot help thinking it is all my fault."

Miranda put her arm around her. "That's a mother's prerogative, my lady."

Racine stopped, turned, and kissed Miranda on the cheek. "You bring to me the peace of God, Mira, for he truly lives within you."

"Yes, he does, my lady. And he truly lives in you. He has not forgotten you."

She felt a ghost of a smile light upon her lips. "No, you are right. I did not believe for a moment that he had."

"So then, your faith will see you through, my lady." She spoke the words with such confidence Racine couldn't help but believe her.

"Yes, it will, Miranda. And now it is time that I let it do just that. But how hard it is to let go."

When they returned from their walk, Racine went directly to her room and pulled out her copy of the Scriptures. Then she set about calling on God to forgive her sins and heal her troubled heart. It was going to be a long road, she knew. But the Savior would be with her on the journey. Some valleys would have to be revisited, some hills climbed more than once before the varied landmarks were conquered for good. But God would supply all her needs. His love was rich and unending. He would see her through.

CHAPTER ❖ THIRTY-FIVE

"S o this is the mysterious houseguest the village has been buzzing about!"

Sylvie was almost thrown back by the forceful speech that bombarded her from beneath the large, ostrich-plumed hat. She answered from beneath her own hat, the yellow feathered concoction she was wearing the day she had first seen Matthew. It was the only piece of memorabilia she had tucked inside her carpetbag on the flight from France. "Yes, well, we left under such duress . . . the death of my husband . . . that we only felt able to venture out very recently."

"Sylvie Woods, did you say your name was? And your mother-in-law—is she unable to come to church?"

"Doing quite well, but unable, as yet, to face strangers. She and her son were quite close."

The woman frowned, and that frown was quite all Sylvie could manage to see of her face, as the rest was concealed by the quivering brim of her hat. "She should be relying on God now to see her through. Where better to find him than on Sunday in church?"

Sylvie felt her smile go false. "Our Father is everywhere, ma'am. Not just in a sanctuary."

But Mrs. Horace P. Rooney would not be put off. "If we let up on our devotion on Sundays, he's not so near the rest of the week."

Just then, Matthew rescued Sylvie from Mrs. Horace P. Rooney's loveless legalities, flapping over in his voluminous black robes like a protective father bird. "Mrs. Rooney, I see you have met Mrs. Woods at last!"

"Indeed. Been telling her how happy we are to have her here in Swainswick."

Sylvie didn't bother to enlighten the vicar.

He smiled. "I could not have said it any better myself."

"Positively lovely, she is, Vicar. How soon are you expecting the child's arrival?" She directed the question at Matthew.

"Around the end of May," Sylvie informed her, feeling rather tart about now, but trying to sound sweet for Matthew's sake.

"Your husband passed away when?"

If it wasn't so obvious Sylvie would have been angry. "Just over two weeks ago."

"When were in you in France, Father?" Mrs. Rooney asked with a sniff.

"About a year ago." He cheerfully volunteered the information, clueless to what she was getting at. Sylvie was fuming.

That monstrous mouth frowned again. "Well, then. Whatever we can do to help. We do have a wonderful midwife here in the village—"

"And Miranda has overseen her share of births," Matthew reminded the maven pleasantly.

That frown again. "Of course if there should be complications—"

"We have a wonderful midwife in the village," he conceded with a wry smile in Sylvie's direction. "Have a blessed Lord's day, Mrs. Rooney."

The woman pulled her wrap more tightly about her. "I was hoping you'd come for dinner, Vicar, but I'm sure Miranda has something lovely cooking in the oven back at the vicarage."

"As always, Mrs. Rooney, you are correct. But another time, perhaps?" He took her hand and gave it a squeeze. His eyes smiled along with his pleasant mouth. Sylvie couldn't believe the woman's frigid demeanor failed to thaw at the touch of Matthew's warm charm.

"Of course."

And when the hat sailed off like a fully cargoed schooner, there was less of a smile beneath it than there was when it left port earlier that morning.

"I see the charm you exhibited in France wasn't something you toted along just for the trip," she said later, aching to put her hand in his as they made the short walk together back to the manse. "That Mrs. Rooney was even worse than you had warned me of. The old crow." Sylvie muttered the last part under her breath. "To think she was actually insinuating my pregnancy was anything other than—"

"You must excuse her, Sylvie. The older women at St. Jude's . . . they feel somewhat of an ownership over me. 'Tis the nature of the beast, I know, and it is not always something I enjoy. In fact, it can be quite ghastly. But they do rely on me, and when they think my services to them may be in jeopardy . . ." He lifted his shoulders in a shrug.

"I think I understand. What woman wouldn't want you for her slave?" she chuckled. "And such a dependable one at that!"

Matthew rolled his eyes in good humor. "Laugh all you like, but it seems my life is to be spent in your service as well, Sylvie."

"Something for which I am most grateful," she muttered, almost feeling guilty for how quickly she was recovering after the death of Rene. "To think that my husband actually sent me to you, especially knowing how we once felt about each other."

"It proves he loved you more than either you or he realized. Rene would have been a good man if only he had let himself be, if only he had turned to the Savior. Who knows what he might have prayed as he was dying, Sylvie? I shared with him the way of salvation many times. But in the end, in his final act of letting that yacht go without him, to protect you and the child, he lived up to his human potential."

How could she not remember the horrible scene at the dock? "He died with honor."

"It is all any man can hope to do. And now you must live the same way. Bear his son and train him to stand in his father's shoes."

"So much responsibility."

They stood before the door of the cottage, the aroma of roast beef, potatoes, and carrots drifting pleasingly out the open window. The hum of the conversation between Miranda and the countess wound through the breeze. "But you are not alone, Sylvie."

No, Sylvie thought, *I am not alone. All around me are people I love: Matthew, the countess, even Miranda*. And God was kind and loving, strengthening her each day, fortifying her each minute.

She knew she would make it just fine. Rene would have expected nothing less. It was why he had married her in the first place, wasn't it? Well, actually, Rene's reason for marriage had been her fortune. The thought saddened her deeply because it was so true.

⁓

"What do you mean you lost them?"

Claude Mirreault's voice thundered against the rafters of his dining room. Apparently, he had been enjoying a tender filet of beef, but not anymore.

Didier stood sturdy on his feet. He'd been through worse with his boss. Even so, a blush struggled over his gnarled features. "Actually we never found them. London's a big place, monsieur. They most probably disguised themselves."

"I told you not to come back if you didn't find her."

"Yes, sir."

"What have you to say about your failure?"

"That I'm the only man who would have stayed with you this long, and if I had never returned you would have been sore indeed?" Didier raised his eyebrows. He knew Mirreault better than Mirreault himself. And when the big man laughed, he was relieved.

"Have you any idea where they might be going?" The initial rush of rage over, Mirreault became once again a man of business, obviously refusing to give way to unproductive emotions.

"None, sir."

Mirreault tapped his fork thoughtfully against the rim of his plate. His face flashed a quick expression of weariness. "This seems to be altogether more trouble than it is worth. 'Tis not surprising, really, that Youngblood somewhat played the traitor. But it was upstanding of him to pay up for de Boyce. It was the least he could do, I suppose, seeing that he took away any chance for the count to pay up for himself. Hard to get the bank from the bottom of the Seine." He boomed a laugh, then stabbed a piece of steak with his fork. "He has quit Paris for good now, searching for the de Courcey wench himself. And I should be quite satisfied, but I must admit the entire affair rankles me terribly and I am not certain for the reason of this."

Didier shrugged, sitting down when a plate for him was brought in from the kitchen. "Well, sir, I think I know the reason. You've gone lo these twenty years without losing a single payback. If you ask me, Youngblood's paying up doesn't count. No sense in spoiling your record now." If Claude Mirreault went soft, he'd be out of a job.

Mirreault cut off another piece of steak and popped it into his mouth, the devil back into his eyes once again. "Thank you for reminding me, Didier. For a moment I was considering dispensing with the whole affair."

"Money's money, sir."

"Indeed. And the love of it is the root of all evil. Never forget that."

Didier looked up into his master's eyes and shuddered. "I won't, sir." He choked out the words, then swallowed a bite of his meat, cooked a bit too rare for his own liking.

Mirreault tapped a fork against his cheek thoughtfully. "Who knows what secrets Sylvie de Courcey wishes to keep quiet? There may be a way to claim her money yet. Blackmail has always been a game most enjoyable." He laid down his fork, resolved. "Yes, we must find Youngblood, and thus through him the de Courcey wench. Let us hope Yves can keep a trail on him."

"That should be no problem, sir."

Mirreault waggled his fork at Didier. "Didn't you say she was expecting?"

"Soon." Didier nodded. "It shouldn't be long until she delivers."

"Hmm. Have we ever done a kidnapping?"

Didier shook his head. "Don't even entertain the idea, sir. There are a lot of things I'll do, but when it involves children . . ."

But Mirreault was already lost in thought.

～

"Supper is ready, your lordship." A stiff butler bent slightly at his waist as he relayed the news to his master, the new earl of Cannock. David Youngblood suspended his stare at the fire to look up. First at the portrait of his father, then at the same man's butler, now his own servant.

"Any news, Wilby?"

Wilby shifted his gaze away from his new master's face. "I'm sorry, my lord. None since yesterday morning. As you know."

Youngblood heard the insulting tone, but his mind was already occupied with new strategies to reprimand the man's impertinence.

"She is not in London, Wilby. I am almost certain of it."

The butler shifted from one foot to the other. "Most probably not, sir."

"Send word that the house in Scotland should be prepared. I will be leaving London within a week's time. Away from the likes of you, Wilby."

"I'm sorry you feel that way, sir."

"No. I do not believe you are. I see that it is you standing there, but your eyes are the same as his. You have taken up his cause, a cause that, I will not hesitate to remind you, is not your own."

"If that's the way you feel, sir . . ."

"It is. And I will tell you something else, Wilby. Once you have seen to the closing of this house, you will find employment for the rest of the staff, and when that is finished, you will find employment for yourself."

The man's face began to turn pink. "But sir . . ."

Youngblood stood to his feet and strode across the grand entry hall toward the dining room, Wilby at his heels getting redder by the second. "It is a new day, Wilby. I am the earl now, and I shall not have my own staff looking upon me with the distaste you have become so accustomed to experiencing. I'm not the little boy whose ears you used to box, and it would have stood you in good stead to have remembered that. I will be master here, in Cannock, Cornwall, and in Scotland as well. You might want to warn them up there that heads will roll if I find even the smallest amount of disrespect such as I have found here."

By this time, Wilby was shaking with anger, but he kept his voice as calm he could. "You can't do this, you upstart! You'll take all that your father worked so hard to preserve and let it slip through your fingers like sand!" His gaunt face purpled with righteous indignation.

"Do not seek to transform my father and mother into saints!" Youngblood spat. "They were frivolous party goers who cared about no one but themselves. Not even their own children rated high enough on the social roster to be part of their calendar."

"You shan't say such things about them!"

"I will. I am the master here, Wilby."

"Then I am leaving."

"Right now?" Youngblood laughed.

The man turned flustered. "Well—"

"No. You said it, Wilby. Get out, right now. Pack your things and be gone. You will receive no references."

"A reference from you means nothing anyway."

"As you say, then. And if I find you in the kitchens spewing this story to the others, I will have your head." He dismissed the man, who stomped up the front stairs to the servants' quarters. Youngblood bellowed into the hallway. "Mrs. Wooten! Come now!"

The housekeeper appeared a minute later, straightening the small cap on her head, smoothing her apron. A genuine smile creased further her lined face. Youngblood told her of the recent developments. "And if you do all I ask, and do it well, there will be a place for you in Scotland, if you like."

"Oh yes, sir. And for Mr. Wooten, too?"

"Of course. And he shall be my new butler. You may go now. I've worked up an appetite."

She curtseyed and clicked back to the kitchen, where he was certain a tray of scones was baking just for him. Mrs. Wooten had been baking scones just for him ever since he could remember. And they were always served up with tea and kindness, with a little bit of love sprinkled on top. The only bit of love he had ever known. Until his father found out and sent him packing up to Scotland! He was surprised the Wootens weren't dismissed, but they had once, after all, been servants of the illustrious Buckinghams.

Youngblood entered the dining room, feeling somewhat stronger of purpose. He had been putting off the bloodbath, weighted down by his search for Sylvie. But the time for mercy was over. It truly was a new day. He would find Sylvie and there would be a new regiment of staff ready to serve her, meet her every need, and love her as he did.

An antique sideboard almost buckled under the weight of heavy, covered dishes, and the aroma of supper made even the agitated Youngblood hungry. He had searched the streets of London for days, asked a thousand people a thousand questions. Nothing.

She was not in London. He was certain of it. Would he not feel her presence? Would he not know instinctively if she was within several miles of him?

Now, there was nothing to do but wait. Sporting a well-greased palm, an old Scotland Yard inspector was searching for her, starting in Dover. So Youngblood himself would go north and bide his time, maybe even take in a little fishing, strive to become the true gentleman of whom Sylvie was worthy.

Besides, there was someone up in Scotland he very much wanted to see. Someone he had been neglecting for far too long.

Matthew slammed his fist down on the table, upsetting the ink pot and making a mess of his sermon. He roared in frustration. It was market day and the younger women were gone anyway. The countess was napping downstairs. Why not let the raging turmoil out of its cell for a while?

The truth was, he was madly in love. All the feelings he had tried to squelch after he returned from France were back, and stronger than ever. She was here with him. Living under his roof. Blooming with child. And there wasn't a thing he could do about it.

How he was longing to pull her into his arms, to tell her of his feelings. Memories of their time together in France, when they looked deeply into each other's eyes and declared their love, wouldn't stop playing in his uppermost thoughts. What was happening to him? How could he withstand such temptation?

Sylvie had made herself clear enough on the way home from church. *How we used to feel about each other*, she had said in such a cavalier manner. Her words had cut him to the heart. He could hardly believe she had thrown away their love so easily.

Should he confront her? Ask if her heart still belonged to him? Then what?

What if it did? The child was coming. The countess was still here, by her mere presence reminding them all of Rene. It would be years before they could marry under such stressful circumstances.

He had to get in touch with Youngblood. Find out what was going on in France. Truly an awful situation. The spilled ink pot didn't seem so bad in comparison.

"I need a change of scenery," he muttered, as he quickly cleaned up the mess, then slipped on his coat and hat. One of the parishioners, a farmer named Wilson Dudham, had given him leave long ago to take one of his horses any time he needed transportation. Matthew availed himself of the privilege and was soon galloping down the road to the city of Bath, lost in thought.

CHAPTER ❖ THIRTY-SIX

"Mate got into his first fight when he was only four years old," Miranda said, answering Sylvie's question as they took their tea outside in the garden, eating cheese sandwiches and drinking Darjeeling. "He was a handful, my lady. I can tell you that. And I remember!"

The ladies were basking in the warm April day—stretching their legs, feeling the sun warm the material of their gowns. All three had been sewing almost nonstop for the past week, making dresses for Sylvie and the countess. As tending to such work is guaranteed to do, they formed a womanly bond with each other, discussing large matters, small matters, and everything in between. Many stitches were placed amid laughter, many amid tears. "So he's always had a temper?"

"From the time he was born. Of course, I wasn't in the room when Mum gave birth to him, but I was waiting in the hallway and the holler he emitted rang out through the corridors so loudly the entire staff came running. It was as if being forced into the world from the pleasant confines of the woman was a great effrontery to him."

"Isn't it to us all?" the countess remarked. "We are in the womb, safe and warm, and then, without much warning, cold air is surrounding us, bright light, and nothing is ever the same from there."

"Matthew has seemed to be fighting ever since. He was a very strong little lad. But, well, you've both seen that irresistible sparkle he gets in his eyes at times. We could never be upset with him for very long. There are definitely two sides to my brother."

Sylvie set down her sandwich and sipped her tea. "You two seem so close. I had a brother, you know. Guy. He died last year."

"Matthew told me. I'm sorry. I don't know what I'd do without Mate."

"He's a good man."

Miranda lifted her brows and nodded. "Yes. That's always the word I use to describe him myself. Good. Matthew is a very good man."

"Why do you call him Mate?" the countess inquired, now finished with her sandwich and picking at the grass beneath her fingers.

Miranda chuckled. "My father started that. An endearment . . . like laddie or cherie, I guess. When he was five he decided he liked it so much he wanted to be called nothing else. And now, we rarely call him Matthew. Except in the presence of others."

"It's a fitting nickname." Sylvie nodded. "He's such a good friend."

"Yes, to so many people," the countess agreed. "Where would we be without Matthew?"

Miranda smiled gently. "I've asked myself that question many, many times, my lady. God has made Matthew the answer to so many people's prayers. Many years ago he prayed that God would make him a blessing. And so he has."

So Sylvie and the countess sat together, enjoying more stories at Matthew's expense. It was easy to forget they had left a raging storm in France, for neither wanted to face the fact that somehow, someday, they must return and deal with the problem once and for all.

But for now, the English sunshine and the love of Matthew and Miranda was what they needed . . . to heal them, to sustain them, and to ultimately bolster them for what lay ahead.

When Matthew hurried into the garden fifteen minutes later, they were still having fun at his expense. Miranda was more full of stories than a proud mother. "But the best story is what we Wallaces have come to call the 'I'll-have-another-oyster' incident."

Matthew put his hand over his sister's mouth. "And we'll just *keep* it amongst the Wallaces, thank you very much! Besides, I have something to tell all of you. The news of your disappearance, as well as the countess's, has reached our shores."

"Did they find the count?" Miranda asked.

"Apparently, Rene's body was never found. He is presumed missing as well, along with all of you."

Sylvie's eyes turned flat. "Maybe his body will never surface."

"It would not be so unusual."

She rubbed her belly. "He told me to wait until autumn, then to contact David Youngblood."

Matthew nodded. "Then wait until the appointed time. Until after the baby is born at least. Viscount Blackthorne will only complicate matters at this point."

"I agree," the countess said with a firm nod. "Let us leave him out of our affairs as long as we possibly can."

Sylvie knew David held the key. He was Rene's only true confidante. She would find out the name of the man who sought her from Youngblood. But the last thing she wanted was to have the special time of the birth stolen from her by future scandal.

"It's best to leave things as they are until after the babe is born," Miranda said, now knitting a little bonnet. "Let God be God and trust him to prepare your way to freedom."

The man could only be described as a presence. Wavy brown hair grew back from a forthright forehead. A thick beard sprouted from a strong jaw. The piercing yet merry eyes sparkled with intelligence, imagination, and love. His expression assured as well as challenged.

George MacDonald had come. And Matthew Wallace was beside himself with gratitude as he ushered the gentleman into the house.

"Take me right into the kitchen, Mate," MacDonald boomed. "I smell your sister's roasted chicken. And it was an arduous journey to be sure."

Miranda accepted his warm embrace, introduced him to Sylvie and the countess, and seated him near the window where he always sat when he visited. The formalities quickly conquered, Miranda's luscious meal of roasted chicken, ragout of onions, and crusty rolls was eaten with gusto by both of the men as they chatted comfortably. The women, picking at their own food, looked on.

"So, Mate, have you read my book yet?"

Matthew looked down, feeling sheepish. "Well, actually, George . . ." He wiped his mouth. "I'm dreadfully sorry—"

"Oh, don't worry about it," MacDonald interrupted. "If you've known how many people that claim to love me haven't so much as cracked the book open, you'd be astounded."

"Well, *I* read it," Miranda piped up. "And I loved it."

Matthew could have strangled his sister just then. "Typical of Miranda."

"Never a truer woman ever born!" MacDonald effused, obviously happy to hear she had read his novel. "I want to find out later what you thought about it, but first, I'm terribly curious about these two lovely ladies here."

In his usual inquisitive yet kind manner, MacDonald drew the entire story out of Sylvie and Racine, ushering them into his confidence with an ease that astounded the others.

It wasn't long, however, before Matthew escorted him upstairs to his study, in which MacDonald's presence pushed all the furnishings, the books, even the walls into a twilight of insignificance.

Matthew pulled a chair nearer to his desk and MacDonald sat with a contented, full-bellied sigh. "Your sister cooks a meal almost as fine as my Louisa does. Fare like that puts heart into a man. Among other things." He looked at Matthew pointedly.

"It's that obvious, is it?"

"Love, if it is truly that, should be."

"I do not know what to do."

"Do you have a heart, Matthew?"

Matthew smiled. "Too much of one, it appears."

"And did the Creator fashion it?"

Matthew nodded, knowing exactly where the conversation was going.

"Then trust he who knit your heart. If it is truly love that your heart bears for this worthy woman, trust him who made it capable to love her."

"That is it? Could it be so simple?"

"God's will is not a complex mystery, Matthew. You know that. It is mankind and their propensity to order and arrange all things, even the very God they pretend to serve, who hide him in shifting shadows."

Matthew knew he was right. "But her husband is so recently dead, and in my heart I only want to marry her. To make her my own. But that cannot be for a while yet."

"She loves you, that much is certain," MacDonald chuckled knowingly.

"We loved each other before she wed. Now I don't know if her feelings are the same. What I do know is that she needs love now more than ever."

MacDonald slapped his knees and rose to his feet. "Well, then, with the bairn on the way, and the natural father dead, I would say you've a mission of mercy as well as love."

"Isn't love merciful?" Matthew asked, hearing Miranda's footsteps on the stairs. Bringing them tea, he assumed.

"Not always, my friend. And what of Isabelle?" MacDonald wondered. "This delightful Sylvie is not a replacement, I hope."

"No, no. I have loved two women well in this life, George. One was too good for this earth, the other too strong to be cut off so soon. I love Sylvie for all the reasons Isabelle wasn't meant to survive."

"So you do not fear she will leave you as Isabelle did?"

"No. Sylvie simply would not have such a thing."

The next three days of MacDonald's visit proved to be a time of spiritual refreshing for Matthew. Surely God was leading him in the direction his heart so wished him to go. This was the woman he loved, and he knew it was time to do something about it.

~

"I love you."

He could not wait any longer. They were sitting midst a forest of trees that had begun assembling behind the village centuries before when the field was left to the devices of nature and time. A spring softness permeated the air, and the sun was high and clear.

"It is true, Sylvie. I love you."

And so he stood, arms folded protectively across his heart, watching her sitting there so round and beautiful with the dappled blush of the sunshine on her cheeks, eyes shining. A smile sweetly stretched across her face, but she said nothing.

So he filled in the silence.

"I know it is not the right time to tell you. With the babe coming, Rene's passing so soon. But I love you. You are here with me each day. I see you early in the morning, in the evenings, before me at each meal. My love." He reached out and tenderly cradled her cheek. "You have been that since the moment I saw you, Sylvie. And I can no longer live beneath the same roof without you knowing how I feel. You may spurn my love, never wish to speak with me again, but I am a man who deals terribly with secrets. I always have and I always will."

He finished the speech, breathing in deeply. There. He had said it. And there she sat, so still. "Well, Sylvie?"

She held out her hand. "Are you quite finished?"

"Of course."

"I was just making sure. We've lived through this scene before and you know, I do believe it's quite a lovely thing when two people twice get to declare their love for each other for the first time."

He froze, feeling relief, then a passion of emotion. "So you are saying you feel the same?"

Her small hand caressed his sturdy jaw. "I never stopped loving you, my Matthew. Of necessity I pushed you from my mind as much as I possibly could, but only because my heart was still yours. Fear not, for I love you. I always have and I always will." She rapidly blinked, her eyes misting with tears of joy and sweet contentment.

"Oh, Sylvie. My sweet love."

With tenderness, he pulled her into his arms, gently ... awkwardly, taking care not to squeeze her too tightly. His lips touched hers tentatively, then, at the taste of her ... so sweet and fresh, so loving ... he pressed more firmly, unable to be close enough to this woman for whom he would willingly give his life.

They kissed each other hungrily, making up for time that was lost, wondering what would happen now. Finally he pulled his mouth from hers, and she sighed in contentment as he held her quietly in his arms and thanked God for bringing her back to him.

"What now, Matthew?" So certain he had the answer, Matthew realized.

"We wait. Until the babe is born, my love." If the child should be a boy, a whole new set of complications would come rising to the surface.

"Will you love this child, my darling?"

"As it is an extension of its mother, I do not see how I can help but do so."

"What about Rene?"

They searched each other's eyes, and saw the pain of Rene's death, a friend of both, was still fresh. "I think he would be glad you are happy, Sylvie. Don't you?"

"Yes. I do. And it's true then, what you said before, you'll never leave me?"

"Never, Sylvie. I will always be yours. My heart I willingly place in your hands."

The woman before him lifted his broad hand to her mouth and softly kissed each knuckle on the back. "I was always meant to be yours, my love. And I humbly accept your heart, knowing it is a gift from God."

A sudden burst of joy flooded through him, and he stood to his feet and lifted her into his arms. Spinning with the maelstrom of his emotions, he pulled her close and kissed her again. "You have made me the happiest man alive, Sylvie de Courcey. Nothing will ever destroy this moment."

"No, darling. Nothing ever will."

Two shrewd eyes watched the exchange from far away. And an idea sprang to life in the brain that rested beneath the large, gaudy hat. This was quite a development. Quite a development indeed!

CHAPTER ❖ THIRTY-SEVEN

Grabbing fistfuls of sheet, Sylvie yelled out as a contraction ripped through her uterus. Any pain she had ever experienced before this paled in comparison. The countess, standing beside her, swabbed the sweat from her brow with a cool, damp rag. Excitement, apprehension, eagerness touched her brow.

Sun streamed in the open window of the bedchamber, and the breeze followed suit, providing a bit of relief and causing the dust particles to dance in a frenzied manner in the stream of light.

Sylvie breathed in, gasping for air as the pain subsided and the rock-hard mound of her stomach somewhat softened, showing the basest form of the child which lay down her left side. The babe was quiet. Sylvie looked up and smiled weakly at Miranda, who sat on a chair by the foot of the bed. Matthew's sister knew exactly what she was doing.

"Get ready, my lady. Another contraction should be coming soon. The head is just beginning to crown. It won't be long now." Miranda rubbed a sleeve across her sweaty brow.

But by the time the contraction came, Sylvie was too tired to push.

"You must try, my lady. Please," Miranda pleaded. "It's dangerous to stop now."

"Yes, cherie," the countess cooed soothingly, kissing her fevered brow. "If I could do it, you can. You are a strong woman."

"I want Matthew," Sylvie grated. "I want him here with me."

"Get him then," Racine urged. "This child must be born, and safely. If his presence gives Sylvie strength, so be it."

"But my lady," Miranda gently argued. "It is unseemly for a man to be here in the birthing chamber. And unmarried as he is . . . it could cause a scandal. Do not ask it of him. Should anyone find out, it could ruin his reputation."

The countess twisted the rag in her hand, and Sylvie could tell she was trying to hold her temper. "We won't tell anyone, Mira. Please do as I ask and do it now."

"It's useless to argue with her," Sylvie whispered, grateful when the countess put the cool rag upon her brow.

"Leave the decision up to him," the countess said.

Opening the door slightly, Miranda inserted her face into the opening. "She calls for you, Mate."

Sylvie heard his footsteps immediately, as they moved from the couch in the sitting room, down the small corridor, and into the bedroom. Miranda discreetly covered Sylvie until Matthew stood at the head of the bed, holding her hand.

"Another one is coming now!" Sylvie shouted, holding tightly onto Matthew's hand, grating her teeth beneath the weight of the pain, the iron tightening of her womb.

"Push!" Miranda cried. "As hard as you can!"

"Yes," the countess breathed beside her. "Let us see this child now, my dear. His time has come."

Blinded by the rage of agony, Sylvie bore down, pushing with the strength she had forgotten she owned.

"Harder, my lady. Please. Harder!" Miranda urged.

Sylvie didn't know where she found more fortitude. Perhaps it was the firmness of Matthew's hand, the feel of his warm breath on her cheek as he prayed in her ear that more strength would be given her. It was a whirlwind of sight, feeling, and sound, and it spiraled her up, up with an urgency she had never felt before. The child. The child.

"Now!" She screamed a primal shout, her head feeling as if it would explode beneath the pressure.

"The head! The head is out!" Miranda encouraged loudly, grabbing a clean cloth and wiping the tiny face. "One more good hard push, my lady. If the rest of the body is as beautiful as this little face, heaven has lent us an angel!"

Hearing the words of Matthew, still petitioning the throne with a spiritual might, she squeezed his hand and found the strength for one last push.

And the child was born. Sylvie went limp with exhaustion.

"It's a girl!" Miranda announced, as tears streamed down her face.

"A girl!" Sylvie huffed breathlessly. "Give her to me, Mira. Let me see her now."

With a heartbroken wail, the countess ran from the room.

Sylvie grasped Matthew's hand and held tightly, turning her face to look in his eyes. Miranda quickly wrapped the baby in soft flannel and laid her in her mother's arms. The tiny face was soon bathed in the tears of her mother, and the man who stood beside her.

"My baby," Sylvie wept. "My sweet little child." She looked back up at Matthew, knowing only one thing remained to make her life complete. "Marry me, Matthew," she rasped in a tired voice.

"I will," he promised solemnly, as if taking his vows right then.

"Make this little girl your own," she demanded.

"She already is, my love. She already is."

She named her Eve as she said she would, telling those around her bed, "If it was good enough for God the Father himself to use, then it's good enough for me." And for the next three days, Sylvie forgot there was much unfinished business that threatened the life of not only herself, but her dear little daughter. She would worry about it later, content for now to become the mother she had always wanted to be.

Mrs. Horace P. Rooney sat like a queen at court. Two other church busybodies congregated in her parlor as they did every Thursday afternoon, slurping tea and gobbling cakes. The tea was hot, the cake was sweet, and the gossip spicier than anything the biddies had partaken of in quite a while. She was in her glory.

Jonquil Marrison, a woman with the look of an ostrich—long lashes, long neck, long legs, and short arms, took a dainty bite of lemon cake and chewed rapidly. "Let me tell you. I don't think this Sylvie Woods is all we believe her to be. She doesn't sound quite . . . English. There's some twist to the way she says things and I can't quite place it. But she is a nice girl for all of that, I suppose."

"We should give her the benefit of the doubt. But the way they keep that old woman hidden!" Mrs. Horace P. Rooney added, remembering Sylvie's embrace with the vicar in the woods, but not willing to tell all just then. One did these things in stages. "I don't like it a'tall!"

"Nor do I!" chortled the final partaker of scandal tea, India Bellows—a squared off, short woman with wild, dull brown hair and a throat made large by a goiter. "All of them living in that manse . . . at our expense, mind you!"

Jonquil sat back in her chair. Her husband had a finger in every pie concerning the church. "I have to disagree with you there, India. Much as I wish I didn't." She giggled self-consciously as she took two quick bites off her cake. "The women have actually been quite generous to our parish, more than making up for the extra coal their presence consumes."

"Hmm." Mrs. Horace P. sat back with a thump, her ample bosom shuddering under the impact like two of Miranda's puddings. "When you think about what's really going on in that house, now that the baby's been born . . ." She raised her eyebrows.

"Surely you don't think . . ." Jonquil replied, nibbling faster and faster at her cake. "The birth was only a few days ago, and we all know it's impossible to—"

"Oh, *please*, Jonquil!" Mrs. Horace P. put her saucer down on the table in disgust. "Let's not go into *that!*"

Jonquil wiped the crumbs from her mouth. "I just think we might be jumping to conclusions."

"My dear, how could one not!" India Bellows bellowed. "A handsome, lonely man like our vicar . . . a beautiful girl, recently widowed. Estranged from somewhere, I can tell you that—"

"Needy," Mrs. Horace P. interjected. "That's what she is. Haven't you noticed how she hangs onto his every word?"

Jonquil, now finished with her cake, immediately reached for a tea sandwich. "But you can't blame a man for being a man, can you? He's done so much for us, ladies." The sandwich was nibbled to nothing in no time. She grabbed another.

"Heavens, no!" Mrs. Horace P. reassured her with a firm pat on her knee. "Don't you worry yourself in those regards, my dear. It's just a little talk we're having here. Just a wee chat between ladies. This should go no further, mind you."

"Definitely not!" huffed India Bellows.

Jonquil cleared her throat and popped the entire sandwich into her mouth. "Perhaps we should talk about something else."

Mrs. Horace P. Rooney grinned like a mischievous cat. "Of course, Jonquil. What a marvelous idea." The objective was obtained—Jonquil would go home to her husband Geoffrey— and soon the whole church would be abuzz with the news, for Geoffrey Marrison was the biggest gossip of them all!

"Tell us about your grandson, Mrs. Rooney," India Bellows requested. "He should be graduating from Wycliffe Hall in Oxford this year, am I right?"

"Oh, not Oxford. He's a *Cambridge* man. Will be receiving his first church assignment soon. I can only pray God commissions him to a parish nearby. We do love the boy so."

And so the talk continued, and when the moment had come to go with hats and gloves primly where they belonged, poor Jonquil Marrison had quite nibbled away her appetite for the next week.

But she would be back seven days hence. And Mrs. Horace P. Rooney would have plenty of food on hand. She certainly would.

~

The wedding plans began with a simple letter written in Matthew's hand and sent off secretly to Reverend George MacDonald. Even Miranda wasn't privy to the request. Sylvie agreed to marry him only if the engagement and wedding remain a secret, for the countess's sake, until the death of Rene wasn't so fresh.

Dear Friend,

I fear I cannot run from the delightful, provoking, glorious, frightening presence of love. As you are coming in July to address our congregation, might you consider conducting a small, secret wedding ceremony as well? As Sylvie is recently widowed, convention must not be denied. Or rather, let it be denied, but the infraction should not be shouted from the rooftops!

How wonderful it was to see you, my friend. Enclosed with this post is a gift for you from one of the members of our congregation. It was an anonymous gesture, left on my pulpit after the service last Sunday. Realizing you are not one to complain about the less-than-lucrative state of your finances, I am joyful that God has provided for you through one of the parishioners here at St. Jude's.

As always, my love to Louisa and the children. Mira is most looking forward to being with her dear friend once again. In faithful regard, I remain your good friend,

M. Wallace

Matthew sat back, thoughtful, happy. July eleventh couldn't come quickly enough. Nevertheless, he chose not to wish away the weeks in between, choosing to rest in, as his good friend George MacDonald would say, "the holy present."

~

Enraptured, Sylvie gazed down into the serene little face of her baby and felt the same explosion of love burst into her heart that always did when examining the child she had been given. The downy cheeks were still a deep rose. The dark blue eyes were usually sleepy and otherworldly; the burnished, wispy curls that barely rested on the top of Eve's little ears were so soft and comforting. And the ears stuck out just enough to make them endearing and render the child a natural pixie. Sylvie kissed the tips of both.

"*Je t'aime*, Evie," she whispered, the raging emotions of motherhood stirring throughout her heart, mind, and soul. An ecstasy like no other warmed her entire being and flooded her soul with maternal might. Her days were now filled with a parental purpose. She would do all she could to protect this child. A return to France was imminent. It had to be for a woman who would allow no one to destroy her peace again. Her peace ... and Eve's.

"It is hard to believe she is almost three weeks old," Matthew whispered into Sylvie's ear.

She turned around where she sat on the grass outside the cottage. "I didn't hear you sneak up behind me."

They neither kissed nor touched. Not out here for all to see.

"You were too busy kissing that adorable little face."

Sylvie chuckled. "Just when I think I've used up my ration of kisses for the day, twice as many more appear at my disposal."

"Motherhood suits you, my love," he murmured, the warmth of his voice covering her like a caress.

"It's easy to love such a perfect little baby," she informed him with pride. "Isn't she remarkable?"

"Perfectly beautiful ... like her mother."

"And now that her grandmother has accepted her ..." Sylvie was referring, of course, to Racine and the severe disappointment the older woman had experienced knowing the direct male line to the de Boyce title had died with her son. Sylvie, on the other hand, was quite relieved it was a girl. The de Boyce title and what was left of the estates would be inherited by a distant cousin ... and that would be that. Praise God. Her formal ties to the family were broken. There were no legal obligations concerning Eve.

"The countess will most likely dote on the child, and Eve will dote on her in return." Matthew ran a hand over the baby's soft curls again and again.

"The countess is quite infectious in those regards, isn't she?" Sylvie smiled. "This is one child who will reap the treasures of a vast storehouse of love. I have to fight both the countess and Miranda merely to hold this little one! Neither could believe I had the audacity to actually take her outside by myself this morning."

"But you would not have it any other way, would you, my love?"

"Never!" she declared fiercely, holding baby Eve tightly against her bosom. "A child can never have too much love." She remembered what it was like growing up in the cold confines of Chateau du Soleil. "I will never withhold her from the affection of others so that I might succor my own soul."

"Well said. You are a wonderful mother, Sylvie."

"God help me."

"It is obvious he is doing just that."

Matthew sat down on the grass next to his secret fiancée. "Sylvie, there is something we have to talk about. George will be here in less than a month's time."

Sylvie didn't like the way his tone suddenly dropped, then deepened. "What is it, Matthew? What troubles you on a day like this?"

He sighed and picked a long blade of grass. "Have you really thought about what you are getting into, my love, in marrying me?"

"I believe so. We love each other, and believe God has ordained these feelings we hold. What else could there be to worry about?"

"Sylvie, you are marrying a man called to be a minister of Christ. It is a humble calling, one that requires me, and you—if you so choose to accept it—to live meagerly, in service to others. In short, darling Sylvie, you will have to give up the wealth you have obtained in order to be a true servant, in order to allow me to do the work I am called to do without resentment and jealousy on the part of my parishioners. Nothing must cloud my ability to serve the Lord. As much as I love you, my darling, his calling came first, and it always will." He watched her face and reached for her hand.

Sylvie breathed in deeply, feeling hurt by what he had said.

"What is it, my love? Sylvie, tell me."

"I know your chivalry, your loyalty, and your fairness were what caused you to pose the question, Matthew. But do you know so little of my love for you that you really needed to ask?"

"No, Sylvie, I merely meant to put all my—"

"Apparently, I know you better than you know me. I know your heart, my darling. And, so that you will know mine as thoroughly, I will tell you that even such a sum as belongs to me means nothing when compared to the richness of your love. I forsake it all ... and gladly. In fact, I will do so as soon as I return to France and sort out all the unknown details that will restore our lives to order. My father's will is still being sorted out. There may not be much left. I may have to sell off the land to pay off his debts, and whatever is left will be put into Eve's name, to be handed down to her when she reaches adulthood."

Matthew squeezed her hand. "If I tell you I love you one more time, will you become sick of me?"

She laughed, feeling so wanted, so cherished. "You could never tell me enough, my darling. Say it again, and give me cause to rejoice."

"Then, I love you. I love you. I love you."

"And I love you, my Matthew. Your love has transposed my life from sadness to joy."

Just then little Eve stirred from her nap, opened her eyes, and blinked at the bright summer sun that poured down upon her fair, sweet face. Simultaneously, Matthew and Sylvie leaned down and kissed her on top of her wee round head.

Miranda ran into the cottage, a basket full of staples she had brought from the small store in the village swinging on her arm. At such a speed, her skirts were far behind her and she shut them in the door. Her basket sailed through air as she was jerked to a premature halt.

Matthew, making himself a pot of tea, instinctually raised his arms and caught the basket in midflight.

"Oh, Mate!" Miranda gasped. "I just heard the most awful buzzings in the village. Oh dear, it's just too awful to be true!

How can they say such things?" She smoothed her hair with a shaky hand, her birthmark twice as purple as normal.

"Calm down, Mira. I am just making a pot of tea. The countess is in the sitting room reading a newspaper, and Sylvie and Eve are asleep in their room. Have a seat and we will talk about this in a civilized manner."

"But Mate, you don't understand!"

"Everything's better with a cup of tea, Mira. Go hang up your bonnet, wet your face, and take some deep breaths, then tell me what is so important it made you run back from the shop like a jumpy thoroughbred."

Miranda shook her head but did as she was told. Matthew, in all actuality, wanted to give himself time to prepare for whatever it was she had to say. Mira was hardly the type to overreact. Whatever it was must be terrible indeed.

Finally, she reentered the kitchen, her coloring not so high, the fringes of her bangs moist from the washing she had given her face.

He pulled out a chair. "Now, sit down. Your tea is poured and I have sliced you a piece of cake."

"I don't think I can eat anything right now," she informed him, but gratefully took a drink of tea.

He breathed in and planted his feet wide, prepared for whatever onslaught was coming his way. "Go ahead, now tell me."

"The church rumor mill has started grinding again, Matthew, and this time you're the grain that is being ground down to dust."

CHAPTER ❖ THIRTY-EIGHT

Inside the church it was hotter than usual. *Everyone in the congregation must be here today*, Matthew mused, yet wondered why some of the more lackadaisical members of St. Jude's decided to appear on an overly warm June day.

Was it really Easter and he had forgotten?

For a split, irrational second he panicked, thought of his sermon on God's peace to his children, and wondered why he wasn't speaking on the beauty of the resurrection. Chided himself for being so nervous.

Every Sunday it was the same. He wondered why he continued to put himself through this week after week. Then one of the most loyal members of the flock, his farmer friend, Wilson Dudham, with his wife and seven children, filed in without a minute to spare. Each of them waved as he made the procession up the aisle.

Usually most of the congregation paid him scant attention as he walked to the front of the church. But this morning, as they wiped the sweat from their brows and turned down their mouths at something, they stared at him, leaning their arms on the pew backs behind them and tapping their fingers. Some tapped slow. Others fast.

The hair on the back of his neck bristled.

He knew he was in for a to-do, and he was smart enough to know it had something to do with Sylvie. The way many of the ladies' heads turned in her direction where she sat by the baptistry cradling a napping Eve, was the telltale sign that Miranda had been right.

Once at the front of the church, the candles were lit and all the pre-sermon liturgy was dispensed. It wasn't that he didn't care for the liturgy. He loved it. Nevertheless, giving his sermon sometimes rendered him nervous. He merely sought to dispense with the preliminaries so he might address his fears and offer up his personal sacrifice of word and work to those in the pews whom he served and to the God before whom he was accountable.

"Beloved in the Lord," he began, trying not to feel the battery of hostility that some of the members failed to hide. Mira hadn't been overreacting after all! "Will you please rise and recite with me the twenty-third Psalm."

Geoffrey Marrison stood to his feet.

Mr. and Mrs. Horace P. Rooney did as well.

"The Lord is my shepherd . . ." he began, with only a few other voices. "I shall not want."

Marrison pulled Jonquil to her feet.

"He maketh me to lie down in green pastures."

Marrison pulled at his wife's sleeve. She shook her head vehemently, tears overflowing onto her cheeks.

"He leadeth me—" Matthew knew what was happening. Every minister's worst fear.

Jonquil, seeing a slight nod from Matthew, meekly obeyed.

"—beside the still waters. He restoreth my soul."

They were walking out!

The Marrisons, the Rooneys, the Bellows were all out the door. Half the congregation now stood to their feet. But Matthew continued, breathing deeply between sentences to quell the tide of nausea that threatened to drown him. He felt hot; his breath came quickly.

"He leadeth me in the paths of righteousness for his name's sake. Yea, though I walk through the valley of the shadow of death, I will fear no evil—"

More and more members. More and more fathers, mothers, children, grandfathers, neighbors, and some he had considered friends. Almost the entire vestry was caught up in the mass departure.

In an absurd moment, Matthew thought, *I should have been preaching on the book of Exodus!*

"—for thou art with me—"

Yes, Lord, even now.

"—thy rod and thy staff they comfort me." His voice became softer.

May it be so.

"Thou preparest a table before me in the presence of mine enemies." And softer.

Are these not my people, my flock, my friends?

Wilson Dudham's voice, increasing in intensity and volume, imparted him with strength, and relief. The burly man's chest thrust forward, tears of manly, righteous rage streaming without apology down his leathery face. He hopped up on the pew, shouting the Scriptures.

"Thou anointest my head with oil—"

What is this, Lord? What is happening?

"My cup runneth over."

Yes. Lord, I remember your goodness. Do not leave me now. Was it his own voice which was getting stronger with each word? How?

"Surely goodness and mercy shall follow me all the days of my life, and I shall dwell in the house of the Lord forever."

Two-thirds of the congregation was gone.

Matthew slowly shook his head at those whom he knew were his friends all along, and those whom he didn't, but would never doubt again. "Do I go on?"

"Preach to us, Vicar!" an elderly lady hollered. "And let the village know that some of us believe in you and the power of the God you've always served so faithfully and so well."

"Aye, good sir!" Mrs. Dudham stood up on the pew with her hand raised in the air. "Let it be said here and now that there are some who will not abide the idle chatter and poison tongues of the gossips!"

"Preach on, sir!" Mr. Chesser, a cobbler, shouted. And the others agreed, verbally and with adamant nods of their heads.

So Matthew did just that, the support of those who loved him truly holding him up.

But when he returned to the manse, a notice was pinned to his door.

⁓

Matthew took a sip of his tea and stared out of the window.

"They can't just throw you out!" Miranda's voice raged at him. "It simply isn't done that way!"

He was drained, but he knew the best thing for everyone to do was to stick to routine. He would eat his supper, pray, then take a nap. And pray some more. "No, Mira, they cannot. They must go through the proper channels. But do not forget, the Rooneys and Marrisons carry a lot of weight and a lot of money. Whatever they want to happen will happen."

"Just like that?"

"Church for them is about power. They do not know when to be quiet or humble. It is a place to bully others, not serve them."

"But the bishop has been good to you. Jonathan won't let them do such a thing, will he?"

"He's been wanting me to move on for three years," Matthew reminded her. "And if they threaten to pull out their support, he might not have a real choice."

Sylvie was perched on the settee, Eve in her arms, and faithful Dizzy at her feet. "I should never have stayed, Matthew. I'll leave shortly. I'll go to Scotland, to Youngblood's estates there. Surely they will welcome me even if he is not there."

Mira openly displayed her dismay. "That won't be necessary. Once you and Mate are married . . ." She had been told several days before about the coming event, for Matthew hated to keep the secret from his most faithful friend and companion.

Matthew, however, disagreed. "I think the damage is done. We now have to think of a way to repair my reputation and have them accept Sylvie at one and the same time."

"It may be impossible," Sylvie spouted. "I am so … angry, my love. And you, with your temper … how can you sit there so calm?"

Matthew took her hand, and Mira's. "Right now, my rage is so great that to give place to even the most minute aspect of that feeling would be disastrous for both my ministry and the people who are trying to ruin it."

He arose, tamped his hat down upon his head, and walked out.

"What are we going to do?" Sylvie asked Miranda as they sat embroidering late in the afternoon. Dizzy was sleeping by the door. Matthew still hadn't returned, but Miranda wasn't in the least worried. In fact, it was a good sign. It meant he was thinking hard, and praying hard, and would come home more at peace than when he had left.

"I don't know, Sylvie. To tell you the truth, being here at St. Jude's all of these years, with the likes of Mrs. Horace P. and that India Bellows woman, hasn't always been easy. There are a lot of shortcomings I can accept about the human race, so I hope you don't think I'm being too judgmental. But such gossip is something I cannot abide. It's bad enough that the entire congregation knows every detail about everyone else's life, offering up opinions where it isn't their business. But this is talebearing, and false witnessing, and … and …." Much to her own dismay, Mira put her face in her hands and began to cry.

When Sylvie's soft hands descended to her shoulders, Miranda broke even further, fully allowing herself to weep. Her soon-to-be sister-in-law pulled her close and cried with her.

"How can they do this to him?" Sylvie whispered. "I do not care one whit what they think of me, Mira. But how can they do this to Matthew?"

Miranda shook her head and was grateful beyond all telling when Sylvie began to pray. But the peace that passes all understanding was veiled by a heavy curtain of fear and a decided lack of certitude. They had given their lives for these people, only to have it come to this.

The countess relaxed in the garden amidst the blooming fox-glove, which towered at the back of the border gardens rich with the scent of roses and the hues of blue lobelia and purple cone-flowers. Some black-eyed Susans congregated near a small stone birdbath. It was next to the busy little pool that Miranda had set Racine's chair.

Time to be realistic about things, Racine decided, gazing appreciatively around her at the sweet little dwelling—a house she once wouldn't have considered living in. She thought about the group that inhabited its once cheerful confines, two members in particular. They were meant to be together. And they always had been, if she hadn't been so stubborn.

She wiped a sudden tear away, wondering when it was she had come to the opinion that she was so wise, that she knew best what the hearts of others should feel.

A shadow darkened her lap. Sylvie, holding Eve in her arms, blocked out the sun.

"What brings tears to your eyes on such a lovely afternoon?" Sylvie asked, her beautiful golden eyes darkened by yet more concern. For certainly, the situation at St. Jude's weighed them all down.

Racine took a deep breath. "I must ask your forgiveness, child."

"Whatever for?"

"Come, let me hold that little one while you bring yourself a chair. She comforts me so just with her breathing. Sit down next to me and let me explain the regrets we older women are some-times forced to feel once we admit we have made mistakes."

She watched Sylvie drag a wicker chair from the small porch that jutted off the back of the cottage. Sylvie sat down, then took Racine's hand, her eyes sparkling. "Without sounding disre-spectful, I think you're overreacting just a little bit, Aunt Racine. You've done nothing to dishonor me and we both know it."

Racine sighed. "I knew you loved Matthew, and I forced you and Rene to marry, relying completely on your good graces. And now, look at where this has put you. A man seeks your life, and you have born a child without her father alive to raise her. All along you should have been with Matthew. You must forgive me for meddling in your life, child. I wish I could say I did it all because I thought it was best for you. But I knew the type of man Rene was. Deep in my heart I knew. And I thought you could better him. Your parents did not place your hand in his, Sylvie. Rather, I placed his hand in yours. Only it was really too late. This was all a dreadful mistake."

"Darling countess." Sylvie reached forward and put her arm around her shoulders. "There are no mistakes with God. We are both his children. Matthew too. And look down into the sweet face of your grandchild, and tell me she wasn't meant to be here. Tell me God's plans for her are recent and second best." She pulled a handkerchief out of her pocket and handed it Racine.

The countess laughed through her tears. "So you have finally remembered your hankie! You've learned."

"Yes. And so much more. None of it could have been possible. And now, I have precious little Eve."

"And Matthew."

Sylvie said nothing.

"You are unable to deny it, are you not, child? Do not pretend with me any longer, or worry about what my reaction might be. I know that look in the eyes of a man when they come to rest on the woman he loves. I know the blush on the cheek of a woman when she shares her heart with a worthy man." She closed her eyes, remembering. "I know what it is like to love like that."

"I cannot deny it," Sylvie whispered. "I've loved only him since the moment I first saw him."

Racine knew this was right, felt the warmth of their love trickle over her cold, aching heart. "You must marry."

"There's time for that," Sylvie responded gently.

"I overheard the conversation about what transpired this morning in church. You must marry. If not for your own benefit, then for his sake. You have my blessing, child, my full and untainted blessing. Only promise one thing."

"Anything, dear countess."

"Please let Eve always bear the name de Boyce."

"I promise."

Racine felt a wide smile slide across her lips. This was right. She was giving the girl her freedom, something the child had been crying for all of her life. Hugging Rene's child to her, she kissed the baby on the forehead and prayed that Matthew would take good care of her.

It was a prayer she was certain God would answer.

CHAPTER ❖ THIRTY-NINE

Having walked miles of countryside, Matthew returned just after midnight, grimly resolved for the days ahead. He felt stiff and bruised inside and out, but strangely invigorated by all of it. Hadn't he always loved a fight?

"I have decided to see this through," he announced, striding into the kitchen where the ladies were drinking a cup of tea. Sylvie and Miranda both rose to their feet.

"The wedding should take place soon, then," Mira announced.

Matthew looked harshly at his sister, shook his head slightly.

"It's all right, Mate. The countess has given her blessing to your relationship with Sylvie."

"Is this true?" He set his hat down upon the window ledge and held his hand out to Racine. The old woman, looking extremely exhausted, nodded slowly. She put a hand on either side of his face, drawing him down to kiss him on the forehead. "But you are not going to get off that easily, Reverend."

He smiled. "Oh?"

"As Sylvie's only living relative, I believe there is a proper order to these matters."

Matthew bowed and cleared his throat in a formal manner. "Madam, in humbleness, I am asking for the honor of your daughter-in-law's hand in marriage. May I marry this jewel of priceless worth we've both come to love so dearly?"

Racine held her hands over her heart. "My blessing is yours." She extended her hands toward him.

He kissed the backs of both her hands. "I promise I will make her happy."

Racine tilted her head. "I know that, dear boy. I wouldn't have given you her hand otherwise."

Matthew winked in Sylvie's direction. "Well, George will be coming to St. Jude's soon; we might just as well have him do the ceremony!"

"I don't know why you didn't think of it sooner, my love!" Sylvie laughed out loud, the sound so rich in the midst of the turmoil that was raging about them from all sides. Matthew was comforted by this. Their love for each other, given them by God, would see them through many more storms life would blow their way. Someday, they would look back and laugh at Mrs. Horace P. Rooney and her ilk. Someday they would clearly see the hand of God.

⁓

The plans, set in motion weeks before, came out into the light. At least as far as the family was concerned. The wedding would still be a secret from the troublemakers at St. Jude's. Matthew, rightfully so, Sylvie felt, wanted to fight the accusations for their own sake, and not appear as if he had acquiesced and entertained the lies of Mrs. Horace P. Rooney and her cohorts. He had already written to the bishop and was awaiting his judgment on the matter.

George MacDonald's letter, expressing he would be thrilled to officiate for the couple, arrived a week later, and Miranda and Sylvie found themselves in a dither with preparations for his visit. Two weeks passed, and they were into July. Only six more days until the wedding. Sylvie looked upon Matthew each day with wonder. How she could have ever doubted God's love for her was a mystery. For even in the darkest days of her life, Matthew had always been set aside just for her.

Sylvie gathered a length of sheer silk with a quick running stitch. "We are making this ensemble in record time!"

"Monsieur Worth could do no better!" Racine pronounced.

"I didn't know it was even possible to sew so quickly!" Miranda blew, as she cooled the tips of her fingers down. "This dress will be magnificent. The skirt is so full!"

The countess selected another bit of lace from the pile beside her and appliquéd the delicate scrap onto the bodice with tiny stitches. "I rather like this idea of being married in white."

"It's all the rage!" Miranda gushed. "Ever since Queen Victoria wed Prince Albert in a white gown."

"Albert in a white gown?" the countess gasped.

"Oh, no, forgive my grammar. It was Victoria wearing the white gown!" She laughed.

"Whoever wore it first, I think it is a lovely way to give oneself to the man you love." Racine patted Sylvie's knee.

Sylvie looked up from the shimmering veil. "I do too, but isn't this going a bit too far? I am a mother, for heaven's sake. And it's a secret ceremony! Why go through all this trouble just for us?"

Miranda knit her brows. "Humor me, then, would you? I always planned to make this exact dress for my own wedding. I dreamed up the design years ago, and it's so beautiful I think it would be a shame to let it go to waste."

The countess clucked her tongue in a mild rebuke. "Listen to me, dearest Mira, you will get to wear this gown one day. I know there is a man out there for you, a loving, humble man who will take as good care of you as you do him."

"I agree!" Sylvie said.

Miranda shook her head but kept a smile on her face. "I leave the hoping to you two then. As for me, I'm surrounded by those I love, and even though this situation at church grows worse each week, I am content to rest in the Lord. Not that I have much choice, mind you."

"I think it is horrible the way they have cut Matthew's salary by half!" Racine stormed. "How can they call themselves Christians?"

Miranda cocked an eyebrow. "You'd be surprised at what Christians will do to each other all in the name of the Lord."

"How can they do that, Miranda?"

"Well," Miranda sighed. "St. Jude's is a mission church. It isn't self-supporting. The archdiocese contributes quite a bit of the funds. The church itself has refused to pay their share of Mate's salary. What's coming to him is the portion from outside the church."

"What is worse is that Matthew refuses to take any money from us," the countess added. "If he does not soon learn to accept my help I shall be forced to find a new home. After all, it will not be possible to feed me and Sylvie and Eve and … and everybody!"

"God will provide for us," Miranda assured Racine. "He's never let us go hungry yet."

The countess wouldn't let it go. "Still, if I was not so aware of God's presence all day, I swear I would call down all sorts of curses upon those horrible women."

Miranda sighed. "Unfortunately, Countess, they are already cursed by the hardness of their own hearts. I don't know how this will all come to rights in the end. But it will. And hopefully they will be stronger in the Lord for it all."

"Hopefully, we all will be," Sylvie agreed.

The countess's mouth became an angry line. "You both are more Christian about it than I am. I just see them wounding three of the people I love most in the world, and I wish nothing but bad things upon them!"

Miranda laughed. As did Sylvie.

Racine continued. "So you pray for this old sinner, girls."

"And for me as well," Sylvie invited. "I've found myself sinning many times over since this has erupted."

Miranda went back to her sewing. "Thank goodness God is faithful even when we're less than godly. I see my whole world falling apart right now, yet I know God is sovereign. He has to be."

Sylvie wondered if she would ever possess such an enormous, daily faith like that owned by her soon-to-be sister-in-law.

A knock sounded from outside and Sylvie, checking the baby sleeping in the cradle beside her, arose and opened the door. "Mr. Dudham! What brings you here today?"

He held a letter in his hand. "Was in the village . . . pickin' up a few things for the wife . . . and the post came through. Told Mrs. Winslett I'd bring these over to you."

Sylvie took the letters and invited Wilson in for tea. But he raised his hands in apology. "Thank you, no. Got to be gettin' back home. Good day to you all."

Halfway down the walk he turned back around and took off his cap. "We've been prayin' for you. Thought you'd like to know."

"Thank you, Mr. Dudham," Sylvie said. It was no surprise that a man so humble and kind was a good friend of Matthew's.

When he was gone, Sylvie gently shut the door and turned to face the ladies. "Well, let's see who these are for!"

She turned over the envelope and saw Matthew's name written in a clear, yet sprawling handwriting, one she had come to know well.

Gasping for breath, she held onto the door frame for support, dropping her head in utter confusion. Behind it, the other letter was addressed to her in the same writing. She tore open the note, her eyes riveted straight to the signature at the bottom.

"What is it? What is it, child?"

Sylvie handed the envelope to the countess, then dropped onto the sofa. "It's from Rene. He's still alive."

"Praise be to God!" The countess stood to her feet. "He's alive! My son is alive!" Tears of joy poured from her eyes, and she pulled Miranda into a tight embrace.

Sylvie could only hear at that moment. Her eyes were shut against what at first seemed like an awful truth. Rene. Alive. She cast the veil aside and prayed for strength. For the countess's sake, as well as her own. Standing to her feet, she took the countess into her arms and cried with her, tears of joy and relief mixed with tears of sadness, loss, and guilt.

"Read the letter!" the countess commanded. "Please, Sylvie, read the letter."

Sylvie looked at Mira, eyes imploring her.

"Let me," Miranda said. "I'm the only one not crying."

~

Matthew felt the blood drain from his face at the news.

Oh, dear God, he prayed. The world spun around him as he placed his hat on a chair and sat down. Sylvie was pale and quiet, petting Dizzy softly. The countess and Eve were napping in her room.

"I'll make us some tea," Miranda volunteered.

"Go ahead, Matthew," Sylvie said, her voice raspy and thick. "Read it."

The words swam before his eyes, and he rubbed them. Took a deep breath.

Dear Matthew,

Most likely you think me dead, and for a time I believe I was. Indeed, I came to consciousness several minutes later, I assume, in the water, and was pulled up out of the water by a passing boat. I really don't remember much. But it was a miracle to be sure, yet I can't help but wonder if my death would have suited the matter much better. An old woman and her daughter nursed me back to the state of health I now enjoy, meager as it is. First I must inquire as to the welfare of my wife and mother, and, I assume, child. I trust my letter to Sylvie made it into her care. Most likely they are still with you in Swainswick. Of a surety you have taken good care of them. Which is why I entrusted them to you. Always you have been so faithful to all of your callings.

As you see, there is no address at which to contact me for my whereabouts change daily. I am doing much in Paris to rectify the situation of which Sylvie most likely informed you. Claude Mirreault, for that is the man's name to whom I owe a great deal of money, has finally heard that I am still alive, and seeks diligently to find me. There must be a way to bring this man to his knees and so erase my own debt. But to do so would only incriminate myself. I have done more than even Sylvie herself is aware, and hopefully the knowledge of these deeds will die with me.

Now, from the talk I have heard, Mirreault seeks Sylvie's life yet again, knowing I will inherit her fortune. He will get the money any way he can, and the talk is it has become a personal matter. My source says Mirreault had a man in Britain searching for her. Unfortunately, she couldn't say where the search was primarily taking place. Presumably London. When I asked if she heard talk of Scotland, she said no. Apparently Blackthorne is searching for Sylvie as well over there. I'm sending word to him even as I write you.

Sylvie must go to Youngblood's estate in Scotland and await my return. In the meantime, I am trying to rectify the situation here in France and pay back as much of the debt as I am able. My home in Paris, and the bit of treasure left therein, is being sold privately. Only Jean-Francois, my personal secretary, knows of my present whereabouts. The proceeds should be enough to satisfy Mirreault. But why should you care about such details, other than for Sylvie's sake? I know you love her well, and apologize for coming between the two of you once again. As I said, my death would have better served everyone involved, but I am too much of a coward to take such matters into my own clumsy hands.

Mother will certainly be glad to hear of my survival. Give her my love. As I have requested many times before, Matthew, pray. Pray for a miracle, for though I deserve nothing, I am a man most desperately in need of God's intervention. I shall remain always in your debt for the gracious care you have given my family.

R. de Boyce

He handed Sylvie the letter. She read it quickly.

"Mine said as much," she offered, handing it back to him. "Oh, Matthew." She lifted her hand to her mouth, the tears beginning afresh.

He didn't know what to do. He couldn't take her hand, couldn't gather her into his arms. She was another man's wife. And had been.

Suddenly all the kisses, the tender words, the warm embraces scratched at his conscience, and he stared at her helplessly. Wanting only to comfort her, to help her, he found he had not strength to do either.

The earl of Cannock preferred to ride north to Scotland, rather than be driven by his coachman or pulled by a behemoth of a steam engine. Remembering what he learned about medieval men, how they would ride ahead of their pleasure carriages, a vehicle made for women, he had made it a habit of journeying most everywhere on horseback. Sylvie, he was sure, would rather ride beside him, not stuffed into a musty old coach. She didn't seem to be a creature made for such stifling confines. Made to have a sun-warmed face and breeze-cooled hair . . . that was his Sylvie most certainly.

His journey was proving to be pleasant enough. Although, looking for Sylvie's face in each town he passed, asking questions of the inhabitants, left him exhausted by the time he fell into bed each night at the inns along the way. A very long journey indeed.

It had been disheartening to receive the message from Rene. His work, suddenly doubled, was far from over now. Hopefully Sylvie would be found before her husband arrived. It didn't matter whether or not Rene lived if Youngblood couldn't find Sylvie. Why hadn't the Frenchman told him Sylvie's whereabouts in his note? Blast the man again!

And yet, the memory of stabbing Rene de Boyce was something he tried not to recall. All the murders were beginning to abrade his soul like an ill-placed seam on a tight-fitting garment. He wasn't enjoying this sense of conscience a bit. Yet, he had never been comfortable in this world, had he?

"I am becoming much too soft," he mused as his horse galloped between the cities of Lincoln and York. It was an almost welcomed thought . . . if he wanted to become the man that Sylvie de Courcey would fall in love with, that was.

And yet it went deeper even than his feelings of love. As if a voice was whispering inside him that there was a consequence for sin, and that there was a greater love which covered even the blackest of deeds. There must be . . . or he was surely destined for the dark, eternal night which lay beyond the fortress of his life.

The conversations he had with Matthew at Oxford came trickling into his memory, slowly at first, then in a torrent. Words he hadn't thought of for years resounded in his brain. And, surprisingly enough, even to himself, he decided that the dark, lonely road on which he traveled, no man in sight for miles, was a perfect, even profound background for such weighty contemplation.

Matthew Wallace. He thought perhaps Sylvie would have gone to Bath, considering her feelings for the man. But his inquiry to the vicar came up empty. "As far as we know, the countess de Boyce is not staying in Bath," was the reply, or something like it, written by Matthew's sister.

Another empty avenue down which he had traveled. But he would find her. He had to.

⁓

They departed for Scotland the next day. In Bath, Sylvie boarded the train with Eve and Racine, feeling nauseous, tired, and confused. Neither she nor Matthew could think of anything to say, and so she departed almost wordlessly with only his awkward "Goodbye, then," suspended between them in the steamy air of the station.

As the countryside sped by, Sylvie saw none of it. Her eyes were dry and sore, and if she could have cried, she would have. Unfortunately, there would be more than enough time for tears, her entire life in fact, for her love for Matthew would never die . . . that much she knew for certain. That Eve would know and love her father was the only reason for any sort of joy at all.

She felt selfish—wounded and wondering why life had turned tail and sent her spinning back to where she had started.

In her grief she held Eve closely against her, and purposed not to look at the peaceful, happy face of Racine de Boyce beside her. For such a sight would only shatter the tiny fragments of her broken heart into dust.

⁓

Racine prayed as she had never done so before. For Rene. For Sylvie. For Eve. How much she loved each person who now bore the same name as she. She prayed for her son's safety, knowing that he was in great danger. For Sylvie she petitioned God's throne for peace, and for Eve, strength.

It was only the sweet grandchild, now sleeping in her mother's arms, which kept her from questioning God. Surely this little child had always been in his plans, for no human being, from the moment it began life in its mother's womb, was a mistake. Racine prayed that somehow Eve's presence would provide the succor her mother needed at this time.

Never again, the old woman promised herself. Never again would she meddle in the life of anybody else. It was a lesson hard learned, and unfortunately, she wasn't the bearer of the brunt of it all. She was merely a tortured bystander, begging God to intervene on her behalf for those she loved so dearly and so desperately.

Wondering how it would all work out, she sent a special prayer heavenward for Matthew Wallace, the one who had lost the most.

CHAPTER ❖ FORTY

David Youngblood, well seated on a gray Arabian, galloped beneath the raised portcullis of the gatehouse and into the inner bailey of his castle. His great-great-grandfather had manhandled the fortress away in a London card game at which he openly admitted to cheating and dared anyone to do anything about it. The eighth earl of Cannock had been as tempestuous and blustery as the Scottish highlands, more rugged than the craggy glens, more colorful than the heather that bloomed late summer on the surrounding hillsides. He had always been only a figure in a painting to the young David, but the cragged lips and the crooked teeth bound the lonely little boy closer to the swaggering, arrogant man than mere blood could ever have done. He wanted to be just like Lord Reginald Youngblood, and up until now his deeds would have shocked even that infamous ancestor whose harelip had failed to stop him as well.

Situated about six miles northwest of Peterhead, on the River Ulgie, the castle was a massively thick structure, continually lived in since the day the original stone keep was completed a century after the reign of King Robert the Bruce. Having never known a moment's disrepair, it stood proud and a shade arrogant for all the weathering it had done. The tales of love and revenge concerning the fortress had been spilling in front of hearths for centuries. It courted intrigue, it seemed, and each generation that inhabited the region had its own story to tell. Youngblood figured another scandal was soon due. He'd sorely hate to disappoint the superstitious highlanders round about.

The sea breeze from the coast weighted the air. Youngblood breathed in deeply, proud eyes surveying the many acres which were now his own.

Of all his recently inherited castles and lands, this estate was, and had always been, his favorite—the castle simply called Greywalls. He had spent much of his childhood here, away from his parents in the more fashionable south of England. Wandering the halls and hills in solitude, he had found two pastimes that dominated his childhood—drawing and fishing. And sometimes, when the weather permitted, he would enjoy them simultaneously on the banks of the river, a little sack of bread and cheese beside him. Most times, he put together his own luncheon, the staff too busy to bother with the deformed little boy about whom they had been given no concrete instructions and with whom they had no idea what to do.

His fingers itched to get around his fishing pole, maybe catch a trout or two, make a little fire and enjoy his favorite meal. Already he could taste the crispy, blackened skin of river trout, the tender, moist flesh within melting on his tongue.

Boyhood memories.

How long has it been since last I was here? he wondered as he dismounted, and a servant rushed out, a lad he did not recognize. He would recognize almost no one on this visit. He had made certain of it.

"Your name, lad?"

"Angus, sir. Angus Malcolm MacDowell."

"Very good, Mr. MacDowell. The house prepared, then? I am staying for a while, I believe."

"Ready and waitin', m'lord. All's weel."

"Been working here at Greywalls long, Angus?" He smelled of horses and hay, and the way he was stroking Persia's flank informed Youngblood that the lad loved beasts more than man. Smart little fellow.

"Nay, your grace. Just helpin' oot in the stables."

"Do your best and you will find you can do very well in my employment."

The boy, about six years old, looked up and smiled broadly, apparently unaffected by Youngblood's malformation. "Aye, sir! Mother's been tellin' me the very same!" Much to Angus's apparent dismay a groom walked up, bowed to the earl, and led the horse away.

"Your mother sounds like a smart woman, then."

"Aye, m'lord. She's the cook!"

"And what is her name, young Angus?"

"Why, her name's Pamela, my lord," the lad reported as if the answer was perfectly obvious.

By this time their words were echoing in the vast hall, unused in an official capacity for years, but kept the same to remind the inhabitants of the original purpose of the castle. Swords and axes hung high up on the walls; cabinets filled with precious silver pieces lined the far wall. All Youngblood's now. Every last piece of it. "And does she cook a fine trout?"

Suits of armor leaned forward on their stands almost as if they were trying to hear the answer.

"Aye." Without a thought, he took Youngblood's hand. "The finest fish you've ever tasted east of the Spey. Me Grannie lives west of the Spey."

Youngblood leaned down on his haunches with a laugh. "Does she cook it till the skin crisps nice and brown?"

"Aye. An' the other parts just melt in your mouth like butter on hot bread! Do ye wish to be havin' some for your tea, m'lord?"

"Yes, Angus." He stood to his feet. "I do believe I would. In fact, would you catch it for me yourself?"

His eyes widened. "Truly?"

"Have you a pole?"

"Aye, that I do, m'lord! Me da' just fashioned me a new one! He's the new carpenter. Most of the old servants decided to leave some days back, sir. Me mother said 'good riddance to bad rubbish.' But you'll not be regrettin' me da' workin' for ye!"

"Splendid. Then your orders are set. Off you go!"

"Sir?"

"Yes, lad?"

"You look like the man in the picture over there. Just like him."

"Yes, Angus, I certainly do."

"You're lucky then, sir."

Youngblood was taken aback. "Why is that?"

"Well, I've been lookin' at that man for many months now, an' I figured that he was a one-of-a-kind sort o' gentleman. Mother says things that are one-of-a-kind are the most valuable."

With that, the boy ran toward the back of the house. A small voice caused Youngblood to wheel around to face the stairs.

"Papa? Ith it really you?"

He drew in his breath, felt his mouth go dry. "Yes, Elspeth, it is me."

How she had grown in the past eight years. She was eleven now, slender with long black hair. She hid her mouth behind a slim hand. He didn't know what to do next. The child's mother, one of his many past mistresses, was dead nigh on two years, and he hadn't even bothered to return for the funeral.

"Do they feed you well here?" It was all he could think to ask. He felt so stupid, and yet he didn't resent the feeling for it was well-deserved.

"Aye, thir. I am weel." Her brogue—even with its speech impediment—pleased him for some reason, so unlike her mother's and his mother's.

"And do you read?"

"Aye, Papa."

"Who told you to call me that?"

"Mother. Thee thaid ye'd return one day."

"Did she now?"

"Aye, thir. And tho ye thee, thee wath right."

"Take your hand away from your mouth!" he ordered harshly. "Within these walls is the only place such a sight is welcomed, so you might as well take advantage of it, girl!"

She lowered it slowly, and the sight of her deformity, worse even than his own, repulsed him so greatly that he hurried into his study and slammed the door, his heart racing.

⁓

Matthew and Miranda had left Swainswick as well, to sort things out. And now they were in London, at the home of the MacDonalds, seeking advice.

"Am I wrong?" Matthew opened his hands, looking up at his friend with imploring eyes. "Is it selfish to want a marriage, children? A houseful of laughter? Love that fills the heart?"

"God meant us to love like that, Matthew." MacDonald opened his hands as well. "How can this be wrong? And who would I be to judge?"

It was true. There George MacDonald sat with three children upon his lap, the picture of contentment, though they had been hard pressed to round up two extra helpings of dinner when Matthew and Miranda suddenly appeared on their doorstep two hours before. Miranda had talked him into a brief holiday to London, to clear his mind and think about the situation at St. Jude's in a more rational manner. They had left Swainswick, virtually on the heels of Sylvie and the countess, with a purse holding their meagre savings.

"Perhaps I should just be content in the state I am. Like the apostle Paul says."

MacDonald shook his head, his Scottish brogue warm and soothing. "There is not much I can say to you right now, is there, my friend, that would help? You and your sister are welcome to stay here with us as long as you wish until you decide whether or not to return to St. Jude's and fight what I consider to be a ridiculous battle. I have been down that road before, Matthew. You cannot force your love on the unwilling. But I would suggest another course to you. Go home."

"Home? But didn't you just say—"

"Not to Swainswick, Mate. To Leeds. Go remember what it was like to be a boy. Remember what it was like to be safe in the strong arms of parental love, to smell the grass and to trust God in ultimate simplicity."

Matthew crossed his arms, uncrossed them. He stood to his feet. Then sat down. He couldn't impose the expense of a stay on the MacDonalds. Yet he couldn't go back to Swainswick just yet. But to go home? Back to that huge, luxurious house with all its fine crystal and carpets? How could God's will be found in such surroundings? He asked George as much.

MacDonald squeezed his children tightly. "He was able to call you to the ministry of the gospel in that house, was he not?"

George was right, that was the only place for him now. "I suppose there's really no place else to go, is there?" He felt too resigned, too complacent. Wasn't one supposed to attack life and its problems? Hadn't he decided he would fight to the end.

"Cheer up, Mate!" Miranda said late that evening on a northern train bound for Leeds. "You'll be able to get that birthday present in record time!"

Matthew looked sadly over at his sister, saw the love in her eyes, and smiled in spite of his inner turmoil. He took her hand and raised it to his lips. Miranda had that way about her. She wouldn't tolerate melancholy. Not while God was on the throne and the final, ultimate battle had already been won.

"George's Louisa tells me there's a church near Huntly that needs a pastor," she informed her brother. "Maybe we can take a trip north to Scotland soon."

"I thought you didn't like Scotland, Mira? What was it you said? Too wild and barbaric?"

She thrust forth her chin. "Well, maybe I did. What do I know, though? And think of what Christ must have thought coming to us? Talk about a passel of barbarians we humans are! And besides"—she put her hand on his arm, becoming grave— "St. Jude's is a lost cause. I know that now."

"You believe that? Really, Mira?"

Just what was God trying to tell him anyway?

"Yes, Mate. I do."

"What about the Dudhams and the others?"

"They're the minority. Your work is done. God is leading you on now. Can you not see that?"

"But all those years of work, to come to this? Fleeing from the conflict? We even left poor Dizzy behind!"

"Oh"—she waved the irrationality away—"Wilson's brood will take care of the fellow. Do not fear, brother, God has use of you elsewhere. And it just may be that church in Scotland. I'll be with you still. You know I always stand ready to share in your work."

There wasn't a truer word ever spoken, but Matthew wasn't ready to commit. "Let us just go home for now, Mira. We will wait a bit, listen a bit, and see if we hear the still, small voice of God."

"As you wish, Mate. It's always a good time to wait upon the Lord."

Matthew sat back in his seat, closed his eyes, and tried desperately to pray. Finally, he rested in the fact that the Holy Spirit himself would intercede on his behalf, for he knew not what words to silently utter.

Miranda interrupted his confusion. "Would you call Moses a failure?"

"No." Matthew didn't hesitate. "Of course not."

"Well, then." She sat back in her seat. "You see, then."

Matthew didn't have to ask, remembering how Moses, temper high, killed the Egyptian and left Egypt. Fleeing. He lifted one corner of his mouth. *At least I'm not leaving because I murdered somebody!*

"Could be worse, eh, Mate?" Miranda said with a knowing smile.

"Just needed you to point that out, Mira. Like you always do."

God help me if she ever finds a husband, he mused. Then he began praying and this time, knowing he was being led to another land by the very hand of God, he found the words.

"Why are you so sure about leaving, Mira? There is something you are not telling me." He always knew when Mira was keeping a secret. She had no talent for it either.

"You remember when Moses struck the rock?"

"Of course. Not firsthand knowledge, mind you," he joked.

"Well, I did a little striking of my own," Mira said, her face bright red, "in the village the day before we left."

"Oh, Mira," he began, his voice dropping. "You didn't—"

"I couldn't help it, Mate!" she rushed to defend herself. "Mrs. Horace P. Rooney was standing there in such triumph as I was trying to dicker with the grocer over the price of the cucumbers, almost begging him to lower the price so we could afford them. I . . . I lost my temper."

Matthew held back his laughter, knowing this was not a laughing matter to his sister. "What did you do? Did you hit her?"

She shook her head fiercely. "No. I yanked that ridiculous hat off her head, threw it in the road, and stomped on it. The flowers on the brim went flying, let me tell you! And I cried, 'Fie on you, Mrs. Horace P. Rooney. Fie on you!'"

"You actually said 'Fie?'" He couldn't contain the laughter now. "'Fie'? Why 'fie'?"

"I don't know!" she started giggling nervously. "I just don't know what came over me! She was standing there so . . . so Elizabethan . . . or . . . or something . . . that to say 'shame on you' wasn't good enough!"

Matthew's shoulders began to heave with laughter. "Well, sister, you may not have stricken the rock, but you stomped on the hat, so I guess *you* will not be going back into the Promised Land anytime soon, will you?"

"No. That is why we must go to Scotland instead!"

"George might say Scotland is the Promised Land." He was still laughing, grateful to be given a moment's relief.

"Maybe he's right, Mate. But we'll never find out unless we go and do a little investigating?"

"Like Joshua and Caleb?"

"Why not?" She gave him a hug. "Let's just hope they're not all a bunch of giants!"

"Are you certain it's safe to transport all this money on foot?" Jean-Francois, the count de Boyce's secretary stammered. "Remember the last time I took a large amount of money on the streets of Paris! A nightmare to be sure, monsieur!"

"Trust me, Jean-Francois, no one knows of this but you and I. You will be quite safe, I assure you." He whispered, as he looked around with darting eyes, praying no one would recognize him. Camille had dyed his hair black, but the color was beginning to fade . . . and these old garments she had found him . . . well . . . at least there was someone in Paris he could trust! He couldn't complain there. Camille had taken him in over a month ago and hadn't given up his presence to Mirreault. It still shocked him that her love for him was that true. He regretted succumbing to temptation with her, but he found he just couldn't resist her sad eyes any longer.

No matter. He was going back to Sylvie now and all would be like it was during the winter. And he had a child now! As soon as he parted company with his secretary, he was heading to Le Havre where the yacht had been secretly docked for months. He had refused to tell even Camille of its location, no matter how much she begged to know.

He would soon be off to England. For good, if he was lucky.

He handed Jean-Francois a slip of paper that gave Claude Mirreault's address. Then he tipped his threadbare hat with a final "Au revoir" and headed toward the train station. He purchased the cheapest ticket he could, sat in his narrow seat, and took a long, deep swig of paregoric.

He slept, his dreams riddled with grief and guilt and fear.

CHAPTER ❖ FORTY-ONE

It was amazing how one could punch a man, bind his hands and feet, and still he wouldn't answer a simple question. Didier paced the floor of Claude Mirreault's study, staring daggers at Jean-Francois Gauttier, the secretary of Rene de Boyce. It had truly been a surprise when he had turned up, cash in hand, to pay off another large portion of his employer's debt. He confirmed that de Boyce was still alive, but naturally refused to give Mirreault his whereabouts. Of course, Didier was left with the responsibility of finding out!

"Come now, you fool!" Didier exploded. He'd reasoned with simpletons before, but this man could have tutored a raving lunatic in the fine art of spreading a communicable madness! "Do you realize how much money is in here?"

Jean-Francois lifted his chin, but his eyes held a healthy amount of fear. "I am a man of honor, sir."

"Does Youngblood know he is alive?" Didier asked.

"Yes."

Didier wheeled around, backhanding the man across his jaw. "Idiot! I will have the whereabouts of the count. And I will have it now. Do you hear? It is for his own safety!"

"I hear you." The secretary rubbed his rounded jaw painfully, eyes darting around the room. "But that doesn't mean I will obey you. I do not believe a word you say when you tell me you do not seek the count's life."

"Of course not," Didier smirked.

"Someone tried to kill him down at the wharf," Jean-Francois accused. "And who else could it be but your organization?"

Didier crossed his arms, curious. "What has Count Rene de Boyce ever done for you that you give him such loyalty?"

"I could ask the same of you concerning Claude Mirreault."

"Just answer the question!"

"Why, my father was his father's secretary, and he rescued me when the thieves attacked me for the payroll. Surely you heard about that."

"Oh, I heard." Didier couldn't help but chuckle at this one. This man really was one of the most stupid people he had ever met. "And have you figured out why he was so close at hand, just as the crime took place?"

Jean-Francois turned mute.

Mirreault's henchman leaned back on the desk in his boss's study and examined the secretary thoughtfully. "Perhaps ... perhaps I'm just not getting through to you. Perhaps you need to be persuaded by another, more dramatic means. Sit there in that chair. I'll return shortly. Do not attempt to leave, or you will most certainly regret it."

Didier hurried into the garden where Mirreault was learning the fine art of watercolor, a most delightful-looking teacher perched upon his lap as she showed him how to work with a dry brush. She was giggling while her pupil tried to do everything but paint.

"Sir." Didier cleared his throat.

Mirreault turned impatiently. "What is it now, Didier? Can you not perceive that my wish to be left undisturbed grows greater by the second?"

"Yes. I'll be brief."

"You'd better be!" His former life on the streets burst through in his speech. "Uh, do go on."

"Jean-Francois will not talk. I'm asking permission to take the matter a step further."

Claude grimaced. "Why do you need my say-so? You've always done well enough without obtaining my permission. I asked you to learn the whereabouts of Count de Boyce. How you do it is up to you! How unfortunate he failed to show up at Camille's doorstep like we thought he was going to do. Unless, of course, Camille was lying to us when she said she hadn't seen him."

"Camille cannot abide the count. She'd willingly give him over to us!"

"Go on, then," Mirreault dismissed him.

"Thank you, sir."

Didier turned, amidst a new, even more annoying rain of girlish laughter. Jaw set, he knew what he must do.

Three hours later, he entered the study, where Jean-Francois still sat, a pistol pointed in his direction by one of Mirreault's guards.

"Go," Didier ordered the flunky, who left presently. He escorted a lovely, blindfolded young woman into the room, his gun held firmly to her temple. She was shaking with fear, her blond curls vibrating in time to her quivering shoulders, arms, and hands.

"He had just left for Cherbourg, when I set out!" Jean-Francois blurted out at the sight of his daughter.

"Then where?" Didier tightened his grip on the girl's arm and she cried out.

"Please, don't hurt my Claire!" the secretary hollered.

"Tell me all that you know!"

"He's stopping off in London first!" Jean-Francois babbled. "For just a few days. That is all I know."

"Is he going to the earl of Cannock's after that?"

"He didn't say."

Didier twisted the girl's arm a bit. "Papa!" she cried.

"I swear to you!" Jean-Francois screamed. "I don't know where he is going after London."

Silence ensued as Didier examined the secretary. The mantel clock gonged the half hour.

"Get out of here," Didier ordered suddenly, cursing beneath his breath as he roughly shoved the girl in her father's direction. She sobbed as she was led from the house and up into the carriage in which her father had arrived.

"Blast them all!" Didier grated between his teeth as he stomped back into the chateau. If this situation wasn't getting to be more trouble than it was worth, he didn't know a thing about a life of crime. He'd always felt such an enjoyment at what he did ... and as far as he was concerned there wasn't a crime out there that couldn't be called "a crime of passion." When Claude Mirreault found him on the streets picking pockets twenty years before, he had remembered their childhood days together and took pity on his friend. Didier felt important now, each deed for the sake of his master and friend another tightening of the cord which bound him more firmly to the wealthiest criminal in all of Paris. Perhaps all of France.

Still, dealing with such insipid people couldn't help but be bothersome. Take the count, for example ... there was a dull one. Buried in a grave of his own digging and too stupid to find the simplest way out of it all. If it had been himself, Didier reasoned, he would have sailed away in that big family yacht and disappeared to some far-off corner of the globe a long time ago. But the count was too foolish, too tied down. It was why Didier himself never bothered with women, never had time for even the most casual of sexual or emotional encounters.

Light and easy. Keep your feet swift, and just off the ground. That was his philosophy and one that stood him in good stead for many years.

He was scowling when he marched into the sitting room where Mirreault was smoking a cigar, drinking a brandy, and reading an ancient volume probably in some ancient language. Thank heavens the girl was gone.

"You don't appear to be happy, Didier," Mirreault observed as he set the book down and swizzled his brandy. "Had enough of this affair, I assume?"

Didier felt his brow harden and crossed the room to pour himself a brandy. He took a sip and scratched his pate. Why had he talked his boss out of dispensing with the matter altogether? Who was the stupid one, eh? Here he was, doing all of the legwork as usual, Claude making all the money. "You could say that."

"Well?"

"He's on his way to Cherbourg, then over to England to reunite with his wife. After a stop in London. The secretary had no knowledge of the young countess's whereabouts. But I think it's safe to assume she'll be meeting him at one of Youngblood's estates. Our source says he is in Scotland. It's the most logical place for the count to flee to. Although this is only guesswork, it's the only lead we have to go on as to her whereabouts."

"I do not think it is guessing at all. The count is stupid. He believes Youngblood to be his closest friend, so where else would he rendezvous with his wife? It is only a miracle that he had eluded us for so long here in Paris. Someone is protecting him to be sure, someone here in our camp."

"Our network is large and varied. It could be almost anyone. But whoever it is hasn't given himself away by saying too much. Smart man."

Mirreault took another sip of his brandy. "So convenient for David, is it not? Kill the husband and have the wife waiting there to fall into his open arms!" Expecting Mirreault to curse, Didier was surprised when a wide grin burst on the large face accompanied by a chuckle and the words, "Blast it, but I like the man's style. He reminds me of myself."

"Yet you said yourself he's growing careless," Didier reminded him with a tip of his head.

"There must certainly be, as they say, 'a method to his madness.' You had better drink up and be going, then."

"Already? I can easily make it to Scotland before the count, especially as he is going to London first."

"You must catch up to the count in Cherbourg, warn him of Youngblood's intent. You see, Didier, the purpose of your journey is threefold. First, warn the count and so render Youngblood ineffectual. Then, kill Sylvie de Courcey, and if by any chance you cannot achieve your first objective, at all costs you must protect the count from Youngblood. If Rene de Boyce dies, you might as well not bother coming home."

Didier stood to his feet and made for the door. It sounded like a welcomed invitation . . . to walk out of the chateau and never return. To be his own man again.

"Oh, Didier!"

"Yes, sir?"

"Take Yves with you just in case it gets to be too much for one man. And send someone over to deal with Monsieur Jean-Francois. He has become privy to a bit more information than I am comfortable with."

"And the daughter?"

"Have her brought to me. A right pretty little filly she was."

Didier chuckled. Claude would always be Claude . . . a man with an eye for the ladies and a mind for destruction. He had been comfortable with the volatile situation for years. Why leave now? Didier smirked. "And after you're done with her, sir, there's an opening in the scullery, you know."

Mirreault wheezed a laugh, coughed a bit, then cleared his throat. The eyes of the two men met, their loyalty to each other plainly evident.

"Sir?" Didier reached into his pocket and wiped his brow. "Did you really mean what you said this time? About never coming back?"

"No, Didier. This will always be your home. I'm surprised you haven't realized that yet."

So it was true, Didier supposed. There really was honor among thieves, even so seasoned and hardened a thief as Claude Mirreault.

⁓

No matter what happens, I am the one who will suffer! Camille sat alone at a café, drinking cup after cup of coffee. She was agitated and heartbroken. All the men in her life were after Sylvie de Courcey. Mirreault wanted her dead, wanted her money. Rene wanted her to be his wife and the mother of his child. And the viscount, most painfully of all, wanted her to be his wife, his everything.

Poor little Camille, she thought.

It had been difficult pretending to love the count this last time they spent together. But she had to protect him. If he was dead, she would just hang up her hat and go back to the country. As long as Rene was alive, and Sylvie was alive, their marriage would be intact. And Youngblood would not be able to pursue the young countess.

She had to keep them all alive! Unfortunately, she knew Rene wouldn't take her advice to spirit Sylvie away to America.

It was a heavy burden indeed, and the love of her life was in the middle of it. If only he would love her as she loved him, then Sylvie would be safe and so would Rene. She would kiss Mirreault good-bye and leave without a backward glance.

Yes, she would.

⁓

It was a small church with an overgrown cemetery. The iron fencing surrounding the consecrated ground buckled and swayed like children playing crack-the-whip on a frozen pond. One tomb, raised above the ground, was spotless, the grass around it clipped neatly, a wreath of summer blossoms resting serenely on top. Lily petals trembled in the breeze and the roses entwined in the greenery spilled their perfume to the favor of anyone close by.

Matthew breathed in deeply through his nose. Scratched an eyebrow, surprised by the lack of tears.

Isabelle Brae Stratford-Mann, born April 5, 1832, died June 15, 1850.

He had loved her well. There was no regret there. She had shown him how to love, how to be loved, for she had known how to love strong and to love with excellence and without reservation. Isabelle had fostered in him that need for a loving wife and children of his own. Sylvie, he thought, had been the answer.

Not so.

So he stood by this grave, wondering what God required of him now. Was this his way of saying, "Marriage is not the path I've chosen?" Or perhaps, "You must go on. Don't hold Sylvie to you like you did with Isabelle. Don't mourn for another decade. Don't let love pass you by again."

Was there another woman for him somewhere? Or was it to be Mira for the rest of his life?

Isabelle. Sylvie. And now Eve. That sweet little face still haunted him, having already come to love her as his own. His heart broke at the thought of the dear wee one who slept so peacefully in his arms in the evenings after supper as the women would sew and chat.

Matthew bowed to the will of the Lord. He knew a heart to love again would be his, if God so chose to bring someone else into his life. A heart to belong only to the ministry of the gospel would be his as well, if that was the divine plan for his life. But God was enough, no matter the future. He had to be. And Matthew knew this. Hopefully soon his heart's sentiments would echo what his head knew to be the case.

He plucked a rose from the wreath Mira had given him to bring, lifted the blossom to his nose, and breathed in the fragrant perfume. Strangely, he was comforted by it. God made the rose. He made all the roses, and roses would continue to bloom until there was no more earth from which they might sprout.

⁓

"Why no, sir!" the harbormaster shook his head in bemusement, searching through lists indelibly etched into his mind for the past five years. "The count de Boyce's yacht was never moored here, so far as I know anyway."

Didier tapped his foot, feeling hot and agitated. "Are you certain? He's not just paying you to say this?"

The man looked truly puzzled. "No, sir. I don't believe I've ever seen his ship before."

Didier knew he was telling the truth. A seasoned liar always recognized the genuine article. Well, maybe not always. He'd thought surely the secretary had been telling the truth when he said the count's yacht was moored in Cherbourg. And with a gun to his own daughter's head! Didier thought he had seen everything.

The man was probably already dead. Unfortunately for them. Not that it mattered; they would be out of time anyway if they went back to work the truth out of the man. The loyal simple-ton act had fooled him, he hated to admit.

Well, on to Scotland, then, to await the count's arrival. To pick up the pieces, or keep them from being dropped altogether.

CHAPTER ❖ FORTY-TWO

Sylvie looked about her with relief as the northbound train crossed into Scotland. The countess had absolutely insisted on visiting an old friend in London for a couple of days and replacing some of their dowdy, homemade dresses with some fashionable new clothes. Too weary of heart to argue, Sylvie meekly went along with the plans, wondering what happened to the woman she had come to France to take care of so long ago? The countess had been so changed by the news of Rene's letter, caring only for herself and her son. When he wasn't around she was much more sane, much more rational. It was as if her crazy love for him blinded her to all else. Probably living in such humble surroundings as the Wallace's cottage had been hard on her as well, and she was just itching to spread her wings a little bit. She even told Sylvie as much when they had stepped out of the cab and into the fashionable pedestrian traffic of Bond Street.

"I know this seems selfish of me, my dear," she had twittered, as they made their way into an exclusive dress shop. "But I just want to experience a small piece of my life again, if only for a little while. And not only that, Rene will soon be with us, and I would so hate for him to see me like this."

Sylvie, on the other hand, was quite comfortable in her garb. The Lord knew, they were the type of dresses she had grown up wearing. And despite the countess's vehement protests, she chose not to buy herself a more extravagant wardrobe. Only she knew the money in the de Courcey coffers was limited. She was curious to find out what the final figure would be once the lands were sold to pay off the debt. But that was fodder for future rumination, she knew.

So now here they were, riding off to yet another destination, the countess looking like a fine, plumed bird in robin's egg blue, and Sylvie a plain little sparrow in dove gray.

David Youngblood felt his heart thrill at the sight of Sylvie, so womanly now and holding a baby in her maternal arms. Motherhood had softened her yet more, made her more appealing if it were possible. Even the homely dress she wore was enchanting. And the weight she still carried from her pregnancy made her that much more delectable.

"Sylvie!" he cried, hurrying forward from his post near the tracks. "Countess." He bowed, never one to forget good manners.

Sylvie was genuinely delighted. "You came to fetch us yourself! I thought you would. Countess said you would send a man round with a carriage. But I knew better!"

He was touched deeply by her familiarity with his ways, or rather, her presumed familiarity, he corrected himself. But more than that, he was touched by the depth of her eyes . . . so sad and worn out by trial upon trial . . . and trying to be so brave and cheerful.

"You must be relieved to find your son is alive," he said to Racine.

"Of course. Relief hardly describes it."

Youngblood could believe that, if the strength of his feelings along the opposite vein were any indication. He put his hand on the small of Sylvie's back, her waist broader than he had remembered from before, and ushered them from inside the dark station at Peterhead to his waiting carriage.

She was here. Sylvie was here with him, and he could begin to woo his heart's first and only love. How would she feel about Elspeth? By the way she cradled the babe in her arms, he knew she would love the girl as her own daughter. He'd have to remember to tell Mrs. MacDowell to send Elspeth up an extra tart for dessert tonight.

"Your husband said he'd be coming as soon as possible, maybe even next week," he reported. "At least that is what his message relayed."

"It may be even sooner than that!" Racine gushed. "Oh, I cannot wait to see his face again. He whom I thought was lost . . ."

Her voice trailed off leaving an overly dramatic silence that David Youngblood wanted to grind out of his ears. These women who coddled their sons!

"What makes you frown so?"

Youngblood was pulled from his thoughts by Sylvie. "Nothing for you to worry about, darling. I am, however, happy you are safe and here with me. Both of you." He turned to the countess. "My home is yours and all that is within is at your disposal. I hope you realize this is most definitely the case, and will take full and utter advantage of the situation."

"All I wish for is a nice hot bath," Racine informed him tartly with a downturned mouth.

"Me too," Sylvie smiled. "And perhaps a nap." She pushed a wisp of red hair off of Eve's smooth forehead. "For both of us."

David Youngblood felt his breath leave him at the sight. Such beauty. Such love. *Oh, how I adore you*, he thought, thinking if he could only take her hand in his he would be satisfied.

That was a crazy thought. He could never get enough of Sylvie.

"I've hired on a girl from the village to help you with the baby, and of course you'll both have ladies' maids as befits your station."

"It seems you've thought of everything, David," Sylvie remarked, her body sagging with fatigue, her eyes filled with gratitude.

"I'm sure there's much I haven't anticipated, but I've tried my best, my lady, to make you happy."

"You do make me happy, David. You always have." She stepped into his coach, and the earl of Cannock knew he had never heard words more welcomed, or more sweetly spoken in his life.

Sylvie could plainly see that David had been doing all he could to make them comfortable. In the three days since they had arrived at Greywalls, simple meals were keeping them healthy; riding and walking each day was keeping her fit. In the evenings, he encouraged her to pour out her heart to him. Always, always, he would take her hand sympathetically and tell her that one day it would be all right. And she chose to believe him. It was all she could do. God was still with her, she knew that, and she relied upon his mercy and his love to usher her through every minute. Matthew was gone. Loving him was not her choice to make anymore. But she didn't feel dirty inside, as if she had sinned by loving the vicar who had returned her love with a strength she had never known. Indeed, she was nourished for the life that lay ahead of her. It was a strange situation to be sure.

She was utterly thankful that their physical relationship had not gone further than a few kisses. God had protected them most certainly. Most of the time she tried not to think about Matthew, for she couldn't help but feel guilty that she had turned to him so soon after Rene's death, that she had dragged his heart down a path that led to more pain and heartache.

The day after she arrived, David surprised her with a shy visitor. Or rather, a hitherto before unknown inhabitant of Greywalls.

"This is my daughter, Elspeth," he had announced simply, forthrightly, and without further explanation. "She will be joining us for all our meals from now on."

The child stood with her hands at her side, head bowed. Sylvie's heart broke at the sight of her, feeling Elspeth and David's pain, knowing what it was like not to fit in inside your own house. That would not happen as long as she was beneath this roof, she decided firmly.

She patted the chair next to her. "Then she shall sit here, beside me, and we will get to know each better as only girls can."

Elspeth raised her head and smiled a smile that was quite gruesome yet utterly beautiful at the same time. "Thank ye, ma'am. Thank ye ever tho much." Her words were extremely hard to understand, but somehow, Sylvie managed, translating her "th's" into "s's."

By the end of the meal, Elspeth and Sylvie were chatting like old friends. "Do ye ken, ma'am, if I may hold your wee bairn sometime? Maybe tomorrow? I've theen ye thittin' in the garden together from my window up in the nursery."

"You may hold her as soon as supper is over with, Elspeth. We'll go up together."

"An' if she be thleepin', ma'am?"

"We'll wake her up. Mothers love nothing so well in the world as to see their babies waken. The sweetness in their eyes makes life worth the living."

It was true. She could face anything life had to offer as long as Eve was in her arms. And so, after supper was over, she took Elspeth by the hand and led her upstairs, longing to see her daughter, aching for Elspeth who had tucked her hand in hers and said, "I with with all my heart my own mother had loved me even half tho much ath you love your daughter."

⁓

"Well, it is nice to know I have not completely lost my skill at finding missing individuals." David Youngblood hurried up the hill upon which Sylvie, Eve, and Elspeth were sunning themselves. A small spread of tarts and pastries sat on a plate between them.

"We're here in plain view, David," Sylvie laughed, smoothing the crumbs off her plain green gown. "I'd hardly call that a major accomplishment!"

The words were spoken with the familiarity one old friend feels for the other, and no offense was taken. He was finding he didn't take offense at much these days, and the freedom such an attitude imposed was life changing.

He plunked himself onto the blanket, reached for a custard tart, then leaned back on an elbow as he downed it in two bites. Elspeth watched in apparent fascination, eyes shining with love at the sight of her dashing father in his slim breeches and shining black riding boots. As dashing a man as she had ever seen, no doubt. Youngblood wondered why he had stupidly deprived himself of such affection for so long. Then remembered the child's lazy mother who had grown fat and unkempt on the money he sent for their upkeep. He had fathered other children, but only one who took after himself, and so, since he had handed down the deformity, he felt it was up to him to take care of her.

"I was not speaking of the ladies of the house, actually." He reached for another treat. "You have visitors coming up the drive. In fact they might be waiting for you by now."

To his delight, she paled. "It's not Rene already, is it?"

He swallowed the pastry. "No, no. This is going to be a surprise indeed. Totally unexpected. It did not take me long to track them down, either, I might add."

Sylvie's brows drew together as she thought. There was only one answer. "Agnes and Rupert!"

He clapped his hands and picked up the final pastry. Highland air stepped up the appetite, he supposed. "Very good, my lady. Yes, that is exactly who!"

Sylvie bounded to her feet and pulled David to his. She threw her arms about him. "Thank you, David. Oh, thank you! I can't believe you'd do such a wonderful thing!"

Soon, he told himself, relishing in the feel of her body so close to his, the softness of her bosom and her tummy, still a bit round and soft. *Soon, I'll do all the wonderful things you ever dreamed of or could even imagine.* If only Rene would arrive more quickly! "I just wanted to see you smile, Sylvie. You do not do it nearly as much as you used to. I thought maybe the sight of Agnes and Rupert . . ." He shrugged.

She quickly kissed his cheek, pulled out of his embrace, then scooped Eve from Elspeth's arms. "Will you bring back the blanket and the plate?" she asked the girl.

"Go on, ma'am. I'll take care o' everything!"

Youngblood watched in triumph as Sylvie, Eve pressed tightly against her, bounded down the hill toward Greywalls. Mesmerized by the fluttering gown, the dark hair streaming in the breeze, the fact that there was actually a spring to her step, he was surprised when Elspeth stood to her feet and asked if he was ready to go. With the blanket folded neatly under one arm, the basket of plates and linens hanging from the other, she began the trek home. She stayed directly in the middle of the path Sylvie had made through the long grasses.

He observed his daughter for a span. Examined her slender form, the graceful way she swung the basket, then looked up at the dramatically tall cloud formation overhead. She belonged to this land. Made by God. People were more than mere mouths, weren't they?

To be sure.

"Just a moment, Elspeth!" he called, hurrying forward to catch up, casting aside any more of those sentimental thoughts. "Hand me that basket like a good lass. There."

He took the basket from her hand and they walked home together . . . saying nothing.

"Agnes!"

Sylvie literally screamed the word in her excitement as she ran across the bailey and up into the keep. Agnes handed Rupert a bundle and hurried across the great hall where they had been examining the suits of armor and laughing.

"Miss!" Agnes cried, encircling Sylvie in an embrace so powerful, so maternal, so unconditional, that Sylvie felt as if she understood, in a small way, what it was going to be like to enter heaven.

Tears poured forth in such a current, so unexpectedly, that Agnes, stroking the back of Sylvie's head, said softly to Rupert, "Take the lad upstairs, ducks. He needs his nap. I'll warrant you could use one too after the long drive."

Rupert tended to Agnes's wishes, and Sylvie felt herself being led to a bench near the great wall fireplace. It was as if she had been waiting for Agnes to truly let go of the emotions that had been boiling within her. Agnes, loving Agnes, just cooed, "There now, lovey" or "Poor, sweet child." She stroked Sylvie's hair and every once in a while joined her with her own tears.

But the tears could only flow for so long. Finally they began to share the stories of what had brought them both to England. Several hours later, Sylvie took Agnes, with their babies, outdoors to stroll over the hills. The blooming heather blanketed the landscape like a purple quilt of sundry shades, some hills glorious amethysts in the sun, others shaded by passing clouds to appear like velvet. Agnes couldn't stop talking of Adam, their new son.

"So you see, Miss Sylvie, he may not be the most beautiful baby, but he's ours and we've ached for a baby for so long!"

"Why, Agnes, he is perfectly wonderful!"

Agnes smiled down at little Adam. "Well, my lady, you have to admit, he isn't what you'd call beautiful. Not like little Eve there."

"He's made in the image of God. Isn't that enough?"

Agnes smiled broadly. "You're learning, aren't you? And yes, he is made in God's image, and although it is quite a homely little face that smiles up into mine, I love him well." Agnes was exactly right. Adam was quite a plain baby. His face was coarse and unrefined, and he was so large for his age it was almost shocking. When they compared his foot to Eve's, they could hardly believe how much larger Adam's was, and with only two months' age difference! Naturally, they had already had a good strong laugh over the babies' names!

"Rupert seems thrilled with him."

"Oh, he is. Calls him 'my big man.' He rolled over when he was just four weeks old, you know! This little one has made the exile from France a bit easier to bear. Seeing him grow and change so quickly has given us a proper perspective on what life should be about."

Sylvie laid a hand on Agnes's arm. "I never believed the charges for a moment. It was Rene, you know. He was selling off the items himself."

"We figured that out. He's turned life upside down for everyone."

"Unfortunately, yes. I don't know what I'm going to do when I see him. How I'll react. I'm frightened, Agnes, if you want to know the truth."

Agnes's eyes were their black, snappy selves. "'Tis a good thing I won't be here when he comes!"

"Anger is only the half of it for me. I've come to pity him to the point of despisal. How anyone can be so irresponsible, so stupid, so . . . so weak!" There, she said it. "If I never saw him again, I do believe I'd be the happiest woman alive! He's destroyed any chance of happiness I might have ever had. And for what?"

"Opium is a powerful element, my dear. We can't understand its power. He's going to need your love, however little he deserves it."

"And that's what frightens me, Agnes. There's no love left for him"—she patted her heart—"in here. Nothing. Other than the love I am commanded to have for him in Scripture."

"'We love because he first loved us,'" Agnes quoted.

"Rene was always my friend. And now, I don't even feel the most remote bit of kinship with him. He compromised the safety and health of everyone who ever cared for him."

"But he's Eve's father, my lady. You must not forget that. You must forgive him, and go on . . . for the child's sake."

Sylvie reached out and smoothed a hand over Adam's round head, then touched Eve's curls. "I've forgiven him. It's just that

I don't like him anymore. Though I never felt that fairy-tale kind of love that I felt for Matthew, I always liked him. But even that is gone."

"Well, you thought he cared about you, but his actions have spoken the opposite."

"Yes. It's obvious now that was never true. Hopefully, he'll be detained in London for quite a while. I received another message from him yesterday telling me he has a few matters to attend to."

Agnes shrugged. "It's only putting off the inevitable, dearie."

"Perhaps, but as I have my whole life to live with the man, I might as well postpone the torture as long as possible."

They walked along a bit further, circling around to a meadow fenced in by a stone wall. Contented cattle stood still and stocky in bovine stupidity, the sun warming their reddish coats as they grazed. Sylvie envied them.

"Do you miss the English vicar?" Agnes asked without warning.

"Oh, Aggie." Sylvie turned toward her and grabbed her hand. "More than you'll ever know." She turned her face to the breeze, jutting her chin stubbornly against the flow of air. "I wouldn't despise Rene so much if I didn't."

"How long do you plan to stay here at Greywalls?" Agnes's words interrupted her thoughts.

"Until all the trouble in France is past, I suppose. I still have no idea what has been going on, and most times I simply don't want to know."

Agnes said nothing. They laid out a light blanket in the sun, rested the babies on their tummies, and patted them to sleep.

"Is it my imagination," Agnes began, "or does the viscount— I mean the earl—seem to be softening around the edges a bit? I can honestly say that I don't positively hate the man anymore!"

Sylvie laughed, grateful for the lightening of the conversation. "I've never hated him! He's really a delightful person, Agnes. You just haven't seen it before now."

"No. You were just blind before this, ma'am. There's something happening to him. I know about these things."

"Maybe it's Elspeth."

Agnes rubbed a hand over her son's back and smiled a gentle smile that Sylvie knew was just for Adam, because of Adam. A mother's smile. "It's amazing what a child can do, my lady."

Sylvie gazed down at her own sleeping baby and had to agree.

CHAPTER ❖ FORTY-THREE

O h, for heaven's sake, Mira, we have servants to do that! Put that platter on the sideboard and get in your seat, please. Our soup's getting cold and it's all your fault!" Mr. Mervyn Wallace's thick mustache vibrated with each plosive that burst from between his lips.

Mira chuckled at her father's blustery antics. "Father, calm down. You know Dr. Krebbs told you that you must stay calm or you'll make yourself sick. Tell him, Mother." Mira turned toward her mother for support. Mr. Wallace did the same.

Mrs. Wallace held up her small hands. "No, you don't! I won't be put into the middle of things anymore! I've grown much older and twice as wise since you and your brother left home, Miranda. I'm saying nothing, Mervyn."

Matthew applauded. "Bravo, Mother. Bravo. It is nice to know you really can teach an old—"

"Mate!" Miranda broke in, horrified. "How can you say—"

"Oh, Miranda." Mrs. Wallace waved away her consternation and her eyes met her son's. "It's just Matthew. We've been treating each other like old shoes for years!"

Matthew laughed. It was good to be home. George had been right. The past three days he was remembering who he was, and what he was put on earth to do, to glorify God and enjoy him forever. In fact, he was leaving for Scotland in less than a week to see about that church near Huntly.

Their kindly butler, a jumpy man nicknamed Cricket, interrupted the happy meal. "There's a visitor, sir . . . madame." He bowed to each of the Wallace parents. "A count de Boyce."

Matthew stood to his feet, feeling horror and concern at the same time. "Show him in, Cricket. By all means."

Cricket's old, watery blue eyes bounced up at the ceiling in quiet frustration. "He's asking for a bath and a change of clothes first, sir. Shall I have the maids draw one upstairs in the lilac room, madam?" he directed the question at Mrs. Wallace.

"Of course, Cricket. Of course."

He politely withdrew, closing the intricately carved pocket doors with a noisy slide.

"Mate, will some of your old clothes do?" his mother asked.

"No, Mother. Rene is taller than I am."

Mrs. Wallace pushed out her chair and patted her husband's shoulder. "That new suit of clothes that was just delivered will have to do then, Mervyn." She turned toward her son and raised her eyebrows with a sigh. "'As we have therefore opportunity . . .'"

"Looks like God's got a job for you to do, Mate," Miranda remarked, eyes suddenly sad.

Matthew felt his molars grind together.

Mrs. Wallace laid her gentle hand on top of his head as she walked past him. "Yes, well, Son, let's just hope you really can teach an old dog new tricks."

"'The heart of the king is in the Lord's hand!'" Mr. Wallace boomed from his seat at the head of the table. "Now let us eat!"

⌒

David Youngblood stared down at the note, delivered to him just minutes ago. It was 4:25 A.M. The writing was childish and blocked, such a contrast to the elegant appearance of the woman who had penned the words inside. Words of warning. Feebly disguised.

I must give you warning, even to the detriment of myself, that the beast is sending a man after you. He told me of your plans to kill beauty's husband and will thwart your attempt by killing you first. I did all I could to protect him up until now so that you would never be able to claim his wife as your own. So that your feelings for me might return. But now your life is at stake and I must sacrifice my own happiness to warn you. You and only you were ever my heart's true love. Beware, darling. Be on your guard.

Blast! Youngblood crumpled the sheet of paper, nevertheless grateful to Camille. He would make sure she never wanted for anything again.

"Will you be sending a reply, sir?" the messenger asked, dark rings of fatigue squeezing his bloodshot eyes.

"No. Ask Mrs. Wooten to give you a bed for the night, then you may return to France."

"But sir," the man said, hesitation rendering his voice shaky, "the lady was most distraught."

He hurried over to the wall safe, hastily negotiated the lock, then threw a bag of coin to the messenger. "Then give her my thanks, and tell her that her services will no longer be required. Ever."

Rene was coming, and bringing some unseen guests along as well, it seemed. David walked across his bedchamber and poured himself a bit of whiskey, Scotland's finest, and thought about what he should do.

⁓

"If Sylvie hates me now, I do not blame her." To Matthew, the misery in Rene de Boyce's face and voice was altogether pitiful and painful to the ear, if not to the heart. And the way he was swallowed whole by Mervyn Wallace's new suit of clothes didn't do anything to render him less pathetic.

Matthew swallowed and sat down on the chair opposite. There was no fire in the grate that evening, for it was quite warm. The garden doors were spread wide, circulating the summer air somewhat. He still had not recovered completely from the surprise of Rene's visit on his way to Scotland. They had already resolved to travel to Youngblood's estates together, or rather, Rene had begged Matthew to come along and lend his support.

When the young nobleman had cried on his shoulder, saying he couldn't face this by himself, Matthew knew he should go. When Rene reported that Mirreault may have already sent men after Sylvie, he knew he would go. Thank goodness, Miranda agreed to accompany them, knowing Sylvie would need her support too.

But now, it was quiet. The rest of the Wallaces were in bed and Matthew sat with Rene, who rolled cigarette after cigarette. "You sure you don't have any brandy, Mate?"

Matthew shook his head. He personally did not have any brandy, and he wasn't about to raid the kitchen on his friend's behalf. The last thing Rene needed was to dull his conscience even further.

"Sylvie will not hate you, old man. She'll simply need a little time to readjust."

"It is a wonder you don't hate me as well. If you were not a minister, if it was not your calling to love all men, I am sure you would be filled with disdain."

Matthew agreed inwardly but said nothing about it. "There is no use wallowing like this, Rene. The future is yours. Sylvie is yours. Be glad about that."

The count shook his head, rubbing the sparse blond stubble on his chin. "But it is worse than you think. There is much Sylvie does not know, my friend. I do not know how I can face her now. I have been haunted by my deeds, and every day the need to confess to her grows greater. Foolish, I know." He tapped his cane on the floor in agitation, stubbed out his cigarette, and began to pace before Matthew's chair. "I do not know how long I can hold out before I spill everything before her. I am a man who has trouble denying what he perceives to be a need. I have not been able to talk to anyone. If I did, I might feel better about it all."

"I do not have the power to grant you the absolution you crave, Rene. Only God does. And although confessing to me is not as good as confessing to God and those you have harmed, perhaps it will help clear your mind, show you what to do, illuminate further what you have to lose by telling everything."

Silence suddenly reigned, thickening with each tick of the large, walnut grandfather clock near the door. Matthew picked up a pen from off the desk and began to fiddle with it, studying the ink-stained nib, wishing he could be any place else just then.

"I killed them. I killed them all!"

Rene blurted out the words as he heaved, and a sob came forth. He choked back the many more that were obviously stored up within him.

Matthew set down the pen. "What are you talking about?"

"Monsieur de Courcey, Collette, Guy. They are all dead because of me."

He felt as if he had been hit by a train. "At your hand?"

"No. But because of my weakness."

Rene de Boyce's side of the story erupted into the room, filling in all the gaps that Sylvie's story failed to expose. Matthew sat as one paralyzed, unable to move at the wild bevy of words that assaulted him like a gang of London street urchins. He couldn't ask the questions which piled up, there was no room for interruption. Rene's voice softened and rose as the story dictated, then, finally spent, the tale almost completely told, he threw himself into his chair and wept loudly.

"I tried to fool myself that the death of Armand and Collette really was a work of Armand himself—a result of a drunken madness. I thought he killed himself and his wife because of Guy's death! But I know better now."

"Who then?"

A look of fear passed across his face. "I do not know. One of Mirreault's hit men, to be sure."

Matthew didn't move. He knew he should comfort the man, but he couldn't, not when Rene had taken away everything from his own wife, Sylvie, the woman Matthew loved with his entire being. Surprisingly enough, that familiar rage didn't rise into his throat as he thought it would. Suddenly it was as if God was lending him his eyes.

"How could she ever forgive me?" Rene gasped. "How?"

"I don't know," Matthew breathed. "I just don't know. I don't ... know what to say to you, Rene."

"How could I have done it?" he wailed.

"The question now is, what are you going to do about it?"

Rene nodded. "Perhaps Sylvie will forgive me."

Matthew was suddenly angered by this man. "This isn't about Sylvie anymore, man! It's about what is right and what is wrong! You must expose this Mirreault. You must make restitution."

"But what about Sylvie! Mirreault seeks her life. She needs my protection! And worse, if he should get to her, Eve will need a parent."

Matthew wanted to belt him across the jaw. "Stop this nonsense, Rene!" he grated between his teeth. "Heavens, man, your appetites caused the death of three innocent people! If you expose Mirreault, he will not have a chance at Sylvie's fortune."

"I could be sent to jail for all the stealing I've done, Matthew."

"You chose your fate when you allowed the deaths of the de Courceys. Jail is more of a luxury than they had."

Rene's eyes went wild. "You won't tell anyone, will you, as a man of the cloth?"

Matthew wished he could. "You know I cannot."

The room filled with silence. Matthew, still angry, consciously kept his hands from balling into fists. That his Sylvie should be saddled with such a man for the rest of her life was too much to bear. "You don't deserve her, you know," he said. "You never did, and you never will."

Rene began to cry again. And Matthew left the room, left the house. All night he walked the city of Leeds, dreading the trip to Scotland come morning. *One year you're tending to a small, boisterous flock in Swainswick, the next you're in love with a married woman and trying to intercept assassins,* he thought bitterly.

Oh, God, he prayed. *Let me see your hand. Please, Father. Show me what to do, use me, and above all, protect Sylvie and Eve.*

Eventually, the sun came up. As it always would, until God declared otherwise. He made the trek back home and found Rene still sitting in the study, the contents of his tobacco pouch almost gone.

"Until you seek the forgiveness of God himself, Rene, I do not see how Sylvie, or anyone else, will ever forgive you." The words sounded cruel, even to himself, but it was the best he could offer.

Rene rolled one last smoke. His hands shook ferociously, but Matthew offered no help. "You have told me such things before, Matthew. I do not know how God can really help me now. Or even if he would want to."

"He is your only hope at this point, my friend. I have been telling you that for years."

Rene shook his head. "It has been so long. I have forgotten most of it, I am sure." His foot tapped in agitation; the tone of his voice was an invitation of itself.

Matthew gently took the cigarette from between his fingers and set it on the desk. "Then let me refresh your memory." *Oh, Lord, help me now.* Here was an opportunity to share the gospel of his Lord and Savior, and he didn't even wish to do so. How did he ever come to such a point?

But the presence of the Holy Spirit was the victor and the love of God, as found in his gracious, merciful plan for mankind, poured from the mouth of his servant, Matthew Wallace. How the Christ, the very Son of God, paid for the sins of humanity, every sin, no matter how dark, by his death upon the cross. For Rene's sins. If he would only believe.

"'Believe on the Lord Jesus Christ and thou shalt be saved,'" Matthew quoted simply as Rene listened patiently, foot tapping ever more slowly as the words seemed to filter through his pain.

They left the next morning on the earliest possible train.

It was still early, darkness covered the skies, and Rene wondered why he was going through with this. The soft snores of Matthew Wallace were hardly comforting. They only served to remind him that he hadn't had a good night's sleep in months and hadn't slept a wink in three days. Miranda was sleeping as well, he noticed, slipping the laudanum from out of his pocket.

Rene took a heavy swig from the small brown bottle, then grimaced. Before, his opium habit had always been so civilized . . . smoking a pipe, lying side by side with a beautiful woman, eating peasant food. Now it was a slug here, and a slug there, and life had ceased to be improved by its consumption.

He was weak and skinny and filled with a blackness that seemed to be eating him from the inside out. Matthew was right; he should turn himself in and be done with it. Mirreault would be powerless if he was in prison. Before corking the bottle, he took another quick sip, then closed his eyes and waited for it to take effect.

"You shouldn't be drinking so much of that, my lord." Miranda's soft voice skirted around the corners of his mind. He opened his eyes.

"Yes, thank you, I know."

"I mean it. It's not making it better. It's drawing you further down."

"I know that too." Rene knew she meant well, and was comforted by it somewhat. But it was too late.

"And if you take too much of it at one time—"

"Yes, yes. I know that too. But to be honest, Miss Wallace, I think it might be better for everyone if I did just that. Never to awaken. Think of it."

Miranda sat up straight, her eyes wide and blazing. "But you mustn't say such things, my lord! Why, it's sin!"

Rene smiled. "Life isn't always so cut-and-dried, Mira. At least not for men like me." *Men like me*, he thought. God help the world if there were more men just like himself.

Miranda took his hand, but her sincere warmth did nothing to make it better, nothing to make it all go away. He laughed harshly. "I'd love to kill myself, Miranda. But I'm too much of a coward."

Miranda patted his hand. "The Savior can help you, my lord."

"The only way God can help me is to send a bullet straight to my heart."

CHAPTER ❖ FORTY-FOUR

Sylvie was sitting in the garden, enjoying the scent of the late-blooming roses as she hummed Eve softly to sleep. As wonderful as Scotland had been, the clear air, the charming warmth of the people around her, she knew it was but a small drop of ointment on a large abscess. The time was coming when she had to go back to France, presumably on Rene's arm. And what were they going to face once there? A man named Claude Mirreault. *If Matthew was in this kind of trouble*, she thought, *he would go back to take care of it alone and leave me and Eve here in safety.* Not that he would ever be in this kind of trouble. But with Rene, she knew it was upon her shoulders to set things to rights.

Little Angus MacDowell, the servant boy, came running into the garden. "M'lady! M'lady! There's visitors gettin' oot the coach in the courtyard. The master isna' home yet and me ma sent me to fetch ye."

She stood to her feet. Youngblood had been gone for two days on some urgent business in Perth. He was planning to return that afternoon. "Who is it? What do they look like?"

"A man wearin' nothin' but black—a preacher, I'm supposin'."

Matthew Wallace.

"An' a vera skinny man with hair the color o' the sun."

Rene. *Oh, dear God,* she prayed, not knowing what else to say. She started through the door that led to the great hall. Angus followed, not done reporting yet. He was a thorough lad if nothing else, Sylvie had noticed.

"An' there's a tall woman with long white hair, an' berry juice on her face. Must've had a wee accident durin' lunch!"

"Go tell your mother to put on some tea," she ordered him, hoping against hope he wouldn't say anything rude to Miranda. There just wasn't time to enlighten the lad right now. "And then, get Elspeth to fetch the countess. She's in the library working on a puzzle."

The lad ran away, his kilt jumping wildly about his spindly legs.

As she hurried across the massive room, the group entered through the door. Rene first, then Matthew, then Miranda. Matthew, of course, saw her first and pointed her out to her husband.

"Sylvie." Rene could barely look her in the eye as she arrived at his side.

"Rene." She forced a smile on her face, tried to sound cheerful, but was failing miserably. "How are you?" she asked.

"Fine, and you?"

"David's been feeding me well, giving me good company. You don't look well."

He sighed and Matthew interrupted. "Mira and I will see to the bags."

Rene only nodded.

"I'm glad to see you are alive," Sylvie said, knowing that, at least, was the truth. She wouldn't wish anyone dead.

"It was a rough recovery."

She pulled Eve's blanket down, exposing the child's face. "Here she is, Rene. This is your child, Eve."

Rene looked upon the child even as Sylvie looked upon him. His features softened, his eyes moistened, and then, a look of total devastation passed over his face. He reached out his hand, long fingers touching the downy cheeks. "Oh, Sylvie," he whispered, "she's a beautiful child. She looks just like you."

"Rene! Rene! Oh, my sweet boy!"

The countess's voice overwhelmed the scene as she hurried down the steps. She pulled her son into a long, hard embrace, weeping and carrying on. Rene, it seemed, didn't even have the strength to hug her back.

She pulled back to look at him. "Oh, but you're tired, Rene. You look terrible, so thin and exhausted. See how you still need your mama? Come with me; I'm taking you right upstairs and tucking you in bed. I've had your room made up for days!"

"I'm having tea sent around," Sylvie offered, but was ignored. The countess had failed to look at Sylvie even once.

Rene offered up no argument, just followed his mother up the stairs and out of sight.

Sylvie stared after them, not knowing what to do . . . until Matthew came back inside.

"May I?" he asked, holding his arms out toward the babe.

She smiled up at him. "How is it you always know the right thing to say and do?"

But he didn't answer. He took Eve from her and held the baby tightly to his chest, kissing the top of her head. It was his way of saying, *I may not be able to show my love for you, but we can love this child together*. Or so Sylvie thought.

Despite the circumstances of his arrival, his presence was a balm. A healing balm. For Matthew Wallace would never offer a temporary medicine to an aching wound, he would offer up healing. It was what he was put on earth to do.

"So he came to see you?" she asked.

"Yes. I was at home in Leeds, and he stopped in to spend the night on his way north. Mother and Father had always enjoyed his company back during university days."

"He's in terrible shape. Tomorrow I'm going to start getting him off the opium. There's no sense in putting it off."

"You have done it before, you can do it again, my love . . . forgive me, I mean my lady."

Sylvie shook her head wearily and pushed back a stray tress that amazingly enough was now littered with several white hairs. She had noticed it that very morning. "Last time I cared what happened to him."

"And you still do!" He grabbed her forearm. "You must care for him again. You will care for him again." His voice sounded desperate, urgent.

"Oh, Matthew," she cried, tears spilling from her eyes. "I'm so glad you've come. We will see this through together, won't we? You will help me, won't you?"

He closed his eyes, breathed in deeply. "Yes, of course I will, Sylvie. I don't know how. But you know I will do all I can to help you."

~

Didier dropped down on a pile of leaves he had gathered several hours earlier and made himself as comfortable as possible. The wooded expanse about three hundred yards from the west side of Greywalls was the perfect area from which to watch the gatehouse.

"Well, he's arrived, Yves. Just as I thought."

"Mmmph." Yves chewed on a piece of clover he had plucked earlier as they scouted the area, dressed as one of the many wealthy tourists who combed the hills of Scotland in summer now that Queen Victoria had rendered the Highlands a fashionable destination. Unfortunately, David Youngblood wasn't making their job easy. Out of town, they were told. They did buy word, however, that he would be returning that very day.

"I know Youngblood won't do anything to the count before tonight. He would view it in poor taste. We will wait as well. We must see to the girl as she sleeps."

"We?" Yves raised a brow.

"All right, you must get the girl tonight, as that kind of assignment is more to your liking. I'll keep an eye on Youngblood. Most likely he'll bring Rene into his study for some brandy. I'll watch him from that oak tree in the east garden, or perhaps from near the garden fountain."

"Who was that man in black?" Yves continued chewing, a patch of sun breaking through the canopy of leaves overhead to brighten his hair to a brilliant strawberry shade. He did very well with the women, actually, Didier admitted grudgingly.

"A vicar, no doubt. Nobody to worry about. Just an old friend from his Oxford days."

Yves snorted a laugh. "A religious man . . . and a Protestant at that! No trouble there. He'll be too busy turning the other cheek. Do you think I might go into the village for a spell? Find a woman? I was looking forward to having a little turn with that secretary's girl."

Didier rolled his eyes. "Don't remind me of that one. To think he escaped before our men could get to him. I wonder where he could have gone? He fooled even me, Yves. And that is saying something."

Yves snorted again, more derisively this time.

"What was that for?" Didier demanded.

"Crime is a youthful venture, old man. You should have quit years ago."

Didier slapped the fellow upside the head, laid back in the leaves, and closed his eyes. But he wondered whether or not Yves was right. He'd saved up enough money from his association with Claude Mirreault; maybe he'd do what the count de Boyce should have done, maybe someday he'd take his small fortune and disappear into the night. "I may have my age against me, not that fifty is ancient, mind you, but my discretion is my ultimate friend, and you, young man, should learn to have a little of that. You won't be going into this village to prowl like a needy tomcat. We need to finish the job with as little ruckus as possible."

Yves snorted again, placed his hat over his face, and was soon snoring. But Didier continued to ponder the deed that lay before him.

"A toast!" David Youngblood raised his glass, and the rest of the diners echoed the movement of his arm, although clearly lacking their host's gusto. Wine sloshed gently over the rim of his cut crystal goblet. He was feeling wonderful.

"A toast." They answered.

"To the future. May it be filled with love, happiness, and fulfillment."

"The future."

They lifted their glasses to their lips and drank, but he and the countess were the only two who wore smiles. He found that terribly ironic.

Dessert arrived, but was picked at by the rest of the party. Finally, Sylvie made her exit. "Do forgive me everyone, but I feel a little tired tonight. Please excuse me."

"I'm tired as well." Miranda daintily dabbed at the corners of her mouth. "I shall accompany you upstairs."

The countess agreed that an early night would be most beneficial after the exciting day.

"Papa?" Elspeth asked. "Will we read together as usual tonight in the library?"

David turned to Matthew with a smile. "Would you mind entertaining the count for a bit in my study whilst I attend to my fatherly duties?" In truth, the half hour he spent with Elspeth in the evenings had been gratifying. Presently they were enjoying the boyishly wicked antics of Tom Jones.

"As you wish, my lord," Wallace answered. And Youngblood felt pity. The man loved Sylvie as well, that much was obvious, and how could he blame him for that? There was nothing to really worry about, was there? Matthew Wallace was going on to Huntly in the morning and most likely would never be heard from again. Whatever feelings Sylvie had for the religious man, he was certain he could change them. There wasn't a woman alive who couldn't be wooed. And he had plans. Sylvie de Courcey would be wined, dined, and given all that her heart desired.

And so the group dispersed to their respective destinations. In the library, Youngblood scraped a brass smoking stand across the floor, pulled out a cigar, and settled down next to Elspeth on a leather davenport. She smelled of the heather on the hills, her sunburned face merry and kind. He took her hand and closed his eyes as she began reading chapter five.

⌒

Youngblood awoke an hour later as the wall clock chimed ten. Elspeth was gone and in her place was a little note that said she loved him. He tucked it into his pocket and stood to his feet. *Tonight is the night!* he thought with excitement. A slim length of rope lay coiled in a desk drawer; the brandy decanter was full. He could hear his own voice explaining it the following morning when he apparently found the body. *I left him safe and sound around midnight. I can only assume Claude Mirreault finally caught up with him.* Oh, he'd put them all in a dither, to be sure. And yet, it wasn't going to be as easy as before. Not by a long shot. The little note from Elspeth suddenly weighed heavy in his pocket.

Youngblood heard the murmur of voices from inside the study, the vicar talking about God and forgiveness and whatnot. He placed his large hand upon the doorknob and pulled. "Gentlemen!" he effused, obviously interrupting a grave conversation and not caring a whit. "Care for a third?"

Rene tottered to his feet, and Youngblood noted the strain on his face. "Please! Come right in. We were just finishing up, were we not, Matthew?"

"You do look a bit tired, my good man," Youngblood said, wanting only to get the vicar out of the room. If Camille's message was accurate, the count's protectors would be arriving soon. If they hadn't done so already. He had posted a few extra men out and about. But he knew Mirreault's men, and he knew they could get by anyone. He'd simply have to keep his wits and protect himself. Trust only himself, as he had always done.

The vicar stood to his feet. "Perhaps you are right. It was quite a journey today. And I must see to Miranda's comfort."

Now there was an interesting woman, Youngblood had to admit. He had sat next to her at dinner, and her intelligence was remarkable. And the way she bore her birthmark so comfortably, without a trace of embarrassment or apology. A woman to be admired, yes, but adored—no. He wondered if she would consider becoming a governess to Elspeth? Certainly she was possessed of the social graces, and was kind and learned, a worthy teacher for his daughter, indeed. He'd talk to her in a day or two, after the furor died down.

He hadn't foreseen Wallace's arrival, but having a vicar on the scene around Rene's death and subsequent funeral would be most advantageous. Healing for all involved. And as soon as the last spadeful of dirt was on the grave—off he would send him! Without a moment's hesitation. Then, he would woo Sylvie most thoroughly, a courtship which she had been denied, a courtship she deserved. He was going to take his time about it, not frighten her with transparent intentions. With cords of affection and caring, he would inextricably bind her to him. Did she not already rely on him in a manner of speaking? Of course! Agnes and Rupert's visit was merely the first step. Women don't love men for who they are, he reasoned, they love them for what they can get out of them.

But there was a more important objective to be obtained tonight, one upon which all the others hinged. Unfortunately, it was going to be more difficult than he had thought. He hadn't killed in a while, and with Elspeth in his life, human existence seemed a bit more precious. Just a bit, mind you.

"Well, then." He cleared his throat. "Good night, Wallace. Lovely to have you here at Greywalls. Please make yourself comfortable and stay as long as you wish."

The vicar bowed like the gentleman he was. "Thank you for your hospitality, my lord. But my sister and I shall be leaving tomorrow morning for Huntly. May I come back to visit on my way back through?"

Youngblood nodded.

And with that, the vicar left the room, calling after him, "Think about what I said, Rene. It is your only hope." Then he was gone completely.

David Youngblood sighed with relief. "Religious men can be so boringly zealous, eh? Well, Rene, here we are, just like old times. More brandy?"

Rene nodded mutely and handed over his empty glass.

"Amazing the way all this worked out, isn't it?" Youngblood went on as he poured the drinks. "Presumed dead for months, and now, here you are! A father of a beautiful daughter, a loving wife to come home to, an ecstatic mo—"

"Sylvie does not love me. She did not before, and she certainly will not now that she's aware of my . . . addictions." His tone was dull.

Youngblood handed him back his glass, now brimming with the amber liquid. "But you were so close! Such amiable companions. Come now, it cannot be that bad, can it?"

Rene stood to his feet, leaning heavily on his cane. "Enough, David. You alone know how far this all has gone. You are reprobate, but I never thought you capable of murder."

Youngblood raised his brows in surprise. "Meaning?"

Rene shook his head sadly. "I may not be a strong man, David, but I'm not stupid. A mask? Really, old man, how could I have not figured out it was you who tried to kill me down at the dock?"

"When did you realize this?" Youngblood asked.

"Not long afterwards."

"And you sent Sylvie to me?" He couldn't hide his incredulity.

"She is safer with you than almost anyone else. If you'd kill me to get her, you would kill anyone who tried to do the same."

There was a certain twisted logic to it, Youngblood admitted. "So why did you come to Greywalls, then? You know now I am not your friend and never was."

Rene pressed his palms hard down the tops of his thighs. "I seem to be a man without friends these days. Only Mother—"

"Oh yes, dear Mummy!" Youngblood interrupted. "She never fails to keep you from assuming responsibility for your actions. No matter how far you show your petticoats, she refuses to believe you are anything less than an angel."

"At least she believes in me."

"She's afraid not to. Imagine what she would think if she knew you were responsible for the death of her dearest friend." *Blast!* Youngblood thought, *I've spilled the beans now.*

"What are you talking about?"

Youngblood shrugged, remaining outwardly calm. Come to think of it, Rene would be dead soon, so why not empty the bucket completely? If confession is good for the soul, well, the soul of Rene de Boyce needed to know just what sins were charged to its lengthy account.

"The de Courceys, of course."

"Guy was killed by a highwayman. Armand shot himself and his wife."

"Armand shot no one. Claude Mirreault arranged it all."

Rene turned a paler shade of white. "No. He was going to, but Armand did the deed before he could send his man."

Youngblood shook his head. "I was that man. Believe me, Rene, Armand was so drunk he wouldn't have been capable of shooting an elephant at close range."

Horror took over Rene's stare. "*You?* You killed Sylvie's parents? How could you? You love her!"

"How could I not!" Youngblood spat, thinking of his own parents. "That pathetic man who never once told her he loved her, who used her as a packhorse. And that woman! Heavens, there was someone ripe for justice. Always clinging to her daughter, casting off her responsibilities upon her."

"So you've justified your murderous actions?"

"Oh, please. I fully admit that I'm an evil man. The least you can do is the same."

Rene sighed, his mind obviously working. "So you've been in Mirreault's employ all this time I thought you were my friend." He spoke slowly, as if trying to get used to the idea. "I do believe you deliberately brought about my dissolution. You encouraged my gambling, provided opium, and even Camille was part of your strategy to gain my fortune. It all makes perfect sense now."

Nodding a grudging approval, Youngblood clapped his hands slowly. "Bravo, Rene, bravo. You're smarter than I thought. And to think it only took you a few years to realize the truth!"

"So am I right to assume you were Guy's killer as well?" His tone was softly accusing.

Youngblood felt his throat spasm with a sudden rage. "You vile pig! How dare you transfer your own lack of loyalty onto me! Though you might compromise your friendships for your own gain, to save your own hide, I would not! I loved Guy!"

Rene's voice turned steely. "I may not be loyal, indeed, I may be the vile pig you accuse me of being, David. But is it more honorable to pretend an affection, to act out a friendship with someone merely to add to one's financial interests?"

Youngblood shook his head and sipped his brandy. "Had you been less self-absorbed, you might have noticed I didn't care for you one whit."

Rene shrugged. "The point is, I know now. You took all my money for Claude Mirreault, therefore you, directly or indirectly, were the cause of the destruction of Sylvie's entire family."

"And you hope to find absolution in my guilt?" Youngblood mocked.

Rene said nothing.

Youngblood spoke slowly and evenly. "You utter weakling. It's always someone else's fault, isn't it? Trying to transfer your guilt upon my shoulders won't take away your own. Yes, I pulled the trigger that killed Sylvie's parents, and I willingly bear the burden of that. Now be a man and shoulder your own guilt. I didn't force you to gamble away your fortune to the point of such desperation. Each day you made a conscious decision to go deeper and deeper down the well. Each day you could have looked me in the eye and said, 'Enough is enough.' But each day you came by my place begging for more."

Rene's eyes darkened, as though a full realization of his own damnation had just flooded his soul. "It is as you say. I'm no better than you are." His hands shook violently. "I wish I was dead!" he wailed.

David Youngblood raised an eyebrow and crossed his arms. "That, my friend, is something that can definitely be arranged."

"What?" Rene's head snapped up. "What did you just say?"

Youngblood walked around his desk and pulled open a drawer—slowly, smoothly. "I said . . . it can be . . . arranged." He pulled out a gun and slipped it into his pocket.

Rene's eyes closed at the brief sight of the cold metal. "Of course, you would know that better than anyone. And right now, I do believe I am glad for it."

Youngblood's throat went dry, but he held in his anger. "I've never made excuses for who I am."

Rene sighed. No anger, just a grim resignation accompanying his words. "Everything would just be perfect for you, wouldn't it? Sylvie would be yours. No more attending her night after night during my absences. You would have the firstfruits, not the leftovers."

"We both know she deserves better than you, Rene."

Rene grimaced. His slender hands pulled at his blond hair. "Kill me now. I want to die. I have destroyed any happiness I once had, any chance of future happiness that might have been. Some mistakes can be fixed. But not these. Do what you will."

Youngblood stood as stone, watching the man before him . . . remembering the lad at Oxford, the youth with a spring in his step and a smile as sunny as his hair. The bold, infectious laughter he once had owned and used to his every advantage. Then the Paris days and the way he had destroyed the young count for a man named Claude Mirreault. He was right in a way, Rene was. It really was all Youngblood's fault. The kindest action to take would be to put Rene out of his misery.

He turned back toward the desk. And opening the drawer, he pulled out the slender length of rope he had placed there earlier that day. He slid it into his pocket alongside the gun. "Drink up, old man." He poured more brandy into another glass and handed it to Rene, who took three immediate gulps. "It will all be better come morning."

"Make it painless," Rene said, his voice dull.

Youngblood refreshed Rene's brandy. "As you wish."

CHAPTER ❖ FORTY-FIVE

A dark, starless sky cast no image of itself in the reflecting pool of the garden. The wind had died down completely, leaving behind nothing but the torpid breath of a summer earth. Didier mopped the perspiration from off his brow and cursed the heat. Some of the locals had proclaimed this the hottest July they'd ever lived through. He could well believe it.

"Do another search through the grounds, Yves. Make sure we are as alone out here as we were before."

Yves left his place behind the brick wall of the pool, moving like a great yellow cat, eyes one with the darkness. From the bailey, music played. "The White Cockade." Loud and filled with Celtic urgency, most of the servants were now in attendance. Shouts, whoops, wails, and the stomping of feet bolstered the atmosphere and lent the Frenchmen a kindlier atmosphere in which to steal the life of others.

Didier looked without wavering through the open doorway of the study. Inside the events seemed normal enough. Conversation, brandy, a cigar—as yet unlit—bandied about in the graceful hand of the earl of Cannock. Nothing threatening. And the poor count, almost witless in his weakness, a shell of a man, no doubt.

He smiled again.

Claude would be thrilled with the state of the man. Easier to manipulate him, easier to steal the de Courcey fortune from under him like a carpet runner from beneath the feet of a tot. Things were working out nicely, indeed.

But tonight would tell the final tale to be sure. As long as Yves did his job, and he was able to keep the count from being annihilated by Blackthorne, the final mountain would be conquered and de Boyce would be theirs.

The glory that would be his filled his thoughts, and his eyes lost their focus as he pictured a new life in a warm, exotic land of his own choosing.

What?

Didier was hoisted alarmingly out of his daydreams by the sudden cessation of music ... and there stood Youngblood, brazen and strong, tightening a length of rope in his hands as Count de Boyce's head lolled about his shoulders in drunken elasticity.

He began to run along the brick path. Heart beating wildly. Breath heavy. Old.

Where was that blasted Yves?

Rene felt the pressure of a rope around his neck, felt himself slipping off into another dimension, one where death was in the past, and darkness was luscious and never ending. There was no hope. This was for the best.

Nevertheless, he felt himself begin to struggle when the air in his lungs was depleted for good. He felt himself scratch and pull at the rope, kick his feet, and twist in his chair. Anything to cool the burning in his lungs. An urgent panic filled him with a lively need. Was death what he really wanted? And like this?

Eve's tiny face swam before him, and the feel of her little body in his arms as he held her before supper caused him to fight against what was happening to him. And Sylvie—he didn't want to die now, doomed to be despised by her forever.

Behind him, David Youngblood was pulling more tightly. He could feel this. And he expected the man to be laughing as he did so. But there was no sound. No sound until someone came crashing through the set of doors that led into the garden. Rene could see the sudden intruder out of the corner of his eye.

Didier?

He struggled more, and Didier raised a pistol in the air, even as Youngblood dropped the cord and reached for his gun. But the English noble wasn't quick enough. Didier pulled the trigger, and Youngblood's body jerked beneath the impact of the bullet. Youngblood's gun fell from his fingers, and his body crashed heavily to the ground.

Another man, tall and blond, ran into the room, breathing heavily. "I heard the gunshot."

Didier spoke to him. "Go up and take care of the young countess. Now. We haven't much time."

Rene gasped and gasped, receiving the cooling air into his lungs. He watched helplessly as Yves ran from the study and disappeared into the darkness of the main hall. Didier spun around and hurried back outside into the garden, fading into the night.

Just then, Matthew Wallace slid into the room. "I heard a shot!"

Miranda was at his heels. She cried out at the sight of Youngblood, wounded and bleeding and unconscious.

Somehow, Rene felt himself rise to his feet. "Mirreault's man," he croaked, voice damaged by the rope, "he's gone to get Sylvie."

"See to the earl, Mira," Matthew ordered his sister, then pulled Rene out of the room.

⁓

"Do not move, madame."

"Don't hurt my baby!"

Sylvie threw herself in front of the cradle, smashing her kneecap against the pointed rocker. Eve's cry sounded, the baby alarmed by the jolt. A large man loomed above her in the room, this young Frenchman with yellow hair and familiar eyes. "Who are you?" she cried.

"It is not your baby I want, madame." He bowed, eyes glittering. "It's you. Time to pay up on the debt your husband owes. Get up now and the baby won't be hurt."

"You've come to kill us, haven't you? Me and Rene?" She refused to move from the cradle. "You've finally found us."

"I'm not going to kill your husband, if that is your worry. My boss has plans for him . . . if Youngblood doesn't get to him first."

"David—trying to kill Rene?"

"For the love of you," he smirked. "And it's easy to see why he feels that way." He reached forward with his left hand to touch her hair, eyes suddenly blazing with a base need that had gone unfulfilled for too long. "Of course, David has killed many others. Your mother, your father."

She slapped his hand away. "I don't believe you. David would never do anything like that."

Yves stood up straight—the mood broken by the loud contact of her hand. "It doesn't matter what you believe, for now you are going to die. And I will see you struggle and beg for your life, even as your brother did."

His fingers wound into her hair, and as he pulled her to her feet and slid a derringer from a holster strapped to his calf, Sylvie screamed as loudly as she could. Eve's startled cry wracked against the stone walls of the castle. The world seemed to slow down. The cradle rocked ever so slightly, the curtains swirled from their rods like tortured ghosts writhing in agony.

It was all coming down to this now. The sins of the father were being visited upon the mother, and Eve would be left without her. A motherless child, an orphan in all practicality. *I must live*, she thought, struggling now. *I must live. Fight!*

But the man was strong and he held the gun steady to her head.

"No!" she screamed. And as she did so, Matthew Wallace burst through the door, followed by Rene.

Oh, the vicar charged like a wounded bear, grasping the wrist of the intruder. Red rage lashed him into a frenzy, but the killer was a cold man called to a purpose. He pushed at Matthew with all of his might, and in the spare second he was afforded as Matthew climbed back to his feet, he inhaled and aimed, ready to fire. Sylvie readied herself as Rene was suddenly galvanized into action. She heard the explosion of the discharge.

Then, felt nothing.

Using his cane, Rene had propelled his body between the assailant and his wife, his chest accepting the bullet. Sylvie watched in horror as the force of the shot sent his body flying through the air, to land like a limp puppet upon the lavish carpet.

"Rene!" Sylvie screamed, standing to her feet as Matthew stood to his.

The intruder lifted the gun again ... then, a shot went off. Yves's brows raised in surprise, and he crumpled to the floor.

Miranda stood behind him, shaking as blood pooled on the floor in front of her. She cast Youngblood's gun aside and fell to her knees. Sylvie grabbed Eve from her cradle as Matthew turned over the body of the killer and grabbed his gun. Sightless eyes stared in death up at the ceiling.

Sylvie knelt down by her husband, tears falling onto his dying form.

"Sylvie," Rene rasped, blood on his lips, trickling from his mouth. "Let me see her one last time. Let me see you."

As if in a dream, Sylvie brought Eve close to her father. Sylvie kissed his face. "You saved my life, Rene."

A frail smile lifted one corner of his mouth. "Don't tell her ..." he coughed, "who I really was, my ... dear. Let her think"—he grimaced in pain—"that I was worthy of her. Worthy of you. That I was a ... a hero."

"You'll be all right, Rene. Miranda"—she looked up and handed her the baby—"call a doctor immediately. See, Rene? A surgeon will be here soon. You'll be better in no time."

"No." He shook his head ever so slightly. "I'm dying now, Sylvie. Let it be."

She firmly took his hand. Never in her heart did she want something like this to happen.

He sucked in a rasping breath. "You are so . . . strong. You will . . . raise her . . . to be strong. Like you?"

Sylvie's heart broke in that moment as it never had before. But she gave him a tremulous smile. "I will do my best, Rene."

"Promise me that."

"I do. God help me, I promise, my husband."

His eyes began to close, and she squeezed his hand more tightly. "Did that man there really kill Guy?" she asked.

He nodded. "Through Mirreault's orders."

"And my parents . . . it wasn't my father who pulled the trigger, then, was it?"

"No," he confessed painfully. "David Youngblood did the deeds, again by Mirreault's orders, so that I might gain your fortune."

Sylvie couldn't believe it; she felt her head reel under the news. A quick intake of breath sounded from the doorway, and Youngblood stood there, bloodied but alive, noticed only by Sylvie. Sylvie looked at him, beseeching him silently. Youngblood said nothing, just held himself up by the door frame, then stumbled out of sight, back down the corridor.

There was time later to let the world fall apart, she decided, feeling the strength she had once taken for granted return with a vengeance. Rene was dying now, and she couldn't do anything but bid him good-bye, willing him a peace he didn't deserve but one she wished for him anyway. Forgiveness would have to come after he died.

"Send me Wallace," Rene commanded, voice shaking.

"I am here." Matthew knelt down.

"Read me a prayer, Mate," Rene requested, the words lighter than a whisper. "Tell me a story. Anything to ease this pain."

Sylvie held her hand to her face and cried as Matthew told him of a criminal who died long ago, a criminal who died alongside the Savior. And she remembered that her sins as well sent the Son of God to the cross. In God's eyes, without the Savior, she was no better than her husband, no better than Youngblood. Matthew's voice was a comfort to her as well. "'This day you will be with me in Paradise,' said the Lord. Rene, my dear friend, it is never too late as long as you are living."

But it seemed Rene didn't hear. However, as his hands went limp, his lips began to move. No words came forth. And that is how the count de Boyce slipped into eternity.

Sylvie threw herself upon him and wept.

It was all over now. His final act had been his greatest. Her husband had died saving her life.

She lifted a tearstained face to Matthew. "Do you think he prayed for forgiveness? Did he come to know the Savior?"

"Only God knows, my love."

He pulled her to her feet, and when she felt his arms go around her, she succumbed to a well-deserved state of unconsciousness. Matthew would take care of everything.

Matthew showed the doctor into the bedchamber. "They're already gone, I'm afraid."

The doctor needed only to look at them to come to the same conclusion; nevertheless, he knelt down, felt their pulse, and opened their eyes. "Hmph," said the gruff Scotsman. "I'll have to call in the authorities on the matter, you know."

"I'll be available to tell you anything that I know."

"Good."

Miranda stepped forward, wiping her sweating brow with a handkerchief she had pulled from her pocket. "There's another body, I'm afraid. Down in the study. The earl of Cannock was shot tonight as well."

Dr. Matheson blew an impatient sigh between his thin lips. "Goodness, then. It's this house. It has to have a scandal every fifty years or so. Let's go down, then."

A bevy of servants had gathered in the hallway. The doctor shut the door. "No one is to go into that room until the constable has arrived. Where is the countess de Boyce now?" he asked.

"She's with the count's mother, bearing the sad tidings," Miranda said as they started down the stairs. "A sad day, indeed, Doctor. I suppose someone will have to notify the earl's next of kin."

"Yes." He agreed. "A terrible mess here. Terrible."

Matthew opened the door to the study. "His body's in here." They entered the room.

"What?" the doctor asked. "What are you talking about?"

Matthew could hardly believe it. He turned to Miranda. "Are you sure he was dead when you came upstairs?"

"As sure as I can be." Her mouth dropped open, for David Youngblood, the earl of Cannock, was gone.

CHAPTER ❖ FORTY-SIX

Sylvie gazed over the Champagne countryside, her heart reeling beneath a whirlwind of emotion. The steps of Chateau du Soleil were solid beneath her feet, the grapes were heavy on the vine, and her hand was firmly protected within the stable warmth of Matthew's grasp.

"And here we are," he whispered in her ear.

"I wish it didn't have to be like this. I wish our life together might have begun in a carefree manner."

He put an arm around his wife of two weeks. "It did, Sylvie. Remember our walks with Dizzy? The evenings in front of the fire at Maison de Fleur? Remember those days?"

She turned to him. "How is it—"

"—that I always seem to say the right thing?" He laughed and kissed her softly. "You bring out the best in me, my love. You always have."

She smiled. "It's just my job."

They turned and gazed once more at the vista before them. Once Armand's, once hers. But no more. It was all gone.

"You feel good about this decision?" Matthew asked. "About selling the vineyard?"

Sylvie had never felt more right about anything in her life, other than saying "I do" to Matthew. "It's better this way. Now, the money will go in the bank, under Eve's name."

"You are an incredible woman," he said, pulling her closely to his side. "To give up so much for me. I had no idea I was marrying such a wealthy woman!"

Once the land was sold there was more than enough to take care of the outstanding debts and deposit a large sum in the bank. She chuckled. "Not anymore. I'm just a threadbare former countess in need of care and understanding." She truly meant it.

So much had happened in the two months since Rene's death. Grief stricken, the countess had returned to France, to her daughter Cecile's home in the country. Rene's cousin had assumed the title and, a rich man in his own right, had agreed to care for her financial needs. Youngblood was never found, and indeed, a manhunt was on for the killer of Armand and Collette de Courcey. And how many others? Sylvie wondered, her heart broken at the deeds of her friend. His lands and title passed on to his next of kin. Miranda was hired by the new earl of Cannock, Youngblood's uncle, to be a governess to Elspeth. She was already locking horns with Tobin Youngblood as to how the child should be educated, and Sylvie knew the earl was in for quite a ride with Miranda around. Matthew had taken the church in Huntly, leaving the gossips of St. Jude's behind for good.

"Do you know how much I love you, Sylvie?" Matthew asked her as, for the last time, they watched the sun go down over the de Courcey vineyards.

She turned to him, wound her arms around his neck, and caressed the black curls at the back of his head. "I think I have a good idea."

He kissed her sweetly, with the promise of a passion in which he would enfold her later that evening. She responded, as she always did. They were together forever. She wouldn't dwell on the circumstances that enabled them to love now as they did. She would only rest in the fact that God was directing their paths, and he had joined them together. Down the same road they were now traveling, hand in hand, loving God and loving each other.

It was all for which a woman could ask.

"Are you ready?" she asked, looking in wonderment upon the man she had vowed to love until death.

"To go back to Scotland?" he asked, his arms tightened around her.

Thinking of the quaint little cottage in Huntly they would occupy on their return, she nodded. "Let's go *home*."

"Oh, Sylvie, don't you know it yet? You are my home."

Sylvie felt the tears wash over her eyes and she fished into her pocket for a hankie. "Oh dear," she mumbled. "I've forgotten my handkerchief."

"You don't need one anymore." Matthew smiled into her eyes and kissed away her tears.